LiT
Part V – Darkness Comes

I0641324

Maxwell F. Hurley

LiT
Part V – Darkness Comes

FICTION4ALL

A FICTION4ALL PAPERBACK

© Copyright 2023
Maxwell F. Hurley

The right of Maxwell F. Hurley to be identified as author of this work has been asserted in accordance with the Copyright, Designs and Patents Act 1988

All Rights Reserved

No reproduction, copy or transmission of the publication may be made without written permission. No paragraph of this publication may be reproduced, copied or transmitted save with the written permission of the publisher, or in accordance with the provisions of the Copyright Act 1956 (as amended).

Any person who does any unauthorised act in relation to this publication may be liable to criminal prosecution and civil claims for damages.

ISBN 978-1-78695-826-6

Published by
Fiction4All

This edition published 2023
Fiction4All

This book is dedicated to the victims of
sexual assault and rape.
Don't let them take your power.
Contact someone, tell your story.
The strength you possess,
is far more formidable than you realize.

This book contains scenes that deal with the
aftermath of rape.

PROLOGUE

Sometimes it seems to surround you, the pain, the shame, the fear of the reaction from the ones you trust most. A constant feeling of uncleanliness and self-doubt that you should have done something different. The perception that we can control the actions of others is a lie. The Dark feeds this to hide their plans for dominance, to ensure the Balance leans in their favor. The first step is understanding you are not alone. No one is immune to such travesty; it could happen to anyone, even the most elite and strongest of them all.

INTRODUCTION

Nights like this were just horrible for Steven. The never-ending failure after failure sometimes actually made him sick to his stomach. He kept on thinking, *Why do I put myself through this?* He knew why–the hope of getting his life back on track with the help of his roommate. Calvin dragged him out of their apartment, where he was perfectly content to have a night of wallowing in self-pity. The only escape from that gray feeling was writing his novel. Now, he was no Maxwell F. Hurley, but it got him away from thinking about losing his job with Scarlett.

Scarlett Roberts: the smart, funny, caring, attractive, rich media socialite, moved to this pathetic town from California. So, where she went, Steven followed as her personal assistant. There was no doubt they had a great working relationship. They clicked, even though her life was like that kid's game…the one where you had to put the shapes in the holes before vibrating them out. Never once had he dropped anything she requested; he was able to anticipate most things she would require. Then, four months after he arrived, the F.O.R. gave him the gut-wrenching phone call. That stupid organization only spent a couple of minutes explaining how they knew what was best for her. The kicker was they asked Steven to become a member to show him absolute power, but he would have no contact with Scarlett. Anger engulfed him as he told that manipulative cult to go to Hell.

It may have been the wrong move; Steven was miserable now. When he was her assistant, he was somebody. Now, he was approaching his mid-twenties– no job, no girlfriend, and right now... he was sitting in the corner of the bar with the music blaring so loud it vibrated inside his head. To make things worse, his night was about to end up like most others. It was almost time to go home alone, while his roommate would pick up any girl he wanted.

Calvin was a pilot for the fire department. He airlifted wounded firefighters who were dropped in by helicopter to fight forest fires. His mocha skin combined with his tall, athletic build was his arsenal as he confidently approached girls. Steven was short, balding from the back of his head, and spent most of his free time writing stories he never shared with anyone. Why couldn't he just go home? He needed to find a job.

Calvin was a lifesaver, though, and becoming a good friend. He listened to Steven from the initial impact of what happened with Scarlett. The solution he had, to no surprise, was to find a girl to take his mind off his troubles. So, from time to time, he's been trying to get him a willing girl, usually meeting with a collapse. Maybe tonight would be the night. Calvin motioned for him to join him with a group of girls on the other end of the bar. With a deep breath and a sip of liquid courage, Steven got up from the table. He tried to hide the pain from banging his knee on the table. It hit him just right to make him limp.

"You okay, man?" Calvin put his arm around Steven.

Steven tried to hide the pulsating throbbing of his leg. "I'm good. I think the table shrunk on me."

Calvin didn't waste any time trying to promote his friend. "My man here was the personal assistant to Scarlett Roberts."

The girls were leery if he was telling the truth or not. "The Social Media Diva?" the brunette girl asked him as she downed her shot.

Steven nodded. "Until recently. I'm Steven."

"I'm Mindy. This is Eve," the girl standing closest to Calvin introduced.

"Scarlett Roberts? What happened? Did you get fired?" Eve asked as she finished her drink.

This line of questioning was getting uncomfortable. "Long story, don't really feel like getting into it."

"I don't believe you." Mindy was checking her phone. "Any proof?"

Steven reached into his pocket to show the photo album on his phone. There were pictures of him and Scarlett at a couple of parties together. One time they went kayaking to a small island in the middle of this lake for a photo shoot. Then he showed her the time she brought him to Sweden for a Christmas ski trip sponsored by the F.O.R.

"Wow, you weren't kidding." Eve genuinely seemed impressed. "You really were her assistant."

Steven smiled as he snuck a peek at one more photo before putting his phone away. "It was a good job. If you know anyone who needs a personal assistant, let me know." He tried to joke, but it came off a little pathetic.

"Let's see your qualifications; get us new drinks." Eve handed him an empty glass. "Let's see if you can get it right."

Steven immediately knew they were Manhattans. It was one of the rare drinks that Scarlett didn't care for. Calvin was shaking his head not to do it, but Steven couldn't help himself. If he got them drinks, then perhaps it would show them he was something special. The girls smiled when he returned with the drinks. They took a sip, then left the two guys and joined a different bunch.

Calvin blew it off as he went to talk to another girl, but Steven just stood there, dumbfounded. How could that happen? Another incident that proved he wasn't anything. Calvin was on his way to secure a night with a different girl. That meant Steven was on his own, just like always. It was that time to go home for an escape into his fantasy world on his computer.

First, he had to get his jacket from the table… if no one stole it. A little surprise was at the table. The seat was now occupied by a beautiful girl sitting alone. The closer he got to the table, the more he could see how stunning she came off. "That's my coat." He pointed. The girl turned to get the coat and slowly grazed her fingernails across the back of his hand. The air was clear as Steven's nerves started to make him sweat. Perhaps, this was the spell to get over Scarlett… he meant, from losing his job.

Steven didn't know what time it was when he rolled over in his bed to feel the empty spot where his mystery girl once lay. The aroma of her perfume was still in the room. This night was truly a treasure. He got out of bed to see the nice sight of his lady of the night, still here, staring out the window. "Truly a beautiful view." He slowly walked up to her. "I was hoping you didn't leave." Very gently, he moved her purple hair out of the way as his other hand went to go around her waist.

"DO NOT TOUCH ME!" she screamed as she turned around. In an instant, Steven was being held in the air by his neck. He tried to pry her strong hands from his gargling throat. The mysterious lady threw him down onto the end table next to the couch. Pieces of the furniture scattered, some of the smaller pieces of wood lodged in his body. The next thing he knew, he got thrown across the room. Pieces of drywall covered his beaten body. The last thing he saw before passing out; it appeared misty wings came out of her back before she jumped out the window.

CHAPTER ONE

Alex's hometown of Copper Top Mountain seemed different now that she was back. There wasn't a small feeling because the town had grown exponentially. Maybe it was the fact she knew the Dark was rising along with it. Even though she still couldn't sense them, it still felt encompassing. Her long, black, weaved hair lifted up a bit as she turned around to ensure Komptin was still behind her. Alex caught herself doing that a lot lately; since she couldn't feel his Lite either.

The massive German shepherd moved up to join her side. He enjoyed the scratch of the ears as they both left Marty's to grab a double cheeseburger. Tonight, they were going on a hunt for nothing in particular, but secretly, Alex was hoping to run into Shawn. He was a Demon now, who went by Merik. They were due to have a much-needed little chitchat. Still, before that happened, it was burger time. Normally, she would sit outside to enjoy the night, but she felt old sitting amongst all the teenagers. One of the girls did catch her eye, though.

She wore dark eyeliner with long jet-black hair. Her smile was contagious as she held hands with a boy with light brown hair dressed in nice clothes. Alex didn't want to stick around there. "Come on, Komptin. Let's get out of here." She licked her fingers as she threw her wrappers in the garbage. The only thing she kept was a vanilla milkshake she planned on mixing with her Apollo energy drink. The two hunters from the Lite began to walk through town as a preliminary expedition. Alex was still teaching herself to rely on Komptin more to notify her of any Infiltrators or Demons in the area. It was not a pleasurable experience getting attacked on her blindside.

The hunts were difficult enough, but with her sense of the Dark being stripped away made it a lot harsher. Admittedly, that wasn't the worst of it. The connection to the Lite, which seemed to balance her... was severed as well. That left a constant feeling of cold emptiness from not being able to feel the warmth. She still had her powers, but it just wasn't complete; she felt abandoned.

Alex sipped on her energy milkshake as she started up the stairs to her home church. Anne was unlocking the padlock. The makeshift plywood doors were basically just to keep the innocent person honest. It wouldn't take much if someone really wanted to get into the church. The church renovations were coming along, but much slower than Anne would probably like. The F.O.R. really did a number on it before they left. Though, seeing Anne always brought a little joy to Alex. It was weird she was here so late. With stealth, Alex was able to lean into her ear. "Whatcha doin here?"

Anne jumped with a small scream. "Alex!" Her chipmunk-cheeked surrogate sister grabbed her chest. "You scared me." Anne was never good at hiding her emotions. It clued Alex in that something was up when she noticed Anne kept looking over the Lite Sentry's shoulder down the

15

road. Her best friend had a nervous expression. She would be a horrible poker player.

Alex turned around to see what she was staring at. There wasn't anything coming… not even Komptin alerted to anything. "What are you doing here so late?"

"Just had to get something," Anne said with a bit of nervousness in her voice. She escaped into her purse, perhaps trying to find a reason for being there.

"Really, what?" Alex playfully toyed with Anne. Alex pried open Anne's purse with one finger. That, full out, told Anne that Alex knew she was hiding something.

Anne playfully slapped Alex's hand. "Nothing big. Just something I need for tomorrow." She opened the plywood doors to the echoing chamber of the church.

Alex stared at Anne with squinted eyes. "Okay, let's go get whatever it is, then."

Anne made a scrunched face. "Really, you don't have to. I can get it myself." The Lite Sentry stared at the Church Historian. "Fine, Alex. Come on." Anne made it to her office rather quickly, as if trying to rush Alex out of there. She went to open her door but dropped the keys. "Ooops," she nervously laughed.

At first, it was kind of cute, but now Alex was getting annoyed. "What are you hiding, Anne?"

"Nothing, I had to get…" Anne got her office door opened to immediately start scouting the room. "My report files. See, I need to finish it for the Council." Anne seemed relieved that her idea had come to her. Almost a taste of pride that she came up with that so fast. Now Anne was telling the truth, but there was something else. Alex could tell because she was nonchalantly gazing down at her watch. "Shouldn't you be hunting right now?"

"I'm going right after I leave here." Alex studied Anne some more. "Why? Are you trying to get rid of me?"

"No reason. I mean, I'm not trying to get rid of you." Alex watched Anne put her handwritten reports into the briefcase. The Council didn't like to use computers for the reports for fear of hackers. So, everything was handwritten, and four times a year, a Vatican liaison would come to take the files.

"So, you're not trying to get rid of me?" Alex was studying her reaction. Anne was trying to think of something to say but couldn't. "Anne?"

"I really should get going, Alex. It's getting late." The two of them left after locking her office. Alex escorted Anne out of the church. They both turned to leave the grounds when, in the far distance, a pair of headlights appeared. Alex caught Anne shutting her eyes as if hoping Alex didn't see them.

It was rare Alex trembled from nerves, but the sight of the car caused her body to shiver. Alex already knew the answer to the question she asked. "Who's in the car, Anne?"

***

"Kameron," Midnight calmly called out to her friend. Her attention was on the road as Kameron

17

blankly stared while driving. "Kameron," a little louder. Kameron continued, didn't say a word as there was no emotion. "Kameron." Then a small thud came from underneath the car, leaving the carcass of a rabbit in the road.

Scotty was sitting in the middle of the backseat. The only movement was his eyes from above his phone before looking back out the rear window. After shaking his head in disbelief, he went back to his phone.

Midnight just slowly positioned herself to view Kameron, who continued driving with a blank stare. "Want me to drive?"

"No, why?" Kameron grabbed his bottled water from the cup holder.

Midnight faced forward. "No reason. I'm sure Bugs Bunny over there didn't feel a thing."

"What?" Kameron put down his water.

"Nothing. Something on your mind?" Midnight verified their flight information on her email.

"No." Kameron remained stoic, but he did move his eyes a bit as he saw a sign for the Catholic Church.

Scotty chimed in from the darkness of the backseat of the small car. "Why are we leaving on a red eye?"

Midnight started to speak in her defense. "It was the only flight we could get back. Whose turn is it as Air Marshall?"

"Yours," Scotty pointed out. "I don't think it really matters. I can't sleep on planes anyway."

"I don't think I'll be sleeping much," Kameron interjected.

It was quiet before Scotty unexpectedly asked, "Do you think Paige is playing both sides of the fence?"

Midnight scowled at Scotty. "How can you say that?"

"She's part of the Council," Kameron reminded him.

"Yah, because everyone tied to religion is stand up." Scotty went back to his phone to look at needlepoint catalogs online.

"Why would you even think that?" Midnight was still in shock over Scotty's remark.

Scotty put down his phone. "Think about it. She has access to find all these former F.O.R. members. She just happened to directly supervise Lane, who turned out to be one of those Demon things. He never went after her during that fight."

"No, she sent us to find Alex," Kameron reminded him.

"Yah, and when we did, there were Demons there, where we almost died. All ends cleaned up nice and neat," Scotty pleaded his case. "I'm just saying."

Kameron and Midnight both made eye contact with each other. He did have a point. They pulled up to the church, where Anne and Alex were on top of the stairs.

***

Alex felt the blood rush to her face when the car pulled up. Even though she hardly had her pale face turn red, she could feel a couple of shades turn. She turned to Anne, "Kameron?"

Anne closed her eyes as she nodded. "He just came to say goodbye. He's leaving on the red eye tonight." She put her hand on Alex's back. "This might be a blessing in disguise."

"How do you figure?" Alex stared at the car, waiting for some sort of movement. "He wants nothing to do with me. He's the one who is leaving."

"You broke up with him." Anne prevented her voice from rising. "All he wanted to do was be there for you."

Alex didn't say anything; all she did was stare at the car. Then some movement finally came as the back and passenger doors opened. Alex's heart skipped a beat when that happened, but then it just turned out to be Kameron's new friends from San Diego.

She didn't really get to know them all that well. All she knew was they got thrust into this war. The agent with brown hair was a cocky thing, and the tight-bun blonde was a very governmental type of woman. Alex couldn't help but think she and Kameron were perfect for each other. They would probably end up together. "Good for him," she found herself saying aloud.

"Sweetie?" Anne asked her.

Alex could barely be heard. "Nothing."

The driver's side door opened, then out came Kameron, who confidently came around the car to join the other two. He stood there, barely off church property, staring at Alex to make the first move. Alex almost thought it was just to show he didn't fear her no matter what. The two just stared at each other, which was very uncomfortable for the other witnesses of the 'Alex and Kameron show.'

Anne rubbed Alex's back before she headed down the stairs to greet the group. "Hello, I don't think we've officially met. I'm Anne, the Catholic Council Historian." She offered her handshake.

Midnight was the first to accept the offer. "Midnight."

"That's a unique name." Anne was always curious about how people got unusual names.

"My parents were a little hippy, so naturally, I joined the Secret Service," she joked.

Anne smiled. Then she offered her hand to the other agent. "I'm Anne."

Scotty put down his phone and eyed Anne. "I'm Scotty. My parents watched Star Trek."

"Nice to meet you." Anne turned around to see Alex and Kameron still hadn't taken their eyes off each other.

"This is a bit awkward." Scotty went back to his phone.

Anne walked over to Kameron, only taking his eyes off Alex to hug Anne. "Thank you for rescuing her," Anne whispered in his ear.

Kameron very quietly replied so only Anne could hear it. "You just tell me where to be."

Anne fought herself from crying at the conviction in his voice. She just didn't understand why Kameron and Alex couldn't just get back to how they were. "Just be patient." She felt him pat her on the back as if he understood what she was referring to. She smiled at him as she pulled away. Kameron went back to staring at Alex with no emotion on his face.

Midnight decided to try to break the silence. "What happened to the church?"

Anne welcomed the conversation. "Oh, the F.O.R. decided to start an unscheduled remodeling project. They completely tore the place apart."

"It looks like it was a beautiful building at one point." Midnight eyed the tension between Alex and Kameron.

"It really was. We'll get it there again." Anne noticed that Scotty wasn't really paying attention to what was going on. "Would you like a tour?"

Midnight checked her watch. "We'd love one."

Scotty immediately commented. "Nope, don't want to."

"Yes, you do," Midnight insisted.

Scotty continued to play on his phone. "Nope, really don't."

Midnight slapped him in the back of the head. "Yes, you really do."

"Ow, what the..." He rubbed the back of his head. Then the expression on Kameron's face as he stared at Alex convinced him otherwise. "Oh, why not? I would love to explore a building of false promises from an abandoned parent figure."

Anne was taken a bit aback by his reaction. "So, I take it you're not religious." Midnight cleared her throat as if telling her not to go down that route.

Scotty lifted his head to confirm. "Ah, no."

"Well, you can enjoy the architecture then." Midnight grabbed Scotty's hand. "Come on."

22

Scotty reluctantly followed her up the stairs. Anne was fast enough to get ahead of them to unlock the door. Alex didn't move; she just stared at Kameron. Midnight stopped next to her.

Alex broke her stare down with Kameron to turn to the blonde woman. "Thank you for saving my life."

Midnight just kept her eyes forward on Scotty who was getting uncomfortable as he went in with Anne. "All he wanted was to get to you." She turned to Alex with a business card in her hand. "If you need anything, you can call me."

Alex took the card. "Thank you." She turned back to Kameron. Komptin moved his massive head to look at Alex, then at Kameron, and finally back to Alex before joining Anne back in the church, where he morphed into his gargoyle state.

Midnight joined the others, leaving Alex staring at Kameron. The two didn't move. Alex just locked eyes with him. The only movement he made was putting his hands in the pockets of his black trench coat. It must have been a couple of minutes before Alex got fed up with Kameron being so stoic. "Are we just going to stand here and stare at each other?" Kameron shrugged his shoulders. This made Alex blow up. "Well, you're not going to say anything?"

Kameron was calm. "What do you want me to say, Alex?"

His calmness infuriated Alex even more. To the point of yelling. "Say anything!"

Without skipping a beat, he just replied, "Anything."

Alex stepped off the stairs. She just wanted to hit him. How calm he was... Did she mean anything to him? How could he act as if he didn't care about her? Luckily, Anne came out of the church with Scotty and Midnight.

"We need to get going," Scotty shivered. "Thanks for that," he sarcastically said to Anne. "Take care."

Anne sighed heavily.

Midnight joined Anne. "Don't take it personally; he's really a good guy."

"No, I'm not!" Scotty yelled from the bottom of the stairs.

Anne smiled at Alex. "I know what it's like to have complicated friends." She rubbed Alex's back in support. The three agents were at the bottom of the stairs, staring up at the two girls and the dog.

Alex resisted the urge to run to Kameron; she wanted to feel his embrace again. She started to breathe a little heavier. It actually made Alex a little sick to her stomach.

"I don't want this to be goodbye," Anne told Kameron. All Kameron did was nod, prevented from saying something, as for a moment, his facial expression turned to sadness before he buried that feeling. "Take care. Have a safe flight."

"Can't wait, love the red-eyes." Scotty opened the door to the car before turning to Alex. "Thanks, it was fun, especially having a gun stuck to the back of my head." Midnight kicked the door to get him into the car.

"No problem, anytime," Alex gave a quick quip back.

Midnight saw the tension was still thick between her friend and Alex. "Maybe next time you can save us."

"Count on it," Alex assured her. "I owe you one."

Anne and Komptin walked down to Kameron to hug him goodbye. "We'll take care of her."

"Thank you." He knelt so Komptin could say goodbye. Anne and Komptin moved off to the side in hopes Alex would come down or Kameron go up. It seemed like an eternity before Kameron just hurt Alex more, when he said, "Alex."

"Kameron," she returned, as it was evident now she was fighting her emotions as she watched him get into the car to leave for the airport. Alex closed her eyes before starting to walk down the stairs. "I'm going on a hunt. Let's go, Komptin." The second she got off the church property, her eyes flashed blue, and her fists ignited as she headed toward the woods.

***

"Where is she now?" Gron rubbed his hand over his face with agitation.

Merik stood tall in front of the leader of the F.O.R. as he explained how the popular social media diva was now in the F.O.R. study, putting together the plan on how to use her influential status to positively boost the F.O.R. through her social media platforms. "She didn't really enjoy scrubbing the grease bins from the kitchen."

Gron chuckled. "No, I didn't really think she would."

Merik sat down in front of Gron's desk. "Has her dad asked about her?"

"No, Geoffrey is only focused on becoming a Host. He and Nicole should be ready for infiltration in a couple of days. I need you to set everything up for that." Gron got a text from Misluna with a picture of the gift she got from Gron. An unintentional sneer came when he saw how she enjoyed the gift.

"That's secretary work." Merik was disgusted.

Gron didn't really like his minions complaining about the tasks he assigned. If he weren't so low on Demons and Infiltrators, he would've torn him to pieces. "Well, go back to work, and remember. The Sentry is probably hunting you."

Merik thought about it. "Do you think she's mad?"

"Not as mad as the other one," Gron came back with under his breath. "Speaking of which, time is getting close; we need to find her."

"She could be anywhere. Any reports from outside Copper Top?" Merik sat back down on the couch.

Gron kept it close to the chest on how low they actually were on Infiltrators and Demons. With Vandor being trapped inside the Dark Conduit, no new Infiltrators have been available for resupply. "The Dark within the twins will draw her to stay near the biggest concentration of the Dark, which is here."

"What if she goes to Heaven?" Merik thought he actually had a legitimate question.

Gron looked at him as if he'd said something completely stupid. "I just told you, the Dark of the twins are keeping her close to here."

"Won't the Lite sense them growing?" Merik stirred his drink with his finger.

"Misluna explained that her Lite would hide the Dark inside." Gron double-checked the list in front of him. "Paige hasn't moved up?"

Merik shrugged his shoulders. "Not my department. Maybe if we show her Infiltration, it will motivate her a bit more."

"She was moving up so fast and then became stagnant." He started to tap his pen on his desk. He pushed the button to the intercom on his desk.

"Yes, my leader," an attractive voice came over the intercom.

"Find out where Paige Cass is," Gron commanded.

The young lady immediately replied back, "She is currently in San Diego."

Gron was impressed that she got that so fast. "Got it." He sat there for a split second. "Send for her for Infiltration."

There was a pause before the secretary replied. "Forgive my failure, Leader. To be Infiltrated or guest of the event?"

"Guest." Gron lifted his finger off the button. "Damn, she's a good secretary." Gron got up. "Come on... let's go talk to our little social media diva."

27

They started down the dark, musty hallway to the study. Gron stopped at the base of the stairs. "Do you have someone picked out for the first night the twins are here?"

"Without Salamor, we can only guess. Of course, we can just grab Anne or the Sentry's boyfriend."

"Ex-boyfriend," Gron corrected. "No, if we grab one of them, the Sentry would know something is up, and we can't have her disrupt the twins." They continued down the hall to the front door of the study room. They peeked in the window to see the young social media influencer was hard at work. "How much longer does she have in her punishment?"

"Next week," Merik was staring at the attractive social media influencer. Her flawless mocha skin and shiny black hair with green streaks were truly stunning.

Gron couldn't help but see the diva had bags underneath her eyes. Merik opened the door for Gron. "My leader." The Surrogate, who was over-watching Scarlett, frantically stood up. Scarlett was immediately on her feet, almost in a tremble. Gron liked that, when she first got with the F.O.R., she was an arrogant socialite who needed some grounding. Now, she knew who Gron was.

"To your command." She opened her arms and bowed her head.

"Damn right." Gron lifted her face with his finger. "I own you."

"I give myself to you," she replied.

"Your own father signed away his rights to you. Your mother abandoned you." He stared coldly into her eyes. "I'm all you have."

"I don't need them. The F.O.R., under your leadership, provides everything I need." Her soft-skinned hand was resting on Gron's finger.

"And how are you going to pay me back for all I do for you?"

"By recruiting all I influence to benefit from F.O.R. teachings." She calmly recited her intentions to Gron.

"And what are those teachings?" Gron continued to drill her.

"There is no God. The only power is the one you teach me. To learn to accept absolute power when I'm able with open arms."

Merik chimed in, "What were you doing in the Head Watch Office?" Scarlett put her eyes to the floor, almost trembling. "Speak!"

"I wanted to give myself to him," she bluntly said.

"What?" Gron's eyes opened as a burst of laughter came out.

Scarlett turned her head in shame. "His power and responsibility that you entrusted to him to make sure we are safe. I wanted to show my appreciation."

"You've got bigger daddy issues than advertised." Gron shook his head at the thought of the two of them together. Gron turned away, with Merik following him. "Lurk is the one who caught her in his office?"

Merik turned to stare at the young girl who was back to her studies. He was thinking about how he wanted to get with her before that nasty, fat Demon. "Actually, it was one of his Surrogate Guards. Lurk was notified."

"Huh," Gron turned to see the influencer's back, who was deep into her books. "Well, get her what she wants."

***

A little food came up from the thought of giving herself to Lurk, the head of the Sentinel Guards. That excuse was the only thing that came to mind. There was no way she could let anyone know Eric's role in her plan. Scarlett and Eric were working on getting the key to the Rejuvenation Room but were about to be caught by Lurk. They had to act like Eric was the one who caught Scarlett.

The F.O.R. Action Review Board was thrilled she was caught breaking the rules. It was very intense, and it almost seemed cold in the room. Shawn was heading the review board with Misluna at his side. Having her sperm donor of a father staring at her with disappointment was just the icing on the cake. They grilled her for over an hour on F.O.R. protocol.

At the end of the meeting, she was busted down to Serf, which she had never been before. She came into F.O.R. with a high rank due to her popularity as an Influencer. For the past week, she had been sleep deprived and forced to only eat barely cooked rice with some disgusting hamburger. In all her life, she has never had to do manual labor. Her dad hired people for that. As part of her punishment, she's had to do lawn work, bathroom cleaning, and doing the nasty laundry of the F.O.R. Legion Members. Those were volunteers to take the journey on the Map to Absolute Power in promoting the F.O.R. agenda to rid the world of religion. She was Scarlett Roberts; the only thing more than her friends on social media was her dad's money.

Her black hair with green highlights still seemed slimy from the grease bin she was scrubbing earlier this morning. The smell of her hair confirmed she still came off like a redneck state fair. After tonight, it was going to be different. She was going to get her life back. Eric was going to help her escape– but there were conditions.

Eric had been in a secret relationship with Kaylee. A cute little blonde girl who worked in the video production staff with Scarlett. Relationships were forbidden until after you gained Absolute Power. That happens when you show your dedication as a Provisionary. Kaylee was a Surrogate about to become a Provisionary until she found out she was pregnant. A person could hide a pregnancy for only so long, so she told her Provisionary Supervisor after she let Eric know.

They immediately stripped her and yelled at her as they dressed her in a black and maroon outfit. They told her she was a disgrace and had to decide whether to abort the baby or keep it. If she killed the baby, she could gain Absolute Power. Although, if she kept it, she would get kicked out of the F.O.R.

Scarlett thought for a second that she should get herself pregnant. There was an ugly rumor that people who left F.O.R. were never seen again. Some people say they were hunted down and killed. Regardless, when Eric approached Scarlett to tell her he could get her out of the F.O.R. Compound, she jumped at the opportunity. The only requirement was that Kaylee had to come with her. Nope, there wasn't going to be one more second of her on this compound than needed.

"Scarlett!" the supervisor of the study hall yelled at her, at the same time, a semi's airbrakes sounded from outside the window.

She jumped from the fact she was daydreaming of a better life outside this compound. Her heart started to race, and cold fear shot through her body like lightning. The truck was here early. If she were sent to Rejuvenation, it would be all over. There would be no escape. Scarlett had to take a gamble. She wasn't going to stay here one second more than she had to.

The sound of her getting up from the chair caught the supervisor's attention. "You still have three hours, Serf."

Scarlett could tell he was trying to create a false sense of hardness. She had seen this guy before. He had a kind heart and he followed the rules of the F.O.R., but he wasn't comfortable with the hardships the organization put people through. Scarlett could exploit that. She cautiously approached him. "I have a problem."

He looked from side to side to make sure he wasn't caught talking to her without berating her. "What is it, Scarlett?" he softly asked.

"I'm having female issues," she told him. "You know, down there." She pointed down.

He closed his eyes with disgust. "Isn't there a pill for that or something?"

It took everything for Scarlett not to laugh. "Not yet. But there are products in the bathroom I'm going to need."

"I'm not supposed to let you out of my sight," he told her.

"You want to watch?" She put the supervisor in an uncomfortable position.

"NO!" He shivered over the thought. "Just go, be back in fifteen minutes. Don't risk anything stupid, like sneaking food or anything like that."

"You have my word." Scarlett made it down the hall to the nearest female bathroom. Her nerves were so high that she started to hyperventilate a little bit. She calmed herself down before taking off her shoes. She needed to ensure she didn't make a sound as she snuck down the hallway. The main door was down the hall, but that wasn't an option. The Sentinel on duty was watching the door.

Getting out the main door was never the plan anyways. Eric had told her the room with the cribs had a broken latch on the window. Below was a shed she could drop onto to get to the Rejuvenation Room. The key to the padlock keeping Kaylee sealed off would be placed inside a water bottle. That bottle would be in the rain gutter attached to the roof she would use to get down to the shed.

Scarlett carefully started up the stairs, almost cringing at every noise the stairs made as she stepped on them. She carried her shoes in her left hand as her right hand was holding onto the cold iron rail. Very few members were allowed to use these stairs. Eric was the Lurk's protégé, so he was able to follow him up there to go over the security requirements for the compound. That was when Erik saw the window, his inspiration to formulate his plan.

She continued to walk on the side of the hallway. It was long and dark, with a dirty maroon carpeted floor. The air seemed more chilled, as her flight or fight response was screaming, "Run." She continued down the hall as she hugged the wall attempting to present as little of herself as possible. Scarlett noticed a picture of the Leader, Roger Somberson, standing in a power pose as if he was looking down at her. The second picture was of a brunette male. Scarlett stopped and stared into the eyes of the gorgeous man. His physique was almost flawless. It seemed as if he had this weird black fog in the background. Scarlett had to shake off her mesmerized stare at the painting. The last picture of the three was one that really freaked her out.

It was a dark figure with a pale white face. His white face was partially covered by his big black hat tilted close to his eyes. His long black stringy hair did its best to cover the rest of his face. Scarlett had to do a double-take as she thought the eyes of the man were following her every move. The next door was the room where Eric told her to go.

The door slowly creaked as she snuck in where two black cribs were sitting in the room. In between the cribs were what seemed like shackles. This was not right. There was something wrong about this room. She ran over to the window, where she saw the water bottle in the gutter. Inside was the key to get Kaylee out. She was about to open the window when she heard someone coming. There was nowhere for her to hide. She quickly ducked underneath one of the cribs.

The floors creaked as three people came into the room. Scarlett closed her eyes as they were surveying the room. One of the voices began to speak. "Gron, there's still no sign of the carrier of the twins." There was no question about it. That was Shawn speaking. Scarlett was trying to figure out who Gron was.

Movement from one of the feet headed towards the window. "We need to find her and just follow her. If we try kidnapping her, she'll fight it. Could damage the twins." That was Roger Somberson. "Merik, there's a water bottle stuck in the gutter."

Scarlett's heart just sank. First, she didn't know who Merik was. But, if they went out and got that water bottle in the gutter, they would see the key in there. Then she would be done for. "I'll ensure it's taken care of." That was Shawn's voice. Scarlett couldn't help but think about what was going on with all these different names. What was with these twin babies? This was getting out of hand.

"My leader," the third voice said. Scarlett knew that voice. Anger and disgust filled her body. Oh, how she wished she could just go off on him. Her father continued to talk. "We need to go over the financial statements regarding Mayor Paroyale."

Roger moved back to the center of the room to the two of them. "What do you want to do with Scarlett?"

She had to control her breathing as they started to talk about her as she hid underneath the crib. Her dad replied to the Leader, "If she doesn't comply, throw her into Rejuvenation."

"Get her to create multiple videos supporting F.O.R. actions. When she finishes a good three months' worth, then throw her in the hole."

"I say keep her in there until she complies," her dad suggested almost irritatedly. "She needs to know that the F.O.R. is the way to Absolute Power."

The three left the room, talking about booking all the contractors in the immediate area. Scarlett waited a bit longer before sliding out from underneath the crib. She went over to the window and put on her shoes. She opened the window and pushed the screen out onto the roof. It made just enough noise to scare her that somebody might hear it. The roof was dry when she stepped out on it. It was difficult to lift her body an inch off the ground while crawling to the bottle with key.

The grease bin she was cleaning earlier had the lids closed. She gently dropped on top of it to get to the ground. The shadows concealed her as a roaming Sentinel was conducting a check. To the left of her was the semi-truck being unloaded of materials for the compound. Scarlett was tempted to just make a break for it, but she promised Eric to get Kaylee out of there.

Scarlett made it to the Rejuvenation room, where she unlocked the padlock. The door opened to a pure white room with one blanket on the floor. In the corner of the room was just a hole in the floor to go to the bathroom. F.O.R. propaganda was blaring over a speaker system. Kaylee was in the corner of the room in her black prisoner clothes with her hands over her ears. She was trembling as she leaned in the corner, bashing her head against the wall. Scarlett rushed over to her. "Kaylee, come on, we've gotta go." The mixture of noise and F.O.R. brainwashing was hurting Scarlett's ears.

The little blonde girl pushed Scarlett away. "No, I need to promote the F.O.R. I need to prove my worth to the Leader."

"Come on, Kaylee." Scarlett grabbed her arm again, trying to pick her up.

"No, I need to rid the world of religion. I need to do my part." Kaylee started to shake uncontrollably.

"Damn it, Kaylee. Eric can only hold the truck for so long." Scarlett was getting to the point where she was going to have to leave her.

"Eric." Kaylee looked at Scarlett in confusion. "The baby, our baby."

"Yes, the baby's safety. We need to go." Scarlett now had Kaylee's help in getting up. "Are you with me?" Kaylee nodded with confusion in her eyes. It was as if she was working on instinct alone. "Let's get the hell out of here."

She followed Scarlett out of her tortuous domicile of the past two weeks. "Where's Eric?"

"By the truck at the back gate. We need to get to the fence without getting caught." The two hugged the fence line, hiding in the shadows whenever possible. They made it to the edge of the fence line where it met the gate.

A couple of the lower Serfs were unloading the truck. Eric was monitoring the offload with his supervisor as it came over the radio that there was an unaccounted F.O.R. member. This was no doubt, Scarlett. She was due to report back to her Surrogate. The truck started up its massive engine. It seemed to roar as a warning. This was going to be it.

The gate was opening, but there was no way for them to squeeze between the truck and the gate. The truck started moving; then, an alarm came over the radio. The Sentinel in charge halted the truck. "Wait a minute."

The truck driver rolled down his window. "What's going on?"

"Just a routine security check. We need to double-check your cab." The Sentinel stepped back to get him out.

"No, you don't," the truck driver told him. "What gives you the right?"

The Sentinel held up a piece of paper. "You signed right here upon coming into the compound that you and your vehicle are subject to a complete search upon entering the premises. You, sir, are on the premises. Now, get out."

"If this is some bullsh…" He stopped himself as he got out of the vehicle. The truck hissed from the air brakes.

Eric happened to see Scarlett and Kaylee on the fence waiting for the opportunity. With the alert going, there was no way for them to break free without being noticed. Then they wouldn't be able to make it.

Kaylee locked eyes with Eric as the truck started back up from being cleared. They would have to follow underneath the truck while it moved, but there was a Sentinel on the side where they were. The chance of escape was rapidly decreasing. The truck was starting to move; fear was no doubt on the faces of the two girls as for sure they were sure to be caught.

Eric knew Kaylee was about to get caught with Scarlett. He mouthed over to her, "I love you." He handed the clipboard over to his over watching Sentinel.

"Where are you going?" the Sentinel asked as Eric started moving to the other side of the semi-trailer.

Kaylee whispered over to Scarlett, "What's he doing?"

Scarlett watched Eric hop down the loading dock. "I don't know."

Eric waited for the perfect opportunity when the trailer was halfway through the gate before throwing himself underneath the wheel of the truck. Scarlett covered Kaylee's mouth from screaming as they watched Eric's body get pancaked between the tire and the blacktop of the driveway.

The truck immediately stopped as the driver got out of the truck. "What was that?" The sight of the mangled body almost made the big trucker faint. "Oh my God, I swear I checked my mirrors."

The Sentinels from the guard shack got on the phone. Their view was blocked by the truck. All attention now on what was left of Eric. Scarlett knew what she had to do. "We have to go, now!"

"Eric." Kaylee stood there dumbfounded.

"If we don't leave, then we are going to get caught. They will kill your baby; Eric's baby, and he'll have sacrificed himself for nothing." Scarlett was starting to get worried as she saw commotion in the background. "We have to go, now."

Kaylee gathered what energy she could on top of controlling herself from not crying to follow Scarlett underneath the trailer to get around the gate. They snuck out the other side of the truck and took off, running into the thickness of the forest toward the highway. In the distance behind them, they heard the scream, "We have two on the run."

The sounds of alarms from radios on top of the chatter coming over the airways on the location of Scarlett and Kaylee seemed to get closer and closer as they ran. Kaylee had always been a runner, but Scarlett wasn't much of an athlete. She was falling behind as Kaylee moved ahead.

Scarlett turned her head and saw three people chasing her, with what looked like a bear. She was now starting to breathe harder as her eyes started to tear. Her vision was starting to get blurry. She turned back around to see their chasers. For a second, she thought she saw the bear and one of the people with glowing red eyes.

Scarlett bumped into Kaylee as, for some reason, she was standing still. When they fell to the ground, their faces were buried in the dirt. They lifted them to see they were at the feet of a skinny petite girl with a pale face. Her eyes were glowing a neon blue, as well as her hands. The monstrous creature behind her was purple-skinned with glowing blue eyes. The two girls held each other tight, not knowing what would happen next.

***

Kameron stared out the window of the small plane to begin their trip back to San Diego. Even though he wasn't acting as Air Marshall for the flight, he wouldn't be getting any sleep on this trip. Scotty was reading a needlepoint magazine, while Midnight was meeting with the flight attendant.

He saw that Kameron was looking at the cover of his magazine. "I'm just looking for my next one to do."

"What's the most detailed one you ever did?" Kameron asked him, getting situated in his seat. There were only a few people on this flight besides the agents, so it would be a relaxing flight.

Scotty tried to blow it off, but a hint of pride colored his statement. "I did this angel one time. That was really a test of skill. I was really into it, even gave up a couple of Friday nights to work on it. A lot of blood was drawn." He showed him the tips of his fingers.

"What'd you do with it?" Kameron leaned over to him.

Scotty shook his head, "I don't know." It was obvious he did know but was playing it off. "Funny, I thought they were all made-up bullshit, but now…"

"Can I ask what caused you to lose faith?" Kameron finally came out with the question that was a faux pas.

Scotty leaned towards Kameron as well, "Sure. If you, tell me… about what's going on between you and Alex." Scotty saw Kameron start to clam up. "See, we both have issues, don't we?"

Midnight came back and sat behind Scotty. "Looks like there are only six people on this flight, counting us."

"If you want, we can switch around, get some sleep," Kameron offered. "I'm not going to get any."

"Me either." Scotty smiled at the stewardess across the plane. "Do you think me and her could…"

"No," both Kameron and Midnight told him.

Scotty chuckled before going back to his magazine.

Midnight buckled in her seat for takeoff. "You know, I'm really going to look forward to getting back to just doing paperwork for a bit."

"It's been an interesting couple of days." Kameron felt the plane start to move backward.

"That's putting it mildly." Scotty was studying the ground crew.

"What are you looking for?" Midnight asked him.

He turned to speak to her. "Do you think that purple-haired angel would sit on the wings of the airplane like in the movies?"

"That would be Devine." Kameron gave him the name of the angel.

"Yeah, it would be." He turned his attention back to the wing of the plane as it started to take off.

Midnight just shook her head. "Sometimes you're just a child." She grabbed a magazine she picked up from the store to pass the long flight home. Kameron stared out the window as the plane was waiting for its turn to take off. "Let me ask you something."

Kameron got situated. "Yes."

"What's with you and ol' girl? Why did you end it?" Midnight asked him while still reading her magazine.

"What makes you think I ended it?" Kameron continued to watch the plane get situated for takeoff.

"Finally." Scotty was doing some math in his head. "You finally admit you guys were dating."

Kameron adjusted in his seat as the engine started to rev up. "It just wasn't in the cards, okay?"

Scotty and Midnight glanced at each other before Scotty went back to his needlepoint magazine. He just continued to read as he said, "Funny thing about cards. You can stack the deck in your favor."

Kameron turned his attention back to outside the window. The plane raced down the runway, and it started to take flight. The landing gear locked inside the belly of the plane, and the aircraft started to turn into its flight path as it continued to climb. Kameron gazed at the forest below him, where he thought he saw a neon blue light.

***

Alex stood over the two girls as they held each other tightly, not knowing what to do. "Get up," she annoyingly said to them. "I can't do anything with you cowering on the ground in front of me." Behind them were three people and an Infiltrator. Alex had to do a double-take, one of them was the spitting image of Kameron. The three of them started to cautiously approach Alex. The only hope was that they weren't all Demons because then, Alex would be in for a very rough night. "Come on, get behind my purple-skinned friend here."

"Lite Sow." The medium-sized man with glowing red eyes took command of the others.

"Well, that's one, two counting bad breath over there." She pointed to the Infiltrator, who was more than likely circling around. Alex wasn't too worried since Komptin would probably take him while protecting the two girls.

"We just want the girls," one of the people explained to Alex. It was obvious he didn't want anything to do with her.

"Well, that makes you a Provisionary." Alex was still surveying the situation. "No Demon would give up a chance to call me some stupid name or something." For some reason, the plane above her caught her attention.

"You'll die tonight, Lite Harlot," said the third person.

Alex was immediately extremely annoyed, "And there it is. Okay, I was trying to have a moment there. I have a lot on my mind."

The first Demon attacked Alex as the Infiltrator lunged at the girls. Komptin tackled the Infiltrator, and they started to fight until one of them dropped. Alex wasn't too worried about the girls, as Komptin would die to protect them. That left her with two Demons and one Provisionary.

Alex blocked the punch from the Demon as she quickly grabbed it into a headlock to spin it around and kicked the other Demon in its side. The Demon she had squished between her arms grabbed hold of her scarred side and dug into her skin. Alex screamed in pain as her eyes flashed and flipped him on the ground, driving her knee onto the Demon's forehead where she actually heard a faint crack from the skull. She formed a knife to finish him off but was tackled by the Provisionary.

"Are you out of your damn mind?" Alex picked herself up with ease as she threw him into the Demon she'd kicked earlier. She picked the Demon up that was on the ground from colliding with the Provisionary and tossed him into a tree. The Provisionary got up and stared at Alex. Her eyes flashed neon blue enticing him to make a move. The man took off in the opposite direction in a frantic scare. Alex rolled her eyes before turning her attention to the Demon sprawled out with an indentation on his forehead. "Gross." Alex pointed to her own head.

The possessed man felt the small crater on his forehead. His eyes flashed red, and he showed his teeth. He let out a massive roar for all to fear, and then got hit with a Lite Blast from Alex. The force pushed him into a broken branch of a dying tree. He was stuck on the tree, preventing him from getting away. Alex calmly walked up to him with a knife formed in her hands. "It only takes two, Lite Sentry."

"Shut up." Alex jabbed the knife into the upper chest of the Demon, causing him to disappear into the ground. Alex turned around to see Komptin shred apart the Infiltrator's body with his claws before tearing the head off with his massive jaws. She walked up to him and gave him a hug. "You okay?" He snuggled up to her with his massive head to tell her he was fine.

The two of them started walking toward the girls. Alex stopped in her tracks. "It feels like I'm forgetting something." She shrugged it off as she continued toward the two girls holding each other. The light, brown-skinned girl got in front of the small blonde one. "Don't hurt us," she pleaded.

"You really think I'm going to hurt you? I just saved your ass." Alex lifted both of them off the ground. Komptin morphed down to his German shepherd state next to Alex.

"We really have no idea what's going on," the small blonde one pleaded.

"Why were they chasing you?" Alex asked as she was studying her surroundings. "It really feels like I'm forgetting something."

One of the girls said, "We escaped the F.O.R. compound, then we got chased by those things. They were going to kill us."

"Yep, pretty much," Alex told them, still looking around. "Did I lock up the church?" She asked Komptin. "That wasn't it." She turned back to pay attention to the girls. "You look familiar."

"I'm Scarlett Roberts." She had almost a surprised look on her face that she didn't know who Scarlett was.

"Sounds familiar." Alex looked at the blonde-haired woman.

"I'm Kaylee Whithers," she said as she stepped closer to Scarlett.

"I'm Alex. This is Komptin." She scratched her dog behind the ears.

"Can we go now?" Kaylee pled to Alex.

"Yah, let's get you to a hospital," Alex told them, looking around. "Scarlett Roberts? Aren't you that social media influencer for the F.O.R.?" Alex snapped her fingers.

"Not anymore." Scarlett helped Kaylee through the woods.

Alex took a couple of steps before stopping to look at Komptin. "Are you sure we're not forgetting something?" Then the Demon that looked like Kameron dropped from the trees causing Alex to fall to the ground. Komptin immediately morphed to protect the girls from any other attack.

47

Alex grabbed the Demon by the throat as she got off the ground. Her entire body did a quick flash of blue before lifting him in the air. With tremendous force, she slammed him onto the ground with a thunderous fury. She started to punch the Demon with more passion than the others. "You left without saying anything! Not one word! You left without saying goodbye! I LET YOU LEAVE! AHHH!" Alex screamed as she punched faster and faster. The Demon's face was becoming disfigured. Komptin let out a spine-chilling roar. This startled Alex enough to stop her attacks. She stood up to stare down at the broken Demon. His face was barely recognizable. She grabbed him by the shirt and stabbed him in the chest with her Lite. Alex took a moment to close her eyes as the body of the Demon melted. She calmly turned to the girls. "Ready?"

Both the girl's eyes were wide open with shock. "Did you know him?" Scarlett asked.

Alex glanced back at where the Demon disintegrated. "No, why?" She innocently went by the two F.O.R. escapees to get them to the hospital.

Kaylee and Scarlett both mouthed, "Wow."

***

Merik was standing near Gron, overlooking what was left of the body of the young man who threw himself under the semi-trailer. The smell of blood was getting the hiding Infiltrators a bit riled. Merik saw that Gron was far from happy. Merik could tell he was having a hard time controlling his anger in front of the cops who were taking a report. The shaken truck driver was giving his statement to the cop. There were a few secret Provisionaries in the department, but none of them were at the scene. This irritated Gron; he wanted this to be done with.

Merik leaned to Gron. "Want me to kill him?"

Gron turned to Merik. "Don't be stupid. He has no reason to die."

"What about the detective?" Merik could feel the Dark in him wanting to be unleashed.

"We can't kill him now." Gron saw a pair of headlights come up to the gate. Out of the car came the Prosecuting Attorney, Michael Johnson. He was met by the police detective, who briefed him on all that was going on. "Great." Gron stepped off the stairs to greet the attorney.

"Roger," Michael approached the F.O.R. leader. "Another dead body at your compound?"

"Watch yourself, counselor. This is the only one." Roger got a text from Misluna that she enjoyed her present. If he wasn't handling this situation, he would call her to hear about it.

"Interesting that he would throw himself under a semi-trailer," Michael told him as he studied the scene.

"Tragic," Roger tried acting as if he cared.

Michael was looking around the scene. "You think if he was going to commit suicide, there would have been signs. Did you know of any?"

"We offer confidential counseling sessions to all our members. I don't even have access to them. If you want to see them, get a court order. Speaking of which, I do believe you are trespassing. There are no charges against me, nothing to prosecute, so shoo away." He motioned with his hand for Michael to leave.

"I heard rumors of former F.O.R. members being murdered," Michael mentioned.

"Rumors, just rumors. If they died, there's no connection to us," Roger told him. "Give my best to your daughter and her brother." Roger snapped his fingers. "That's right, my bad. I guess just your daughter."

Michael didn't say anything. "I guess we'll see you around." He said something to the detective before taking a final look at the semi-trailer as he got into his car.

"Want me to kill him?" Merik eagerly invited his services.

"How stupid can you be?" Gron shook his head in disbelief. "If the Sentry finds out we killed her father, it would send her into battle mode. We can't risk it with the twins. They need to finish their task; that's all that matters. Everything else can wait." Gron motioned for Merik to follow him.

Merik and Gron turned the corner of the building, where he grabbed Merik by the throat. Gron's eyes glowed along with his fists. Merik thought for sure he would perish at his will. "What?"

"You better find Scarlett and that girl she took with her." Gron was furious.

Merik grabbed Gron's hands, trying to break free. "What about the twins?"

"You're too incompetent to handle such a task. I'll take care of it." Gron let go of Merik. "If I wasn't so short on Demons and Infiltrators. I'd kill you right here. Consider this your performance feedback."

Merik watched Gron call over Lurk to give him his thoughts on the situation. Merik decided to head home. The driveway fit his house, as it was small and needed repair. This dwelling was so beneath him. Being a Demon, he didn't need lights on to see in the shadows, so his electricity bill was cheaper. He sat down on the couch in the blackened house, drink in hand. He deserved to live in the compound; no –he deserved to run the compound.

Back when he was just Shawn, he ruled the high school. He was the king of that castle. He had any girl he put his sights on. Gron, who was Roger at the time, was a pitiful primate. The little runt couldn't even get with Alex. Considering how easy she is, that just proves Gron was a failure. So how did he get in charge of the F.O.R. while Merik was just a minion?

"You could be the face of the F.O.R.," a voice from behind him stated.

Merik turned his head around. "That is not possible."

Then the voice came from the corner of the room to right in front of him. "I can make it happen."

"No, what I'm talking about, is that you're here." Merik stood up from the couch to get another drink. "Gron needs to know you are here."

A pair of eyes appeared out of the dark. "I can make you the leader of the F.O.R."

"Gron is the Leader." Merik leaned on the bar.

"It could be you." Salamor appeared behind Merik through the wall.

"I'm listening." Merik took a sip of his drink.

Salamor perched himself on top of a hutch in the room. "The twins. The twins are the key."

Merik walked over to the living room window, staring out into the distance. "How?"

"I know where they will be delivered," Salamor quietly spoke from the shadow.

"Then Vandor will show his appreciation to me." Merik smiled.

"You'd be somebody. Somebody that everyone should worship." Salamor knew he had him. "Not Gron."

"What's in it for you?" Merik knew Salamor had his reasoning for his offer. "What do you want?"

Salamor started to fade away. "Just keep this between us. I can give you everything you want. It just has to maintain the secrecy that you and I will share."

CHAPTER TWO

The hospital waiting room was surprisingly quiet. Alex sat guarding two girls she found in the woods near the F.O.R. Compound. There was a feeling of happiness rescuing the girls, but she was disappointed that she didn't come across Shawn. That's who she would have liked to come face to face with for a *long uninterrupted* conversation. A Demon-possessed Shawn, who called himself Merik now, just infuriated Alex on how he seduced Anne. The way he treated her. He just left Anne on the ground near the lake, feeling miserable. She had and still does, feel like she betrayed Kale by allowing him to be with her.

Alex could relate. She was by no means an angel. She and Kameron had split up when he got transferred to San Diego. On top of that, her connection to the Lite was severed, causing her to have a consistent feeling of cold emptiness all the time. Her reliance on Komptin to notify her when the Dark was present had increased. She gave her friend a scratch behind the ears while he was sleeping at her feet. The German Shepherd lifted his massive head, leaning into her hand as she hit all his favorite spots. She sat back in her chair to wait for the girls to be seen. Time was standing still.

Scarlett sat between Kaylee and Alex. It was almost as if she was protecting Kaylee. "Are we safe here?"

Alex just continued to read her phone. "Yah, you're fine."

"What if they attack us here?" Scarlett jumped at the sound of the door to the emergency room opening. The calmness from Alex amazed the young socialite.

"They won't. The one thing the Lite and Dark have in common is neither of them wants full out public knowledge of the war." Alex was looking at the door and then at her watch. "Ugh."

Scarlett was trying to find out what she was waiting for. "Why?"

"The Dark fears they will lose because people will knowingly go to the Lite. The only way they can win is to secretly convince people to turn their backs on the Lite." Alex went back to her phone, scrolling through some social media videos.

Kaylee leaned over Scarlett. "Then why doesn't the Lite announce it?"

Alex shrugged her shoulders. "Probably because faith needs to be induced by free will, not fear." The doors opened to the emergency room again, and to her shock, her dad came into the hospital. "Dad. What are you doing here?"

"You first." He sat down across from the three of them. Michael patted Komptin on his back. The big dog welcomed the acknowledgment.

"I was out for a walk and found these girls running from the F.O.R. Compound." Alex was still paying attention to the door. Her face showed that she wasn't happy.

Her dad gazed at the door to see what she was looking for. "Okay." He turned his attention to the two girls. "Scarlett Roberts, Kaylee Whithers?"

"Yes." Kaylee adjusted her stance as she held her stomach.

"I'm Scarlett." The social media influencer admitted.

"I'm US District Attorney Michael Johnson. I have some questions about your recent residency at the F.O.R. compound."

The doors to the emergency room opened again. This time, a man was holding a greasy brown paper bag. "Alex Johnson?"

Alex stood up with excitement. "Right here." She grabbed the brown bag from the man after giving him some cash. The sound of the brown paper bag rustling caught the room's attention. She quickly unwrapped a double-cheese burger and took a big bite– ketchup seeped down the side of her mouth as she chewed. Alex realized the room was staring at her ravaging the sandwich down. "What?" Behind Alex, the emergency doors opened again to a man being helped into the hospital by a larger black male. It looked like the man being helped into a wheelchair was beaten.

The security guard quickly came over to assess the situation. "What happened?"

The man helping his friend stated, "I came home and found my roommate lying on the floor in our apartment. I thought he was mugged, but nothing was taken." The security guard yelled for a nurse.

The man in the wheelchair began to speak, "It was the girl. I'm telling you, it was the girl."

His friend interjected, "He keeps talking about this girl jumping out the window. Our window was broken, but we're on the fifth floor, and there was no one below it."

"She flew, she flew," he was mumbling.

"Did he take any hallucinogens?" the caring nurse asked.

"He wouldn't voluntarily." The roommate was concerned.

"She had wings come out her back and purple hair." The man was taken off into the back of the room.

Scarlett moved her head towards the man. She didn't get a good glimpse of him, but he sure sounded like Steven. It must have been her imagination because he probably would have moved back to California by now. Her thought was interrupted by Alex digging in her greasy brown bag.

Alex grabbed another burger as she offered the girls the rest of them. "I need to go check on something." She whistled for Komptin to join her in the elevator. The doors opened, and the hallway was eerily quiet. The two fighters for the Lite knew where the chapel was located. They both hesitated before entering the room. In front of all the pews, on her knees praying, was Devine. She wore some rather baggy clothes compared to what she usually morphed into. "I took a shot that you might be here."

"I do not wish to be bothered." The angel's body did not move.

"Devine, you okay?" Alex cautiously approached. "Want to talk about it?"

"I wish not to be disturbed." She got onto her feet, about to move but stopped. "Will he live?"

"Luckily, he'll live. You could've killed him." Alex looked down at Komptin, who was approaching her with caution as well. The purple-haired angel just slowly nodded. "Devine, was that your first time?"

Devine could not face Alex. She started to walk towards the door. "I must go."

"Do you have questions about sex?" She now knew how her mother felt talking to her about it. This was quite awkward for Alex. Devine started to walk by her. "Devine, there can be some mixed emotions…" Alex placed a gentle hand on Devine's arm.

"DO NOT TOUCH ME!" Devine yelled at her. She grabbed Alex's arm and pushed her away, causing her to fall on her back in the chapel aisle. Devine left the chapel as Alex got up to follow her. There was no sign of her in the hallway. Alex didn't know what to do. She decided to go check on Scarlett and Kaylee.

***

Anne barely got any sleep. She had nightmares all night about her and Kale fighting over her being with Shawn. The weather must have been changing because she was getting a small headache. All she could do was lay there in bed, staring at the ceiling fan as it spun around. She didn't like the fan blowing at night, but Kale needed it to sleep. There were times she tried shutting it off, but she never ended up sleeping well.

Her cell phone startled her when it started ringing. She moved the Bible she was reading last night to get to it. "Good morning."

Alex was on the other end. "Hey, morning, we have a little situation." Alex went on to tell her how she ran into two girls that escaped from the F.O.R. Compound.

"Are they okay?" Anne sat up in bed. The pulsating throbbing in her head hurt.

"They're being discharged from the ER now," Alex told her. "The thing is, they don't have anywhere to go. My dad said the sheriff's office is short-staffed with the United Won setting up here to counteract the Darius King protestors; they have no one to watch Scarlett and Kaylee."

"What do you suggest?" Anne swung her feet around to put her slippers and bathrobe on.

Alex covered the phone to make sure no one heard what she was about to say. "The safest place for them is the church."

"It's not even close to being finished renovated." Anne entered her bathroom and opened the medicine cabinet to get pain pills.

"I know, but we need to do something," Alex told her. "Hang on a second." Alex started talking to her dad before turning back to talk on the phone. "Let's meet at the church, okay."

"Okay, sweetie. Give me a bit, okay?" Anne hung up the phone. She put the pills in her mouth and washed them down with water she cupped in her hand. She closed the medicine cabinet to a figure with glowing red eyes in the reflection. It was standing outside her bedroom window. Anne screamed as she turned around… but there was no one there. It almost felt like her racing heart was about to come out of her chest. Luckily the sink was there for her to grab onto when her legs turned to jelly.

Anne took a second to calm down before starting the shower. For some reason, she wanted to close the door. After her hot, steamy shower that she really didn't want to get out of, Anne got dressed. Her dyed black hair wasn't something she liked. She checked the salon appointment openings on her phone. By the grace of God, they had an early appointment to change it back to her light brown hair.

"Mom, Dad?" she yelled for them as she was going down to the kitchen. There was no answer, so it would be assumed they had left for work. The house was quiet. Anne cut an English Muffin in half and grabbed the homemade peanut butter from the cupboard. She waited for the toaster to finish gazing out the window over the sink. Normally, deer or animals are eating the salt block and bird food her dad put out there. There was nothing out there, not even a squirrel. There was plenty of food, but no sign of anything.

"Anne," came a whisper in the distance from down the hall.

She shook it off. It was so distant that Anne just played it as her imagination. The muffin popped up. She had to spread the peanut butter quickly to properly melt. The honey she lightly drizzled was from her dad. He started to raise bees last year, and surprisingly, it was good. There was a sudden movement in the field. Anne could feel her heart begin to race, but then she saw that it was a deer coming out of the field. It had its head down and slowly approached the salt block. It seemed as if the deer were leading the charge because the rest of the animals started to approach. Squirrels, birds, and even a small rabbit came out of the woodwork to eat their morning meal.

Anne finished her breakfast and brushed her teeth. She ensured she had enough time to make it to the hair appointment before she said she would meet Alex at the church. Even though it was going to be a nice day, Anne grabbed her jacket on the way out the door. On the porch was a fifty-dollar bill on the ground. Anne picked it up to study whose it could be. Perhaps her parents dropped it. It had a weird substance on it, as if someone had sneezed into it. Her phone beeped to remind her of the appointment for her hair coloring.

* * *

Kameron must have slept a total of an hour and fifteen minutes before the phone rang. "Kameron," he said in a very groggy voice. Paige was on the other line telling him that he needed to come in. "Okay." It was all he could say before putting his head back into the pillow to groan into it.

Even though Paige told him to come straight in, Kameron had to shower first. He was so tired. He,

Midnight, and Scotty were talking the whole trip. They talked about work, the new career path they seemed to stumble onto, and then they talked about everyday life things. It was one of the most relaxing flights.

"Hey, buddy," a voice said. "Hey!"

Kameron jumped in the back seat of the taxi he called. There was no way he was in any condition to drive, especially if there was traffic. "Sorry, what's going on?" Kameron forgot for a second where he was.

"We're here, man." The longhaired taxicab driver shut the car off.

"Thanks." Kameron handed him a twenty-dollar tip.

"Thanks, dude." He held up the bill to make sure it was real.

The elevator ride up to the office almost put him back to sleep. He passed the office door to see the office cubicles under construction. The conference room had a new temporary table. The other agents talked about the surprise remodel with all the new furniture Paige got. In the back of the conference room, Scotty and Midnight were sleeping on each other. Midnight was out cold on Scotty's shoulder while he was drooling onto her hair.

Kameron nudged them. "What's going on?"

Scotty snorted when he wiped his mouth. "I don't know. I was just told to come in." He shrugged Midnight, who was passed out on his shoulder. She didn't really move so he slapped her face to wake her up.

"Ow." She hit him in the chest and went back to sleep. "Go back to bed."

Scotty leaned over to her. "Get up!"

"I'm up. I'm up." Midnight rubbed her eyes. "What are we doing here, anyway? Aren't we on comp days?"

"I don't know, but I'm tired." Kameron saw the San Diego PD SWAT come into the room. "This is interesting."

Paige followed them into the conference room with Weston behind them. "Okay, sorry for the short notice. We just got one hundred percent confirmation that the arsonist who set fire to Marchester & Payton Law Firm is located at this apartment complex." The slide show on the television screen showed a rundown building. "Remember, this guy knowingly killed twenty-one people in that fire he set. I want to thank San Diego PD SWAT, who got organized on such short notice to help us out." She turned the floor over to the SWAT Commander. "Sergeant Nelson."

"Thank you." The man with gray hair came up. He was in shape, and it was obvious he was a hard knocks police officer. He held up a picture, "This is our target. His name is Corwin Train." The man was an older man. His face was sunken in a bit and his shoulder-length hair was black with a hint of gray in it.

"Looks innocent enough," a younger officer said as he was smacking his chewing gum from nerves.

"Don't be fooled. This man was a demolition expert in the Marines and got his master's degree in

Fire, Arson, and Explosion. And to top it off, he's a member of F.O.R," the commander briefed.

Kameron and his two friends made eye contact with Paige and Weston when he said that. "What's the extraction plan?"

"Take him alive, obviously, but if he puts any of my men in danger, we're dropping him." The commander went to the next slide. "Alpha Team, you're going to breach the door, followed by Beta. Our Federal Task Force will only come onto the scene once it's secure."

Paige chimed in. "That's Kameron, Midnight, and Scotty."

Scotty put his head back. "This sucks. We've had like two hours sleep," he quietly said to Midnight and Kameron.

The commander concluded the briefing. "We go in, apprehend the target, and we all go home to our families. Rapunzel, you can get your haircut." The group laughed at their teammate with long blonde hair.

"And deny the ladies what they want?" He jokingly played with his hair in front of the group.

"Yeah, beauty tips," another member teased. The group was playfully mocking his hair, giving him fake kisses. They all left laughing to go get into their gear.

"He does have nice hair." Midnight caught herself admiring him. "Not bad looking either."

Scotty put his head back onto the wall and closed his eyes. "I want sleep."

Paige approached the sleepy agents as they were falling asleep in her conference room. "Sorry, guys.

I know you're tired." Kameron showed her with his thumb and finger that they were just a little bit tired. "I'll make it up to you, I promise. The one thing the Council does is appreciate all who help."

Kameron opened one eye, "So, we're all officially in the Council?"

Weston made sure the doors were closed before speaking. "Yes."

"How much does it pay?" Scotty still had his eyes closed.

"Well, without being greedy, you won't live paycheck to paycheck." Weston joined next to Paige.

"Plus, you'll still have your paycheck and benefits from here." Paige was studying the file on the arsonist.

"Nice." Midnight was still leaning her head on the wall with her eyes closed. "Just one thing added on to that."

Weston asked, "What's that?"

"Can we have it not reported to the Friend of the Court?" Midnight asked out of curiosity.

Kameron turned his head over to Midnight for an answer, but Scotty was the one who spoke. "That jackass ex-husband of hers collects alimony from her."

"He got a good lawyer." Midnight was obviously irritated at the thought of her former husband.

"I'll see what we can do," Weston snickered. "How'd it go with the Sentry?"

"We found her," Kameron answered with no emotion. "She's in Copper Top Mountain."

Paige stopped studying her files. "Copper Top Mountain, near the F.O.R. Compound?"

"Yes." Kameron now put his head on the wall.

"Well, that's convenient." Paige closed her files. "Look, right now, I need you three to, well, one, wake up." She kicked them.

"I'm up." Scotty shook his head to clear the cobwebs. The other two rubbed their eyes.

"Two, can you see what you can get out of the target?" Paige turned around to make sure no one was coming into the room.

"Like what?" Kameron asked, getting out of his seat to try to wake up.

Weston added, "The Council says that they're dealing with something they've never seen before, but that's all they're giving us."

"Surprise, a religious organization withholding valuable information," Scotty nudged Midnight to get off his shoulder again.

Weston came to the defense of the Council. "They're not telling us because they don't know."

Kameron got up to stretch. Paige said with a sympathetic tone, "How's the Sentry?"

"She's fine," he quickly snapped. "I'm going to go get the spare vests."

***

Anne just finished getting her hair back to normal. There was no doubt about it; it felt good. Every time she passed a window, she couldn't help but admire how well it turned out. The town seemed to be a bit busier than usual. Copper Top

Mountain wasn't always the biggest town, but it has grown a lot since the last time she lived here.

The town was thriving, but there seemed to be a tension in the air. Anne went into a coffee shop to get a muffin and something to drink. There was a group of people having a coffee, talking about how Darius King perpetuated the movement of reverse racism. They were wearing coats that had a symbol on their shoulder that seemed familiar. It had the letter 'U,' and inside of it was the number "1."

"Hey, Anne, what can I get you?" the woman asked from behind the counter.

"Hello, Rhonda." Anne studied the display. "Can I please get a banana nut muffin and a pumpkin spice latte?

Rhonda processed the order before getting the coffee. "Big plans today?"

"Just work." Anne got a text from Alex stating Father Richard, and Father Carl were flying into town in a couple of hours. Alex couldn't pick them up, so she asked if she could do it. A sudden shot of nerves went through her body. The fear of running into Shawn haunted her thoughts. The memory of how he treated her after she allowed him to be with her. Even though Kameron helped her deal with the feelings, she still felt somewhat guilty for betraying Kale's memory. Alex said she talked to Shawn about it but didn't say much about it. Knowing Alex, she probably punched him.

Anne really didn't have enough time to get back to the church to do anything productive before needing to pick the priests up. Inside her car, across the street from the coffee shop, was a book she could use to kill some time. It took a bit before she was able to cross the street with her muffin and coffee in hand. For some reason, she wasn't comfortable leaving them unattended. The book was in the back seat of her car. She placed a picture of her and Kale as a bookmark. Across the street, she saw Kate ready to go into the coffee shop.

They made eye contact, staring at each other. The last time she saw Kale's mom was at the park, where she left Anne crying at the park table when she was trying to give her some of Kale's childhood items. Anne shouldn't have done that. The feeling of going over to apologize overwhelmed her. Then the fear of having her know how she betrayed Kale was overwhelming. The only thing Anne could do was get into her car to head to the airport.

The airport was busy with a lot of people running around to get to their destinations. Occasionally, Anne would gaze up from her book to see if Father Richard or Father Carl were coming out from behind security. She went back to her book, reading the theoretical implications of the Catholic overture in Eastern Europe. An excited scream from a couple of girls caught Anne's attention. They were hugging each other with enthusiasm. Anne smiled at the sight of the friends reconnecting.

In the background, Anne saw Shawn in his airport neon yellow vest with radio in hand. Anne could feel her breath shorten at the sight of him. She hoped he didn't see her, so she buried herself back into her book. She was getting into the theories the book was reporting until she felt the presence of two individuals approach her.

"Excuse me, ma'am," one of them said as they surrounded her.

Anne placed her bookmark in her book before closing it. "Yes." She went to stand up.

"Please remain seated." One officer held out his hand to keep her down.

Her heart rate started to pick up its pace a bit. "Is there something wrong? Is Alex okay?"

"I don't know who Alex is. We're checking in on you. You've been here for two hours." The one who took control of the talking stepped forward.

"I'm sorry about that. I'm here picking two people up from the airport. I'm just using the extra time to catch up on some reading." Anne showed them the book.

"That is enjoyable reading for you?" He was trying to figure Anne out.

Anne smiled and nodded.

"There are concerns that you might be scouting the area." The officer called over the radio, advising the situation was under control. "What time is your friends' plane arriving?"

Anne was happy to see both priests coming out from behind the security gate. Anne waved to them. "There they are now."

Both of them were wearing their collars, and Anne was happy to see them. Even though she knew this was deescalated, it was still nice that this showed even more she wasn't a threat. Father Richard came up to the three of them. "Hey, Anne, is everything okay?"

The lead officer removed his hat. "Sorry, Father. We're just conducting a routine security check."

"No need to apologize to me." Father Richard put his briefcase down to put his jacket on.

"Of course." The lead officer turned to Anne. "Ma'am. I do apologize if I made you uncomfortable."

Anne noticed the officer, who still had his hat on, just rolled his eyes. "I get it." She got up from her seat to gather her belongings.

"Have a nice day," the officer offered to her. "Fathers." He nodded his head to the two of them. The other officer walked away, voicing his objections on how he handled that.

"What was all that?" Father Carl watched the officers disappear.

"I was just here for a while reading and someone probably thought I was acting suspicious. How was your flight?" Anne put on her white coat.

"I thought last-minute notifications of getting on a plane were over in my life." Father Carl rubbed his eyes from being tired.

"Where's Alex?" Father Richard started following Anne out to the car.

"At the church with our guests." Anne showed them to the car. They got to the car, and someone had scratched an F.O.R. symbol on the hood of her car. "Oh, come on." Anne looked around to see if there was anyone in the area. "This isn't even my car."

Father Carl peeked over at the cars next to Anne's. He didn't want to mention that none of them were touched.

***

69

Kameron wasn't comfortable with this situation at all. Even though there were two teams going in to secure the room before they got into it, he still was uneasy. "I got that same feeling as the day I got shot."

"I'm not feeling the greatest either." Midnight adjusted her vest. "This is squishing the girls."

Scotty perked up. "Really?"

"Not a comment from you," Midnight warned him.

Kameron motioned for them to be quiet as they were about to breach. "This is all wrong." He wiped a bit of sweat off his head. The humidity in the building was thick. Being in all that gear didn't help either.

"Yah, I'm not liking this much either," Scotty agreed to both Midnight's and Kameron's surprise. "We shouldn't be here."

"They're on the countdown." Kameron pointed to the team.

The SWAT Leader gave the go-ahead to breach the door. A member of the team knocked on the door. "Corwin Train, we have a warrant for your arrest." The next member swung the battering ram to open the door. The sound of the door crashing sent the team into the apartment. There was a quick pause before the team leader told them to clear the apartment. The Beta Team followed in and cleared the rest of the apartment.

The SWAT Leader was called into the scene. He left the federal agents alone down the hallway to join his team. After what seemed like an eternity, he came out and pulled his hooded mask off. "Scene is clear. You need to come see this."

Kameron led the way and entered the room. As soon as they entered the room, they saw a man hung upside down on the wall. His body was shaped like an upside-down cross. There were multiple cuts across his body, arms, and legs. The only piece of clothing he had on was an old t-shirt draped on his crotch.

"Oh my, God," Midnight said aloud. Five of the team members, including Midnight, made the sign of the cross on their bodies.

Kameron forced himself to get closer to the body to study it. "Is it rigged with anything?"

The Team Leader came to join him on the other side of the body. "Doesn't look like it?"

"Why is there a number four scratched into it?" One of the officers' face suddenly turned pale.

"It's the symbol of the F.O.R. They must have carved it before stringing him up." Kameron wiped his hand over his face. "It didn't look like the place was broken into before we got here."

"So, the killer knew him." Scotty slowly advanced toward the body. He placed his hand on Midnight's shoulder. "You okay?"

"Yah, I'm good. Go on." She motioned him over to the body.

He took Kameron's spot on the other side of the body to look at it. Kameron shifted to the front of the body. The Team Leader joined him. "I'm going to call this in. I need to state the obvious. Don't touch it."

Kameron nodded as he continued to compute the scene.

The young SWAT Member joined his side. "What are you thinking?"

"I'm wondering why there's a body?"

Midnight and Scotty both made eye contact with each other before turning to Kameron in confusion. Scotty softly said, "Because he's human." It was code enough for SWAT Members to think it was a joke, but both Kameron and Midnight knew what he was talking about. Demons and Infiltrators disappear when they're killed.

The Team Leader called over the radio that Crime Scene Investigators were five minutes out. The SWAT members left, leaving the three in the room alone. "We have five minutes. Make it count." Kameron started to scour the apartment.

"What are we looking for?" Scotty asked as he started to scan the apartment.

"Anything." Midnight picked up envelopes with her rubber-gloved hands.

"Preferably any connection to F.O.R." Kameron went to the kitchen area to look through the cupboards. He smiled when he found a box of Hostess cupcakes in the pantry but quickly got back to business. There wasn't much of anything in the refrigerator.

"Nothing in the bedroom!" Scotty yelled. "This guy led a pretty boring life."

"If you consider grand arson with murder boring." Midnight peeked out the window to see if anything was out there.

72

The three of them met in the middle of the living room. "I got nothing." Scotty covered his radio, advising that Crime Scene was on its way up.

"Me either." Midnight yawned. "I want to go to bed."

"Me too," Scotty told his friends.

"But I want to sleep in mine...alone." Midnight started to head out of the apartment.

"I'm stopping off at Harry's for their lunch buffet before I go home." Scotty followed her out. "They can take me home. Did I ever tell you about their driver's program?" He started to say as they left the apartment. All Kameron heard from Midnight was, "Stop."

Kameron was leaving when he got a phone call from an unknown number. "This is Kameron." This was a phone call he wasn't expecting. While listening to the other end, he noticed something behind the door. "Hang on, one second." He bent down to pick up a rosary with his pen. It wasn't anything special, but there was confusion about why such a powerful Catholic symbol would be here in this apartment. "Sorry about that," he went back to his phone. "You want me to do what again?"

***

Devine was perched on the church's steeple, staring down at the Lite Sentry's father talking on his communication machine. Alexandria had rarely talked about her dad. As far as she knew they didn't always agree on the topics of discussion. Devine gracefully moved to the other side to catch a better view of the man. He seemed like a nice primate; she didn't understand why the Lite Sentry and he didn't really get along.

There was movement below that caught her attention. Devine saw the Sentry was carrying a drink. She walked toward her father and handed it to him. He took a sip of it as he was talking on the device. Why would the Sentry do that if they don't get along? Devine then saw him hug his little girl and kiss her on top of her head.

They do love each other, but they don't agree. This confused Devine. Was she supposed to love this Demon? This wretched, foul, disgusting...Devine grabbed her stomach as it was coming to pain. It wasn't a pain she had felt before. This was coming from inside her body. She took off to the clouds in the hopes of feeling better. It seemed as if the higher she flew, the sicker she became.

The lights below of the human community were behind her now. For some reason, she had the feeling of wanting to leave, but yet needing to stay. Then a sharp pain like a bunch of small spears inside her came out of nowhere. She grabbed her stomach as she crashed into a field of corn. There was a trail from her crashing as she was now covered in mud. She screamed in pain as tears dropped down the side of her face. What was happening to her?

***

Alex was checking up on the new guests in the church. The coffee she gave her dad seemed to wake him a bit. There was no doubt he was tired. She felt bad that he was taking on the F.O.R. in this manner. He had no idea what he was up against, or did he? If he did, there was a chance he knew what her role in this war might be. Alex shook off that line of thought because she was sure he would confront her about it.

She set the two girls in what she assumed would be her bedroom when all the renovations were done. It would seem time wasn't her ally to discuss it with Anne and Father Richard. Even though she still didn't have any connection to the Lite, she still wanted the security of staying in the church. There wouldn't be any objections to it, well, except from the jackass.

She slowly opened the door to see the girls under some blankets and pillows that Alex had gotten from the store. Her dad and the sheriff provided security while she ran to the new Purch-Mart. Initially, she went to the old building, but they built a bigger one across town. The door creaked a bit as she shut the door to the girls who were fast asleep. Alex turned around to see her dad approach with the sheriff.

"Hey, Dad." Alex motioned for him to be quiet. "They're fast asleep."

"Come with us." He smiled, letting her know that things were okay. He waited until they were in one of the priest's offices. The office was in complete shambles. "They really did a number on this place."

"Yes, they did." Alex looked around with sadness at the remnants of what she considered her home.

"You should get some rest," Michael told his daughter.

"Isn't that calling the pot a kettle?" she halfway joked with him.

Michael snickered as he was waiting for the rest of the saying, "Touché." He kept on looking at his phone with a worried face. "I'm going to go home after we talk with the priests."

"Waiting for an important phone call?" Alex felt she overstepped a bit but didn't really care.

"Just debating if it was the right one." Michael put his phone away.

Alex poked her head out in the hallway when she heard Anne and the others. "Anne, we're in here." The three of them joined Alex with her dad and the local sheriff.

"Hello." Michael shook the hands of the priests. "I'm US District Attorney Michael Johnson, this is Sheriff Pearl."

"I'm Father Richard, the Dean of the church. This is Father Carl, who's in charge of administration." Father Richard removed his glasses to wipe the sweat off his shiny bald head.

"We would like to discuss your most recent guests down the hall." Michael leaned against the wall. The weight of his eyes was getting heavier by the passing second.

"Okay," Father Richard nodded. "Anne is our Historian. She will be here for an official recording capacity."

Michael and Sheriff Pear nodded.

Father Carl quickly came in. "Alex, there is no reason for you to stay. You can leave."

There was no hiding Alex's face of disgust. "What?"

Father Richard tried to think of a way she could stay in the meeting, but he couldn't justify it. Therefore, he thought he would excuse her with a code stating that he would talk to her later about it. "Alex. We'll talk later about grounds that are in need of cleaning after this meeting."

Alex got the hint, but she still wasn't happy. Anne knew Alex was upset. If Alex didn't know any better, she could have sworn that Father Carl snickered a bit. All she could think of was that she was lucky they were on church grounds. "If this ain't some bullsh…"

"Alex," Father Richard warned her.

"I'll be in my office," she let Father Richard know. She gave Father Carl a sarcastic smile full out telling him what she thought of him.

She gently closed the office door. Father Carl was about to speak when they heard from down the hall: "He's such a jackass."

Alex continued down the hallway, irritated at how she got kicked out of that meeting. She's the one who killed those Demons and Infiltrators, well, her and Komptin. How much blood did they spill on the forest floor? "There's no reason for you to stay. You can leave." She was sarcastically talking to herself coming into the congregation hall. Alex jumped a bit when she saw a figure sitting in the back pew. It startled her enough to raise her fist, and she immediately found herself being tackled by the two Guardians of the Conduit. Arome and Omeila had her pinned to the floor.

"What are you doing?" Alex yelled. "I wasn't going to hurt her. I just wasn't expecting anyone here!" Alex was quite amazed at how strong they actually were.

"Arome, Omeila. She cannot sense the Lite, remember?" Celestial just remained seated as Komptin kept his head on her lap for her to pet. "I am sure you can let her off the floor."

"As you wish." Omeila let go of Alex, not taking his eyes off her.

Arome seemed to give Alex another push as to say they could kill her at a moment's notice. "Watch your actions, Sentry." He joined Omeila as they went forward to pray.

"They're pleasant." Alex pushed herself off the ground. "Can I hug you without any repercussions?"

Celestial smirked as she moved over a bit to give Alex a comforting hug. "Of course."

Alex sat next to the angel in a moment of serenity; it wasn't the warmth of the Lite, but it was a close second. Komptin enjoyed the scratches behind the ears from both beings. "It hasn't been a good day so far."

"Depends on the point of view," Celestial told her. "For those two girls. This is a fantastic day."

"Kaylee lost the one she loves," she reminded her. "She will be in pain.'

Celestial gazed down at Komptin as she scratched his head. "She will find it again."

"That's not fair." Alex put her head on Celestial's shoulders.

"Why do you say that?" Celestial started to fix Alex's hair.

Alex just stared at the Guardians praying. "She misses Kale so much. Why can't she find it again?"

"Anne is not healing because she is not open to it," Celestial told Alex. "You cannot tell her to move on. Even God doesn't have the power to take that away from her. Only she knows when she is ready."

Alex continued to rest her head on her Godmother's shoulder. "I guess when we lose someone we love, we all handle it differently." For some reason, Alex thought about how badly Devine was hurting when she saw her at the church. It wasn't her place to tell Celestial what happened, but maybe she should say something to the Conduit of Lite. Then again, she might push Alex into divulging what Devine had done.

***

The three agents just wanted to get to their respective beds. Paige invited them into her office. Midnight and Scotty took the two chairs in front of the desk, almost sleeping. Kameron took his spot on the wide windowsill. The ocean was calm, and it truly was a gorgeous day, but he just wanted to go to bed.

"I guess we have no lead now." Paige reviewed the photos of the body.

Kameron was studying her reaction. Despise what Scotty said, Paige truly seemed upset over the death of this arsonist. "He was dead for about seven hours. Surprisingly, no witnesses, no cameras, nothing."

Midnight and Scotty both were about to pass out. Paige snapped her fingers. "Hey, hey, you'll be out of here in a bit, just hang in there for a couple more minutes." Paige showed the pictures to Weston. "Anything else?"

"I need to go to bed." Scotty slouched more in the chair.

"Soon." Paige turned her attention to Kameron who seemed like he had something else on his mind. "What's going on, Kameron?"

"I just got word back from Copper Top Mountain. The District Attorney up there has two young girls who escaped the F.O.R. Compound." Kameron continued to stare out the window.

"You're shitting me." Paige turned her attention to Weston. "We need to tell the Council this."

"On it." Weston grabbed his phone from his pocket as he left the office.

"Why did they contact you?" Paige was now enthused in her tone.

Kameron continued to stare out the window. He made sure not to make eye contact with the group for some reason. "They're going to be key players in taking down the F.O.R. up in Copper Top, but the Sheriff can't spare anyone to watch them."

"So, he asked you to provide security?" Paige asked him. Kameron nodded to her. "It's your call. I can make it happen on my end."

Kameron saw that Midnight and Scotty were barely awake. He thought about how his personal stake in this almost got them killed. He was just about to answer when Weston came into the office. "The Council is very happy. I haven't heard them this excited in a long time."

"The District Attorney asked Kameron to provide security for her." Paige pointed over to her agent with her pen.

"Let me call them back." Weston didn't leave the room this time. He just called them. Midnight and Scotty were shocked that Weston was speaking Italian while on the cell phone. There was a pause as Weston was listening to the Council on the other end. "Kameron, are you willing to go get her?"

"I've been up for over twenty hours," Kameron told him. "That's another eight-to-ten-hour flight."

Weston waved him off, "Don't worry about that. That's the least of your worries."

Kameron thought about it. "Who would know where we were?"

Paige chimed in, "Just the people in this room." She sat back in her chair. "Do you have an idea where to take her?"

"I do." Kameron stared back out the window.

"Can I go home and shower first?" Midnight got up from her chair.

"You don't have to do this?" Kameron appreciated the sentiment.

Scotty mumbled with his eyes closed. "I'm not going back to Copper Top?" Midnight smacked him in the back of his head. "Not without a shower first." He rubbed the back of his head.

81

"Really, guys, you did so much already." Kameron secretly thought he couldn't do this without them.

"It's either that or process the paperwork for the POTUS Asian trip." Midnight saw Scotty about to sleep. She smacked his leg.

"Ow." He rubbed the spot she hit him. 'I'm up. I'm up."

"Thanks, guys." Kameron smiled. "Scotty, I'll need you to get the safe house ready."

"No problem," Scotty assured him.

Paige's private phone suddenly vibrated. She read the text causing her face to become pale. "I don't know how to take this."

Midnight rubbed her eyes. "What's wrong?"

"Roger Somberson just told me to attend an Infiltration ceremony." Paige had fear in her voice.

"If he tells you you're ready for the Infiltration…" Weston told Paige.

"I know." Paige closed her eyes and took in a deep breath.

"Will you get possessed by one of those things?" Kameron asked her.

Paige just sat at her desk. Weston came by her side to offer support. "No."

***

Alex opened the door to Osiah's old office. Actually, she guessed it was now her new office. She took a moment to study what was left in the empty room. It was probably her imagination, but Alex could still hear him.

She remembered after she had rescued him from Vandor's attack on the school playground, they both grabbed Marty's burgers before coming back here. They were sitting around eating burgers and talking. He was at his desk with his feet on it. Alex thought he had blood on his orange beard, but it turned out to be ketchup. Komptin was lying down next to Alex sleeping as she sat on the floor next to him.

The two of them talked about so many things. Alex told him how she had just found out that she was really Kale's sister. He smiled as if he knew all along. Osiah began to tell her there was a special connection between the two of them. Alex went on to tell him about how Kale had such a crush on Anne. He just sat back and listened to Alex talk about all the gossip spreading around the school about her. Osiah never judged her, even when she made light of the fact that half the rumors were basically true. He just told her, "Little Spitfire, the strange thing about Blue Gold is that it's so rare, that when you gift it to someone, they will never let it go."

Alex never really thought about what he meant by that. He always said she had a heart of Blue Gold. She didn't realize she was holding the angel from her necklace in between her fingers. Komptin was sitting down next to her as if he too was remembering Osiah. Komptin had such sadness in his big brown eyes. With comforting smiles, they both entered the office.

The desk seemed still intact. She lifted the chair up from the floor. The wheels on it still worked smoothly as she glided it back and forth. She gently sat down in the chair. Komptin went to the corner of the office to lay down. "Do you want your bed from DC?" Komptin's ears perked up. She laughed. "Okay, okay. I'll get Megan to send it." The massive German Shepherd came to Alex and started licking her with excitement. "I get it, I get it. You're happy."

He started to play around with her. She moved from the desk to start wrestling around with him. Komptin knocked her down to be on top of Alex as he licked her. Alex forgot how powerful he actually was since she herself had no power on church grounds. For the first time in what seemed like an eternity, Alex laughed.

"Alex," a voice from the doorway came.

She looked up from the floor to see Father Carl standing in the doorway. Alex playfully grabbed Komptin by the face to turn it to hers. "You're supposed to warn me of danger." Alex kissed her dog on the forehead before getting off the floor. "What?"

"We need to talk." Father Carl just came into her office as if he owned the place.

At first, Alex's first reaction was to tell him this was her office, but she was just being childish. Father Tom was the first to offer the olive branch, and he turned out to be someone she really respected. Maybe this will be just the same. She playfully hopped up on her desk. "Whatcha got, padre?"

"We need to talk about your attitude. Look, it's no secret you have a problem with me being here." Father Carl went to the window.

"Thought I hid that," she sarcastically winked at him.

"Ms. Johnson, this is a one-way conversation." Father Carl got stern with her.

"Excuse me?" Alex was taken aback.

Father Carl wasn't joking around. "Look, there is more going around than you realize, and I'm being considered to join the fight against true evil."

Alex kept quiet, but not because she was brought down by him. Just because she wanted to know where he was going with this. "Okay. Go on."

"There is a fight out there between good and evil. If you haven't noticed, there are many people who need God, but they are rejecting Him. As a priest, it's my job to show them the warmth of God. Do you even know the feeling of His warmth?"

Alex angrily hopped off the desk. "Don't you dare say I don't know what it's like to miss His warmth." Komptin barked at her. Thank goodness he did that because that broke her focus. Alex put her finger up in Father Carl's face. "Don't you dare."

Father Carl knew she wasn't backing down, but he wasn't going to either. "You ever disrespect me like that again in front of others from outside this church, and I swear, on my collar, you will never work for this church again. You got that?"

Alex got a text from Anne to say she needed some help. "Fine …Jackass." She intentionally bumped his shoulder as she passed him. It took all her might to control her temper, but she managed to calm herself down to see Anne in her office quite upset. "What's wrong?"

Anne got herself a cup of coffee. "My contractor just quit on me. He said the building material from another project came in early, so he is dedicated to that one." She sat back on the wall to scratch her back. "You look upset too."

"Oh, I just miss Father Tom." Alex chuckled. "Never thought I would say those words at one time."

Anne thought back when he gave his life trying to protect her. "He was a good man. I take it this is about Father Carl."

"I know the Council is short on priests, but, come on." Alex looked around the office. "Do you happen to have…?" Anne opened the small fridge she had in the office to get her an Apollo. "Thanks."

"Do you have a minute to talk, sweetie?" Anne asked her.

"Of course," Alex told her.

Anne grabbed her jacket. "Let's go outside." Alex followed Anne outside of the church. The two of them sat down on the steps. "Strange, isn't it?"

"What's that?" Alex saw Komptin coming from the side of the church.

"Being back here." Anne took a second to watch a pair of doves flying off. "I think I owe you an apology."

"For what, Anne?" Alex took a drink of her energy drink.

Anne was having a hard time coming up with the words. "For betraying Kale like I did."

Alex turned to Anne. "You did not betray Kale. You were in a lot of pain, and I wasn't there for you. I should be the one apologizing to you."

Anne had a tear drop. "But you were going through so much and still are. I was being selfish."

Alex fought back from crying with her. "I'm learning to manage without sensing the Lite. Some moments are better than others. I should have been a better friend, sister, to you. Why didn't you tell me you are hurting so bad?"

Anne had more tears drop from her eyes. Komptin came to snuggle up to Anne in comfort. "I don't know. I guess I didn't want to because I was afraid of healing, forgetting him. I miss him so much."

Alex immediately followed suit with Anne as her eyes were starting to blur. The only thing the two of them could do was hold each other. "Anne, I miss him too. I will never forget him. When you love someone, you will never forget them when they are gone." Alex adjusted her body so Anne could lean her head on Alex's shoulder.

"What about Kameron?" Anne acted as if she knew something.

The sound of Anne blowing her nose almost made Alex laugh. The remembrance of Kameron leaving left a lump in her throat. "I'm afraid that's a door that will never open again."

Anne would never betray Kameron's trust by telling Alex what he said. It wasn't her place, but she wished so hard her two friends would get back together. "What would you do if it was?"

Alex was about to answer when a delivery truck stopped in front of them. "Excuse me," the man yelled from the truck. "I'm looking for Anne McClure."

"That's me." Anne raised her hand. "These must be the Bibles." Anne and Alex got up to sign for the box. "Can you bring it into my office?"

"No," the man rudely came off. "No inside delivery." He showed Anne the delivery instructions. The man, with a United Won pin on his lapel, got out of the truck to open up the back door. "You know this printing company is the exact same company that prints that Darius King propaganda."

"I didn't know that." Anne signed for the package.

"I can't believe the Catholic Church supports companies that print that kind of material," he said with disgust.

"Hey, watch it." Alex came off the stairs to join Anne. "We just got it printed from there. The Catholic Church isn't offering an opinion on anything."

"Actions speak louder than words," he told her. "Actions speak louder than words."

"And repeating yourself doesn't make you right." Alex made sure she was off church grounds in case something started happening.

"Alex," Anne warned her. "It's fine." She turned her attention to the driver. "Thank you very much." Anne opened up the box. Underneath the lids were a bunch of F.O.R. Roadmap to Absolute

Power guidebooks. "Sir, excuse me. This isn't mine."

"Yes, it is." He locked the door. "You signed for it; you opened the package. It's yours." The truck started as he coldly stated, "Have a nice day."

"What a jerk." Alex turned to Anne who picked up one of the books.

Anne flipped through the pages of the book. "I need to find out where the Bibles are."

"What should we do with these?" Alex picked up a book. On the back was a big picture of Roger. "He just looks evil."

Anne said softly. "He looks like the man who killed my husband." Anne turned to Alex. "I don't want these in the church."

"I'll take care of them," Alex assured her.

***

"Mr. Somberson," an elderly lady came into the office.

"Who are you?" Roger looked up at the late fifty's woman coming into the office with a notepad.

"I'm your new secretary, Beatrice. You can call me 'Bee' for short." The woman in an iron-pressed skirt that went down halfway between her knees and feet. Gron stared at the wrinkled-faced woman standing in front of him with dishwater blonde hair with some mixed gray in. He looked at her, tilted his head to look behind her, then back at her. "Is there something wrong, sir?"

Roger went back to paperwork. "Just curious who I'm going to have to kill."

"Ms. Luna hired me last week," Beatrice confirmed. "Speaking of which, her plane lands at two."

Gron looked at his watch. "Damn."

"I sent the limo to pick her up, and then from there, I asked the driver to swing by to take you to the meeting with the mayor." Beatrice was reviewing her notepad. She pulled out a pencil from her hair to check something off her list. "After the meeting, you have the Road Map to Absolute Power orientation meeting at six o'clock. Then you have the fundraiser down state for the Atheist foundation. It's black tie, so I had your suit dry cleaned and will be on your plane for your trip. I also put Ms. Luna's dress in the plane for the event."

Gron sat back. "Wow, okay."

The phone rang, and Beatrice grabbed the phone from Gron's desk. "Mr. Somberson's office." She sat there and listened for a moment. "No, he is not available for an interview at that time. Call back next Monday to set up a time. Have a nice day."

Gron never really liked saying no to interviews. "Who was that?"

"A reporter for *Cross Over News*. They are an upcoming news agency claiming to report strictly news where they just report the facts. They like to give the story, then interview one side, then the other, and for the final twenty minutes of their program, they have both sides sit down to discuss the issue." Beatrice wrote down. "The founder is a deep heartened Christian. He usually ends the show with a motivational quote from the Bible."

The leader of the F.O.R. rolled his eyes. "What is your views on God?"

"What God?" She came back with. "So, what would you like me to tell them next week?"

Gron nodded. "Keep them dangling. Have them think they'll get me on their show, but never commit."

"To your command." She wrote it down in her notes. A message on her phone came in. "Sir, the limo is downstairs waiting for you." She went over to the closet and grabbed his coat. As he put it on, she wiped off some of the lint off his shoulders. "There you go, sir."

"Nice." Gron turned around. "At first, I thought I was going to terminate you, but I think I'll keep you around." Gron looked in the mirror at himself.

Beatrice handed him his briefcase. "I appreciate that, sir. Also, a Paige Cass called to confirm her attendance. She didn't say to what about, but she said you would know."

"Good," He turned to Beatrice. "Misluna is down in the limo?"

"Yes, sir."

"My meeting is in a half hour?" Gron calculated the time in his head. "I think I will reward her for hiring you."

"Of course, sir." Beatrice turned back to head to her desk.

On the way to the mayor's office, Gron showed Misluna how much he appreciated his new secretary. The driver had to take the scenic route.

Some remnants of drink glasses were shattered throughout the back of the limo. Misluna was fixing her outfit while Gron was tightening up his pants.

"I think you missed me," Misluna snickered as she dabbed at a little bit of her blood dripping from her neck from Gron biting her.

"Don't count on it. How'd you like your gift?" Gron straightened his tie in the mirror.

"It wasn't a Sentry, but oh, was it fun. He had no idea it was coming. He was like, 'oh, the F.O.R. sent you?' and was all proud. Then I was savoring every slice. It was so much fun." Misluna was looking throughout her purse. "Damn, I have to work in two days. I lost my rosary."

The intercom from the driver came on. "Sir, we have arrived at the destination.

"Do you want me to come up with you?" Misluna was applying her lipstick.

Gron sat there and thought about it. "Might as well."

They sat there waiting in the lobby of the mayor's office. They sat there waiting for twenty minutes before Misluna finally said something to Gron. "What's taking so long?"

"It's a power play. He's making us wait." Gron continued to review his schedule for the upcoming week. "That new secretary already got the reservation at Giuliana's."

"I knew you would like her." Misluna went to the mayor's secretary, who was staring at Gron for some reason. Misluna always knew he had a way with the girls. This girl was a little bit older than he was, but that didn't matter to Gron.

The secretary didn't take her eyes off Gron when she answered the phone. "Yes, sir." She hung up the phone. "Mayor Paroyale will see you now." She opened the door. As they walked through the door, the secretary said, "Ma'am." Then with almost contentment, "Roger Somberson."

The mayor, who was taller than Gron and well-built, stood to shake hands with the F.O.R. leader. "I apologize for the wait, but it's just work, work, work."

"I take it you weren't expecting it to be this hard." Gron took off his coat to hand it to Misluna. "This is Misluna, she's my personal assistant."

"I see." Mayor Paroyale shook her hand. "I understand you had an incident at your compound last night."

"A very disturbed individual," Gron simply replied. "Just tragic."

"You didn't see that coming?" the mayor asked, sitting back down at his seat.

Gron glared at him. "You can't see everything coming. Unfortunately, what you don't see coming can get you killed."

"Yes." The big man stared Gron down. "Let's get right down to it. Your little organization out there is a plague on this town. You don't think I see you buying building after building, along with properties under false companies?"

"Really? I figure the plague on the town is still coming." Gron quickly came to defense.

"And that is?" Mayor Paroyale was trying to see where he was going.

"Rumor has it, United One has been coming into town to counteract the protestors for Darius King." Gron took a look at his fingernails. "Very potentially volatile situation you got there."

"There are some growing concerns, but nothing you need to worry about." The mayor was obviously bluffing on the position the town is in.

"I can help you. Let me get a F.O.R. liaison on your staff. Our program has proven to show great results in conflict resolution."

"Really? You, conflict resolutions? I don't think you have a great history of conflict resolutions." The mayor was basically dangling bait at Gron.

Gron bit at the lure. "What do you mean?"

"Rumor has it, you put two of your classmates in the hospital. One of them later on was killed by an unknown assailant when your building burnt down," the mayor called him out.

"There is no record of that. No charges, all hearsay." Gron was upset but calmly got up from his chair. "And congratulations, you will now hear from my lawyer."

Misluna blew the mayor a kiss as they left. The two of them went by the secretary who immediately got up to go to the mayor's office. The two members of F.O.R. got into the limo. Gron didn't say a word until the doors of the limo closed. "We're going to kill him."

***

Anne sat in her office with a picture of Kale in her hand. It was of the two of them on a weekend getaway when they were in college. It was late fall in their sophomore year. He told her to pack her bags for two overnights. He wouldn't tell her where they were going. They said goodbye to Alex before getting into Anne's car. Kale still couldn't drive long distances, so he just gave Anne directions while he sat in the passenger seat.

They ended up at this tiny bed and breakfast in a quaint little town. It was so peaceful. All they did was be with each other. They went for a walk in the woods, and ate a romantic dinner by the fire. Saturday morning, they just laid in bed together; he held her while they talked. Then he surprised Anne by scheduling her for a local author reading. Anne smiled at the memory of how miserable Kale was sitting through it, but he didn't say a word. He just gave her a loving, supporting look when he saw how much fun she was having. There was no doubt– that's when she knew she truly loved Kale Moler.

A knock on the door interrupted Anne's thoughts. "Excuse me." Kaylee was at the door to her office.

"Hello." Anne put her picture down. "How's it going?"

"I'm okay." The small blonde hair girl sat down in front of her desk.

Anne got up to close a filing cabinet and put the picture of Kale on top of it. She kissed her fingers before pressing them against the picture.

"How did he pass?" Kaylee asked her.

Anne turned around. "What makes you think he passed away?"

"Just the way you look at the picture." Kaylee started rubbing her stomach.

"He was murdered by a monster," Anne admitted.

"Was it this war?" Kaylee got up and started to walk around the office.

Anne noticed she was worried about something. "What are you worried about?"

"I lost someone I loved," Kaylee told her. "Now my baby is going to grow up without his father."

"Your life isn't over." Anne could see she was really worried. "Who knows what's in store for you? You just need to be you, inside of here." Anne patted her chest. "You'll be fine."

"They're taking us away to an undisclosed location." Kaylee grabbed a Bible and started thumbing through it. "My mom was religious."

"Is she still?" Anne joined Kaylee at her side.

"I don't know. I ran away when I was fifteen. That's when I joined F.O.R. I wanted absolute power." Kaylee chuckled.

"Ever think of looking into it yourself?" Anne was trying to give Kaylee much-needed support.

"I've done bad things." She handed the Bible back to Anne. "Dr. Smithon is looking over Scarlett right now. After that, we leave for our safe house to prepare to testify, once they bring charges to the F.O.R." Kaylee wiped a tear. "I hope I have the strength for this."

Anne handed her the Bible. "Take this. Whenever you feel scared, weak, or feeling like the Dark is going to overcome, just give this a try."

Kaylee smiled as she nodded. "Thank you." She gave Anne a hug.

Alex came into the office. "Hey, Dr. Smithon would like to see you now."

"Thanks." Kaylee left as she showed Anne the Bible to thank her.

"You okay, Anne?" Alex came into the office.

"I'm fine, sweetie." Anne grabbed her jacket. "I need to get something to eat. You wanna come?"

Alex thought about it. "No. Dr. Smithon wants to see me about my little issue I'm still having."

Anne liked the fact that Alex was starting to make light of the situation of being disconnected from the Lite. It told Anne that Alex was becoming Alex again. She liked that. Anne decided to go to Kate's restaurant. In a way, she wanted to run into her. Perhaps it was time to clear the air with her. Nerves shot through her body walking into the supper club. The waitress approached Anne.

"Can I get you something?" she asked as she logged into the machine.

Anne didn't even need to see the menu. "I'll take a Caesar salad with a side of garlic cheese bread."

She typed it in. "Anything to drink?"

"I'll take an unsweetened iced tea with lemon." Anne was scouting the room. "Is Kate around?"

"No, she's with Jessica at the hospital," the waitress told her.

"Oh my God, is she okay?" Anne could only imagine that she was attacked by the Dark.

The waitress took Anne's credit card. "She's fine, and so is the baby."

Anne smiled as she held her chest. "Jessica had her baby."

"A healthy ten-pound boy," the waitress told her. "It won't take long. I'll be right back."

Anne sat down on the waiting bench. She texted Dan congratulations on becoming a father. He replied with a very tired Jessica holding their baby. She couldn't help but be happy for them. Anne went to get her food from the waitress. "Thank you." As she was leaving, she accidentally bumped into a tall man. "I'm sorry."

"It's okay. I like it when our bodies smash against each other." Shawn stood tall in front of her.

Anne started to breathe in short heavy breaths. "Shawn."

He leaned over to Anne. "I missed you. I don't understand why you won't let me in." He stopped for a second moving eyes to the sky. "Oh wait, maybe you have."

Anne was starting to hyperventilate. "Shawn, … I… I can't…" Anne tried to say.

He just smiled at her.

"Anne?" A voice came from behind them both. It was Kale's mom, Kate, who returned from the hospital. "What's going on here?"

Before Anne could answer, Shawn interrupted, "Oh, Kate, I'm sorry you had to find out this way. We were hoping to tell you at a better time." Shawn moved next to Anne.

"About?" Kate looked at Anne. "Anne, are you feeling okay?"

"She's fine. She just wanted me to tell you how we're a couple now. Something I've dreamt of since high school."

"Shawn...we...are not together," Anne finally got out. It was obvious she was trying to catch her breath.

"Then, why did you pull me down to make love?" Shawn asked her in front of Kate.

"I think you need to leave," Kate demanded. "Anne would never..." Kate saw the guilt on Anne's face. "Anne?"

Anne grabbed her chest as she walked out of the diner. She stopped to put her head down below her knees. Then she started to gasp for air before all she saw was blackness.

***

Alex put on her shirt as she finished her medical examination. The nurse was writing down notes as Dr. Smithon was giving her instructions. "Okay, physically, you seem fine. Still no connection?"

"Nope," Alex told her as she tied her black woven hair in the back.

"I'm still researching. Try not to lose faith." Dr. Smithon was packing up his bags.

Alex finished getting dressed and ran into Scarlett in the hallway. "I hear you're leaving us tonight?"

"They're taking us to some location, we won't know where until we get there. I just want my life back." Scarlett looked around to make sure no one was listening. "Do you happen to have a phone on you?"

"Yes, why?" Alex handed her the phone.

"I just want to see what's been going on." Scarlett logged into her account to see the social media transactions. "Things were so much better when I had my assistant."

Alex was watching her carefully. "I wouldn't post anything, unless you want the F.O.R. to know where you are."

Scarlett thought about it before handing her the phone. "I guess we are getting some protective services while we're hiding." Scarlett gave a smirk. "I get my own Kevin Costner."

"They broke up at the end of that movie." Alex whistled for Komptin. "Don't get involved with bodyguards, they're nothing but heartache." Komptin joined Alex as she went for a hunt. Okay, it wasn't a hunt... more like a stroll through the woods.

Not too far from the church, Alex found Devine sitting on the logs staring into the woods. She was sitting still, staring into the thickness of the forest. It was quiet, as if the animals of the forest knew there was something wrong.

"Devine?" Alex slowly approached her.

"Sentry," Devine acknowledged as she continued to stare. As Alex approached the angel, Devine slowly turned to watch her.

"Hey, you're not going to throw me to the ground again, are you?" Alex tried to joke to lighten the mood.

Devine turned back to the woods. "I do apologize for throwing you to the ground."

"It's okay." Alex stood next to her. "Do you want to talk about it?"

"There is nothing to talk about." Devine tried deflecting the conversation.

Alex moved in front of her. "I know there are a lot of questions. Mixed feelings, confusing thoughts, fear of what your parents are going to say." Alex had a flashback of her first time. She was fifteen, and the guy was a junior. It wasn't romantic or anything. It was in the back of his pickup truck during a football game. "If you don't want to talk to me about it, maybe you should talk to Celestial."

Devine instantly grabbed Alex by the throat and slammed her into the ground. "You will not speak of this to anyone. Do you hear me? Promise me. She must not know what happened."

"Okay, okay. I'll let you figure it out." Alex tried to pry off Devine's hands. Komptin barked to let her go.

Devine extended her hand to help Alex up. Alex hesitated, before she allowed Devine to help her. "Sorry."

"No problem." Alex rubbed her neck. "I got the hint." Alex's phone vibrated. She answered the phone when her demeanor got serious. "Okay, bye." She turned to Devine. "How fast can you get me to the hospital?"

***

Alex finally got through to the hospital admissions to get back to Anne. She was lying in the bed with a heart monitor attached to her body. Alex hugged Anne rather gently, almost in fear of breaking her. "Are you okay?"

"I'm fine," Anne told her as she returned the hug. She peeked over at Devine, who stood over Alex's shoulder. "Thanks for coming, Devine."

"What is wrong with you?" she flat out asked.

Anne situated herself. "I don't know. The doctor will be in here soon."

"What happened?" Alex sat down on the bed to put her hand on Anne's leg for support.

She hesitated at first before speaking. "I went to get something eat and I ran into Shawn." Anne could see that Alex was face turned serious as she continued her story. "he said some things, and then Kate came in. Shawn told her what we did."

"How did she react?" Devine as well as a strange look on her face.

Anne dropped a tear while her heart rate started to pick up. "She was so disappointed and hurt over how I betrayed Kale."

"Anne, calm down." Alex happened to see the monitor.

The doctor just happened to come in to help. "Ms. McClure, I need you to take deep, slow breaths." He started to breathe in slowly for example. "Follow my breathing." Anne started to follow his breathing to calm herself down. Once he got her breathing under control, he listened to her chest with his stethoscope. "Good."

102

"Ladies," the doctor turned to them. "I'm Doctor Clark. If you would excuse us."

"Can they stay?" Anne asked him.

"Of course." He smiled. Doctor Clark glanced at the chart one last time. "The good news is there are no issues with your heart."

"Thank God." Anne leaned her head back against the wall. "Then what happened?"

"Looks like you just had an anxiety attack. Have you had them in the past?" Anne shook her head. "Family history?"

"No, my grandfather had a mild case of high blood pressure, but that's about it." Anne was trying to think back.

"Do you exercise?" he asked her as he took down some notes.

"Three to four times a week," Anne let him know. "Mainly cardio."

"Good. Any other unexpected stress lately?" he asked her.

Anne hesitated before Alex jumped in. "She might be pregnant by a real monster."

"Alex," Anne snapped. "I told you, I'm not pregnant."

"Would you like to relieve her mind?" Doctor Clark asked her. "It wouldn't take long."

"It would settle this once and for all," Alex pointed out. "Then I have no point but to shut up." She winked at Anne.

"Well, in that case." Anne smiled. "Let's get it done."

Doctor Clark laughed. "Okay, lift up your gown just enough to show your stomach." He squirted the gel on Anne's body before putting the ultrasound on her. He moved it around to different spots on her body.

"What are you doing?" Devine was intently studying what the doctor was doing.

"Checking to see if there is anything growing inside." The doctor was studying the screen.

Devine stepped closer to the machine. "That machine can see inside of a person?"

"Yes." Doctor Clark moved over the last spot. "All clear. Nothing growing."

Anne wiped the gel off her stomach. "Feel better?"

Alex was still worried, but at least she knew Anne was out of the woods. "Yep."

Doctor Clark was wrapping up the visit. "Okay, Anne. I'm going to prescribe you a bronchodilator inhaler. Use it when you feel another attack coming."

"Thank you, Doctor." Anne was starting to get ready to go.

"The discharge nurse will give you everything you need. Take care. I'd like you to follow up your primary in the future." The doctor left the room after saying, "Ladies."

Once the discharge nurse left. Alex escorted Anne out of the room. "Coming, Devine?" Alex asked the angel.

"I am going to go to the chapel," Devine gave her intentions.

"Okay, see you later. Thanks for everything." Alex smiled as she escorted Anne out of the room.

Devine made sure there was no one coming before she closed the curtain to the room. She turned on the machine before laying down on the bed. The angel applied thick liquid gel onto her stomach. She pressed the machine down. The screen showed pure blue light around the screen. In the center of the screen was a white circle with two black figures. Devine increased the view to see a closer look at the two figures. They seemed to be facing away from the screen until she pressed harder against her stomach. At the same time, they moved their heads. Each figure flashed a pair of neon red eyes before turning back away from the screen.

CHAPTER THREE

Anne and Alex decided to visit Jessica and Dan in the maternity ward. Bless Alex's heart, she didn't say anything about being in the emergency room. Their baby was so big and adorable. It truly was the love child of the two of them. Dan held his baby with such pride.

Father Richard came to the hospital to pick the two of them up. He took Anne back to her car before going to the church. Anne started her car to head home after receiving her prescription from the pharmacy. For some reason, she really wanted a chocolate milk. She was enjoying the drive home while she drank her milk, when she noticed a cop car closely following her.

She knew she was about to get pulled over. The car was following entirely too close not to. Then behold, the lights came on. There was a small spot over on the side of the road to pull over. She wiped her mouth of the milk as she rolled down the window. The built, white male cop came along the passenger side while a dark-complexioned cop asked for her license and registration. "Good evening, ma'am. Do you know why we pulled you over?"

"No, sir." Anne was positive she wasn't speeding. Then she started thinking that maybe she had rolled a stop sign.

"You don't have registration tabs on your license plate." He continued to review Anne's car registration.

"What? I saw my dad put them on last week," Anne was flabbergasted at that. "Do they fall off?"

"Not really." The police officer continued to study the plates. "Hang on, one second, ma'am." He motioned for his partner to meet him behind the vehicle. They both walked to the front of the vehicle with Anne's paperwork in her hands. Then they came back to the window. "Is there a problem?"

"Your back license plate doesn't match your registration or front plate," she told her.

"What?" Anne was in complete shock. "Not that I don't believe you, but can I see?"

The cop thought about it before saying. "Slowly, come out of the vehicle, and you can see for yourself."

Anne did as he asked so she could see the plate that didn't match. "I swear I didn't know."

Then the other cop chimed in, "Someone probably just took your plate for the tab. It happens on occasion."

"Here, this is just a warning to get it taken care of. The DMV will tell you how to get it replaced." The cop handed her the warning ticket. "Be sure to stay safe out there."

"I will. You the same. Thank you." Anne pulled into the driveway with her traffic warning to see a strange car parked in front of the house. "Mom, Dad, you would never believe what just…" Anne stopped in her tracks, just frozen with shock.

"Anne," Shawn said as he was at the dining room table across from her parents. They were sitting there having coffee together. It seemed as if he had been there for a while. His coffee cup was empty, with a plate full of crumbs in front of him.

Her dad did not look happy. "Anne, your friend Shawn stopped by to talk to us."

Anne tried to control her breathing. She grabbed her inhaler from her prescription bag to use. "What are you doing here?"

With disappointment in her mom's voice, she said, "He told us what happened."

Anne closed her eyes. "Mom."

"Anne, we'll talk about it later." She was stern in her voice.

"But Mom," Anne tried to defend herself from feeling this horrible.

"Anne, I said we will talk about it later." She turned her attention to Shawn. "Thank you, Shawn, for telling us what happened. We'll talk to our daughter."

Shawn politely got up. "Mr. and Mrs. McClure, it was a privilege talking to you." He acted like he hesitated as he went for the door. Anne flinched when he put his hand on her shoulder. "Anne, I always just wanted to be someone special in your life. Maybe someday, I can be." He smiled at her as if he was emotionally hurt by her actions. "I'll see you around."

Anne inhaled some of her medication. She made sure he left before she started to speak. "Mom, Dad. Let me explain what happened."

"Anne," her dad said. "You are an adult who is trying to deal with something that I can only imagine what you're going through. All I can do is leave you with this advice."

"Yes." Anne was ashamed to speak about this to her parents.

"Watch yourself," her dad told her.

Her mom chimed in. "You need to be careful."

***

Alex was applying her make-up in the bathroom attached to her old room. It almost reminded her of being back in high school. She fluffed her hair before tying it into a band. The sapphire angel on her neck was glistening. Her fingers ran over it as she remembered the night she admitted to herself how she felt about Kameron.

"You okay?" Her dad's voice came from the side of the bathroom.

She smiled at her dad, who was leaning on the door. "I'm fine, Dad. How about you?"

"I'm surviving," Michael told her as he stared at her.

Alex embarrassingly laughed. "What?"

"Just that I'm really proud of you." Michael just admired with fatherly love at his daughter.

"Are you dying or something?" she joked.

"Not that I know of," he told her. "Can I ask you something?"

"Sure." Alex finished putting on her make-up to go on a hunt. "How do I look?"

"Beautiful, as always." Michael turned her to face him.

"Okay, now you're scaring me." Alex tapped his arm. "Whatcha wanna ask?"

"Do you still love him?"

Alex was not expecting that question from her father. He had never taken interest in her social life. "It's complicated."

"No, it's not," her father spoke with confidence.

Alex paused for a second to think of her response. "Dad, I..." She just couldn't answer.

Michael recognized the difficulty of Alex answering that question. "I got my answer." He was about to say something to her but stopped. "I just want you to be happy. You're my daughter; I want what is best for you."

"You think Kameron is best for me?" Alex asked the question, but she already knew the answer. "It's too late. I doubt I will ever see him again."

Alex could tell there was something he wanted to say, but all he said was. "I love you." He gave his daughter a hug. "I have to go see your guests off."

"I'm going to go out." Alex returned his hug. The only thing she left out was that she was going to secure the perimeter to ensure the Dark doesn't attack them. Alex got a text from Father Richard of the time Alex needed to start her Sentry work. That meant she had a while before she needed to be out in the woods.

Komptin was sleeping hard on her bed. Alex sat on the bed to pet her dog. He didn't move, he just sat there and slept. "Komptin," she whispered. He just continued to sleep. "Komptin," she said a little louder. He was still sleeping. "Hey," she nudged him. He opened up one eye that was glowing blue. "Come on. We gotta go."

They both made it to the church with Father Richard outside having a cup of coffee. "Hey, father," Alex greeted him.

"Hey, Alex. What are you doing here?" He verified the time.

"Just have some time to kill before I go.... kill.... the Dark." She felt awkward saying that.

Father Richard closed his Bible. "Can you sit for a second?"

Alex sat down and opened an Apollo Energy Drink. "What's going on?"

"I understand you and Father Carl had a little talk," Father Richard started.

"He pissed me off," Alex told him. "He kicked me out of that meeting."

"Yes, he did. Granted, it wasn't the most subtle." Father Richard put his bible in his bag. "He's not a member of the Council, yet. Meaning, I'm recommending him probably by the end of the month."

"When will you tell him about me?" Alex was a bit hopeful she could give him a live demonstration.

"Slowly. When he gets introduced to the Council, we'll deliver the rest of the information slowly." Father Richard noted. "Just give him a break. He is going to have a hard time accepting everything."

"He got mad at me for 'disrespecting' him." Alex rolled her eyes.

"He kind of has a point." Father Richard again gazed at his watch.

"Why do you keep looking at your watch?" Alex asked him.

"Anne? How are you feeling?" Father Richard saw that Anne was coming in.

"I'm fine. Just that my parents had a visitor that I wasn't expecting. I didn't need that." Anne sat down next to Alex. She leaned over to pet Komptin who was fast asleep by Alex's feet. Alex rubbed her back in support. "What are you guys talking about?"

"Father Richard is going to recommend Father Carl to become a member of the council." Alex shook her head in disbelief.

"I think he would be an asset." Anne checked her watch.

Alex noticed that as well. "Maybe."

Father Carl came from the parking lot of the church to sit down with the three of them. "Good evening."

Everyone said hello to him but Alex. Then she was kicked underneath the table by Father Richard. "How are you, father?" Alex rubbed her shin.

"Just checked on the girls. They are ready to go." Father Carl sat down with his notepad. "What time is the security detail supposed to be here?"

"I got a text that they should be here in a couple of hours." Father Richard checked his watch.

"Once they leave, I need to send the VCC-153 up to the Council." Anne reached into her purse to grab some gum.

"Well, I guess I should get going. Can't keep my date waiting." Alex was about to get up, but Father Carl stopped her.

"Can you just wait a minute before you go to the bars?"

"I wish." Alex sat back down. "What's up?"

Father Carl opened his notes. "I was thinking of bringing awareness back to this church. With everything going on, we need to show our community that we are here for them."

"How do you expect us to do that?" Father Richard was babysitting Alex on her reaction.

"I think we should have a fall festival on Halloween. Since it falls on a Saturday this year, we could have it just before Trick or Treating starts."

"Pre-gaming for the kids, nice." Alex actually thought it was a good idea.

"I like it. Let's talk about it tomorrow afternoon." Father Richard indirectly tapped his watch over at Alex, who understood what that meant.

"Well, I'm off to get myself into some trouble." Alex got up. "Come on, boy." Komptin slowly got up and stretched before joining Alex.

Father Carl made sure she left before speaking. "I take it she doesn't know that her ex-boyfriend will be providing security for our guests."

Father Richard shook his head. "She has enough troubles she has to contend with."

***

The blood on Kameron's hands wouldn't come off. He had tried repeatedly to wash them in the sink. The body of the dead girl was lying on the kitchen floor. She had two bullet holes in her chest and one in her head.

His sister, Michelle, was sitting on the kitchen table with legs crossed, looking down at the dead body. "I can't believe you did that. What were you thinking?"

"I didn't mean to, I didn't want to," he explained to her.

"Really, Kameron? You did everything you could to stop it?" Alex said as she came into the kitchen with Komptin in a gargoyle state, growling at him. "You said you loved me, do anything for me, and you abandoned me when I needed you most."

"No, you pushed me away," Kameron explained as he continued to wash the blood off his hands. They were starting to sting from becoming raw.

"You didn't fight for me. You left me, you abandoned me, anything I do is your fault," Alex told him with glowing red eyes.

"How could you do that to her, Kameron?" Michelle joined Alex at her side. "You're a real piece of shit."

"There's nothing I could do," Kameron explained.

"There's always another option." The girl with the bullet holes in her body got up from the floor. "Because you failed. I'm dead. I was someone's daughter." The girl put her arm around Alex. "No wonder she doesn't want you back."

114

"This blood won't come off." Kameron continued to scrub his hands.

A man with a white face and a big black hat appeared behind him. He had soulless eyes as he slowly put his hand on Kameron's heart. "I remember you and your pure heart." He dug into Kameron's chest as he started to pull out his heart.

Kameron screamed as he sat up in the sleeping pods. He tried to catch his breath. The clothes he had on were drenched in sweat. The flight attendant, Mason, approached Kameron. He sat down next to Kameron. "Are you okay?"

As plane rides went, this one was the best he'd flown. Neither he nor Midnight had to be an air marshal. The council had put them on a private flight. It was nice. They each had their own private pod to sleep in. The only people on the plane were the two pilots and one flight attendant.

"I'm fine," he said as he wiped the sweat off his face with his hand.

Mason returned with a couple of hot towels and a glass of water. "Here."

"Thanks." Kameron drank the water before wiping his face with the hot towel.

"Do you want to talk about it?" Mason grabbed the items from Kameron. "I'm basically a bartender of the skies." He gave Kameron a concerned smile.

"No, there's nothing to talk about." Kameron situated himself when he noticed to the left of him, on the other side of the plane, Midnight started to wake up.

"Wow, I can get used to flying like this." She stretched herself out.

Kameron got up to stretch. "I wouldn't get used to it."

Mason got notified they would be landing soon. "I'll have everything set for our guests' flight by the time you get back."

Kameron nodded. "Thank you." He turned to Midnight. "Are you sure you want to do this?"

"I think we need to make sure Paige isn't playing both ends against the middle," Midnight told him. "Scotty does have a point. I'll leave for the F.O.R. Compound straight from the airport. I'll let you know if there is any movement that you should be worried about."

Kameron got up to go put on his suit in the back of the plane. "Sounds good. This just doesn't feel right."

***

"Mayor Caesar Paroyale," Maria Rodriguez came into his office holding a package.

"Yes." He was getting his coat on. "Is this important because I have to get to my son's birthday party at..." He was looking around his desk.

"Party Pizza Palace," Maria told him. "Here's his present."

"I was hoping it would get here in time. Thanks for wrapping it. He's wanted this new video game. I had to pull a few strings, but I got it." He smiled as she handed it to him. He stared at it for a second. "Can you rearrange my schedule next week to get me some time to pick Hector up from school?"

"I'll make sure it happens. The police chief called again. He said he needs to talk about the growing tension in the town between United Won and the Darius King protestors." She handed him the note.

He grabbed the note to read it. "What's your thoughts on all that?" he asked, trying to get a young person's view on the racial tensions growing in the town.

"I think that cop shouldn't have shot him," Maria told him. "He had a weapon on him, but there was no proof he was reaching for it when he moved his hands."

"Well, forty-eight percent of the country agrees with you. Unfortunately, another forty-seven percent say the shooting was justified." He read the message. "Okay, let's see if you can get a meeting with the sheriff, Qawi, and the United Won leader, what's his name?

"Mack Righteous."

Caesar laughed. "Are you serious?"

"That's what he calls himself." Maria wrote it down. "Can I ask you something?"

"Make it quick?" Caesar grabbed his briefcase.

"Do you think Roger Somberson is evil?"

Caesar closed his briefcase. "I think there is more going on out there than we realize." He saw the time on his watch. "I gotta go." The mayor ran to his car parked in the back of the building where he thought he heard a low growl. His imagination was playing with him because he thought he saw a pair of glowing red eyes. The watch beeped to let him know that his son's party was about to start. He dialed his wife on the car phone. "Hey, honey."

"Please tell me you are on your way." She sounded like she was a bit stressed.

He started laughing. "Are you missing me or just need more help?"

"I've got twenty-ten-year-old kids running around here. I need you," she playfully yelled at him.

"I'll be there." A loud explosion came from his car. "Damn it, I just blew a tire. I'll be there as soon as I can."

"Want me to call a tow?" she asked him just before telling a kid not to shove straws up his nose.

He laughed. "I wasn't always a politician; I do know how to get my hands dirty. It won't take me long."

"Be careful. Love you." She went back to settle down the kids.

"Love you, too. I'll be there soon." He got out of the car to see that he had a flat on the rear tire. It was so odd for him to have a flat in the rear of the car. Both sides of the road were bordered by cornfields. Changing this tire was going to be difficult with no light. The trunk opened, but he stopped, listening, as he thought he heard a strange sound. Caesar made sure there was nothing around.

The tire was under some carpet in the trunk. The noise got louder yet; he could have sworn it sounded like a growl. He had no weapons on him. The only thing he could do was climb back into his car if a wild animal attacked. The blackness of the

118

corn fields seemed to add more mystery to the sound that was getting closer.

He snapped his head around at the growl that seemed to come right from the edge of the corn. "Oh shit," he said loudly. The sound of something big was stalking him. A faint outline of a bear seemed to move. It suddenly vanished when a car stopped behind him. "Thank God." He thanked someone for coming by.

"Gotta flat?" the man said as he approached Caesar.

"I must have run over a nail or something," he replied to him.

The man came up to see the damaged tire. "Yep, it's flat." He turned to Caesar. "Hey, aren't you the mayor?"

"That's right. I'm late for my son's birthday party." The watch on his wrist told him that now he wasn't going to make it on time.

"Well, let's see what we got." He leaned into the trunk.

"It's freaky out here," the mayor told him. "I'm so glad you stopped. My imagination was playing tricks on me. I thought I saw something in the field over there."

"Oh, I wouldn't worry about him. He's the least of your worries right now." The man turned his head to show his glowing red eyes. The sharpened teeth sunk into his body just as he screamed. The claws of the beast shredded into the skin to tear his body to pieces.

***

Alex decided to grab a vanilla milkshake so she could mix it with her Apollo Energy Drink before heading to guard the perimeter. It tasted so good. It was a comfort food she was desperately needing. The town was quiet as the air was getting much cooler at night. Alex thought it probably wasn't smart drinking a milkshake when it was cold, but she really wanted one.

Father Richard wanted her to go to make sure the F.O.R. didn't bother them with transporting Scarlett and Kaylee. Alex couldn't really wait for them to leave because progress on the church was halted with them there. Though, the church was coming along nicely. Alex knelt to pet Komptin on the head. He seemed a little down today. Alex figured it was because he missed Kameron. Truth be told, she did too.

Alex made it to the edge of town, where the woods seemed to instantly begin. Alex never thought she would miss hunting in D.C. Maybe because that was where she was the happiest. She was so content living in St. Michael's. Her relationship with Kameron was strong, and Anne was so happy being with Kale. Sentry life wasn't easy, grappling onto happiness was important, because it would seem it wouldn't last.

Osiah had warned her about the travesties her choice would make. Honestly speaking, she was handling it fine. The problem came when she lost her ability to connect with the Lite. She'd been so cold since that happened. It wasn't a physical chill, but a constant freezing of emptiness. No matter what she did, there was no feeling of the warmth from the Lite.

The disconnection from the Lite also caused her inability to track the Dark. She had to rely on Komptin to lead her to evil. However, at times, it seemed more challenging than most. Then, a scream from a distance caught both their attention. That type of scream usually went with death. Alex and Komptin both glanced at each other with flashing eyes before taking off down the road.

Just past the tree line, there were two cars up ahead. They were parked on the side of the road, surrounded by cornfields. Alex saw a figure standing over another one. The man saw Alex coming and turned toward her to attack without hesitation. He took a couple of steps before realizing who she was.

"Sentry?" The Demon almost seemed shocked to see her, not knowing what to do.

Then from the side, an Infiltrator came and tackled Alex. They rolled on the pavement, causing scratches on Alex's arm. Her hands stopped the Infiltrator's mouth from biting into her neck. She managed to roll the Infiltrator over to get it off, giving herself some room to plan her counterattack.

Komptin jumped at the Demon. The Demon dodged out of the way leading to Komptin hitting his head into the car. The Demon immediately began to punch Komptin on the side of the head. The gargoyle tried to get up, but the Demon kept stomping his boot on the side of Komptin's head.

The Infiltrator lunged at Alex. She stepped to the side, giving her the opportunity to kick it in the midsection. It bent over from the pain. She turned around to grab its head to drive into the road's blacktop. The continued assault on the beast was furious until she came to the point when she decided it was weak enough to dissipate. She jabbed a Lite Spear into the side of its head. The beast cried out in pain before disappearing into the ground.

There was a quick moment of relief until she saw her hunting partner being beat down by the Demon. Alex shot a Lite Beam at the Demon, which made him fall to the ground. He got up and immediately started running off into the cornfield. Alex ran over to Komptin to make sure he was okay. He slowly got up, shaking the cobwebs out of his head. "You okay?" Alex asked him. He flashed his eyes to assure her he was fine. Alex nodded before they ran off into the field to chase the Demon.

They chased the Demon through a field that led into the woods. They seemed to have lost it in the thicket of the forest. Alex shut off her glowing fists as they started to stalk their prey, or perhaps they had become the prey. They stealthily hunted through the woods and came across a clearing. It wasn't a natural clearing, it almost seemed as if it was on purpose. Even though Alex couldn't feel it, she didn't like this. The two hunters remained on the perimeter of the clearing.

It was only a couple of minutes before the sound of a large group came through the woods. A single movement started coming up next to her. Alex stayed still, hidden in the bushes on the forest floor, to see what was approaching. The movement was coming closer. If it was the Dark, they would be

122

stupid. The noise they were making was just enough to warn anyone they were coming.

Alex was about to tell whoever it was to leave, but then some other noise came across the way. The individual closer to her was coming. They were going to be in danger from what was coming out of the other side of the woods. The figure was getting closer. Alex was hidden in the bushes when she grabbed the blonde woman by the mouth. Alex very easily pulled her down to the ground.

Midnight's eyes were huge, as she wasn't expecting to be manhandled like a ragdoll. Alex motioned with her finger to be quiet and then pointed to the clearing. A group of people dressed in dark maroon cloaks came out of the woodwork. The black candles were burning a dark red flame. Roger was in a black robe with a red rope tied around his waist. His eyes glowed a dangerous neon red.

In the middle of the circle were two people wearing black pants with white button-up shirts. One was a brunette female, and the other was a tall black man, both on their knees. Roger stepped up, taking down his cloak hood. The girl seemed to enjoy his hand being placed on her face in a tantalizing fashion. Alex couldn't tell who the people in the cloaks were since their faces were hidden.

"To his command!" Roger yelled out to the group.

The group replied in unison. "To his command."

"The Dark is the foundation of life. It is always there. The Lite moves, it takes energy. The Dark is everlasting; we are nothing but existence in all things. Darkness doesn't move in like the Lite, we are forever there. It may be hidden by the lies the Lite produces, but we are forever there. The primates who show no worth in becoming Demons must be ruled over. Without the Dark, the primates war among each other; they fight each other over the most irrelevant of items. With the Dark rule, they will comply with a glowing fist." He raised a glowing red fist in the air as the crowd cheered. He turned to the girl. "Do you accept absolute power?"

Without skipping a beat, she answered, "With open arms." The girl spread her arms open as a dark mist appeared out of the woods to form into an Infiltrator. The black beast lunged into the girl. The force of infiltration knocked her back. She rose with glowing red eyes.

"And who do we have now?" Roger asked her.

"Craxil." She stood proud. "To his command."

Roger turned to the other person. "Do you accept absolute power?"

The man took two deep breaths before answering. "With open arms." Another mist formed into an Infiltrator. It ran and lunged into the male on his knees. A high-pitched scream came from the Infiltrator as it was halfway stuck inside the human. The man screamed in pain as the Infiltrator tried clawing out with its back claws. The shredding of body parts haphazardly scattered on the forest floor from the Infiltrator, trying to escape its deadly fate.

Alex had to let go of Midnight's mouth to cover her ears. Midnight and Komptin both tried to shield themselves from the ear-piercing noise. They watched the man drop to the ground while mixing his screams with the Infiltrator's. Alex couldn't help but feel sympathy for the two beings. The woods were suddenly silenced, with Roger staring at the body.

Roger, whose Demon name was Gron, turned to one of his underlings. "I thought he was ready. You told me he was ready."

"Gron, it's impossible to know if they are ready without Salamor." The Demon feared the repercussions from their leader.

Gron grabbed one of the shorter people in the cloaks. The hood came off to see a short blonde female. Midnight immediately recognized her. Gron shoved her face down to the body. He pushed her face straight into what was left of the creature and human. "You see that. Taste it. You better be ready. You're going to be the next one. I'm tired of waiting for you."

"What about the bodies?" a familiar voice said from one of the people in cloaks. Alex couldn't place where she heard it before.

"Let them rot." Roger went off in a fit of rage. The others started to follow him back into the woods towards the F.O.R. compound.

Alex waited a bit before getting up from the ground. "Huh, that was interesting." She walked over to what was left of the bodies. The two bodies were mangled. Alex couldn't help but think of how painful that must have been.

"Interesting?" Midnight was holding her mouth, preventing her from vomiting. "That's all you have to say?"

"Never saw that before." Alex pushed the Infiltrator's body with her foot. She saw that the Infiltrator was starting to dissolve, but the human body just stayed there with a big hole in his chest. "What are you doing here anyways?" Alex continued to stare at the body.

"Came to check on something," Midnight explained. She wasn't positive, but it looked as if Paige was telling the truth of her commitment.

Alex turned to her. "Wait a minute. If you are here," Alex hesitated a bit. "You and Kameron are the ones picking up the girls." Midnight didn't say anything as Alex started in the opposite direction of the F.O.R. compound.

***

"He's cute," Scarlett whispered to Kaylee. "Maybe this won't be so bad." The two of them watched Kameron talk with the priests and District Attorney about the situation. The two young girls were being escorted by Anne to the car.

"Ready to go?" Kameron joined the girls.

"Where are we going?" Scarlett was getting itchy to know where she was going to be hiding from the F.O.R.

Kameron made sure no one was listening. "The only people who know, are the ones who need to know." Kameron opened the door to the car. "Now, ladies, we must be going."

Scarlett rolled her eyes. "Whatever." The two girls were about to get in when they approached Anne. "Thank you." Scarlett hugged Anne.

"You're welcome." Anne returned the hug.

Kaylee then got her hug from Anne. "I cannot thank you all enough."

"Just take care of that baby." Anne pointed to her stomach.

Father Carl and Father Richard, both gave them hugs goodbye. Father Carl gave a blessing. Kaylee seemed to be looking around. "Where's Alex? I'd like to say goodbye as well."

Kameron got a message from Midnight that she was at the airport. "It's time to go."

The girls nodded as they got into the car. The two priests shook Kameron's hands before heading back into the church. Alex's father stayed behind with Anne. "Kameron, I cannot repay you for what you are doing."

"Don't worry about it." Kameron seemed to be checking his surroundings for something.

"Then let me give you this," Michael offered. Kameron turned his attention to him. "My little girl is one of the toughest people I know. I have never seen her so hurt and vulnerable until you two broke up. I don't want to know the details on why you did, but I just thought you should know." Michael shook his hand and left for inside the church.

Anne smiled at Kameron. "He's right."

"How are you doing?" Kameron was trying to change the subject.

"I think I'm losing my mind at times. I hope I'm not becoming paranoid or something," Anne joked. "But I'm getting better."

"Call me if you need anything." Kameron didn't know what he was doing.

"I will." The two of them hugged. "Love you," Anne told him in a sisterly fashion.

"Love you too," Kameron replied in kind. "Take care of her."

"That should be your job," she whispered.

Kameron got into the car with a pit in his stomach from not wanting to leave. He started the car. The headlights illuminated the Lite Sentry standing in front of the car. Honestly, for some reason, he wasn't surprised. He took in a deep breath before shutting off the car. "I'll be right back." Scarlett and Kaylee looked at their rescuer and protector shining in the headlights.

"I don't think we should get out of the car." Kaylee could feel the tension build.

Scarlett watched the big German Shepherd join Anne as the two of them entered the church. "I couldn't agree with you more."

"Alex," Kameron greeted her.

"Really, you were just going to leave without saying anything, again." Alex resisted the urge to get closer to him. There was a slight movement, but she decided to take a few steps back.

"I'm not here for personal reasons." Kameron calmly put his hands into his pockets. "Besides, I didn't see you stick around to see me."

"I didn't know you were coming," she snapped back at him.

"And would you have stayed or protected the perimeter while I escorted them to safety?" Kameron slowly motioned his head to the girls.

"I do what I need to do." Alex could feel her emotions start to get the best of her.

"So do I," Kameron got a message from Midnight that they needed to get going. The time was nearing that he would have to leave.

"You have to go?" Alex asked him, now having her arms crossed her chest.

Kameron nodded.

"Okay, bye," she coldly told him.

Kameron snickered out of disbelief. "Really? Okay, bye." He went to get back into the car.

"What do you want, Kameron?" Alex forcefully asked him.

"A little emotion would be nice." He stopped before getting into the car.

"You're one to talk." Alex clenched her jaw.

Kameron turned back to the Lite Sentry, standing just off church property. "You think this is easy for me?" He faced his head away to look at the woods.

"I wouldn't know there, Stoneface Jackson," Alex quickly came back with.

"Stonewall," Kameron corrected her. "Besides, you're strong. You'll be fine."

Alex instantly got angry. "Fine? Do you know what it took for me to get over you?!"

Kameron turned to face Alex. "Okay, Alex. Message received. Take care of yourself." Kameron went back into the car. Scarlet and Kaylee were giving Kameron sympathetic eyes. "What?"

"Nothing," Scarlett answered him.

Kaylee put her hand on Kameron's shoulder. "We can go whenever you're ready."

Alex walked angrily up the stairs to the church as the car drove away. She didn't say a word as she walked past the two priests who happened to witness the scene. Father Richard knew not to say anything to Alex even though every instinct as a priest wanted to chase after her.

"She really loves him?" Father Carl gave off a little sympathy.

Father Richard shut the door of the church as it echoed throughout the sanctuary. "Yes."

"Just something I never thought I would witness." Father Carl double-checked the doors to make sure they were locked. "Does she know about the Council of Religions?"

Father Richard took a deep breath. He didn't think he was quite ready to know her true role in the fight. Although, this was an opportunity to get Father Carl's feet wet a little bit. "She was their administrative assistant as a liaison for Cardinal Frank and Father Tom. She met Kameron when Cardinal Frank was shot. The F.O.R. kidnapped Kameron, tortured him, and Alex helped Kameron's supervisor rescue him."

"And while that was going on, Father Tom got shot by the F.O.R.," Father Carl concluded.

"And I think that is why she has trouble talking to men of the cloth." Father Richard took out a breath mint from his pocket. He offered one to Father Carl as he graciously accepted.

"Is that why she stays here and continues to work for us?" The two of them walked down the hall to the outside of what would be their future offices.

"Yes, in part. Right now, what we need to do is prepare for the opening of this church." Father Richard peeked into his destroyed office. "The Dark is growing stronger and upsetting the Balance."

"I want to do my part," Father Carl told him with conviction.

"You'll have my recommendation, pending one minor thing I have to let you in on, but we'll get there," Father Richard assured him.

"Alex won't be my assistant, will she?" he nervously asked.

Father Richard laughed. "No, you get to pick your own."

"I'm thinking Megan would be a good pick. I would like to get her inducted into the Council, pending my approval." Father Carl yawned.

"I think she would be a good fit. I'll talk to Cardinal Joe."

***

Devine watched a pure of heart leave the church grounds with two of the primates. The angel hung on top of the tallest steeple of the building. Off in the distance, she saw the Sentry approach from the forest. The tormented angel turned her head to face the cross directly above her. The feeling of something moving inside made her feel uncomfortable. She put her hand on her stomach while thoughts of confusion entered her mind on what she should do.

"They will blame you for what happened. You are something impure and dirty." Salamor floated in front of the angel.

"No, they care for me. They would understand." Devine stared down at the Lite Sentry, who was now outside the church talking to her friend. "But I feel so unclean." That was all she could say.

"Guilt." Salamor floated to the other side of her. "This was all your fault. How you are dressed makes it easy for them. You allowed a Demon…"

"Quiet," Devine commanded. "They would not think less of me."

"Ask them. Ask them without telling them how you let a Demon…" Salamor disappeared.

Devine followed the Sentry to the back of the church. There was no way the Sentry would treat her like that. She viewed Devine as a sister. The angel dropped down behind the Sentry without making a sound. Devine sat down at the picnic table where she was sitting.

Alex jumped from not expecting Devine to show up. "You scared me."

"Not my intention." Devine sat down at the end of the table.

Anne came out from the back of the church. "Hello."

"Pure of Heart," Devine acknowledged.

"Why didn't you tell me?" Alex asked her flat out.

"I didn't want to hurt you." Anne sat down. "Were you ready to see him?" Alex didn't say anything. "See."

"She is protecting your feelings," Devine told the Sentry who was battling her own emotions.

"I get it." Alex drank her energy drink.

Anne smiled. "Well, some of us actually need sleep. I'm going to go home. Good night."

"Night." Alex watched her leave. "I really do get it."

"Get what?" Devine turned her attention back to Alex.

"Protecting my feelings. That's why I cannot tell her about Shawn becoming a Demon." Alex had an Apollo next to her that she started to drink.

"Why would you not tell her that?" Devine was starting to fish for answers.

"Can you imagine how disgusting and low she would feel knowing she let a Demon do that to her?" Alex shivered at the thought. "I know I couldn't live with myself. Just knowing a vile, disgusting creature was…yuck."

"You would look upon yourself with revolting sickness," Devine described the emotion.

"See, you get it. You would die before you let something like that do that to you." Alex turned around to see Komptin come back from the woods. "Hey, where have you been?" Alex started to say, "You know Devine, maybe I should…" Alex turned to the angel, but she was gone.

Devine flew far from the church. She found herself wanting to be near the F.O.R. compound for some reason. Why would she want to be near something full of so much evil? She fought hard from landing near the compound. The forest offered solitude away from judging eyes. She didn't want to hide like some sort of animal. She hated feeling like this.

The angel landed in the alley of town. She morphed into pants and a green shirt. The streets were busy when she wanted to confront the thing that did this to her. There were multiple establishments where he might be. If the Sentry was with her, she could find him easily. She was about to give up until she caught sight of him. Devine started to shake. There was no reason for this, but it was happening.

The Demon turned around to see her on the sidewalk. He told the group he would be right back. He surveyed the surroundings as if making sure it was safe. He confidently confronted the angel who put her face down facing the sidewalk as she shivered and couldn't move. He lifted her head with his finger to meet his glowing red eyes. "You did, didn't you?" He smiled as he winked at her before leaving to rejoin the group.

Devine ran in the opposite direction from the Demon before taking flight. The only place she found solitude was at the lake. She was cold, alone, there was no one who understood what she did. What she allowed him to do. She grabbed her stomach as she rolled over on the grass. Her stomach started to stretch. The pain caused her to scream in agony.

Salamor appeared next to her. "See, I told you. They will find you disgusting. What you allowed him to do. The pain you are feeling, this is your punishment. You have no one to blame but yourself."

CHAPTER FOUR

Anne slept in until late morning. It was a welcome rarity. It was much-needed rest before her meeting about putting together the fall festival. After the meeting, she had to meet with a new contractor about the church renovation blueprints. The architect had the plans up at the city office to get approval. The remote was on the end table for her to turn on the television. She switched to the local news for the weather because she wanted to go for a bike ride before work. The news was reporting how the mayor was killed last night near his car. What was left of his body was found underneath his car. It appeared the jack slipped as he was underneath it and crushed his body. Anne read the weather on the bottom of the screen as it would have seemed to be a good time for a ride.

She hurried to change into her riding clothes. A sudden rush of sadness always hit Anne as she was riding Kale's old bike. He had given it to her after Roger attacked him. There was always guilt associated with riding it. When he was alive, he loved riding so much. He always assured her that if she didn't ride it, it was going to be sold. The garage door closed as she clipped into the pedals to head down the road.

For some reason, she wanted to head to Lake Tilly. It wasn't the lake where she met Kale, but it was a small lake on the side of the road that was nice. It was so small they didn't allow motorboats on the water, only kayaks and canoes. It wasn't a good swimming lake because it was so full of lily pads and algae. Kale said he went swimming there once and got a weird rash. The lake was peaceful, quiet. Almost a little too quiet. The only sign of life was a fish making a wake in the water as it took off from near the shoreline. She pulled over to use the restroom that was near the lake.

Anne finished using the outdoor restroom when she noticed her bike wasn't in the spot where she thought it was. She could have sworn she put it on the right side of the door but now it was on the left. Anne shook it off as if having some mental block. The ride back home was something she needed. It cleared her mind, and that was something she desperately welcomed.

She hopped off her bike and opened the garage door. After parking her bike in the garage, she grabbed an apple and peanut butter from the kitchen to calm her stomach. On the way to her bedroom, she took off her shirt and noticed a wilted red rose on her dresser next to her make-up. It seemed it was there for a while, but she didn't remember putting it there. She slowly picked up the rose as its thorns pierced the skin on her fingers. "Ow." Then she screamed as something hit her window. Outside her window was a dove with a broken neck. "Poor thing."

Anne went outside the back door to grab the dove to bury it, but when she arrived outside her window, it was gone. Then there was rustling in the long grass on the edge of the lawn. Anne slowly walked backward. *"Maybe a bobcat took it or something*," Anne thought to herself. She continued to back up as she bumped into a person. She screamed when she turned around to see her dad's scarecrow, he was making for a yard decoration. Her heart was racing. The alarm on her phone told her she needed to get ready for work. If Anne was honest with herself, she couldn't wait to go.

Anne got to the meeting a bit late, but they were gracious enough not to say anything. Father Richard and Father Carl were going over some details of the church while Alex was chewing gum. Her feet were up on a chair as she was going through some videos on her phone.

"Alex," Father Carl annoyingly called out to her. "Do you think you should be on your phone?"

"Conducting research," she said without skipping a beat. "See." She turned her phone around to a video of Scarlett promoting the F.O.R.

"Right," the priest turned to the brown wavy-haired girl with black-rimmed glasses. "Anne."

Alex peeked up at Anne. "You okay? You're never late." She went back to her phone looking at videos that were not research.

"Just my imagination playing tricks on me. You know, Halloween and everything." Anne sat next to Alex.

They sat down at the meeting to begin planning the fall festival. It seemed as if everything was coming together. Anne took down notes as Alex was thinking about something else. More than likely, it was about Kameron.

"Also, we got some good news," Father Richard announced. "There has been some shifting around

138

of personnel per the Council." Alex just moved her eyes over to Father Richard when mentioning the Council. Alex took that as Father Carl knew about the Council of Religions, but she didn't know if he knew about her. "We are going to be training a new admin assistant for the Council."

"K." Alex was just moving her eyes around the table.

"I thought I was supposed to do that?" Anne chimed in, almost worried as if she was failing in her duties.

"Honestly, Anne, the renovation of the church is far worse than expected. I want you to just pay attention to that along with historian duties."

Anne was actually a little relieved at the news. She never realized how much she had on her plate until someone took some weight off. "I understand." Anne went to her notes. "What's the name of the admin trainee?"

"It's going to be Megan," Father Carl informed the group.

Alex fell out of her chair. Everyone looked to see if she was okay. Komptin was asleep in the corner; all he did was open an eyelid to check to see if she was okay. Then he went back to sleep.

"I'm okay, I'm okay." Alex put her hand up as she slowly got up. "You've got to be shitting me?"

"Watch your language," Father Carl scolded.

"I just can't get away from her." Alex got up and went to a cooler filled with ice. She pulled out an Apollo. She gazed over at Anne.

"Appliances are near the end of construction, but I'll try to find you a garage fridge someone is selling," Anne assured her. "Are you hungry?"

"I could eat." Alex slapped her leg to get Komptin. He slowly got up to join her with a quick hug from Alex.

Anne gathered her notes. "I just need to put these away." Anne's phone started to ring. "And take this phone call." Anne put the phone to her ear. "Hello, Ted, how are you?" Anne continued to listen. Her face went from one of ease to one of anger. "What do you mean you have to back out? Yeah, I better get my deposit back." Anne continued to hear what her former contractor had to say. "There's no other contractor within two-hundred miles that will take this job." Anne closed her eyes. "I apologize the way I came off, but can you do it after…" She was getting nowhere. "I understand. Thank you." Anne hung up the phone.

"So, it's going to be a bit longer for my refrigerator?" Alex gave her a small smirk.

All Anne could do was laugh. "Can we go eat?"

"Yes!" Alex walked out with Komptin at her side.

***

Kameron didn't say much on the flight, and matter of fact, neither did Midnight. They arrived in the small airport in the desert. Kameron put on his sunglasses as they exited the plane. "You okay?" he asked Midnight as she stepped off the plane stairs.

"We'll talk when we meet up with Scotty." Midnight turned around to help Kaylee and Scarlett. She leaned over towards Kameron. "Are you okay?" Kameron didn't answer.

Kaylee put on some glasses the pilots gave her. "Where are we?"

"You'll be debriefed once we get to the safehouse," Kameron informed her. A beige vehicle came up to greet them.

"Ladies." Scotty stepped out of the driver's side. "Your new oasis awaits."

Kaylee and Scarlett both looked to Midnight for confirmation. "He's good."

"I'm the best there is," he told the girls.

Midnight rolled her eyes. "For an STD," she whispered soft enough so only Scotty would hear her.

They continued to drive off the airport. Kameron jumped in the very back, while Kaylee and Scarlett were in the middle seats. Scotty and Midnight were in the front. As they drove, Scarlett found a constant theme within the small city. There were stores with Martians and little green men everywhere.

"Are we in Roswell?" Kaylee asked.

"As in New Mexico?" Scarlett rolled her eyes. "We're going to be around science fiction nerds."

"A small town outside of Roswell, and no, you're not going to be surrounded by science fiction nerds." Scotty pointed over to a woman in a bikini with green skin marching outside a store. "You think Captain Kirk hit that?"

"What do you mean we're not going to be surrounded by the sci-fi geeks?" Scarlett didn't believe him.

"We have to limit your outings. The F.O.R. may have eyes everywhere," Midnight let them know.

"You know eyes like that dude." Scotty pointed to a guy dressed as an alien who had eyes all over his forehead. "I promise; it won't be that bad."

They pulled up to a descent sized farmhouse in a rural section outside the city limits. "Do we at least have wi-fi?" Scarlett asked.

"Don't post anything," Midnight told her. "This is serious."

"Got it," Kaylee assured.

"Scarlett," Midnight wanted to ensure she understood. Scarlett lifted her hand as if she understood.

Kameron sat up from sleeping. "We here?"

"Home sweet home," Scarlett sarcastically told him.

They all met inside the house. For a farmhouse, it was up to date. Scotty shut the alarm off. "We have cameras that cover the inner perimeter of the lawn. I wanted to put motion detectors further out but the animals kept setting them off."

"The house?" Kameron was studying the house. Outside the living room was a deck with a porch swing. It reminded him of the one back at his parent's house. Last time he was on it was the morning after Michelle passed away. It was the very first time Alex told him she loved him.

Scotty answered him. "Standard alarms on doors and windows. There are break sensors on the windows."

Kameron tapped the glass. "How do you want to do this?"

"Rotate the night shift?" Midnight suggested. "Eleven to six."

"I'm good with that," Scotty told her. "Kameron?"

He nodded. "Can one of you two take tonight?"

"I'll take it," Midnight told him. "Let me get the girls situated and then I'll take a nap."

"Their rooms are on the top floor, second on the left. Your room is across the hall. Kameron and I will share the master bedroom on the main floor." Scotty pointed out.

"Girls, there are some clothes and toiletries in your room. Why don't you get yourselves showered and a change of clothes?" Midnight suggested.

"That actually sounds like something positive out of this whole trip." Scarlett started to walk upstairs.

Kaylee started upstairs, "What about...?" She put her hand on her stomach.

"We have an appointment with an OB. Just to make sure everything is going to be okay with the baby." Scotty walked over to Midnight and put her arm around. "Your big sister," he pointed to Midnight. "And her dashing husband," pointing to himself, "are taking you in to help you with getting your life back together."

"Really, husband and wife?" Midnight told him. "Change that."

"Can't, fake IDs are already created." Scotty laughed.

Kaylee asked, "And if they ask about the father of my baby?"

"Product of a one-night stand. You don't know who the father is," Scotty bluntly told her.

Tears started to fall as she walked upstairs. "Damn it, Scotty. Sometimes you don't think." Midnight went up after Kaylee.

"What?" Scotty was shocked at the reaction. "It was the most believable scenario."

***

Anne and Alex casually strolled down the streets of downtown. They were busy with people as it was market day and a lot of stores had booths and tables set up for selling their products. Komptin was on edge but nothing to be concerned about. "How you doing, sweetie?" Anne asked Alex.

"I'm doing better," Alex started to explain to her. "It's rough at times. I could be right next to a Demon, and I wouldn't know it. It's not so much the hunting part; it's more of being empty, especially inside the church." The two of them stopped at a table with a box full of kittens. Anne picked one of them up as it snuggled up to her. She laughed as it was clawing onto her, not wanting to leave her.

"She likes you," the lady selling the cats told her.

"I never could have a cat." She turned her head to Alex. "Kale was allergic."

Alex forced a smile. It was nice to hear Anne start to mention his name in everyday conversation. There was a definite sound of ease in that sentence. "Why don't you get her now?"

Anne thought about it. "I don't have a place to live. I don't want to bring an animal into my parents' house. Maybe if I get a place of my own." Anne put the small gray longhaired cat back into the box. It gave a small little meow. "She is adorable." Anne scratched the head of the kitten.

They continued to walk down the street. Alex got another Apollo from a vendor as Anne got an iced tea. They found a small table to sit at. Komptin made himself comfortable by Alex's feet. She started playing with her can of Apollo. It reminded her of the time Kameron took her to the Apollo manufacturing factory. It was a nice weekend. They got a nice hotel room with a fireplace and a hot tub. It was such a perfect time.

"You know, when I was asking how you were doing, it wasn't about your situation." Anne took a sip of her tea.

"I know. I was kind of hoping you were, though." Alex scouted the crowd. "I'm afraid I really messed this one up."

"Why do you say that?" Anne asked her.

"I know Kameron. The less emotion he shows, the more he's hurt." Alex let Anne know. "He was completely stonewalling when he left."

Anne thought about it. "You mean stone-faced?"

***

145

"Where's the keys to the backup car?" Kameron came into the kitchen where Scotty was making dinner. He opened the box to the condoms that was a decoy to hide the keys to the car.

Scotty peeked his head over Kameron's shoulder to make sure Scarlett or Kaylee weren't listening. "In my pocket. I went to inventory the getaway bags." He threw the keys to Kameron. "Where are you heading?"

"Town, there are some things I want to get." Kameron checked his firearm. "I shouldn't be long."

"Midnight wants to debrief us when her shift starts. Something about what she saw in the woods when you went to pick up our guests." Scotty tasted the Alfredo sauce.

"I'll be back in a bit." Kameron took off in the car.

Midnight got up to the smell of dinner. She walked downstairs to see Scotty sitting at the table with Kaylee and Scarlett. "What's going on?"

"Scotty made chicken alfredo with broccoli." Kaylee belched. "Excuse me." The table laughed.

"I saved you some. It's in the fridge." Scotty pointed with his spoon that he was using to eat some pudding.

"Where's Kameron?" Midnight opened up the container and smelled. "I hate to admit it, Scotty, but this smells good."

"Wow, a compliment. What's the occasion?" He took another bite of pudding.

"Well, we are supposed to be married." Midnight joined the group at the table.

"That's not how my parents acted," Scarlett finished up her plate. "Dad was cold, and Mom was sleeping with the mailman, pool boy, handyman, next door neighbor, two of my teachers, and oh, yeah, my swimming coach." Scarlett played with the last noodle on her plate. "This is the closest thing I had to a family meal since I was a young kid."

"Kaylee, what about your parents? Do they know where you are?" Midnight asked her.

"No, my parents signed over rights to me to the F.O.R. Roger Somberson provided all that we needed." Kaylee blew her nose into her napkin. "They'll never know their grandchild."

"Your turn, what were your parents like?" Scarlett asked as she had a small bite of pudding.

Midnight stole a piece of Scotty's left-over chicken off his plate. "Typical happy home. Mom was a realtor with comfortable success. Dad worked as a therapist."

Kaylee stole some of Scarlett's pudding. She gave Kaylee a fun scowl. "I'm eating for two," she playfully justified. "What about you, Scotty?"

"Mom jumped jobs a lot until she found something steady as a school secretary." Scotty cleared the table of the dishes not being used.

"And your dad?" Scarlett asked.

Midnight's curiosity caused her to see what Scotty was going to say. This was the most she ever heard him talk about his family. Scotty rinsed off the plates as if he was reluctant to answer. "Dad died when I was ten. He got into a car accident; he didn't make it."

147

"I'm sorry, Scotty." Kaylee was embarrassed. "I shouldn't have asked."

"You didn't know." Scotty rinsed off his dishes.

Scarlett got up to scout out the cabinets. "Isn't there anything to drink around here?"

"Dry house," Midnight told her.

Scarlett turned around. "What?!"

"We can't drink. Were constantly on duty. Kaylee can't drink, pregnant." Scotty put the dishes in the washer.

"And then what about me?" Scarlett asked.

"If we need to bugout. You need your senses about you," Midnight explained. "Where is Kameron?"

Scotty saw the time. "He's been awhile. Let me call him." He called Kameron on his phone. "Kam, where are you? I can't hear you. Say it again." Scotty listened then his facial expression changed. "I'll take care of it. I'm going to call you in five minutes, make sure you answer. Bye." He hung up the phone. "Midnight, can I talk to you for a second?" The two of them stepped outside.

Kameron sat down at a table in the club as he was talking to a girl he met. She was blonde and had a very nice body. She had a low-cut white tank top with pants low enough to show she wasn't wearing any underwear. She sat next to him, very close; there were a couple of times she even kissed him, and he didn't stop her. For some reason, he couldn't remember her name.

"I'm going to get us another round and then maybe we could go back to my hotel room?" She licked the rim of her lips.

Kameron finished his drinks as he stared at the band playing on the stage. "I don't see why not." She came over to Kameron and kissed him before getting their drinks.

"There you are." Scotty tapped him from behind on the shoulder. The server came over. "I'll have lemon-lime soda."

The waitress took down the order. "And your friend?"

"I got someone bringing me a drink," Kameron said as he stared at the band.

"I'll be back." The server smiled as she left.

Scotty sat there staring at his friend. "What's going on, buddy?"

"You know, Scotty. I envy you." Kameron continued to stare at the band.

"Now I know you're drunk." Scotty sat down next to him. "Why do you envy me?"

"You don't let anyone get close. You don't let anyone get close; you don't get hurt. It's a simple action to reaction. If you take away the action, you won't have the reaction. Reaction sucks." Kameron searched the table for his drink.

"What brought you in here anyways?" Scotty gazed around at the crowd. This was not a comfortable environment. "Where's your piece?"

"In the car lock box," he answered. "I swear I didn't plan this."

"I know you didn't." Scotty was relieved to hear Kameron didn't have his gun on him and that it was locked in the car. "But what brought you in here?"

"The band," Kameron admitted.

The music started. It was loud guitars and thumping bass along with thunderous drums. The girl's shrieking scream caused shivers down Scotty's spine. "Didn't know you like this type of thing."

"I don't, can't stand it," Kameron slurred a bit.

"Then, why?"

Kameron pointed to the band. Scotty turned to see a girl with black dreadlocks and dark makeup. She was tall and full of tattoos, but she did remind Scotty of the Lite Sentry. "Ah, I get it now."

Then a beautiful blonde girl came up with two drinks in her hand. "Kameron, here's our drinks. Who's your friend?"

Scotty turned from the band to see the girl putting the drinks on the table. "Cherry?! Cherry Poppz?!"

"That's right, have you seen my movies?" Cherry shyly admitted.

Scotty was searching for his phone. "Please, can I take a picture with you?"

"Of course." She rubbed his arms.

"I'm never washing this coat again," he teased her. He then took a picture with his cell phone of the two of them.

"One more," she told him. While Scotty took the picture, she gave him a kiss on the cheek.

"I could die a happy man right now." Scotty put his phone away. "I can't believe you are here. What are you doing here anyways?"

"Making a movie here about being abducted by aliens. Then I have to seduce him to set me free." She handed him an adult movie flyer.

"I can't believe I met Cherry Poppz." Scotty acted like a little boy talking to an older crush.

"Kameron, do you want to go back to my place now?" She took a sip of her drink. "I have a few scenes I may need to rehearse." She came around and placed her arm around him as she licked his ear.

Kameron nodded. He went into his pocket and handed Scotty the keys. "I'll be back in time for work."

Scotty caught the keys but stopped him from leaving. "Cherry, I really need to take my friend home now."

"I'll make sure he gets to work," she assured him.

Scotty grabbed Kameron's arm. "Kameron, we should go. There is more than one reason you shouldn't be here."

"I'll be back in time to take care of them." Kameron turned to Cherry. "I'm ready."

Scotty maneuvered to prevent Kameron from leaving. "I'll give you the most important reason." The music slowed as the band started to play their version of a ballad. Scotty pointed to the singer with black weaved hair.

Kameron realized the situation he was in. "Cherry, I really need to get back home for work. I'm sorry if I led you on. Really, I am."

Cherry smiled. "Is she the one you are in love with?" She motioned toward the singer of the band.

Kameron stared at the singer as she emotionally sang into the microphone. "Scotty, I think we should go home."

Scotty nodded. "It was nice meeting you, Cherry."

Cherry gave a pouting face. "Nice meeting you guys as well."

The two of them walked out of the club. Scotty was guiding his friend to the car. "She told me she got over me." Kameron fought back his emotions, trying everything in his power to push them down. "She got over me."

Scotty really didn't know what to say to help his friend. All he could do was watch his friend stumble to the passenger side of the car.

**

Devine was on her back, rolling back and forth on the forest floor. She held her stomach as it was stretching. The red of the eyes were faintly coming through her skin. "Oh God, is this my punishment? Is this because I did not die with my sister?" She screamed again as the stars seemed to become a bit dimmer.

"Tell me, Lite Being," Salamor sat on a rock studying the actions of the angel. "Do you still love God even though He ignores you?"

"He does not ignore me." Devine squinted her eyes from the pain.

"Then where is He? Why doesn't He show?" Salamor asked her.

Devine screamed in pain as she held her stomach. The pain started to subside as she was panting heavily. She crawled to the base of the rock where Salamor was sitting. "This cannot last much longer."

"It will be over soon," Salamor whispered. "He will not approve of you."

"He is forgiveness." Devine tried to control her pain.

Salamor floated in front of her. "Do you understand what is happening to you?"

Devine barely opened her eyes to the floating shadow in front of her. "Do you know how this came about?" The pain shot like a shot of lightning. Devine screamed as a bolt of lightning split a tree in half next to them.

"Focus, Angel of Lite," Salamor told her. "Focus on me." Devine screeched as the sharpness seemed to tear her insides. "Look at me!" he yelled at the angel. "Focus on me!"

Devine started panting. "Tell me your fear, Dark Myst." She started to pant to help ease the ache.

Salamor saw a teardrop from the angel's eye. A discomfort from within him started to form. He started to hover over the angel. "I fear my dissipation."

"The Sentry, yes I know she can hurt you." Devine rolled over on her side as she held her stomach.

Salamor stared at the burnt inside of the tree that was hit by the flash of lightning. He floated to meet her face-to-face. "Yes, she can, but there is another way." He floated to her ear; he whispered his darkest secret.

CHAPTER FIVE

"You're telling me the Council of Religions is going to have you become their liaison with one of the newly appointed priests?" Gron asked during an informal meeting in his office. On top of Gron and Misluna being in the room, there was Merik, Scarlett's Dad, who had Paige sitting next to him. They were all sitting around discussing the top issues within the F.O.R.

"Father Carl alluded to it today." She smirked. "Can you imagine if I was able to get to the actual location of the Council of Religions during their annual little get together?" Misluna eyed Gron in a way as if telling him to hurry this meeting up.

He caught the message in her eyes, but there was work that needed to be done before play. "Paige!" he yelled for her as he continued to stare at Misluna.

"Yes, my Leader," Paige acknowledged.

"You're really starting to piss me off." Gron now turned to her with glowing red eyes. "Where are Scarlett and Kaylee?"

"I don't know, I swear," Paige pleaded her case. "I assumed he would check-in so I could track his signal." She could feel her nerves start to rise. "Only the Council knows where he is."

Gron shook his head with disbelief. He then turned to Scarlett's dad. "Well?"

"Well, what, my Leader?" He straightened his posture while still sitting on the couch.

"Any sign of her?" Gron was starting to get annoyed. "I need to know where she is."

"I have complete control of her assets," he told Gron.

Gron swiveled his drinks. "Maybe you should go fishing."

Scarlett's dad nodded.

Merik was looking around the room with confusion. "Why should he go fishing?"

Misluna got up to refill her drink. On the way, she stopped in front of Merik. "It's a good thing you're cute." She playfully slapped him on the cheek. She walked behind Gron's desk as he lifted his glass for her to get him a new one as well.

"Any news on the twins?" Gron started moving the meeting along. "We cannot let the Lite get ahold of them."

"I promise you, with all the power you gave me, they will be delivered to you in time." Merik, for the first time, showed confidence in his statement.

"Okay, then." Gron was a bit impressed by his conviction. "In the meantime. The mayor is out of office, permanently. The Deputy Mayor Gresin is a saint. We may have to get creative to get him out of there. Then, I'll announce my candidacy for mayor. We'll make this town the first religion-free zone where the F.O.R. will be the hub for the morale of this town. My goal is to get the F.O.R. into the schools and workplaces and eventually rid this town of any church that supports the Lite."

"Alex and Anne will fight it," Merik interjected.

Paige's interest rose a bit as Merik mentioned the Lite Sentry.

155

"No kidding." Gron got out of his chair. The town behind him was starting to turn on their lights from the sun setting. It was starting to get darker earlier, he liked that. "I'm counting on it. I need them focused on what we're doing publicly to prevent them from finding out about the twins."

"Do you think the Sentry will fall for it?" Paige interjected. It was the first time she ever voluntarily spoke up during this meeting.

Gron stared at her through the reflection of the window. "She's an idiot, but a tough idiot. She'll be easily distracted by what we're doing. Plus, she hates me. It's an advantage. I'm more worried about Anne. She's got a level head to her."

"Well, there is a way to distract her." Merik's eyes flashed.

***

It was going to be such a nice crisp night to go on a hunt. Alex was really looking forward to it. On top of that, she cut her walk in half since Anne was giving her a ride to her house. Anne just got off the phone with her parents on speakerphone. They decided to take a quick, needed getaway out of town for an autumn vacation.

"You know. We could throw a party," Alex threw out the suggestion. The answer was known even before she asked it.

Anne knew that Alex was being sarcastic. "Sure, Alex, I think we would be those creepy old people who hang out with teenagers."

"Old? We're only twenty-three." Alex just moved her eyes in Anne's direction. "Do you want to go out to the bars?"

"Not particularly. I really don't feel like running into Shawn." Her parents' electric car turned onto the street that led to her parents' house.

Alex went back to her phone. "I may want to run into him," she said under her breath.

Anne turned up the radio. "I like this song." Anne started to sing to the pop music. "Oh, come on, Alex, you know the words."

"No. You can't make me." Alex stood her ground. Anne turned up the radio. "No, Anne, I'm not…" Alex started to sing before they both ignited into the chorus. The two of them laughed as they pulled into the driveway.

"I have to plug my car in." Anne hit the button to open the garage door. Alex continued to sing the song she shamefully liked. "What's that?"

Alex focused on what Anne was referring to. Anne had to do a double-take before she screamed as she covered her face and eyes. Alex ignited her fists as she slowly got out of the car. The Lite Sentry scouted the area as she motioned for Komptin to head to the field. Alex walked up to the dead kitten nailed to the back door of the garage. Alex studied the baby cat stretched out with its legs dislocated.

Anne cautiously got out of the car. "Alex."

"You shouldn't see this." Alex removed the nails from the cat's paws and carefully held the kitten in her hands.

"Isn't that the kitten from earlier today?" Anne fought back from crying.

Alex turned to the garage opening when Komptin came in from his gargoyle form. He morphed down to a German shepherd as he approached the two girls. That told Alex that it was safe. Alex nodded her head to Anne, confirming her suspicions about the dead kitten. "Go get an overnight bag and some snacks. You're going to stay at the church tonight."

"Alex, why do I..." Anne started to say, but then she saw Alex's eyes start to give a faint glow of blue.

"Anne, I'm not arguing." Alex just stared at the dead kitten in her hands.

Anne nodded as she walked into her house, with Komptin following her to ensure her safety. Alex watched her friend go into the house before pulling out the daisy flower that was shoved into the body of the kitten. The Lite Sentry went to the outskirts of the yard where the forest started. Alex gave the baby animal a prayer before burying it in the Earth.

**

"You look like shit." Midnight intentionally slammed some pots and pans together in Kameron's direction as he came down for breakfast.

Kameron sat down at the kitchen table. Covering his ears didn't help the noise from his massive headache. The thumping was causing his stomach to burn from all the alcohol. "I'm never drinking again."

"Famous last words." She handed him a plate with dry wheat toast. "Here, this might help."

"Did the assets see anything?" Kameron made sure that Kaylee and Scarlett weren't around.

"No, they were in bed before you guys got home." Midnight sat down with a ham and cheese omelet she made.

Kameron put his hand over his head. "I can't believe I did that. Did he tell you about last night?" He took a bite of dry toast. The toast was dry, but he could tell it was already helping his stomach. Midnight got up to pour him some water and handed him an electrolyte drink. "Thanks."

"Don't worry about it." Midnight took a bite of her breakfast. "He told me about it."

"I never do that, especially while on duty." He just shook his head out of disgust over what he did. "I need to thank him for helping me out."

"I wouldn't mention it to him. The thing about Scotty… is that he truly has a heart of gold, but he's embarrassed about it when approached." Midnight smiled.

"Sounds like you have firsthand knowledge." Kameron washed down his dry toast with a sip of his drink.

Midnight hesitated before speaking. "Promise me you won't say anything." Kameron crossed his heart. "The day I caught my ex with the weather girl, I ended up at his apartment. I was such a wreck. I spent the night crying in his arms while lying in his bed. He just held me tight as we both fell asleep. I tried to thank him, but he just told me the best thing I could do was not talk about it, to anyone."

"I would have never guessed," Kameron heard the girls move around upstairs. "I could tell there was a connection between you two."

"He was at my side throughout the divorce, my pregnancy scare; I thought I was pregnant with my ex's kid. He's a friend who is beyond family." Midnight saw Scotty coming back from checking the alarms on the property.

"I get it." Kameron finished his toast. "I won't say a thing. You have my word."

Scotty came into the room, knocking the sand off his shoes. "Why did we choose a desert?"

"We didn't choose it." Midnight looked at her watch. "I'm getting tired. I'll take the night shift again. Kameron, Kaylee has that doctor's appointment coming up."

"I remember." Kameron got up. "I need to take a shower."

***

Weston finished his report about the F.O.R. church. He always found it difficult to hide what he truly knew about F.O.R. He noticed Paige's light was still on in her office. He went through the maze of construction that used to be a government office. Thank God that Komptin was here to kill the Infiltrator and Demon. He quietly knocked on Paige's office door.

She was just staring at the wall with a blank stare. "You okay?"

160

Paige shook off her thoughts. "I'm fine. You ever wonder if you are good enough to go to heaven when you die?"

Weston put his satchel down on a chair in Paige's wrecked office. "I lead a good life, remained faithful to my vows, repented my sins, plus I kind of got an inside guy." He smiled. "Why do you ask?"

She returned the small smirk. "Do you think I'm worthy?"

"That's between you and God. Even Celestial herself can't tell you that." Weston could tell his freckled-faced friend was in deep thought.

"That is what my pastor said, minus the Celestial part." She got up and got a bottle of water. Weston took a bottle that she offered him. "You wanna know something?"

"What's that?" He opened the bottle to take a drink.

Paige gazed out the window before going back to her desk. "I appreciate all you and the Council did for me."

Weston suddenly peeked outside the window. "Paige, you're scaring me. What are you thinking about?"

"I'm thinking about coming to peace about my past. I want forgiveness." Paige seemed as if she was about to start crying.

Weston turned back to her. "You have to forgive yourself first." He got up. "I have to go." Paige nodded. "Are you okay?"

"I just hope when the time comes, I'm forgiven." Paige saw her phone light up when Gron messaged her. She opened it, as it was demanding she find out where Scarlett and Kaylee were.

"I have to meet my dad, really quick. Do you want to talk when I get back?" Weston gathered his satchel.

"No, I'm good." She read the message again. "I think I know what I need to do."

Weston headed out of her office before stopping, "If you ever need to talk."

"I'm good." Paige waved to him while forcing a smile. There was nothing she could do to repay him for his friendship. All she could do was take one of those black bastards with her.

Weston acknowledged her before heading down to a local café. He sat down and ordered a tea for himself and a coffee with extra cream. The waitress returned with the drinks as Malkaroy joined his son for a drink. "Hey, Dad."

He was massive, even by angel standards. "How are you doing?"

"I'm doing well. The two assets are secure. What's so special about them?" Weston took a sip of his drink.

"The one girl's son will be a Pure Heart. In this age of such darkness, he must be protected from consumption." Malkaroy couldn't believe the Dark hid Vandor's need for Pure Hearts to remain here for so long. He was more surprised when another Pure Heart put the puzzle together. He truly felt honored that he was able to help rescue her from Vandor's clutches.

"She'll be safe. When will the Lite Sentries be ready?" Weston whispered to make sure no one heard.

Malkaroy shrugged his shoulders. "I have been training one of them. Good set of morals to him, but there is such a lack of confidence in him. I do not know where it stems from."

"Who will he be taking?"

"Scarlett. However, Dinah will be getting Kaylee; she must be the first to be protected. Her son must be born," Malkaroy told him. "Pure Hearts are such an asset in this fight."

Weston agreed. "Yes." The thought of what would have happened if there were no Pure Hearts left in the world frightened him. "What about the other two? Have you heard of their training?"

"All I know; is they are no Alexandria Johnson."

***

Alex kicked the Infiltrator in the head while she stood on top of a big rock. She was on her way back to the church when she ran into two of these Dark beasts. Komptin chased the other one down into the woods. The Infiltrator in front of her shook off the blow from the head. It stood its ground as it portrayed a fighting stance. On top of the rock, Alex had her fists glowing the neon blue of the Lite. The Infiltrator started to circle around as Alex matched the movement. From the back, the second Infiltrator tackled Alex. The pain from her landing on the ground caused her to call out in agony.

Her hands quickly grabbed the mouth of the Infiltrator before it attached to her throat. The other Infiltrator continued to kick her in the side. The drool from the Infiltrator's mouth was starting to drip onto Alex. "Ewww, gross!" she screamed.

She generated enough power to Lite Beam the Infiltrator off her. As the other one went to kick her, she grabbed the leg to twist it. The sounds of broken bones inside the leg clued Alex she'd damaged it. There was an advantage to her now. The Infiltrator was frantic when the Lite Sentry grabbed its leg and threw it into the second one. They both crashed into each other against the rock Alex had previously stood on.

Furious, Alex screamed as she shot another beam into them. Alex ran with full force with a knife formed from her Lite. She was able to stab them both through their chests. They dropped to the ground before disappearing into the earth.

Alex grabbed her side where she'd been kicked. She unzipped her vest and took off her shirt so she could study the wound. It was cut deep, and of course; it was on the charred skin where Alex was stabbed with Sanah's Lite Spear. Alex slowly touched it as she winced in pain. The burning of the skin got her a bit worried.

A sound of something else coming from the woods caused Alex to quickly get dressed. She ignited her fist, ready for another attack. Luckily, Komptin came out of the woods. He trudged up to her with a slight limp. "You okay?" He flashed his eyes with acknowledgment. She smiled at him while she lifted his massive gargoyle head. "It's okay, boy. There are more times than I can count when those black bastards slipped away from me." Alex kissed him on top of the head. "Come on. Let's go see how Anne is doing."

The rest of the walk home was quiet. Alex took advantage of the night and walked unhurriedly. Komptin didn't seem to object. The air was cooling down at night and some of the moisture on the leaves and on the ground was starting to form small amounts of ice. Alex was cooling down from her fight, except for the scar on the side of her body. The burn was slow and just enough for her to notice. The backyard of the church was a welcomed sanctuary as they entered holy ground. The area was starting to take form for the festival. It needed a bit of clean-up, but the building housing the games for the kids was on its way. The night sky burnt bright with stars as she took special notice of Ariel's star for some reason.

The church was dark, as there was no reason for the lights to be on. She quietly peeked in on Anne in one of the spare rooms. She was fast asleep on an air mattress they grabbed from her house. Anne was tightly holding onto a pillow that had Kale's sweatshirt over it. It was a sweet gesture but also sad over the grief Anne was still holding onto.

There could be no fault over that, though. Alex still had no senses. The Dark had taken her ability to sense their presence, which caused more blood on her part to fall to the ground. The worst part wasn't the sneak attacks by the Dark– it was the fact that she still couldn't feel the warmth of the Lite. She was constantly cold and empty, even when she was

165

in a church. Alex quietly shut the door to let Anne sleep as she went upstairs to her office.

A big package was sitting in her office. Komptin started to get excited as he sniffed around the package. Alex tried opening it, but found it difficult. She went to grab a hammer to pry open the crate. A sudden rush of emotion came over her as she saw it cleared of the packing material. The bed Kameron made for Komptin after their first date was delivered. Alex cleaned off the rest of the bed before placing it underneath the window. Komptin jumped into it and fell instantly asleep.

Alex sat down on the floor next to him to pet him as he slept soundly. As she stroked the Komptin's fur, she opened up her phone to find some pictures of her and Kameron. When she realized she had deleted them all, she got a sudden sickness in her stomach. She slammed her head against the wall in disgust with herself. How could she let him get away?

"Alexandria," a soft voice came over to her.

Alex opened one eye to see Celestial with her two bodyguards standing behind her. The Lite Sentry went to stand up, but the Conduit of Lite motioned for her to stay down. "Is Kameron okay?" Alex had a sense of worry to her.

Celestial had a look of confusion to her before answering, "He still walks in this existence. Do you wish me to tell you if something happens?"

"No! Why should I care?" Alex put up a wall, but then it came crashing down immediately. "I would appreciate it."

"You have my word." Celestial had a worried face as she elegantly made her way to the window. "Alexandria." The angel hesitated before asking, "Have you seen Devine?"

Alex got up from the floor. "No, I haven't. Do you want me to go look for her?"

"She could be anywhere," Celestial reminded her. "If you see her, tell her I would like to meet with her."

Alex got fear in her heart. She wanted to tell Celestial about Devine's actions in the past, but she gave her word to her surrogate sister. Devine had done so much for Alex, she thought she needed to do this for her. Alex hoped that Devine knew what she was doing, that she was working out whatever she was going through.

***

Kameron was trying his best to hide his headache from Kaylee and Scarlett as they sat in the doctor's office. He really wished Midnight had been here for this appointment. This was awkward. Kaylee was in the stir-ups with her legs in the air while talking to Scarlett about hoping the medical tools weren't cold.

Scarlett peeked over at Kameron, who was on his phone. "You don't look good."

"I'm fine," Kameron reassured her as he got a random message from Anne. The message just read: "I hope you're doing well. Alex is fine, physically. Please don't shut the door." That heartfelt message was exactly what Kameron wanted to hear. There will always be a sense of sadness for Anne. She has such a big heart. The death of her husband was truly devastating to her.

Scarlett tapped her long fingernails on the counter. "God, this sucks. I need to see what's going on in the world." Scarlett eyed Kameron's phone. "Can I use your phone?"

"No, ma'am," he quickly responded. "It's not worth the risk of the F.O.R. tracking you down."

"They already won if I go into hiding," Scarlett started to argue. "I'm not afraid of them."

Kameron could hear the false confidence in her voice. "Really?"

Scarlett thought back to the torture her own father submitted her to. Kaylee adjusted her body on the table, which made her think back to how heartless the F.O.R. were in brutalizing her. "Can I at least contact Steven?"

That caught Kameron's attention. "Who's Steven?"

"My assistant." Scarlett seemed to turn her head in shame. A memory of her assistant came to her. It was a month before her dad forced her to join F.O.R. Scarlett was getting ready to go out to a club she was scheduled to attend. It was all the buzz throughout Los Angeles. She was supposed to take all these pictures with other celebrities. Her life was so grand, all she had to do was party in expensive outfits, hook up with hot well-known guys, and occasionally get just the right amount of controversy surrounding her. That night, there was a small electrical fire in the club, so they had to postpone the opening a week.

Steven was dressed in a gray shirt and black pants when he came to take her to the club when he was notified. When he alerted her of the fire, she suggested they go to a different club. Then her heel broke, and she twisted her ankle. He picked her up when she fell to the ground and carried her to the couch. They ended up on the couch, watching whatever was on the television. Mainly it was just backup noise. They spent the night talking to each other while she had her foot on a pillow on Steven's lap as he compressed an ice pack on her ankle. It was the most comfortable she had felt in quite some time.

"Too dangerous," Kameron told her. "No outside contact. How do you know he's not F.O.R.?"

Scarlett chuckled, "Stevey is not F.O.R. That is one thing I'm sure about."

The doctor and nurse came in. "Hello, I'm Doctor Amadune, this is Nurse Prate." He sat down. "Let's see what we are dealing with." The doctor continued his examination while Kameron was very uncomfortable waiting for this to be done.

After the appointment was done, Kameron escorted Kaylee and Scarlett out the back to the SUV where Scotty was sitting. He started the car as Kameron put the girls in the back seats before taking the front.

"How'd everything go?" Scotty started moving the SUV out of the alley.

Kaylee spoke up, "The instruments were cold. Can we get something to eat?"

"What do you want?" Scotty asked her.

"I don't care. I'm just hungry," Kaylee told them.

"I guess we can pick something up at that restaurant over there." Kameron pointed over to a small establishment.

Scotty pulled the vehicle into the parking lot. "Can you pick me up a chicken wrap?"

Kameron nodded. "Ladies?" The two of them gave them their order. Kameron went into the small café and ordered. He took this opportunity to message Paige that all was well. She messaged back, stating to keep a low profile.

"I have to use the bathroom," Scarlett told Scotty.

Scotty turned around. "Can it wait?"

"No." Scarlett started shaking her leg. "Come on. I doubt the F.O.R. are going to be in the lady's bathroom in an alien café."

"It's not a good idea." Scotty turned back around to look out the front window.

"Neither is me going all over the backseat of your car." Scarlett started to shift her body around.

"Fine." He messaged Kameron that Scarlett was coming in. He acknowledged back. Scotty turned around. "Put this hat on and sunglasses. Agent Dutcher will point in the right direction inside."

Scarlett rolled her eyes. "I don't wear hats."

"Wasn't an optional wardrobe accessory." Scotty threw the hat at her. "Put it on."

"Ugh." Scarlett grabbed the hat. "Fine." She slammed the door to the vehicle. Inside, Kameron pointed to the bathroom. He sat down at the table watching the entrance to the bathroom. As he was waiting, the employee handed Kameron the food.

Scarlett was inside the bathroom, fluffing her green-streaked hair as she looked in the mirror. The door opened to one of the employees coming in to use the bathroom. The young teenager's eyes opened with shock. "You're Scarlett Roberts."

She smiled at the young girl. "Shhh." She playfully smiled.

"Can I please get your picture?" The young girl grabbed her phone from her back pocket.

"On one condition, can I use your phone?"

***

Steven was sitting at his computer when he answered a video call from a strange number. "Hello."

"It's me, you alone?" Scarlett asked him.

"No other person in the room," Steven told her. "What's going on? I had some people come to my apartment asking about you."

"Long story. Is there any way you have access to my bank accounts?" she asked him.

"I had moved over two million spread out to multiple banks. I have all the information to include your pins on a USB," Steven told her.

"Oh, I love you," Scarlett told him. "Where?"

Steven hesitated. "I think it would be better for me to meet you somewhere to give them to you. Remember that time we went hiking last October? That might be a good place."

"You want me to meet you in Colorado at the Devil's Garden?" Scarlett was confused.

Steven gave a small sigh. "My bad, no, I meant the place we went and found that agate rock you made into a ring."

Scarlett looked at the ring on her finger. "Oh, you mean, you want to meet at that hotel in Niagara Falls." For some reason, Steven's facial expression was becoming annoyed.

"No, I meant, we can meet at that place where you accidentally fell into the water during a photo shoot." Steven closed his eyes in hopes she understood the message.

"You want me in Tampa, why? I couldn't do that. Just have them ready for me in Copper Top. It will be easier for me to get them there. I gotta go."

"It's not worth it." Steven got a little stern with her.

"Just promise me you will be there." She smiled at him. He just stared at her. "Promise me, Stevey."

"I promise, just remember about our time. Bye." He slowly shut the computer down to stare at the man with glowing red eyes and a black monster standing over the dead body of his roommate. Beside him was a small woman with blonde hair.

"Do you think I am stupid?" the man asked him.

"I don't know what you're talking about." Steven sat there motionless.

The man with glowing red eyes circled around behind before whispering in his ear. "The codes you were telling her. Not giving a specific location

172

to meet her." He pulled the chair back with Steven still in it. "How dumb do you think I am?"

The woman with blonde hair spoke up. "He did get her to try to get to Copper Top. So, not a total loss."

The Demon stood up. "True. Where is the USB?"

Steven had a moment of realization of the serious situation he was in. "You know, when a person is in the position I am, they have a choice to make. They can live with the guilt or die with a free mind." He stared straight into his glowing red eyes. "My conscience is clear."

The Demon's face turned to disgust as he shoved his two fingers into the eye sockets of Steven's eyes to pick him up by the head. He smashed his head repeatedly onto the floor until his body became limp. "Paige, let's go. We have to report back to Gron."

***

Devine rolled around in the grass as the skin on her stomach was starting to grow. She couldn't close her eyes any tighter, and she started to cry from the pain. Salamor remained perched on the tree, staring down at the angel down below. The grass was forced down to the ground from her rolling around in that spot.

"Is this what the primates go through?" Devine could barely get out. The movement in her stomach was becoming more apparent. Whatever was growing inside of her was about to come out.

Salamor turned his head away as, for some reason, he couldn't watch her. "No, what you have is forty times worse than they go through. Any primate would die before this was over, including Lite Sentries."

For a split second, Devine's attention wasn't focused on the pain. "Azrael and Cara." Then a sharp pain came from her body. "I do not think I can do this. I am not going to survive."

Salamor floated down to Devine. "Listen to my word, Lite Harlot. You will triumph over this pain. You have the strength. The Dark feared taking on the Guardians of the Conduit; it was almost certain death."

"I am alone." Devine screeched in pain as she held her stomach. "I am irrelevant."

"You are an angel that successfully defended the Conduit of Lite since the Lite invaded the Dark." Salamor floated to a stump in an over-watch position. "Your strength and skill are unmatched." Salamor sensed the twins as the time was approaching. "I need to go."

"Do not leave me!" Devine pleaded to the Dark Myst.

"I must." Salamor started to slowly float off into the blackness of the forest.

***

Gron was enjoying the kingdom he commanded. He loved the fear the Serfs showed as he walked by. Being stuck in his hometown was miserable, but the fact he was a god among peasants made it tolerable.

Halloween was coming soon, and that meant the twins would arrive. There was no sign of them. Gron would have sworn with that much Dark being generated, they could pinpoint their location. Misluna was off to the side of him, giving him the update on the little fall festival the church was planning to improve community relations. Merik was talking to one of the young girls tending the garden. "Merik," Gron called out to him.

"To your command." Merik grazed the cheek of the young girl swooning over the Host. The tall blonde Demon stood straight up off to the side of Gron.

"Meet me in my office in fifteen minutes." Gron continued his survey of the campus. Off in the distance, a car pulled into the gate. It was Jonkyle and Paige coming straight in his direction.

"To your command." Jonkyle bowed. This particular Demon was average height with multiple earrings. "We have some news for you." Jonkyle turned to Paige to tell him the news. Jonkyle liked Paige; he thought she would be a great asset to the organization. "Paige."

"We didn't get the location of Scarlett, but we think she will be coming to us." Paige proceeded to tell him how they got Steve to tell her where her money would be.

"My office." Gron pointed to the office. They walked down the darkened hallway with red carpeting. There were people working in their offices with doors opened as one Provisionary was standing in the doorway.

"Misluna, can I talk to you?" He had a folder in his hand. Misluna stopped to talk while Gron, along with the others, continued into his office.

His secretary handed him a drink with some messages from his campaign manager, Logan. He handed one of the messages back. "Yeah, I'm not doing that. Hold my calls." It was such a good drink. It was the perfect amount of scotch and lemon-lime soda. "Damn, that's good." Paige and Jonkyle stood in front of Gron's desk when he sat down. "This is not good news."

"My leader, she is not going to leave a couple million dollars just sitting there," Paige told him with a tone of voice that was respectful in Gron's eyes.

"I don't give a shit who you are outside these walls, but you know your place." Gron's eyes were glowing red.

"I apologize, my Leader," Paige succumbed. "I meant no disrespect. I'm just trying everything in my power to help the F.O.R. mission to eradicate religion."

"Sure, you are." Gron watched as Misluna came in with a folder in her hand. "We'll see your true intentions in the near future." She handed him the folder while whispering in his ear. After a lick inside his ear, she sat down on the couch, smiling.

Gron opened the folder with a smile on his face. "Now, this is good news." He placed a picture of a young girl taking a picture with Scarlett Roberts in a bathroom. The location of where that young girl lived was on her homepage. "Go get her, Jonkyle." Gron smiled. "Kill her, Kaylee, and whoever else is

176

there. You and three Provisionaries should be able to handle this easily."

"To your command." Jonkyle smiled. "I'll take Paige and two others with me." The Demon smiled at her.

"No. She stays here." Gron sat back down at his desk. "Don't bother coming back until they are dead."

Jonkyle flashed his red eyes and left to go kill the deserters. Paige watched him leave for his mission as she turned to Gron. To prevent herself from fainting, she took a deep breath. "I couldn't use the assets from work. I would have been caught."

"I know. I believe you." Gron continued to write a note to his campaign leader. "You need to prepare for Infiltration."   There seemed to be a pause in time. "You can go." Paige left the office. Gron waited until she shut the door as she left. "Quickly, what's the status of the twins?"

Merik answered, "Trust me."

Gron stood up. "You deliver me those twins, and you will be at my side when Vandor arrives."

***

Paige left Gron's office to head down to her car. She needed to get going back to San Diego for her real job. Plus, she really needed Kameron and the others to know what was going on. She needed to tell them the F.O.R. found out where they were. The F.O.R. knew what town they were in but didn't have the exact address.   There was no doubt it wouldn't take them long to find them. Outside the

177

compound was Jonkyle leaning on her car door. "What's going on?"

"I'm just waiting for the provisionaries." He rolled his eyes. "It would be easier if you knew exactly where they were."

"The Council has them in an undisclosed address. Not even my POC knows where they are." Paige went to his side. "How long do you think it will take to find them?"

"Don't know. I'm not too worried about it." Jonkyle flashed his eyes. "Ugh, I wanna get going. This is going to be fun. I get to kill them all. The only thing that would make this better is if the Sentry was there." Jonkyle got up from the car in an anxious state. "I'm going to go see what's taking them so long."

Paige got into her car to head down the road. It was quite a bit of distance before she knew she could call Weston. She needed to get word to the Council that Kameron's location was compromised. "Come on, come on, Weston, answer your phone." Paige was starting to shake as her F.O.R. phone started to ring. She could hear Weston on the other phone as he answered the phone.

At the same time, she answered Gron. "Yes, my Leader." Her nerves started to rise as all the blood rushed from her face. "I'm going to see if Kameron checked in to convince him to get me the exact address where he's staying."

Weston, on the other phone, was asking, "What's going on, Paige? Can you talk?"

Paige ensured Gron wasn't able to hear Weston on the other phone as he was asking what was going on. "My Leader, if I got the exact address, Jonkyle and the three Provisionaries wouldn't need to search all over New Mexico to find them."

Weston, on the other phone, suddenly became quiet. He knew what Paige was doing.

"Yes, my Leader. My loyalty is to you and the Dark, of course, one hundred percent." Paige closed her eyes. "Yes, it would be my honor to accept Infiltration." Paige saw a car pull up behind her. It was Jonkyle with the three Provisionaries. Paige rolled down her window. "What's going on?"

Jonkyle said with excitement, "I heard you're going to accept Infiltration tonight." He opened the door. "I begged Gron to come to the ceremony. This is a good day." Jonkyle escorted her to his car. "The Provisionary will take care of your car."

Paige hung up the phone with Weston.

"Are you excited?" Jonkyle asked her.

Paige swallowed hard. "I always knew this would come."

CHAPTER SIX

The phone's ring seemed to echo throughout the church. Anne was downstairs showering while Alex was still out on her hunt. Misluna decided to pick it up, "Hello, Saint Thomas, how may I be of service?"

The man on the other end spoke, "This is Weston. May I please talk to Father Richard, Anne McClure, or Alexandria Johnson?"

Misluna grinned. "I'm sorry, but they're not available at the moment."

"This is very important; I need to talk to them," he emphasized.

"I don't think Father Richard or Anne will be in, but Father Carl is here." Misluna watched as Father Carl came in the door. She handed him the phone. "Some guy, asking for Alex."

He covered the phone. "Who is it?"

"Probably one of her one-night stands that she keeps on having." Misluna grabbed some coffee.

"This is Father Carl." He was not in the mood for any repercussions of Alex's nightly ventures. "How may I help you?"

"Father, I really need to talk to Alex. It's important." Weston was emphasizing.

Father Carl was starting to get upset. "If you need to talk to her, call her on her cell. Goodbye."

"Who was that?" Alex walked in, drinking an Apollo while eating a doughnut.

"Look, don't have your private dealings call here. It is far from appropriate to link this church with you," he started to lecture.

"Excuse me," Alex took on the offensive. "You don't know a damn thing about me. And if you would like to know, we can talk about it off church property."

"Alex." Father Richard came in behind them. "That's it. We are going to air this out between you two right here and now." Father Richard's face turned red with anger.

Alex put her hands on her hips in a stance to challenge Father Carl, in turn; Father Carl was in an offensive position. Alex lifted her hand and was about to speak, which wasn't going to be nice words, when Anne came rushing up behind Alex in a frantic state.

"Alex! Father Richard!" She came running in behind them. Anne's hair was dripping with water. It would have seemed she put on clothes without drying off. In her shaking hand was her cell phone. "The F.O.R. knows where Scarlett and Kaylee are."

Alex's eyes got big as she turned around to confirm with Anne. "Kameron." Alex ran upstairs to her office, bypassing anyone who got in her way, to include certain annoying priests. It was the fastest she ever changed clothes. In a backpack, she threw in some clean hunting clothes and started heading out the door but stopped. Komptin was by the window, watching her pack. She knelt down to him. "Kameron is in danger. I gotta go and I don't have time to get the paperwork together to bring you." Komptin flashed his eyes and snuggled up to

181

her to tell her that he understood. "Love you. Watch over Anne." Alex turned and started running down the stairs.

"Alex!" Father Richard yelled.

"Father, there is nothing that you or the council can say to prevent me from going right now." Alex turned to run before Father Richard stopped her.

"There are other Sentries that could go," Father advised.

"Have any of them even fought an Infiltrator yet?" Alex asked flat-out.

Father Richard knew she had a point. "Only one of them has. He barely survived, and it was only one Infiltrator."

Alex gave a quick counterpoint, "And there is no doubt they are going to send a Demon and who knows what else." Alex turned to go.

"Alex," Father Richard tried to calm her down. "You don't have the address."

Alex stopped and turned around. "Let me guess; the Council won't tell it over the phone. It has to be delivered by courier."

"That is their protocol," Anne confirmed.

Father Carl and Megan came outside to see what Alex was doing.

"Father," Alex started breathing heavily to prevent herself from crying. "I don't have time to wait for that."

"You don't have to," Anne said, holding a piece of paper. "I haven't filed it yet."

Misluna was in shock with disgust that she had the address in the church the whole damn time.

Alex ran over to Anne and gave her a hug. "Thank you." The Lite Sentry wiped a tear as she turned to Father Richard. "I have to go."

"And I won't try to stop you." Father Richard signed the cross in her direction. "May God guide you."

***

Gron was speaking to Misluna, who snuck out so she could call him. He couldn't believe the address was sitting in Anne's office the whole time. It would have been easy to send Merik in there with some Provisionaires to grab them. Gron didn't think it was that big of a deal, though. With any luck, Jonkyle would kill the Sentry.

This provided a unique opportunity for Gron. Now that the Sentry is out of town, he can move forward with his plan to become mayor of Copper Top. Merik was on top of getting the twins after their birth. The incompetent Demon had to take off after Paige's Infiltration ceremony tonight.

"Merik," Gron greeted but with a bit of annoyance. "I need reassurance from you about the twins."

Merik confidentially went to grab a drink from Gron's bar. The mere fact that Merik had something over Gron irritated him. He needed Merik; he knew where the twins were going to be. That, and he had some other plans for him. Some fun plans that even Merik would enjoy.

"Is that good?" Gron sat back to put his feet on his desk.

"Smooth." Merik studied the glass. "There's a taste I'm not familiar with."

"Drop of Lite Sentry blood." Gron pointed over to the glass spheres on a shelf in the corner of the office. Merik peeked over to what Gron was pointing at. "I put a couple of drops in every bottle. Just gives it that taste."

"It's good." Merik sat down on the couch.

"Don't get used to it." Gron got a text from Misluna that Father Carl wanted to talk to her about making her job permanent in Copper Top. He couldn't help but smile as he knew she was getting closer to becoming a member of the Council. If she could infiltrate the Council of Religions, then he could find a way to destroy them. That was dreaming. Right now, he had other plans on his mind. "We have a meeting downtown we have to get to. You look pretty sad."

***

Anne was overlooking the building of the kid games and food tables for the fall festival. Some volunteers from a Catholic Church in Westington came by to help with the game's setup. Anne was surprised at how many of them came to help. It was nice to run into Jess again. She hadn't seen him since they went on that one date in high school. That was the night Kale and Anne started their relationship. In the corner of the lot was a kid's game booth where a piñata would be placed. It would be full of candy for laughing children. It was going to be so much fun.

"Anne?" Father Carl called out to her.

Anne turned around to see him holding a folder. "I've got the VCC-153 signed by Cardinal Joe for filing."

"Congratulations," Anne said as she looked over the paperwork. There was a minor issue with how the date was written, but other than that, it seemed as if all was in order. "You are officially in the Council."

"Yes. I just had an interesting meeting with Father Richards and Cardinal Joe." He sat down on the ledge of one of the games.

Anne was interested to see how much they actually told him. It wasn't Anne's place to tell him about Alex. That was something she needed to be here for when Father Richard officially tells him about her. "Kind of life altering hearing all that."

"Life changing," he admitted. "I always knew there was evil in the world, but now I know it actually walks in physical form."

Anne read over the form again. "It's something you'll never forget."

"How much do you know of it?" Father Carl asked her.

Anne was leery on how much she could say. The Council had found out that if they push a new Council Priest into the deep end, it was too much for them to handle. So… they like to gently feed them information over time. "Only what they tell me." Anne headed to her office. "If you will excuse me, father."

"Hey, Anne." He stopped her. "Can I get your advice on something?"

"Of course." She held the file close to her chest.

"It looks like this time next year, they are going to send me to a church to watch over Kaylee and her child. It appears she has no family, and we are going to take her under the church. They want to train her as a Historian." Father Carl picked rock up and tossed it over the fence into the woods.

"It's an important position. The background check isn't pleasurable." Anne remembered what she had to go through while in the Vatican. It happened in the first two weeks; after that, it was actually a pretty good time.

Father Carl picked up another rock. "I'm going to need an admin secretary. Know anyone?"

Anne thought of some people she knew. "None of them are Catholic."

"If you could choose one person, who would it be?" He started to juggle three rocks. Anne was shocked at his talent. "It was necessary to get your mind off of the horrors of war while I was deployed in the desert. I picked up juggling."

Anne thought about it. "Makes sense."

"One person, who would it be?" Father Carl pushed again.

"Alex, hands down," Anne confidentially voiced her opinion. "She's the only one I would want at my side."

Father Carl dropped all the rocks as they came crashing to the ground. "Well, thank God that's not an option. Father Richard was very adamant she was staying here." Father Carl seemed actually relieved to say those words.

186

Anne smirked. "Then what did you need, father?"

"I want your opinion on Megan being my admin assistant." Father Carl turned his attention to someone coming out from the church. "Speak of the devil."

Anne turned to see Megan in the doorway of the church. "Anne, you're going to want to see this." All three of them walked into the church where they were in Father Richard's office. The television hung on the wall had a local television station announcing an interview.

***

"Hello, this is Cindy Mitchell from Television Eight Local News with an exclusive interview. I'm here with some of my old high school classmates, Shawn Mansfield and the leader of the self-help group, F.O.R, Roger Somberson. First of all, I have to say, Shawn, you look great, and Roger, wow, have you changed!" Cindy wiped her head of a bit of sweat off her forehead as she caught herself looking at the two of them.

Roger and Shawn both shyly laughed. "Thank you," Roger played it off. "It's great to see you. I always wondered what had happened since we graduated. I've wanted to get in touch with you."

Cindy smiled. "Well, I hope it wasn't just because of an interview."

"Two birds, one stone." Roger gave her a small wink.

187

"Then we should get right down to it. The positive results coming from the F.O.R. have truly been amazing. I ran into some F.O.R. members the other day at a coffee shop; they are the most polite and respectful people."

"Thank you," Roger graciously replied. "We try our best to bring out the best of the individual by realizing the only power they should look to is within. Once that is achieved, then they can start the roadmap to absolute power." Roger put his hand on Shawn's shoulders. "Not to get into his personal issues, but I was able to help my good friend, Shawn."

"Please, Roger, if it helps people understand what you can do for them, by all means." Shawn motioned for him to continue.

"Well, my good friend here was feeling like a failure, he felt empty, that he wasn't good enough. I taught him lessons that he already knew, and to just to focus on achievement. That if you give yourself to absolute power from within, nothing else matters," Roger told Cindy.

"That is truly amazing." Cindy studied her notes. "And obviously with positive results. Lord knows, we really need some positivity in today's world."

"Comments like that lead to false promises," Roger explained.

"What do you mean?" Cindy leaned into him.

"People put false hopes into a God that doesn't exist. If He did, He is doing a piss poor job with His people. Just look at what is going on with tensions regarding Darius King. Now, we know that the United Won is gaining momentum. That is why the

F.O.R. is dedicated to erasing religion from public view." Roger coldly stared at the camera.

Cindy quickly went to the next question. "Do you think that goes against the first amendment?"

"Not at all. I'm not saying we should not allow you to practice your beliefs, even if they are ridiculous. What I am saying is that, the churches should be taxed because they are a business. If it isn't, then you are not allowed to advertise. That includes displaying any religious symbols. It does this country no good." Roger was done preaching his position.

"Don't you think that religions produce good people who, in turn, do good actions?" Cindy asked him.

Roger turned to Shawn, who looked like he was fighting not to show emotion. "Shawn, I don't have to air this out."

"No, it has to be said." Shawn turned in shame.

"What's going on?" Cindy asked.

"Some of the worst people in this world hide behind their church values. Shawn was courting a girl he had a crush on since high school. He was so nice to her while in school, but she decided to go with a jerk of a guy with a major alcohol problem. I heard while in college, he used to go to strip clubs behind her back. Anyway, I guess evil people are just attracted to evil people. Her boyfriend picked a fight with someone he couldn't handle; he died while trespassing on his property. Shawn was there for her, listened to her, brought her food as a kind gesture, then, she slept with him and just got up to leave him. Treating him like garbage."

189

"Who would do that?" Cindy just shook her head.

"I'm not going to drop any names, but she is currently the historian at the Catholic Church that is trying to reopen. That is why I'm officially announcing my candidacy to recall the acting mayor of Copper Top. I can guarantee you I will be able to eliminate such hypocritical people. I would actually enjoy it."

"Well, with a passion like that, how can you lose?" Cindy said. "This is Cindy Mitchell, signing off."

***

Anne couldn't believe it. She just stood there, trying to catch her breath. Her inhaler was in her pocket, but she was having trouble handling it. Father Richard came to her side. "Anne, breathe. Look at me, breathe. It's okay, breathe." The caring priest guided her to her chair.

Megan just looked at Anne in shock. "Did that really happen, Anne?"

Anne had silent tears dripping down her face. "It wasn't like that. The things he said, about Kale. How could he say that?"

Father Carl approached Anne. "It's propaganda. A little of truth, twisted into lies." He comforted Anne. "This will be tough, but we will get you through this."

"I can't believe that happened. He's the one..." Anne stopped herself out of shame. "What's he doing with Roger, anyways?"

Megan shot it out there. "Sounds like he achieved absolute power."

Anne's eyes widened with fear. With lightning speed, her mind started putting it all together. That was why Alex was all over her about being pregnant; she knew that Shawn had become a Demon. Anne took out her phone to text Alex. *"Why didn't you tell me about Shawn?"*

It was a while before Alex answered. *"You were so hurt; I thought that news would make it worse. Are you mad?"*

Anne thought about that for a second. She knew she was trying to keep Anne's feelings from being hurt. If the situation were reversed, Anne would probably have done the same thing. *"No, I'm not mad. Are you going to contact Kameron?"*

"Not if I can help it. I have to go; my connecting flight is boarding."

Anne requested that Alex let her know when she lands. Most important, Kameron was safe with the others. It wasn't only for her records, but she also cared about this trip. She knew Alex was having conflicting feelings about this hunt. Now she had her own problems she had to deal with. Anne's mistake was twisted and out there for everyone's judgement.

***

Devine held her stomach as she screamed. The movement of what was growing in her body was becoming more active. Devine grabbed the ground

191

at her side. Next to her was a rock she crushed with her hand as the pain shot through her body.

Salamor returned to his perch on a stump in the woods. The pain Devine was experiencing was starting to take a toll on her body. Salamor didn't think she was going to make it through this. That weird feeling again came over his body as he watched her teardrops gliding down the side of her face. He turned his head to stare off into the woods. "You can do this. The night after next, it will be over." Devine screamed again in pain.

***

Kameron sat outside the house in a lawn chair, staring up at the clear sky. The stars were bright and the full moon lit the desert in front of them. Scotty was outside of the fence to verify the sensors were operational. Midnight secured the house's interior to ensure only one-way entry into the house but multiple exits in case they needed to escape.

It was quiet, with only crickets chirping in the night. The mood was quite relaxing. Scotty came down the path leading to the house from the fence. "How you feeling?"

"Better." Kameron drank an electrolyte drink. "How's everything look?"

"Fine." Scotty pulled up a chair next to him. "Scarlett is pretty fine, isn't she?"

Kameron looked back to make sure she wasn't listening. "I just got a coded text that Kaylee will be leaving tomorrow night."

192

"What about Scarlett?" Scotty pulled up a lawn chair. He opened up his backpack as he sat down. He started on the needlepoint project he was working on. It was actually good. There was a relaxation to Scotty, as he didn't have to hide the fact he enjoyed this hobby in front of others.

"I don't know. Apparently, these are new sentries. I don't know how long it takes to train them." Kameron took a sip of his drink.

"Well, it didn't take Luke or Rey that long to become Jedi." Scotty continued to thread the needle and string through the cloth. "It's quiet here. Just the crickets chirping."

"It is," Kameron agreed as he turned around to see Midnight coming out of the house. The fear on her face was obvious. "What's wrong?"

"We have a problem." Midnight showed the picture of Scarlett with a young lady in the bathroom taking a picture of themselves. In the caption it read, "Guess who I ran into today while at work."

"Damn it," Kameron got out of the chair. "Did you talk to her?"

"She knew I wasn't happy," Midnight told her.

Scotty slowly put his needlepoint back into the backpack with a sigh, insinuating that he couldn't believe what had happened. "It's just a matter of time. We should pack up and get out of here."

"Where?" Midnight told him. "This council didn't have a fall-back shelter."

"We're on our own until tomorrow. The new Sentry and trainer should be here to take Kaylee.

193

Until then, I think we should lock down." Kameron checked his pistol.

"If they send one of those supernatural creatures, we're dead," Scotty reminded him.

Midnight double-checked her weapons. "I'll get the girls ready in case we have to bug out."

Scotty cracked his neck. "The vehicle is ready to go. I'll park it right next to the escape exit."

Kameron thought about it. "We should go now. We'll just drive around in constant motion. That way, they can't find us, and we'll just meet back here tomorrow for the transfer of the assets."

"Sounds good to me," Midnight told him.

"Wait a minute." Scotty put up his finger. "Do you hear that?"

"I don't hear anything." Midnight tried to listen for what Scotty was hearing.

"The crickets stopped." Kameron noticed. The three of them stood still as they noticed the power to their house dropped. An eerie quiet surrounded them. "Get the girls to the escape vehicle. We're getting the hell out of here."

Scotty and Midnight agreed as they went to perform their duties. Kameron turned to go into the house, but he stopped. He turned around to look at the desert hills to the left of the house.

***

Alex peeked over a rock, down at the house sitting all by itself in the middle of the desert field. For a moment, she had a familiar sense of a calming serenity, a feeling she hadn't had for quite a while.

It took her a bit, but she was able to find out where they were. The night sky was clear with a full moon illuminating the ground below. Maybe it would be just a night of guarding. There is a chance the F.O.R. wouldn't come tonight. In all honesty, she should go down to contact them. She actually wanted to. Would Kameron want to see her?

The last time they spoke to each other, it wasn't the greatest of departures. This was something else, though. They had a mission to complete; she needed to push her feelings away. They would just get confusing. Alex quickly changed her mind. "They would clear them up," she said to herself. There was no doubt in her mind that she just wanted to see Kameron again. The decision was made for her to go down there to make contact. She got up to go down to the house when she caught a glimpse of some movement below her.

Alex could see four figures start heading for the house. The good news was that none of those figures were Infiltrators. They had human form, but that didn't mean they weren't all Demons. She would have to make contact. Alex started to move toward the bottom of the hill.

Moving through the desert had its advantages for Alex. She could move faster, but there wasn't much cover. She was able to move ahead of the four of them. There was proof that at least one of them was a Demon because she could see the glowing of his red eyes. The other three were behind as they headed towards the house. Alex decided the best course of action would be to meet them head on.

There was really no way for her to give them a surprise attack.

She maneuvered to a spot in front of the group. She cracked her neck as she came out in the open. The ground was hard as she confidently drew the line to the four Demons. She was going to be serious trouble for them.

The four figures noticed Alex stand her ground with her head down. "Lost?" the Demon yelled out to Alex. He obviously didn't know she was a Lite Sentry.

"Nope, just out for a stroll." She raised her head with her eyes glowing.

"Sentry!" The Demon flashed his eyes. He took a fighting stance as the three others looked to the Demon for direction.

Alex was relieved that the three were just humans. That gave Kameron a fighting chance. "Demon," she sarcastically answered back.

"This will be a treat." The Demon grew out its fingernails as it showed its jagged teeth.

Alex lit her fists while flashing her eyes. "Come try to get a bite." She watched the humans start to draw their guns. The fear of being shot wasn't a concern because she knew the Demon would want to take her. The bragging rights of killing a Sentry would raise his status within the Dark. The one thing Demons had a craving for was power and status within the ranks of the Dark.

"Go, go now, kill them all." The Demon pointed to the house. "The Sentry will fall at my hands."

The humans started running towards the house. Alex Lite Beamed the human that was heading in

196

front of the group. She hit him in the head, causing him to fall to the ground in a summersault. The Demon gave a mixture of a growl and a hiss as he attacked Alex.

***

"Come on, get up." Midnight had a little bit of irritation in her voice as she kicked Scarlett and Kaylee's bed as they were sleeping. "Grab your emergency bag."

"What's going on?" Kaylee asked as she was holding her stomach. "It's the middle of the night."

The house was silent. The central air stopped working. Scotty came over the radio in Midnight's earpiece. "Checking the back up for the perimeter alarms."

Midnight acknowledged.

Kameron came up the stairs. "We are leaving, now. Grab the bags and let's go."

Kaylee started to panic. "My baby."

"It will be okay, but we need to go, now." Kameron walked over to the window to see Scotty immediately taking cover behind the truck as if he was being shot at. "Scotty, what's your status? I'm watching from the asset's window."

"Rally in the kitchen." Scotty stayed down as he made it back into the house. Kameron met him in the kitchen. "The truck has two flat tires from being shot. They must have silencers or something."

"That means they're close," Midnight said as she pulled her weapon out.

"The good news is they're human." Kameron peeked out the window. "Because the Dark would just come in for a massacre." Then a bullet broke through the window, causing Kameron to hit the ground. "Get down."

Scotty called over the radio. "Hey, we're getting shot at."

"No kidding, captain obvious," Kameron told him.

Then a bullet broke through the window near Scotty's face with small amounts of glass hitting his face. "Son a bitch!" Scotty stepped back, wiping shards of glass off his face.

"That makes two attackers we know of." Kameron continued to study outside the window.

Midnight came down the stairs with Scarlett and Kaylee in bulletproof vests. "We took a couple of shots upstairs. No damage. Phones are out, and we have no cell service."

"Of course." Scotty snuck to the other side of the window to see if anyone was coming.

"Oh my God, what did I do?" Scarlett started to panic. "I'm going to get us all killed."

Midnight dodged a bullet that came across the kitchen from Kameron's window. Midnight forced Scarlett onto the ground, putting her knee on her back. She motioned Kaylee to hit the ground. "Shhhh."

Kameron signaled he was going to head into the living room. All three agents were suddenly notified by three perimeter alarms of a breach. Kameron made eye contact with two other agents. They all knew they were in a dire situation.

***

Alex stood still as the Demon rushed at her. Just before he reached for her, she bent over, flipping the Demon onto the desert floor. Alex turned to punch the Demon on the ground, but it moved out of the way. The Demon got up at lightning speed as it punched Alex on the side of the head. This blow knocked her down onto the ground. The Demon went to kick her, but she grabbed his foot and then twisted it. The Demon, in turn, found himself back on the ground as Alex kicked the inside of his leg, tripping him onto the ground. She shot a Lite Beam onto the Demon, keeping him pinned against the ground.

The Demon grabbed a rock that was to the side of him. He threw it at Alex, hitting her forehead. This caused her skin to split open as blood started to drip open. "That hurt!" Alex checked the bleeding on her head. She flashed her eyes as she angrily picked the Demon up and tossed it in the air, sending it crashing onto its back on the ground. Alex ran full speed toward the Demon as it tried to get back up, but she clotheslined it from the back of the head, forcing it back into the ground.

She stopped instantly and turned to block the next punch. His counterattack stunned Alex enough for her to lose her momentum. The Demon grabbed her head and smashed it against his knee. He picked her up and forced her onto the ground. "You wanna see how that feels?" He dropped his knee onto her chest and punched her in the face.

"Okay, I'll admit, that hurt." Alex felt a rib crack in her chest. She felt the Demon grind his knee on her chest.

He leaned down to study her. "You are not here just to fight. No, you are here for something else. You are here for love." He smiled at her. "I will ensure every single person in that house is tortured to the point they give up on their God. Then, I will take their lives." He punched her straight in the nose. "Then, when they get sent to Hell, I will ensure Vandor knows which one is the one you love. I'm sure he would like to know."

Alex was still pinned to the ground; the blood from her nose was dripping down the back of her throat. She collected it in her mouth and spit in the Demon's face. The Demon licked it like he enjoyed it. "Gross," Alex observed. This was the distraction she needed. She grabbed the Demon's head to smash it against her own forehead. The Demon fell over, clutching his nose as black blood started to drip out.

"You Lite Whore!" he screamed at her.

Alex rolled her eyes as she got up from the ground. "Seriously, guys. New material." The Demon swung at her, but she blocked it. This gave her the opportunity to deliver an uppercut to his chin. He went flying to the ground. When he landed, his head landed on a rock causing his neck to break. The Demon staggered as he got up. His head was crooked as he stumbled over to her. Alex couldn't help but be disgusted by this shell of a man coming towards her. Alex confidently walked up to him as she checked her nose for blood. She formed a pointed end with her Lite and stabbed the Demon in the chest without breaking stride toward the house.

***

"I got movement at my location." Kameron adjusted his pistol. "One possible hostile." Midnight had confirmed the same at her location. There was a tenseness in her voice as the situation was rising. "Scotty?"

"I see one," he said over the radio.

"Remember your ROE. We can't shoot until they show hostility." Kameron knew full out they were hostile.

Scotty came over the radio. "Because normally, when you go over to someone's house, you surround it before entering." A bullet came through the window, almost hitting Scotty. "Hostility shown." He returned fire, one shot.

Kameron shot at one figure who was moving to cover. Multiple bullets started coming through the door where Kameron was watching. He quickly pushed over a China hutch cabinet in front of the door. "Midnight?" Kameron waited for her confirmation.

"We're good," she confirmed. "They don't know where we are."

"Must be nice," Scotty replied as bullets whizzed by his head.

Kameron sat on the floor with his back against the hutch. Pieces of glass and wood were showering through the living room. His supply of ammunition was getting low. Then an eerie quiet came over as no bullets were flying into the house.

"Why did they stop?" Midnight asked over the radio.

Kameron crawled on the floor to peek out the window. "My guy is just behind his cover. Scotty, what's your guy doing?"

Scotty peeked out the window. "He moved over to the truck and stopped."

Midnight looked down at Kaylee and Scarlett, holding each other in the bathtub shaking from fear. She motioned to them it would be okay before peering out the window. "I've got one with a rifle pointing directly in your direction Kameron."

"I got him. That would make three for sure, then." Kameron checked his ammo. "I think they are humans out there."

"Why would you say that?" Scotty kept an eye on his target.

"Because if they were Demons, they would've just rushed in, and we'd be dead by now." Kameron saw one of the figures step out from cover.

"Kameron Dutcher," he started to say.

Kameron didn't know what to say at first. This was obviously a distraction. He wanted to see what they had planned for them. "Yes."

"We just want the girls. If you kill them, you'll live, and Roger will ensure you are guided on the Map to Absolute Power," the man yelled out. "Two little bullets, that's all you need to do."

"And if I don't?" Kameron yelled back out. Then he took cover as a bunch of bullets started to barrage the house.

"I think you got your answer," Scotty fell to the ground. He crawled up the wall to see if his target was still in his location. He didn't see him, then he felt someone grab the back of his head and smash it against the corner of the wall. Scotty fell back to the ground as he saw a foot coming down toward his face. He was able to deflect the foot and push the guy away from him. The man charged him, tackling him outside the house.

While Scotty was fighting that man, another man quickly went into the house. Scotty went to talk on the radio. The man he was fighting grabbed the radio and ripped it off. The man continued to beat Scotty until he didn't move.

Midnight called over the radio, "Scotty?" It was silence. "Scotty?" Midnight positioned herself on the other side of the bathroom door. "Get down." She motioned to the girls. The door opened to a man with a gun aiming his pistol at the girls cowering in the bathtub. Midnight pointed her gun directly at the man's head. One quick pull of the trigger ended the immediate threat to the girl's life. The body dropped to the ground.

Scarlett and Kaylee screamed, and she told them to be quiet. Midnight kept low to the ground to approach the girls. "We gotta move." Midnight turned to help the girls out of the tub. When she turned back around, she saw another hostile pointing his weapon at her with a grin. Midnight swallowed hard as a shot went off, killing the man.

Midnight was relieved when she heard Kameron's voice, "Are you good?"

Midnight confirmed with the girls that they were okay. "Assets are safe." Midnight peeked out the window. "What about the third one?"

Kameron checked around. "He's still out there. I don't know where he is." He felt as if something bad was about to happen.

***

Alex slowly walked towards the house. This was a time she wished she still had her ability to sense the Dark. She didn't know if there was any Dark around. The result of her handicap meant she had to take her time to get to the house. Hopefully, not too late. The night was still, no movement or sound from the animals that made their homes here. Down the hill was the house where Kameron was staying.

A deep pit formed in Alex's stomach when she saw the house. There was a small urge just to run into the house to find Kameron to make sure he was all right. Alex's instinct took over though. There was something in the air that didn't feel right to her. It wasn't a familiar feeling like the Dark; the only thing Alex could relate it to would be women's intuition. She moved closer to the house, but far enough not to be seen by anyone.

The house seemed to have barely survived a world war. The windows were all shot up with bullet holes throughout the siding of the house. Alex's fears were overpowering her. If she walked into that house to see Kameron shot, she would actually feel sorry for anyone associated with the F.O.R. She took a second to refocus her thoughts; there was no proof he was hurt. Alex did see a man lying down outside. She recognized him. The agent was with Kameron when he rescued her from being burnt alive.

Now, Alex started to breathe a bit heavier, trying to calm herself down. She was about to charge into the house when she heard movement in the distance. It was too noisy to be the Dark; it was human. She saw a man move behind a rock. She decided to come around him to see what he was up to. There was nothing about him that Alex liked. She got behind him without him knowing. He picked up a rifle with a scope pointing at the house. Two gunshots came from the house.

The man adjusted his scope. "I got you."

Alex looked to the house to see what he was aiming at and saw Kameron in the window. For a split second, her body was covered in a neon blue lite before grabbing the head of the man. She easily snapped the neck of the person who was about to shoot the man she loved. The body just fell sideways as Alex stood over him. Alex ripped the scope off the gun to look through it. She saw Kameron with his service pistol out.

Scarlett Roberts came running into Kameron's arms full-out crying. Alex watched as she was being tightly comforted by Kameron. *Did he move on from her?* It was all she could think. Watching Kameron with another woman was something that hurt more than Alex would have thought. She guessed this was what she deserved. She would be a hypocrite if she got jealous as he moved on. Considering all the guys she went through when they initially broke up.

For a second, Kameron seemed to look out the window directly at Alex while she peered through the riflescope. Then he guided Scarlett out of the room leaving Alex's sight. Alex crushed the scope with her bare hands when she realized she had lost him forever. "It's officially over." She wiped a tear before heading out to the hills to keep guard of the perimeter until the Council sent reinforcements.

***

Merik watched Cindy Mitchell lie in bed next to him. She was fast asleep while he thought how easily he could kill her. But he needed her; she was going to tunnel all the information to the town of Copper Top to get Gron elected as mayor. He got out of bed to get a drink of expensive brandy they stole from the F.O.R. compound during their tour. He took a sip of the smooth alcoholic drink as he stared at the full moon that seemed to be glaring back at him. He closed his eyes and smiled as he said, "Is it time?"

"After tomorrow, just as the sun disappears," Salamor advised. "They will come."

Merik nodded. "Then I will deliver them to Gron." He turned to the Demon Myst who was perched on top of the couch. "How's the Lite Angel?"

Salamor hesitated before answering, "She will barely survive the delivery, if she does at all."

The Demon shrugged. "I kind of hope she does, then the icing on the cake as I take the twins is killing her."

Salamor gave no expression. He just flew off as he said, "I will come get you to tell you where her final location of birth will be."

CHAPTER SEVEN

The morning couldn't come quick enough, but it didn't mean they were out of danger. But for some reason, Kameron couldn't shake the feeling they were being well guarded. The girls were gathering what little Kaylee was going to take with her. Kameron could tell that separating from Kaylee was going to be difficult for Scarlett, almost a sense of being alone.

Midnight was nursing Scotty on the couch. The hit was hard from last night, which caused him to be bruised and a little bloody; however, he was going to live. It was far from the two people that were lying in the house. Kameron somberly promenaded into the living room. "I'm sorry I got you guys into this."

"Don't worry about him." Midnight checked on Scotty. "He's just milking this hoping for some porno nursing."

"Doesn't hurt to try," Scotty said underneath his washcloth. "Did you get the third one?"

Kameron shook his head. "No, the cops found a body up on the hillside. His head was twisted completely around."

Scotty sat up. "Why would the F.O.R. do that?"

"Failure?" Midnight suggested.

"Possibly," Kameron admitted. Outside the window he could see a vehicle approaching. It was a white pickup truck with big tires. It stopped in front of the house as a big guy got out of the driver's seat. He was blonde while wearing a set of hiking boots. He gazed around and said something to the figure in the passenger seat.

The passenger side of the door opened as a medium-sized, physically built woman came out of the truck. Kameron didn't recognize her. The most notable feature about her was her bright neon orange hair. She gazed around the desert with disgust before walking around the truck to join the man. They both watched Kameron approach from the house. Kameron unbuckled his holster to his weapon.

"I would recommend you take that hand off that sidearm before you get hurt," the man with a southern accent said as he stood in front of the girl.

The girl got annoyed as she pushed him out of the way. "Move, you oversized primate. I would kill him before he even got that thing out." The girl stepped towards him. "I will remove your head from your body fast enough for you to see your headless body if you move for that weapon."

"And you are?" Kameron heard Midnight behind him, no doubt drawing her weapon. He motioned behind his back for her to hold back.

The man was now leaning on his truck. "Surely, the Council of Religions told you we were coming." He reached into his pocket and pulled out some chew to put in his mouth.

The girl maintained eye contact with Kameron. "I thought I told you not to put that nasty stuff in your mouth around me."

209

He rolled his eyes as he spit out the tobacco on the ground. "Looks like you boys saw some action last night," the man said as he studied the house.

"You still didn't tell me your names." Kameron was now getting irritated.

"Oh, I'm Zeke, and this charming lady with such a wonderful personality is Dinah." The man got up from the truck. "I'm here to save your ass."

Kameron was tired, and he didn't really feel like dealing with this guy's ego. "Who the hell are you?"

The girl very annoyingly said, "He is the Lite Sentry that is to take Kaylee for protection."

Kameron moved his body to see the man. "You're a Lite Sentry?"

The man ignited his hands and flashed his eyes. "These aren't firecrackers, boy."

Midnight came out of the house with Scotty limping behind her. "And who are you?"

The girl with bright orange hair rolled her eyes. "I am the lucky angel elected to train the primate back there."

The man nodded his head. "She must have really pissed God off."

The angel took a deep breath to calm her nerves. "Do you feel that when we got here?"

"Yes," he said. "I don't recognize that feeling; it's not one of those Infiltrators."

"Could be a Demon," Dinah scouted the area. "You are not ready for that."

He stood up. "I can take on anything those Dark bastards throw at me. I did take down one Infiltrator already."

She turned to the young man. "Conduct a perimeter check. If it is an Infiltrator, kill it; if it's a Demon, let me know."

"Whatever, I can handle one little Demon." Zeke was getting annoyed. He got into the truck and handed Dinah a phone. She grabbed it with her finger and thumb as if it stunk. "How else am I supposed to get a hold of you? Just open it like I showed you."

"Just go." Dinah pointed to the hills. "Do not take long." Dinah turned to Kameron. "Is the child bearer ready?"

**

Alex spent the night patrolling around the hillside watching over the house. The rest of the night was relatively quiet. Although, a couple of times, she thought about rushing down to the house to be with Kameron. She watched a truck approach the house and figured it was a police detective or something. Kameron's posture was a bit relaxed, more than usual.

She sat there to watch the group of them talk. One of the people did take off to the hillside, and that got Alex curious about who that was. Alex watched him for a bit. He was moving quite quickly. This person wasn't fully human. It was possible that Kameron was being held hostage. Maybe the Dark got reinforcements. That would explain why it was so quiet for the rest of the night. "Damn it," Alex said aloud.

Alex watched the man move about along the hillside. He was quick but very sloppy. Alex quickly got to the point where she was now following him. She maintained her distance, watching him. Alex occasionally watched the house to see what was going on. She saw that Kaylee was coming out of the house. There was no doubt she was crying.

Was the Dark forcing her to go? Alex needed to know who this guy was. She decided to intercept this guy to find out who he was. Alex jumped from the high ground and landed right in front of the big man. Alex was on guard because she knew it was possible he was a Demon.

The man startled. "Where the hell did you come from?" he asked in a southern drawl.

"What are you doing here?" she confidently asked him.

"I'm the one who's asking the questions, little girl." He got into a familiar fighting stance. "You are not dressed to be hiking. Maybe planning to do something to that house down there."

Alex's eyes got big. *Oh, shit.* This was the Lite Sentry sent to protect one of the girls. From the looks of it, it was Kaylee. The Council was adamant that two Sentries were not to meet. The best thing Alex thought of doing was to get out of this situation. "Nope, my friends were out camping last night looking for aliens, and I wanted to go for a walk this morning."

"You were camping?" The man looked her up and down. "Dressed like that?" He grabbed her. "More than likely, you are that Demon trying to get to that house." He flashed his eyes Lite blue. "I know Demon's Dark is faint, and I can barely sense it."

Alex could only think the remnants of the Demon she killed last night was still in the air. "Let go of me. I'm serious," she said with confidence. "I don't want you to get hurt."

He smiled. "I'd like to see you try. Why don't you come talk to my friend?"

Alex didn't really feel like explaining what she was doing here, especially to Council for contacting the Lite Sentry. She grabbed his hand and twisted, simultaneously kicking him in the chest. It sent him to fall in the ground. "I told you, leave me alone."

The man flashed his eyes and ignited his hands. "I knew it. This should be fun."

He confidently strutted with an immediate swing. Alex dodged out of the way and pushed him a bit down the hill. "Stop. I'm warning you." The man got up and flashed his eyes. He swung again, but Alex blocked it. She countered with an uppercut underneath his chin, followed by another punch across his cheek. This sent him back to the ground.

This didn't stop him. Alex rolled her eyes with annoyance. "Okay, one, you need to think about what you're doing." He swung as she moved her body out of the way; she grabbed him around from his back and lifted him up to throw him on the ground behind her. "Don't be predictable." She had his other arm behind his back, causing him to scream. "Hurts, doesn't it?" She got closer to his ear. "What do you think I would do next? Should you wait until I make a move, or should you get out of this before I go in for the kill?"

With all his strength, he got up from the ground. He lifted her up with Alex still on his back. He ran backward onto a rock, pinning Alex against it. Alex cringed from the hit. "Good. That's it." He went back to do it again, but this time she let go, and he slammed himself against the hard rock. "If I'm not weak enough, don't go for the same major move twice. I could see coming a mile away." The man was starting to breathe a bit heavily. "You shouldn't be breathing this hard. Don't force the Lite; use it. Don't grasp for it."

The man went to swing again but Alex moved out of the way again, this time tripping him, guiding him face first onto the ground. She jumped on a boulder looking down at him. "The problem you have, is that you've probably been a big boy your whole life. Probably been in a fight or two in high school, but in general, people were afraid of you." Alex jumped down off the boulder. "You don't know fear when you go into a fight; there is a good chance you're going to die."

By the house, Alex could see Kameron in the distance. He was hugging one of the girls. This distracted her enough for the Sentry to punch her in the face. She spun around but regained her footing just before he went to punch her again. She ducked out of the way as she punched him in the ribs. He keeled over; for a split second, she was going to grab the back of his head to smash it into the ground, but that would have gone too far. "You need to ask yourself, why am I fighting?"

The man got up and faced her on the edge of being beaten. If Alex were a Demon, this Sentry would not have survived this fight. "I fight to get rid of Dark bitches like you." He generated a Lite Beam pushing Alex against the cliff wall.

Alex couldn't think of anything but that, it hurt, and he just called her a *bitch*. The Sentry formed a knife going to stab her. He charged her, but she dropped to her knees to punch him in the crotch. She stood instantly up, using her head to come up on the bottom of his chin. The big Sentry fell backward, causing a cloud of dust to disperse. "I don't feel like getting stabbed again." She dropped her knee onto the man's chest as he coughed from the pain. Alex knew she had cracked one of his ribs. "You need to ask yourself if you are fighting for you, or for Him." Alex peeked over at the house. For some reason, Alex's mind went to that moment before they attacked the F.O.R. building when Kameron was talking about kids and their potential life together.

Alex looked down at the Sentry, who had defeat in his eyes. He thought for sure he was going to die. Alex felt sad for the young Sentry, but this was a tough lesson that needed to be taught. More than likely, Alex just saved his life. "I have to go. It's been fun." She took off to run into the cliffs.

Zeke lay on the ground, confused on why that Demon didn't kill him. If the situation were reversed, he would have killed her in a heartbeat without even thinking about it. He didn't know how long he lay there when he saw Dinah looking down at him in her battle gear.

She tilted her head in confusion as she studied him. "Did you kill it, at least?"

***

Anne was happy that everything was completed for the festival. As far as she could tell, they were going to be quite busy with kids before they went trick-or-treating. She walked around as some volunteers were talking about the upcoming mayor race.

"He may be F.O.R., but he is a proven leader." The girl continued touching up the prizes for the games.

The other girl in the booth next to hers was finishing her section as well. "But there is just something about him that isn't right. He's a leader of a cult."

"It's an organization that is proven to get kids off drugs and work together. Look at the tensions rising from Darius King. Now that United Won is gaining momentum, who knows what that will produce? Roger Somberson is from this town; he's got all race relations working for a common goal. That is what our town needs, hell that is what the world needs." The girl poked herself with a tack. "Ow." She started sucking her finger.

"You may be right, but it seems like it's at a cost I'm not willing to give." The other took out a first aid kit from underneath her booth to hand her a band-aid.

Anne couldn't believe that people were actually going to support Roger in his endeavor to become mayor. If Copper Top became an F.O.R. haven, who knows what that would lead to? Anne got a text message from Alex that she had boarded a plane to head back home. She said Kameron was safe.

Anne had a sense of hope with her question to Alex. *Did you talk to Kameron?*

There was a bit of time before Alex replied. *No, I'm such a chickenshit.* She put a rolling eye emoji at the end of her message.

Anne smirked because Alex was becoming her old self again. For a while, she was getting worried about her best friend. She was so depressed; Anne was afraid she was going to go down in a spiral and not come out of it. Then there would be no chance for Alex and Kameron to get back together. Kameron fell in love with the free-spirited Alex, not a depressed Alex. Anne knew that once Alex got back to her old self, she and Kameron would find a way to get back together.

Anne went back into the church. For some reason, she wanted to head into the congregation hall. To her shock, Celestial was at the front of the massive room. Anne's heart stopped. She took out her inhaler to take a puff. Fear came out of her mouth as she asked, "What happened?"

Celestial was confused. "Nothing, my dear." Her guardians stayed off in the corner with their heads down in prayer.

"I'm sorry, I just assumed…it was wrong of me, I apologize." Anne did a quick bow with her head.

Celestial gave her a sympathetic smile. "I understand."

217

A young teenage girl with dark skin and long black hair came into the church with a tissue in her hand. "I'm sorry."

It was evident that the young girl had been crying. "Can I help you?" Anne asked her.

"It's stupid for me to come here, I should go." The girl went to turn around.

Anne sat down on the pew. "Wait, what's wrong? Perhaps I can help."

The girl hesitated before coming to sit in the pew behind Anne. "I'm afraid. I'm just confused, and I need answers."

Anne adjusted her seat. "Did anyone get hurt or is in danger?"

"Not physically, but emotionally." The young girl started crying.

"What happened? You might feel better if you say it out loud," Anne told her. "I won't say anything, I promise."

"I'm a volunteer for the Justice for Darius King Group here in town. I'm having a hard time understanding all the hate towards each other. How could such bad things happen in the world?" The young lady was crying.

Anne got up and joined the girl on the other side of her. "I understand. There is evil in the world; it is almost as if it is a war. Unfortunately, with war, there are always good people who get hurt."

"Why do people hate each other just because of the color of one's skin?" the young lady asked.

"I'm not going to pretend that I know the answer to that or even project that I know what it is like having the feeling of being targeted because of something like skin color," Anne opened up to her. "But I do think that it's possible to solve issues like this by talking, showing love for each other even if we don't like what the other person's views are, and have a common goal of peace as God wants us to have."

"Do you think God created a superior race?" The girl wiped her eyes.

"No, it's just another factor that makes all different from each other. Just as blue eyes, brown hair, small, tall, athletic; all those differences make us unique. We all have something to give this world and our neighbors." Anne continued to talk to the girl.

"What can we give to the world to make it work?" the girl asked.

"Well, a small example is we have a fall festival tonight. We are all working together to put on a positive event for the children. If you would like to stop by and see how we as a community can make it better. It is a small progression, but that is better than no progression." Anne handed her a flyer for the fall festival.

The girl read the flyer as she stood up. "Maybe I will. I have to get going. My name is Shanice."

"Anne Moler, I'm the Church Historian. You can stop by anytime if you would like to talk." Anne shook her hand.

"It was really nice talking to you. Thanks, I feel a lot better." Shanice seemed to leave the church with a little more spring in her step.

Anne watched her leave before realizing that Celestial was still there. "Oh, I'm sorry."

"It is quite okay, child." Celestial was looking at Anne with a smile but also as if she had something else on her mind. Komptin had caught Celestial's attention as he slowly walked into the congregation.

A text message came from Father Carl asking if she could pick up the candy from the supermarket. "If you would please excuse me." Anne did a quick bow before leaving the congregation hall. She gave Komptin a quick pat on the head before leaving.

***

It was nice for the three of them to have a Sentry and a Lite Angel onsite until Scarlett was sent with her protectors. Kameron was the first to get up. His body let him know what a rough night he had. His body seemed to announce with every step as he crept down the stairs. Midnight's door was still closed. Scarlett and Kaylee both slept in her room. Scotty was snoring like a chainsaw in the room upstairs. It was no doubt from being beaten up last night.

Kameron sipped on some orange juice as he stared out the window to see the angel training with the new Sentry. It seemed as if Zeke was explaining the fight, he had with the Demon earlier this morning. Kameron, for some reason, was chuckling at the recreation of the fight. It was as if he had seen that before.

He thought he would go outside and watch. "Hello."

220

The angel acknowledged by just a bow of the head. While Zeke said in his southern drawl, "Good afternoon."

The angel quickly swiped Zeke's leg and put her thin sword made of Lite to Zeke's throat as he was on the ground. "Training was not over. The Dark does not have honor; if you are distracted, you die." Zeke nodded with his hands up. With a little compassion, Dinah lifted her trainee up with a little smirk.

"That Demon this morning got distracted." Zeke spit some dirt out of his mouth while he checked his ribs. "I thought I was a dead man."

"I find it rare a Demon would pass the opportunity to kill a Sentry." Dinah morphed into civilian clothes. She was now wearing a white southern-style dress with white and neon orange cowboy boots. Her belt was the same color blue as the Lite she generated with a belt buckle that matched her hair. Her misty halo was now replaced with a cowgirl hat.

"A friend and I were fighting a Demon. He quite easily overpowered us. He was about to be killed when the Demon took off for some reason." Kameron adjusted his stiff shoulder a bit.

"You fought a Demon?" Zeke cleaned off his jeans.

"If you call it that." Kameron turned around to see Scarlett coming out of the house with her fashion sunglasses on. She gave Kameron a wave like she had something on her mind.

Dinah chimed in. "The night the Sentry's brother was killed."

"Yes," Kameron sadly agreed.

Zeke joined up with Kameron and Dinah. "I'd like to meet her. To see if she's as tough as everyone says she is."

Kameron smiled, remembering Alex. "She saved me a couple of times."

Dinah made eye contact with Kameron. "You still love her."

Kameron didn't say anything as Scarlett approached. "How are you doing?"

"Can I talk to you for a second?" The social media diva asked with a sound of humility.

"Excuse me." Kameron escorted her off to the side of the house. "How can I help you?"

Scarlett leaned against the house. "I could have gotten you all killed. I can't shake that."

Kameron tried to ease the situation a bit. "I'm sure you'll have other opportunities."

Scarlett gave a small smile. "I'm not good at admitting I'm wrong."

Kameron gave her a way out. "You don't have to. I know." All she did was nod and wipe a tear before getting up. Scotty and Midnight turned the corner as Scarlett left. "Hey, how are you feeling?"

"Like crap," Scotty told him. "As I was sleeping, all I could think about was how I got involved with this."

"You want out?" Kameron asked.

"Tempting, but no. I'm with you till the end." Scotty rubbed his head.

Kameron turned his attention to Midnight.

"I can't have Scotty be alone; someone's got to watch over his stupid ass." Midnight stepped into the shadows to get out of the sun.

"But it's a nice ass." Scotty turned around so Midnight could see it.

Kameron felt good to have such loyal friends in this fight. "Thanks."

"Don't get mushy on me," Scotty joked. His attention turned to Zeke and Dinah as they came around.

Kameron laughed. "Never." The realization of the situation they were in hit him. "Our location is compromised."

Midnight closed her eyes. "Do you think they will attack again?"

"That is a stupid question," Dinah commented. "Of course, they will. They will bring more than one little Demon to ensure the job is done."

Sometimes Midnight hated the childish arrogance the Lite Angels portrayed. They seem to look down at the normal people that walk the planet. "They'll attack tonight."

Scotty just leaned against the wall with his hand on his head. "This just sucks."

"We're good, but no one could fight off more than two to three Demons, plus Infiltrators." Zeke checked his ribs.

"Alex did." It just came out. Kameron felt bad he said it. This poor guy was in training and the weight of what was asked of him must be hard enough without Kameron signifying he may not be up to potential.

223

Dinah stepped up to protect her trainee. "She also almost got the Conduit of Lite killed because she was being so self-centered." The angel physically approached Kameron. "And do not forget about her impediment."

"Then why does the Dark fear her?" Kameron matched Dinah's challenge.

"Why do you defend her? You are no longer an interest of hers." The orange-haired angel was now getting angry.

Midnight and Scotty both looked at each other, not knowing what to do. The air was tense as if one little thing could blow this situation apart. Then, music started coming from Dinah's body. She was confused at the music playing from her body as she turned around like a dog chasing its own tail.

Zeke tapped her on the shoulder. "It's your phone." He pointed to her pocket.

Dinah picked the phone up with two little fingers. "Here." She dropped the phone in Zeke's hands. She continued to stare Kameron down as Zeke took the phone call.

Zeke listened to the other end of the phone as he handed it over to Kameron. "It's for you."

Kameron couldn't think of who it would be. He was half hoping it was Alex, but that wasn't the case, as Weston was on the other end of the phone. The sour pit in his stomach formed as Weston told him that he hadn't heard from Paige. The air was eerily quiet... as quiet as Kameron handed the phone back to Dinah, who, in turn, gave it back to Zeke. "Paige is missing."

"We need to go find her." Midnight was a bit upset. "If the F.O.R. found out who she really was, then we are screwed."

"And if she got possessed by those black things?" Scotty put it out there. "It was never evident what side she actually played on."

Kameron took in a deep sigh. "I don't think she was infiltrated."

"How do you figure?" Zeke asked as he was about to put in some chewing tobacco.

Dinah immediately smacked it out of his hands. "That is disgusting." The angel turned back to the group. "Because if she was infiltrated, she would make contact and act as if all was well." She cold-heartedly stated, "She is probably dead. I will verify and meet you in Copper Top." She turned to Zeke with a little bit of concern in her voice. "I will speak to you alone." The group watched as Dinah went to talk to Zeke.

"This is wrong, Kam," Midnight put it out there. "We should not bring Scarlett there."

"Weston contacted the Sentry and trainer who will be taking Scarlett. The transfer will be happening there." Kameron had a feeling the same as the morning he was shot.

***

The supermarket didn't have many supplies of candy. What was left would pretty much suffice for the festival. It seemed as if the Lite was shining on Anne because her favorite candy was still there. It only came out during this time of year. The peanut butter toffee with a hint of real peanut butter in the center. Anne picked up a couple of extra bags because she knew she would hide a bag in her desk drawer. If it wasn't against the rules, she would open the bag right here and eat them. There were only a few bags left so Anne got them all.

"Can you believe this lady?" a voice from next to her said.

Anne was a bit startled as she turned around to see a woman holding a cell phone in front of her. "Excuse me?"

The brown-skinned girl wearing a t-shirt with Darius King on the front of it was recording her. "That's right, little white privilege just takes all the candy and don't leave any for the rest of us."

Anne was a little dumbfounded as she looked around.

"That's right. I got you. It is posted right here." The girl got closer to Anne's face with the camera.

The intensity of the situation made Anne feel a bit uncomfortable. "There is plenty of candy left." Anne showed her the shelf.

"Not those ones." She pointed the camera down at the peanut butter taffy.

Anne took half the bags out of the cart. "Would you like these bags?"

"I'm not your charity case," the girl screamed at the camera.

A man with a United Won patch on his jacket came behind Anne. "Hey, she's not stealing like that thug you are supporting. Why don't you read instead of being influenced by the media? Do you even know how to read?" The man stepped out in front of Anne to confront the hostile lady.

The lady's eyes got wide with anger. "Help, help. I'm being attacked by a United Won racist. Help, help!" The lady started shaking and acting hysterically. "Help! Help!"

Anne was looking around in complete shock as the angry man from United Won started arguing with the frantic woman. Then Anne heard her name behind her but there was no one there. She started backing away as some of the employees started to break up the argument.

The fight seemed to be toned down as Anne went to go check out with the candy, minus half the bags of her favorite candy. Anne couldn't believe the feeling of darkness that filled the air as the two were fighting. It wasn't the stale air that Alex always described, but a feeling of hate and tension.

The only small glimmer of hope of escape was that she was the next in line at the checkout. "Hello," Anne gave the cashier a nice greeting.

The cashier was a middle-aged woman who was staring at Anne. She motioned for the supervisor to join her. "I'm not comfortable serving her."

A sour pit filled Anne's stomach. "Did I do something to offend you?"

The lady now turned to Anne, ignoring the twenty-year-old supervisor. "I can't believe you would do that to such a nice man."

"What did I do, and to whom?" Anne was trying to think of all the interactions she had had.

"Shawn." The lady was now stepping back. "To play with his emotions like that. Do you enjoy using people?"

"Ma'am, with all due respect. There is more to the story than…" Anne tried to justify, but the lady interrupted her.

"A typical hypocritical church go'er." The lady acted as if she wiped her clean of Anne. "I'm not serving you. I'm not comfortable with this."

"I understand, Catherine," The young manager punched his code into the machine. "Why don't you take a break?" The girl shook her head as she pulled out her phone to start messaging.

"I apologize for that," the kid told Anne.

Anne took a puff from her inhaler. "It's okay."

The boy was scanning the candy. "Between the Darius King supporters and United Won, and then you coming in, it has been a stressful day."

Anne was appalled at the young man's comments. "What do you mean about me coming in?"

"The whole town knows you were the one Shawn was talking about with Roger Somberson." The boy finished scanning the candy. "That will $76.19."

Anne handed him the church credit card for payment. She didn't say anything. All she could think about was how much of her reputation was being tarnished. She stepped out of the supermarket, where it seemed as if everyone was staring at her.

***

"You're sure you have the twin situation under control?" Gron was getting ready for his television interview while reading over some information his campaign manager had given him. He handed it over to him. "I won't until the twins show they are about ten years old. It shouldn't be long."

"To your command," the man told him as he put the paper back into his briefcase and locked it.

"How do you know where they are going to be?" Gron started to grill Merik on the location.

"Trust me." Merik confidently sat down.

"You have no idea the reign of Hell I will bring down on you if you don't deliver them to me." Gron checked his message from Misluna that the Sentry had just arrived in town. "Damn, I was hoping she would be dead or at least out of town until after tomorrow night." He replied to her message before putting her phone away.

"You son of bitch!" a male voice appeared out of the crowd.

Gron turned around to see Deputy Mayor John Gresin coming towards him with a report in his hand. "John, how can I help you?"

"You linked me to giving money to United Won with city funds!" He threw the papers in Gron's face.

Gron peeked over at the young Mexican girl staring at Gron with hate. "Do you think this is the place?" He gave her a quick wink before turning his attention back to the deputy mayor. "Don't forget paying for male prostitutes while on those business trips to meet up with Mack Righteous." His campaign manager handed him some paperwork.

He reviewed the paper. "This is a bigger work of fiction than that cult you run."

"Your wife and kids won't think it could be far from the truth. I had a really good talk with them at the Copper Club. Right after their tennis game. I told them the F.O.R. would always be there for them. They seemed interested in the program, especially for your little boys, Blake and Daniel." He turned back to the mirror to stare at the scar on his forehead. "Leave the scar. It has a certain sympathetic tone to it." He turned back to John. "I haven't leaked it yet. I'm going to give you a choice. Drop out of the race and support my candidacy for mayor, or...."

The deputy mayor just stood there dumbfounded. "You son of a..."

Gron was admiring himself in the mirror. "I'm going to be mayor. Oppose me and lose not only the race, but your family." He sipped his drink. "Victory is so sweet tasting. I'd give you a sip, but there's no victory for you."

The deputy mayor was about to break down. "I'll make my official announcement tomorrow for your support."

"You can't be serious!" the young Latina woman finally spoke.

Gron peeked over at the young girl. "You're cute. Want your life changed?"

"You already did that." The tension in the air from her was obvious as she stormed out.

The leader of the F.O.R. turned to John, who was watching his assistant storm off. "Don't you double-cross me. You won't like it."

***

Devine rolled in the grass. The pain in her lower abdomen was nothing like she had felt before. In between the pulsating dull pain were the quick sharp spikes that felt like the inside of her skin was tearing. "Why?" she screamed. Inside her growing stomach were flashes of red light. The ground around her was torn up from her grabbing onto something… anything to end the pain. "Celestial, Father, what did I do to deserve this?"

Salamor hid in the shadows of the trees watching the angel scream for any sense of relief. It was something he could not provide her with. He needed to get home.

CHAPTER EIGHT

Alex decided to scout the airport for a bit, trying to see if she could find Shawn. Even though this wasn't a hunt, it was more of a bit of Alex trying to clear her mind. Such an emotional night. Obviously, the majority of what was on Alex's mind was her business with Kameron. Though, running into another Sentry also brought up some unwelcome memories.

The remembrance of what Sanah had done to her was something that raced through her mind. There was the fact that the Sentry was being trained by someone else. Alex knew an angel would be a good trainer, but they were no Sentry. They would have no idea what being a Sentry entailed for a human to become one. The sacrifice, no sleep, battling the balance between having a regular life while fighting Infiltrators and Demons. Alex knew, but then, she was no Osiah.

The airport was decorated with Halloween art from local schools. Mostly they were made up of kid interpretations of witches, ghosts, and whatever monster their imagination came up with. One of them caused Alex to stop… it had a shadow, bear-like creature jumping into a man's body. But that wasn't the most disturbing of the pictures. There were a couple of pictures that had some dark-skinned children running away from a mob of white people. In the picture, it said, "Monsters are real."

"Sad, isn't it?" A lady came up to Alex looking at the pictures.

"So much hate. It's sadder when it starts affecting children." Alex just stared at the pictures.

"They should all go back where they came from." The little old woman had pure disgust in her eyes.

Alex was appalled at what she said. "Why don't you go to your country, where your ancestors came from?"

"We're not ruining this country?" the old lady snapped back at Alex.

Alex sighed. "Tell that to the Native Americans."

The rest of the airport's impromptu hunt was a complete dud. Alex found that Shawn, or Merik as he was called now, hadn't been seen for quite some time. Alex decided to go for a walk in the country. A couple of cars slowed down to see if Alex was okay, but she just waved them off. The woods were quiet; there were no signs of any birds or animals anywhere. Alex didn't like that because that usually meant that there was some major Dark activity afoot. There was a pretty flower that Alex picked as she carried down the road in her slow stroll. It gave her a sense of a sad calmness as she continued on.

The only sound she could hear was her taking a deep breath. She found herself by Sarah's old house. There was a young family living there. Alex saw a swing set with two dogs who perked up when they saw Alex. The house changed. It seemed happy. There were two men working on installing some windows. Alex couldn't help but notice that it was a black man showing the white man some details about the installation. There were two ladies; one white, and one black, teasing the men about the work they were doing. It made Alex smile to see such happiness coming from the house where her best friend was murdered. The flower in her hand was gently put at the foot of the driveway in remembrance of her friend.

Alex didn't know how long she was out when she came to the small building where Osiah lived. It was abandoned, rundown, and falling apart. When she came up to the door, there was a condemned notification on the door. It didn't take Alex's power of the Lite to break in as the door fell off the hinges when she went to see if it was locked. Alex jumped at a sight she wasn't expecting to see. "Komptin?"

Her gargoyle dog was lying down next to an unlit fireplace. He was in his hunting form, sleeping. She slowly walked up, not to startle him. The floor creaked a bit as she knelt next to him, gently grazing her hand against his tough exterior. His eyes opened with sadness when he saw Alex. "I miss him too." She tried to comfort her friend. "You wanna go for a walk?"

He flashed his big gentle eyes in agreement as he stood up. The two of them carefully hiked through the woods. It felt good to have her hunting partner at her side. He seemed to stay close to her side instead of leading the way. It wasn't a hunting walk, more of an enjoyable stroll through the woods.

They stopped at a small stream in the woods to admire the fall colors hovering over the flowing creek. They both ended up at the bottom of Reaper hill, where Kale was first attacked by Gron. It was also the spot where Alex revealed her powers to the people she loved and cared for. Komptin flashed his eyes as he turned quickly around.

"Sentry," a familiar voice came from behind her.

Alex turned around to see the Dark Myst floating in the woods. "Salamor."

The Dark Myst seemed to be on edge as he kept on looking back into the woods. "Why are you walking these woods?"

"Let me ask you something; can you feel my emotion?" Alex opened herself to be read by the tormented spirit hovering before her. He cautiously floated up to her in fear he was going to be grabbed by the Lite Sentry. Probably because she was the only mortal who could kill him. The Myst studied her but shook his head. "That's what I thought." Alex picked up a rock and threw it quite a distance down the creek. "I'm just taking a walk. What are you doing here?"

Salamor made it a point of not looking in the direction of the angel who was about to give birth to the twins. He couldn't have the Sentry follow him while he was off to get Merik. Luckily, he knew something that would keep her busy. "Sentry, head east, the first clearing of the F.O.R."

"Where they perform their Infiltration ceremony?" Alex rubbed Komptin's ear.

Salamor pointed in the direction of the clearing. "There is a shell of a woman."

"I'll go check it out." Alex started in that direction. "Salamor."

Salamor's nerves shot up in fear that he was caught in his plan. "Yes, Sentry."

Alex gave him a warm smile. "Thank you. That was nice. We can give her family some closure."

Salamor watched the Sentry go in the direction of the dead woman. He started to float away but fell to the ground as a warm sensation traveled through his body. The sensation had to pass before he was able to leave to get Merik.

***

Alex made it to the clearing where the Infiltration ceremony had taken place. Komptin was on high alert since they were so close to the F.O.R. Compound on top of being a land of evil. The two of them walked around the perimeter of the circle before seeing a lump that didn't look like anything the forest would produce. There was no doubt about it; the body of the woman Salamor described. Komptin led the way to the body as Alex followed.

The body was a small woman with blonde hair with freckles. What was left of her body was pale from lack of life, with tear stains running down the side of her face. Her eyes had no life behind them as they stared straight up. Alex couldn't help but notice the claw marks around a massive hole in her chest from an Infiltrator as it was trying to escape the potential host. Alex closed the girl's eyes as she gave her a prayer, hoping she was at peace.

Alex turned to Komptin, who was staring at the girl. "Did you know her?"

The massive dog nodded as he flashed his eyes. Komptin started sniffing the ground as he found her wallet in the bushes. It would have seemed she knew she was going to die and tossed it, so hopefully, she could be found. "Paige Cass." Alex continued to look through her wallet, when she noticed something else on the ground that must have fallen out. Her heart skipped a beat as she saw it was a Secret Service badge. "Oh, my God." Alex turned to Komptin when she realized the only way he would know her was when he was in San Diego. "Did she work with Kameron in San Diego?"

Komptin flashed his eyes, acknowledging the Sentry's theory.

"Come on, let's get to the church. I'll have Anne contact Kameron." Alex knew he wouldn't accept a phone call from her. Why would he?

***

Merik noticed outside his window that it was getting darker than expected. That meant the twins were going to be born soon. The pacing was starting to increase as Merik was getting more nervous. There was so much riding on this night. If Merik screwed it up then not only would Vandor not be able to return, but Gron would slowly torture Merik before finally killing him.

Although he did have a small hobby to keep him busy. He picked up his cell phone to call the Catholic Church. Misluna answered the phone.

"Hey, it's Merik. Can you get me one of the priests?"

Misluna chuckled on the other end of the phone. "Sure thing."

Merik waited for a bit before the priest on the end picked up. "Father Carl, is it?"

"Yes, how can I help you?"

It was time to put his college drama class into play. "Father, I just need someone to talk to. Is this confidential, like a confession."

"Yes, of course. Please tell me."

"You see, there was this girl. I cared for her so much, but she just toyed with my emotions."

"That may be a matter of perception. People and their perceptions of their actions are complicated. Have you talked to her?" Father Carl suggested in a caring voice.

Merik was having a hard time keeping a straight face. "I tried, but she just says she wants nothing to do with me. I'm really thinking of killing myself."

"I understand you feeling empty without her love, but God loves you."

Merik was not going to be able to hold it in. "If God loves me, why does he employ such a cold-hearted bitch like Anne McClure?" There was silence on the other end. Merik knew the conflict Father Carl was in. The priest couldn't say anything as this was confirmed as a confession. Merik hung up the phone before busting out laughing.

He turned around to see Salamor perched on top of his bar. "The twins will be born soon. Come with me."

238

***

Alex made it to the church just as the fall festival was starting. Kids were running around having fun. Volunteers seemed to be having a good time while hosting their games to the children. Even some parents seemed to be laughing and having a good time. Alex snuck around the back, hoping not to be seen. This was not the time to find and talk to Anne about what she found in the woods.

She sat in the cathedral where they were trying to get ready for the first service. Komptin walked upstairs to Alex's office, probably to take a nap. Normally she would sit in the back of the massive room, but today, she felt she should sit in the front of the church. In the back of her mind, she was hoping it would make her closer to God, so he could feel her. Even though the room provided some level of comfort, she was still without the Lite, still cold and empty.

"Alexandria," Celestial's voice came from the other end of the room. Alex turned around to see the Conduit of Lite walk down the center aisle. Alex met her in the middle and did a quick bow before giving her a hug. Celestial smiled as she looked down at the Sentry. "It is nice to see you more like yourself."

"But you can't sense anything in me?" There was a small bit of hope in her voice, but she knew the answer.

The beautiful blonde angel just shook her head. "I am sorry, dear."

239

Alex playfully shrugged. "What are you doing here?"

"It is rare that I can play with children at a festival on church grounds. It is an opportunity I cannot pass." She had a bit of excitement in her voice. Then it turned to seriousness. "Have you had any contact with Devine?"

Alex was shocked. "She's still missing?"

"We cannot find her. All available angels are still in search of her. But it is a big planet, and not enough of us to find her. Especially the ocean floor." Celestial turned as she saw kids running in the hallway laughing. "That is such a sweet sound."

Alex peeked over her shoulders at the kids. "Yes, I'll keep an eye out for Devine. I beg you. Please don't leave without saying goodbye tonight."

"You have my word." The angel placed her hand on Alex's face. "If only you remember to take the courage to step into fear after the knock of three."

"What? Really, just once, don't be cryptic." Alex laughed, teasing her godmother. She knew that Celestial had a reason for everything she did, even not telling her the whole story. If she did, it would take away Alex's free will, which goes against His wishes.

Alex escorted Celestial to the festival. "If you will excuse me, but I need to talk to Anne and Father Richard." Alex met with the priest and historian as they saw her approach. "Hey."

"How'd it go, sweetie?" Anne gave Alex a hug.

Alex looked around the festival. "It wasn't what I expected. The festival looks great."

"Thank you." Anne gazed around with pride at what she had created. "Sure is getting dark early."

"It's fall." Father Richard stared up at the sky.

Alex took a deep breath. "I need you to get a hold of Kameron."

Anne peeked over at Father Richard. "He's on his way to transfer Scarlett to her Sentry."

"When he lands, can you call him? There is something I need to tell him." Alex kept an eye on Celestial. She knew she was safe, but it always made her a bit nervous being around people. Alex saw her laughing with the children as they touched her gown.

"Is it something good?" Anne had high hopes that maybe it was to lay down the groundwork for their relationship.

"No," Alex let down her friend. "It's not good news."

Father Richard lowered his voice a bit. "I heard from the Council that a Sentry ran into a Demon in New Mexico."

Alex was genuinely confused. "How'd they know that? I didn't make my report out to them yet."

"There she is. That pure evil of the Dark!" a male voice came from the entryway of the church.

A glass broke as Megan dropped the glass she was holding as she stared at the man who was yelling. She saw that the guy was pointing to Alex. "You scared the hell out of me!" she screamed at him.

Kameron turned from Megan to Dinah who was keeping her Sentry in line. She pushed his arm down. "That was the Demon? That is a Lite Sentry, you knit wit."

Alex and Kameron locked eyes. Alex had such a warm feeling seeing him again, here and safe. She couldn't help but smile as she walked towards him. Then she saw Scarlett Roberts with Kaylee come up behind him. She grabbed Kameron's arm to pull him down to whisper something in his ear. She kissed him on the cheek before leaving with Kaylee to go into the church. Alex's smile went away.

She approached the group. "Nice to see you again."

The new Lite Sentry removed his hat. "My apologies. I didn't know you were a Lite Sentry. I can't feel your Lite."

Both Kameron and Dinah shook their heads to Zeke as if telling him not to go down that road. "Alexandria. I am Dinah," the orange-haired angel introduced herself. "We are here to transfer Scarlett over to Malkaroy and the Sentry he is training."

"Malkaroy is training one of them? They'll benefit from that. He's quite the warrior." Alex peeked behind the group. "Midnight, Scotty. Nice to see you again."

"Nice to be seen. I take it you were the one who saved us?" Midnight asked, full well knowing the answer.

Alex nodded.

"Thank you." Midnight nudged Scotty, who was checking out Dinah from the back.

"Oh, yah, thank you." Scotty tried to recover from being caught. He leaned over to Midnight.

242

"Do you think an angel and a human, could, you know?"

Dinah turned around. "Disgusting, but even then, it is frowned upon." She saw Celestial and her Guardians. "I must speak to the Conduit."

"I'm going to enjoy the warmth of the church," Zeke told her.

Kameron felt for Alex as she watched him with envy going into the church.

Scotty was scouting the area. "Hey, look at that, they have an auction." He booked it over to the auction craft table.

Midnight wanted to see what girl caught his attention but then she realized there was a fancy needlepoint he probably wanted to admire. "Excuse me, I guess I better go babysit him. Nice seeing you again, Alex."

"You too." Alex smiled. She turned to Kameron, who was emotionless. "Then there were two." The two of them just stood there. "We should talk."

"Yes." Kameron showed her the way.

For some reason, Alex wanted to have this talk in the congregation hall. The two of them ended up in front of the room. There was no doubt they both were remembering how he used to hold Alex in the church in D.C. in the dark as they listened to the choir sing. "There is something I need to tell you."

***

Devine screamed in pain as she could feel the movement of the creatures inside her start to move into position to come. She was soaking in a pool of

Earth ground mixed with Lite blood. She screamed in pain as loud as her voice would allow.

Merik heard the scream as he was approaching a hill. "They're coming." The excitement in his voice was overwhelming. He knew this was going to get him to the top of Vandor's servants.

Salamor floated before him and stopped. "I shall confirm the birth. Then you can grab them." He flew over the hilltop to confirm his suspicions. It took him a second before he confirmed with Merik. He nodded with excitement. "They are emerging."

***

Celestial just got done talking to Dinah about her concerns with Alexandria meeting up with the Sentry she was training. She had convinced her fellow Angel that the interaction would not affect the training. Dinah did not trust Alexandria. It was understandable why she had her reservations.

"Celestial, can you come play with us?" one of the children asked. "We are going to try to get Father Carl into the dunk tank."

"Of course, children." Celestial was about to head towards the child's game when a massive amount of Lite left her body to counteract a massive surge of Dark that she had never felt before. She got weak in the knees as she started to fall to the ground. Omeila and Arome caught her on the way down.

"My lady." Arome tried helping her to her feet.

"What is the matter?" Omeila secured her footing.

"The Balance, it is shifting." Celestial feared.

Komptin opened his eyes in full glow as he morphed into his hunting form as he rushed to the window.

***

"You wanna talk?" Kameron spoke as he was talking to a witness of a case. "Go ahead."

"I found the body of a woman. Her name was Paige Cass," Alex explained. "It seemed as if the Dark tried to force Infiltration on her, but she wasn't accepting." Alex handed him her badge and wallet.

"Thank you." Kameron took a second. "I need to tell Weston. Anything else?"

For some reason, that question pissed Alex off. "Why? Trying to get to your little girlfriend?"

"What? Who?" Kameron calmly asked.

"Scarlett. I see how she is all over you." Alex could actually feel herself hurt all over as she said those words.

"Ah, no," Kameron quickly denied it. "We are not a couple."

"Right." Alex didn't believe him, or maybe she did.

"If that is all." Kameron turned around to head out of the room.

Alex yelled at him, "You're just going to walk away?"

"It's what you want, isn't it?" Now Kameron was becoming confrontational.

She matched his stance, not backing down. "Just going to leave like I don't matter. You're just going to go live your life."

Kameron fought back all his emotion to be calm as possible. "Alex, it's your life, you're the only one that has to live it. I just wanted to live mine close to yours."

"Well, you did a bang-up job, moving across the country!" she harshly scolded him. Then Alex saw something in Kameron that she had never seen before. It was pure raw emotion.

"YOU'RE THE ONE WHO LEFT ME!" He pointed directly at her.

Then all the windows of the church shattered inwards, spraying glass all through the air as Komptin gave a massive roar from upstairs. Kameron quickly covered Alex to shield her from all the debris. She looked up at him. "Holy shit, Kameron! No wonder you don't get pissed that often."

"Cute. Let's go see what's going on." The two of them went outside the church to make sure everyone was alright, not knowing they were holding each other's hands.

***

By the time Salamor crested the hill, the twins were lying on the ground, sucking the blood of the Lite Angel oozing from her body. They both had straight jet-black hair. One girl and one boy continued to dip their hands in the body of the angel for more blood. They looked as if they were about a primate's earth year.

Salamor slowly approached the twins with caution. They stopped their feeding on the angel to turn around and hiss at Salamor with their glowing red eyes and fanged teeth. This gave the Angel of Lite an opportunity to try to escape by crawling away. She tried to get up but immediately crashed to the ground, rolling down into a small ravine. The twins screeched with terror as their food source was now out of reach.

The Dark Myst heard Merik start to run through the woods. There was no doubt that he would deliver the twins to Gron. The Demon called out for Salamor in between the screeching of the twins. The angel was starting to cry from the pain.

She screamed for her life to end. "I do not deserve to be a star. End my existence." That was all Salamor could make out in between the weeping within the small ravine.

Salamor knew that Merik would grant the angel's wish to die. Merik was about to reach the twins before he would kill the angel. The Myst looked down at the vulnerable angel who was crying. Salamor hid the shadows to make sure the twins were going to be delivered to Gron. The twins stopped crying at the sight of Merik. He carefully picked them up to make sure they were safe. "Take them to Gron," Salamor thought to himself.

His wish was not granted as Merik spoke to the twins. "Let's kill your mother, shall we? Would you like that?" The twins had no expression as they flashed their red eyes. Merik started to search around the woods for the angel.

Salamor watched his movements as the angel started to sob. Merik heard the crying of the angel as he moved toward the sound. Salamor hesitated before floating down to Devine. "Quiet, Lite Angel. He will kill you." She continued to cry as she held her lower abdomen. "Do you understand? He will end you." Salamor turned to look above the hill as Merik was coming over the top. Salamor hovered over Devine to ensure his black mist body covered her as he stared into her eyes. "Look at me. Stare into my eyes; do not make a sound."

Merik scouted the area to look for the angel. There was no sign of her. The sound of her weeping stopped. His only conclusion was that she must have joined the other angels as a star in the sky.

CHAPTER NINE

"Is everyone alright?" Alex surveyed the area while still not knowing she was holding Kameron's hand. The people in the area seemed a bit confused as to what was going on. Kids were grasping onto their parents while they were trying to figure out what that noise was. The crowd seemed to calm down a bit but was still on edge over the sound of every glass window being shattered in the church.

"What happened?" Midnight came running with Scotty.

"No one is hurt here." Dinah and Zeke were helping some of the kids find their parents.

The new Sentry had a strange look on his face. "I should really go."

"No, you are not ready for what is out there." Dinah moved in front of him, putting her hand on his chest. "The top priority is getting the Conduit of Lite to the doorway."

"But can't her guardians…" he started to argue.

"She is the priority. Then you need to check on the two primates." Dinah pointed her finger to the doorway.

Zeke admitted his defeat as he went to ensure the Conduit would be okay. He cautiously approached Celestial as he led the way to the doorway as Arome and Omelia helped her along. She passed the group and gave Alex a small smile saying she would be okay. Then Alex noticed that she looked down at her hand as it was still holding Kameron's.

Alex quickly retracted her hand from connecting with Kameron. "Sorry, force of habit."

Kameron nodded with a bit of disappointment that she didn't continue with the holding. "It's okay, I need to get a hold of Weston."

Anne approached with Father Richard. Father Carl was telling Megan to go inspect the damage to the church while he politely escorted everyone out. "We should really go back inside so we can talk."

The group of them discreetly went into the church. They decided to meet in the congregation room. Scotty nudged Kameron as he was caught staring at Megan as she started to leave the group to check the damage to the church. He leaned in so only Kameron could listen. "Dude, she's cute in a weird way, but not your type."

Kameron shook off his thought process. "I need to talk to you and Midnight." He turned to Alex as he grabbed her hand on purpose, squeezing it.

Alex knew this was a combination of apologizing for yelling and that he needed to tell his friends about Paige. Holding his hand fit like an old pair of shoes. It felt so good with so many memories. She watched him go off with his team as she turned to Anne, who had a happy smile. "Don't get your hopes up."

Anne just gave her a quick smirk. "Okay, sweetie. What happened?"

Dinah spoke up. "There is something out there." Komptin joined Alex. "Komptin, I am sorry about Osiah."

Komptin flashed his eyes to acknowledge her condolences. Alex rubbed the ears of her hunting partner. "We miss him." She turned to Father Richard. "I need to go for a walk."

"Be careful." Father Richard scanned the area. "I don't like this."

Alex turned to Dinah. "Do you want me to take Zeke, might be good for him?"

Dinah seemed to hesitate before answering. "He is not ready."

"He needs the experience," Alex started to argue. "Hasn't he killed an Infiltrator already?"

Dinah shook her head. "Not by himself. He fought one; it did not go well. I had fought beforehand, weakened it to the point of demise. Zeke barely won, he was bloodied and made many mistakes."

Alex couldn't help but notice that the angel seemed disappointed. It wasn't at her Lite Sentry, but it seemed as if it was at herself. She had never seen an angel have self-doubt. "You are doing a good job. He is learning. It takes time."

Dinah pointed out, "At this time, you took out Infiltrators and a Demon."

Alex didn't know what to say. She didn't have that answer on comparison whether she was that good or was he that far behind in his training. "I also lost my best friend and mentor that night." Anne took a moment to remember holding Kale in her lap after Gron had beaten him. It was the first time she saw Alex and Komptin use their power. "Be careful, Alex."

"I'm always careful." She took one look at Kameron, who turned around to see her. He gave her a forced, uncomfortable smile before turning back to Midnight and Scotty. By the looks on their faces, he'd told them about Paige. "Come on, Komptin. Let's go for a walk." Alex turned around to leave as a bloodied, and bruised Devine came stumbling in before falling into Alex's arms.

***

Kameron stood in the doorway of Alex's new office. Scotty and Midnight ran to a local store to pick up something for her to rest on and a pillow. Alex had her hand over her mouth in complete shock. Komptin sat in an overwatch position to ensure she was safe until the Conduit of Lite arrived, but who knew when that would be. She was really weak when she left.

Dinah knelt next to Devine. "Sister, can you hear me?" She stroked the blood-soaked purple hair as Anne gently washed her body. "Be careful."

"I promise," Anne reassured.

Father Richard joined Alex, who was standing next to Kameron. "Thoughts?"

"I've seen battle scars, but this looks nothing like that." Alex watched Anne get down to her lower front.

"No!" Devine started to thrash about.

Dinah had to hold her down. "Shh, shhh," she quietly tried to calm her down.

Alex came by to put her hand on Dinah's shoulder. "Can you take her to a doorway?"

"NO!" Devine cried. "I cannot go home." Her body started moving again. Both Alex and Dinah tried to hold her down.

"I cannot take her if she does not want to go. To enter a doorway, one must be willing." Dinah moved some of Devine's hair out of her eyes.

"That's convenient." Alex kissed her surrogate sister on the forehead once she calmed down.

Devine's body ceased moving and just stayed still. Scotty couldn't understand how He could allow this, especially in His so-called house. "Is she, is she still alive? She's not moving."

Dinah stood up. "She still lives. Once her existence ends, she will either join her brothers and sister in the sky or melt into the ground."

Anne continued to wash her body. "Most of the blood is concentrated here."

Zeke came into the room. "Dinah, Kaylee is ready to go."

Dinah hesitated to leave Devine, but Alex grabbed her hand. "I swear, we will die before anything else happens to her. She'll be safe."

"Thank you, Sentry." Dinah got up. "Come, Zeke. Now we train together. The Dark shall pay for this."

A determined look on Dinah's face got Zeke nervous. "You mean, it's going to get harder?" They both left to protect Kaylee while preparing for their battles with the Dark.

Scotty watched the angel leave. "Lucky him."

Midnight smacked him in the arm. "Time and place."

Kameron checked his phone. "Weston is here." He motioned for Scotty and Midnight to join him. Kameron was about to leave, but he slowly walked up to Alex, who was still near Devine. He put his hand on her shoulder; instantly she immediately put her hand on his. "She'll be okay, Alex." He leaned down and kissed her on top of her head. "Stay strong for her."

Kameron met Weston outside the church with Malkaroy. "Glad you made it."

"My Sentry is ensuring the flying craft is protected." Malkaroy stared up at the church. "I must go check on my sister."

Weston watched his father leave to check on Devine. "He just found out what happened."

Scarlett had a small bag with her as she joined Weston. "I'm Scarlett Roberts."

"Weston." He shook the hands of the social diva. "We should get going. Dad is going join us at our safe house."

"Is there a chance I can go get something from downtown?" Scarlett asked with a sense of hope.

"It isn't safe," Kameron mentioned.

Scarlett had a genuine concern written on her face. "I really would like to go. It won't take long."

Kameron didn't like the idea. "I don't know."

"I'll have my dad's Sentry meet us there in case something happens. Plus, I think it would be good for him." Weston picked up the phone.

"I'll see if Midnight and Scotty will relieve him." Kameron texted the two of them.

Weston was waiting for his Sentry to answer when he asked Kameron. "Have you heard from Paige?"

Kameron reached into his pocket to hand him the muddy wallet and badge. "Alex found this next to her body."

"Two Secret Service agents will relieve you. Then meet me at a location that I'll text you. Thanks." Weston hung up the phone to his Lite Sentry as he stared at Kameron's hands. "How'd it happen? Did she suffer?"

"I'm not going to answer that." Alex came up to the group. "Malkaroy is with Devine." Kameron nonchalantly moved closer to Alex when she arrived. It didn't go unnoticed by Alex, she welcomed it. "I'm sorry for your loss."

"We need to get going." Scarlett seemed more anxious as they stood there.

"She's right." Weston grabbed his car keys from his coat. "Can you tell Dad where we are going?" He turned to Scarlett. "Where are we going?" She gave him the address of an apartment downtown. "Kameron, do you mind?"

"Not at all." Kameron wrote down the address to where they were going to give it to Malkaroy. He watched the two of them take off to their destination.

Kameron and Alex just stayed there, standing close to each other. It was uncertain, yet welcoming comfort as they stood there. "How are you doing with all this?"

"There is something not right." She turned to him as if afraid someone would hear her. "I found out that my senses taken was caused by someone from the Dark called a Harridan. I'm going to see if Anne has any record of it."

255

"The F.O.R. did it? How?" Kameron and Alex started to walk together to the backside of the church.

"I don't know. Lord knows what I'll do when I find the person." Alex had her fist glowing until they stepped onto the property. The two of them found a spot at a table in the middle of the closed festival. "Kameron, I never truly thanked you for saving my life."

"Apparently, I need to say the same thing." Kameron smiled at her.

She embarrassedly blushed. "Yes, well. Call it even?" Alex hesitated before speaking. "Also, I need to apologize for how I treated you. It wasn't right."

Kameron resisted the urge to grab and kiss her. "It's okay. I get it, the situation you were in." For the first time that he could remember, he didn't know how to act. Was he supposed to kiss her, he really wanted to. Did she want him to kiss her? Were they just going to remain friends? Were they friends?

The two of them stared at each other before Alex got up. "I should get going."

"Be careful." Kameron resisted the urge to hug her. They watched each other, waiting for one of them to make a move. "Go, do what you do." All she did was smile as she whistled for her hunting companion. Komptin came running out of the church as he transformed into his gargoyle state to go find what happened to Devine. They disappeared into the forest as Kameron stayed behind. His mind was full of confusion regarding Alex. This was a situation that he needed to play it slow. He walked into the church annex where the offices were. In the hallway, he thought he heard a voice muffled from behind a door. Behind the door was Megan in a small storage room full of office supplies.

"You scared the hell out of me." She grabbed her chest.

"I apologize." Kameron took a step back. "What are you doing? I thought I heard you talking to someone."

Megan played it off. "Oh, it's nothing. I was talking to Mom when I was looking for another rosary. I lost mine." She grabbed one from the shelf. "I guess I should have Father Carl bless it."

Kameron took a moment. "You lost your rosary?"

"Yep." Megan showed him the one in her hand. "Lucky we have plenty of spares. I guess I should get moving." She stopped herself and then stepped to the back of the room. "Unless you want to come in here with me?"

Kameron got a little uncomfortable as she started to lift up her shirt to show her skin. "Megan, this is not appropriate."

"I have no scars like some other people. Want to see more?" She continued to raise her shirt up.

"If you will excuse me." Kameron left down the hall. He ran into Father Carl who was coming down the hall. "Father, when Alex returns, can you tell her I left to go check on some things?"

"Will do. Why don't you just call her?" Father Carl was putting on his coat.

257

"I don't have her number." He was now regretting deleting her number from his phone.

"I'm heading home, but I'll call her on my way out." Father Carl grabbed his keys. "God bless."

"Thanks," Kameron told him as he was heading out the door of the church. He grabbed his phone from his coat pocket. "Scotty, I need you to look into something for me."

***

Gron just got off the phone with Misluna, who was telling him that something was going on at the church behind closed doors. She wasn't able to find out what it was, but only the people who were part of the Council were going in and out of the room. *"What are you up to, Alex?"* Gron went to get himself a drink. Outside the window, there was a car coming at a high rate of speed. The gate opened, and Gron could see Merik eagerly step out of the car to get one of the babies from the back seat.

Gron picked up his phone to call Misluna to get here now. He rushed downstairs, pushing two Serfs over the edge of the railing of the staircase. The only thing that mattered was the twins. "How are they?"

Merik handed one of them over to Gron. "They are a bit weak. The birth must have killed the angel; she was nowhere to be found." Merik rushed them upstairs with Gron to the baby room that was set up.

The babies didn't make a sound. Their eyes started to slowly lose the glow of the red. They were unresponsive to anything Gron was trying to do. "They must feast."

"What do they need? That baby powder stuff?" Merik was about to leave until Misluna came into the room. There was a sigh of relief when she got into the room.

"How are the children?" she asked in a calm, motherly tone. The skin of the kids was warm to the touch. "They need to eat." Only her eyes moved to Gron as she picked up one of the children. "Time to put those orbs to use. The blood of Lite Sentries."

"I'll go get them." Gron left for his office in haste. He ran downstairs as Serfs were just getting up from the ground. Gron knocked them back over into a plant that was sitting in the corner. He ripped a backpack off a female Serf, causing her shoulder to dislocate as he ran to his office. The orbs were carefully placed in the bag, and he put one of his spare shirts between them to provide extra cushion. With great care, he headed back up to the twins' room for feeding.

Misluna had one in her arms that she handed to Gron. They carefully poked a hole in them to avoid spilling any of the Lite Sentry blood over the floor. Both babies drank the blood before falling asleep. Gron watched as the keys to get Vandor back rested peacefully. "Merik, I'm not one for compliments, but good job."

"Thank you, my leader." Merik smiled at the thought that he may be rising in the ranks in the Dark. "It was no trouble at all."

Gron whispered carefully, "I don't know how you did it, but there is no chance in Hell you rise above me." His eyes turned to a steady red glow as he turned his head to Merik. "And I'll kill you if you try."

Merik nodded out of pure fear. "Yes, my leader." He stepped back by the door in case Gron decided to attack him.

"Now that that is settled. Misluna, when do you need a pure of heart?" Gron walked over to Merik who was pinning himself to the door.

Misluna was mesmerized by the children. "The children will grow at an extreme rate. We'll need a pure of heart within three days."

"My man Merik will get one for you." Gron put his arm around Merik and slapped him on the cheek. "Because if he doesn't, he's dead." The leader of the F.O.R. put him in a headlock and rubbed his head with his knuckles. "Isn't that right?" Merik didn't answer him right away, so Gron grabbed him by the throat to lift him up.

"That's right, that's right." Merik was trying to break free of his grip.

"You can go now." Gron went back to ensure the twins were safe in their beds.

Merik got into his car as fast as he could. There were only two pure of hearts he knew of that were in Copper Top. His car was moving a little fast for the road, but with his Demon reflexes he was able to compensate for it. There was no way he could get one of them from the church, so he would have to scout out on the perimeter and snatch one of them when they left. It was too bad, because he still wanted to have fun with Anne.

He would have to avoid Alex at all costs which wouldn't be too hard considering her senses were gone, but the dog might give him away. It was a chance he would have to take. Hopefully, he could snatch one of them before Alex came back from hunting. There was a spot behind the church that he found would make a good snatch and grab. It was close to his car and secluded enough not to give away his intentions.

***

Salamor carefully kept his distance far enough away from the church. It always gave him such a sickening feeling to enter His house. The time it took for him to float there was much longer than he could have gone. He was procrastinating and weak. He had never used his influence on an Angel of Lite before. If he didn't keep her quiet, Merik would have found her. Why did he care? She hated him, she didn't trust him. The thought of him disgusted her. He should just leave to make sure the twins were safe. Although, something compelled him to ensure the angel was protected.

The Lite Sentry had taken off on her hunt and the only ones left were the big angel who was staying with the one who was hurt. Salamor couldn't help but watch him care for her from the window. She lay in the bed; bloodied, bruised, and beaten to a

point of hopelessness.   Salamor dropped a bit of
that sickening feeling from his body again. He must
be too close to the church was the only explanation
he could think of.

Salamor backed off from the church and sensed a
Demon nearby. The scent was Merik. Salamor
couldn't think of why he was here, but he needed to
leave. Salamor floated around the backside of the
church as he came up from behind him. "Merik,"
he called out to him as he floated down to him.
"Why do you hide on the forest floor?" The Demon
Myst was hoping he did not know of the angel
being brought here to heal.

"I need a pure of heart." Merik studied the
church for any movement he could find. "I know for
a fact there are two here."

Salamor was taken aback a bit.   "There are
others."

"Need one now." Merik thought he saw
movement in the window to see Anne. That's not
the one he wanted but would take her as a last
resort.

Salamor floated back a bit from shock. "The
Sentry will not like that. She will hunt you down
until you are dead."

"Better her than Gron," Merik quickly stated out
of fear.

Salamor knew Merik feared Gron. The only way
out Merik saw was to take the Sentry's pure of
hearts. "I must go."

***

Alex didn't have any luck finding out what was going on with the Dark in the woods. Komptin didn't pick up any scent of the Dark. Whatever was causing Celestial to get weak must have affected him as well because he was lagging back a bit. "What do you say we walk downtown?" He seemed to like that idea.

Some of the local businesses were handing out candy to the last of the trick-or-treaters. The small kids were gone and the only remnants were the older kids. Hints of the bar crowds were starting to come out in their costumes. Some of them were ingenious, but one she saw was in poor taste.

It was a guy with a white t-shirt in zombie makeup. He had fake bullet holes, and blood splattered throughout the shirt. Alex overheard him telling his friends that he was Darius King. Alex wanted to punch him. The ignorance of his actions was appalling. That, and if one of the Darius supporters saw him, he was probably going to get the crap beat out of him.

Alex stopped at a local ice cream shop just before they closed to grab a vanilla shake. It was nice because they even blended the Apollo Energy drink she had with her. The two hunters walked up ahead when she saw a familiar figure. He was talking to a young pretty black girl who reminded Alex of Anne for some reason. She snuck up on Moses. "Does your dad know you're here?"

Moses turned around in fear. "Alex, of course, Pops knows. What are you doing here?"

"This is my hometown." Alex sipped her drink. "Who're your friends?"

263

Moses vaguely answered. "Just friends, I know."

Alex surveyed the group, and they all just stared. They were no doubt telling her that she was not welcome. All of them had contempt in their faces except the girl next to Moses. She smiled at Alex, almost telling her that she should leave before something happens. "Well, enjoy Copper Top. Try a Marty's burger, you won't regret it." She smiled as she started to leave.

"Saltine," one of the members of the group said just loud enough for Alex to hear.

Alex turned around to see Moses telling him to keep quiet. Komptin barked at Alex as she was approaching the kid, but she quickly regained her thoughts. That kid wasn't worth a night in jail for Alex, so she decided to walk down the street. Down the road, she saw Scarlett being escorted by a young-looking guy with short light brown hair. He wore a pair of jeans, hiking boots, and a conservative gray sweater. Alex stood still as the two of them locked eyes.

Alex quickly turned away, knowing this Demon couldn't sense her. She turned to the alley to wait for the imminent attack. The Demon followed her into the alley as expected. "This is not going to end well for you. Turn her over to me." Alex had her arms crossed in the center of the alley staring at him.

"Come get her." The young man stood his ground. Then he flashed his eyes blue and lit his hands.

Alex couldn't believe it. "Seriously?" She knew she wasn't allowed to have contact with any of the

Sentries. She turned her attention to the sky. "This isn't fair." Alex thought she should leave but instead, she just told Komptin to stay put.

The man swung at her, but she ducked out of the way, giving her an opportunity to push him into the wall. "You really need to think about what you're doing." The Sentry shot a Lite Beam at Alex, but she rolled out of the way. She had to retract from shooting one of her own; the last time two Lite Sentries shot a Lite Beam at each other didn't end well. She picked up a garbage can lid and threw it at him. It hit him in the stomach. "Have you ever fought a Demon before?"

"Of course, I have, and many Infiltrators," the Lite Sentry stated.

"Really?" Alex didn't believe him. "Okay, first of all, don't lie. Not your strong suit."

The Lite Sentry approached Alex and swung. She blocked the punch and the knee he tried to give her. She took her other hand and slapped him across the face. "Keep your hands up." Alex let go of him and stood back to see what he would do.

"Come on and fight!" he screamed. He confidently approached to jab her, but she grabbed the arm into an arm bar and kicked the back of his knee. It brought him down to the ground. Alex grabbed the garbage can she got the lid from and dumped it on him, putting the can onto him. He tried to get out of it like a cat stuck in a small paper bag. Alex smirked at the humor when the Lite Sentry slipped on a bottle, landing flat on his back. "Here, let me help you with that." Alex lifted him up and took the can off, spilling garbage all over him.

The Lite Sentry screamed as his fists glowed. He presented many variable attacks, but Alex blocked them all. The last swing caused him to twist his body around. She picked him up from behind and twisted, throwing him onto the ground. "You need to think." Alex stepped a couple steps back. Komptin was laying down on the ground with his front legs crossed enjoying the show. "Infiltrators love to attack when you are least expecting it."

"I'm always ready," he claimed.

"Really?" Alex smirked. "Komptin." He lunged at the Lite Sentry from the side in the gargoyle form with his massive jaw drooling, staring at the Sentry's neck. Alex recognized that look; he thought he was going to die. "Remember that feeling you have right now. It's a feeling you will have quite often. Just don't get used to it; that is when you will die." Alex whistled for Komptin to get off of him.

The beaten Lite Sentry remained on his back, defeated. Alex leaned over to look down at him. Malkaroy joined her in staring down. "Tristan, I see you met Alex." Alex flashed her eyes to show she, too, was a Lite Sentry. Malkaroy helped his Lite Sentry off the ground to see him full of garbage. "Did you at least land a punch?"

***

Alex and Malkaroy were making small talk up the stairs as his Sentry was behind them, trying to clean himself off from his defeat. "Have you ever faced an Infiltrator or Demon?"

Alex didn't know how to answer that question. She didn't want to sound like she was bragging to alter his confidence. So, she let Malkaroy handle it. "She's been at this a lot longer than you." Malkaroy turned around to his Sentry. "You should have no shame."

Scarlett was about to knock on the door, but Alex stopped her by grabbing her arm. "Can you sense anything?" She turned to the Sentry. "What's your name again?"

"Tristan." He closed his eyes. "No, a light sense of the Dark but nothing serious."

"What does that tell you?" Alex asked him.

Tristan just shook his head. "They were here but left."

"Or could be a Demon inside," Alex pointed out. She knocked on the door. "Housekeeping." There was no sound from the inside. "I don't think there is anyone inside."

"What's that smell?" Tristan covered his nose.

"Death." Malkaroy moved Scarlett next to Tristan. She looked up at him and shyly smiled. Malkaroy nodded to Alex, but she stopped herself. She motioned for Tristan to knock the door down as she moved next to Scarlett. Malkaroy adjusted his position, fearing for the safety of his Sentry, but he needed the experience. "Ensure the immediate security of the room, move far enough for me and Komptin to get through."

Tristan nodded as he flashed his eyes as he went to kick the door in. His foot went through the door, but it didn't open. Malkaroy put his hand over his head in disbelief. Alex just did a quiet laugh. "Use the doorknob."

Tristan opened the door with his leg still stuck in the door. Malkaroy and Komptin secured the small apartment. "Alex, we're clear, but…."

Scarlett rushed into the apartment. "God, please no." She rushed into the room to see what was left of Steven hunched over on his computer. The shell of her assistant was wearing the shirt when she last video chatted with him. She tried to hold it in but couldn't.

To Alex's surprise, Scarlett sadly moved his hair out from his eyes. They just stared at the one man who cared for who she was, not what she was. "This is just wrong, he didn't deserve this." Scarlett wiped a tear before it dropped. She would never get out the image of the gouged out sockets on his face where his gentle eyes were once held. Then the real shock came when she bent over to kiss him on the forehead. "I'm done here."

"I thought you wanted the money?" Alex came out and called the elephant in the room. Malkaroy whispered to Alex that there was another body in the other room. Alex nodded in agreement. "We'll call the police when we leave."

"I just used that as an excuse to get him somewhere I knew he would be. The money was going to be used to ensure we, or he would be safe." Scarlett grabbed an ugly cuckoo clock off the wall. "I gave this to him for his birthday. We were in

268

Germany for a photo shoot." Then the sound of it crashing on the floor startled Tristan. Scarlett picked up the USB with the information she needed to get her money from the secret account. "I'm ready to go."

Alex couldn't help but see how much she actually cared for the man who laid dead on the table. The way she acted seemed as if she was ashamed of how she felt. It was sad that she never acted on that, whatever it was that held her back from being with each other. "Nothing should prevent that from happening," Alex said out loud as everyone turned to her.

"What is that, Alex?" Malkaroy asked while showing Tristan some clues revealing that the Dark was here.

Alex realized why everyone was looking at her. "Sorry, I have to go. Komptin." She knelt next to her friend, giving him much-needed love. He flashed his eyes as he knew what Alex wanted him to do.

CHAPTER TEN

Salamor hadn't had action like this since his Master was banished to the Dark. This was a comfortable familiarity that must be completed. The area was full of so much hate among these costumed primates attending a gathering on the street with music and lights. People were laughing, but there still was much tension in the air.

The Dark Myst floated above the crowd to continue his search. The sense of a pure of heart caught his attention. There was no doubt there was one nearby. There was a young primate talking to a female. He approached them, but neither of them was the one he needed. Agitation started to cloud his judgment. Time was not his companion in his search. Although, the scent did get stronger.

This was it. He caught the trail. It moved around the street as it was getting stronger. A pure of heart was close. The primates in his way prevented him from seeing his prize. Then the sea of people parted to show the pure of heart. Salamor froze as he saw the Sentry's love sitting at a table with a drink with two other primates.

This pure of heart was not to be touched. It caught his attention though to see what they were doing here. He started to make his way until he came across a new scent. This one was not pure of heart in front of him. He approached a young female next to another. He was inches away from her face as she held hands with the boy next to her.

This was what he was seeking. The boy next to her was full of hate. Salamor knew that could be used to his advantage. Then something else caught his attention that could complicate his plan. A sense of a Demon was near.

The boy, full of hate, turned to the Demon. "Qwai!"

Salamor quickly gained enough distance not to be noticed. The two primates did shake hands before giving a quick hug. The Dark Myst could tell the primates didn't know his true form. This was not his concern. He had another agenda; he rushed to tell Merik of his findings.

***

Kameron studied the crowd. He started to get that feeling again, like the day he was shot. There was something wrong with the air on this night. It was almost as if the world had pumped hate into the atmosphere. He saw one customer holler at a waitress over a drink. The waitress started to retaliate. The manager was trying to calm the situation down, but he too, was starting to get angry.

"Weird night, isn't it?" Midnight took a sip of her drink. "What is this?"

"I don't know, it was the event special." Scotty took his. "It was cheap."

"It's nasty." Midnight pushed her drink aside.

Kameron was drinking his whiskey and cola, but he asked for it to be made light. "Did you find anything?"

Scotty was eyeing some of the girls who were dressed in costumes that were quite revealing. "God, I love Halloween."

"Scotty." Midnight tapped his shoulder, but he didn't respond. She got up from the table to get behind Scotty. With both of her hands, she moved his head to Kameron. "There you go."

"Sorry." Scotty sipped his drink as well before making a face of disgust. "Okay, you're right, this is gross. Anyways, I put a call into TSA, but I won't hear anything until tomorrow or the next day."

Midnight rubbed her head. "It's pretty weak, Kameron."

"Just a gut feeling," Kameron defended. "But if I'm right…"

"I don't even want to think about it." Midnight leaned back into her chair.

In an unlikely fashion, Scotty turned around to the two of them. "You know, I feel kind of guilty about my thoughts of Paige."

"Not your fault. It's just natural as an investigator to look at all angles." Midnight tried to ease his guilt. "You had a legitimate point."

"My impression is that she had no family." Kameron noticed a man dressed as a zombie that was Darius King.

Scotty lifted up the drink that he couldn't stand. "To Paige. May her sacrifice and loyalty to her cause not be forgotten."

Both Midnight and Kameron were shocked at his toast. They joined together and had their drink in honor of their fallen comrade. Midnight sat back in her chair. "You know, it seems like we've been going nonstop since San Diego."

"Agreed." Scotty flagged down the waitress to order more drinks.

Kameron had a moment of relaxation. "I'm not going to lie, I'm tired as well. I think I'm going to retire for the night and..." He stopped in mid-sentence. Scotty and Midnight both saw what he was staring at as Alex came out of nowhere heading for their table. Kameron whispered so only Midnight and Scotty could hear him. "Not a word of what I asked."

"Of course," Scotty agreed.

Midnight nodded.

Kameron stood up. "Alex. Is everything alright?"

"Fine. I just wanted to let you know that Scarlet is off with her protectors." Alex stood at the table.

The split-second Alex stood at the table seemed like an eternity. Midnight was the first to speak. "Will you join us?"

Scotty turned around to grab a chair behind him. "Anyone using this?" he asked the table. The group told him it was okay to take the chair. "Here you go."

"Thanks." Alex sat down with Komptin at her side. He put his head on her lap so she could scratch his ears.

There was an awkward silence before Scotty finally said something. "So, your dog saved our lives."

Alex lovingly smiled at Komptin. "He tends to do that. Saved mine more than once." The waitress came by with the drinks. Midnight asked the waitress if she could bring something for Alex. "Just an Apollo would be great." The waitress told them she would be right back.

"How long have you been in your current job?" Scotty was trying to strike up a conversation.

Kameron kind of studied Midnight and Scotty as they acted as if they were grilling Alex to see if she was good enough for him. He was curious if Alex felt the same thing.

"Since I was seventeen." Alex turned around to see some arguments between two girls in the far corner. "Isn't it weird people come out just to cause drama?"

"Nothing good happens after two a.m." Midnight turned back to Alex's answer. "Since high school, you've been doing this?"

"Yep." Alex accepted her drink from the waitress. "Thank you."

Midnight stirred her drink. "We're just getting a taste of this. How do you handle it?"

Alex sat there for a moment, knowing it was the warmth of the Lite that gave her the balance she needed to maintain this fight. She turned to Kameron who also knew the answer to Midnight's question. "My connection to the Lite." Alex felt emptier as she said that out loud, knowing her connection had been severed.

"Wish I could have that," Scotty said under his breath.

Midnight heard what he said but didn't pursue it as it was the first time he mentioned something almost positive about faith. "I bet you've seen your fair share of nasty."

"Yeah, but you can't constantly think about that. It will drive you insane. You have to find the humor in life," Alex told her.

"Humor. In this line of work?" Midnight wanted to hear more.

"Oh yeah," Alex started to loosen up. "You have to hear this one. I was on this hunt, and I ended up at the docks in D.C."

Kameron sat back and smiled as Alex was laughing with Midnight and Scotty about her past humorous hunts. It was a familiar feeling of peacefulness. The four of them started to talk into the night, laughing and teasing each other.

***

Anne got a text from Alex telling her about what was going on downtown. Her best friend seemed to have a happy tone to her message. That was confirmed when she said that she wished Anne was there. Even though there was a lot going on, it was good for Alex to relax a bit. Anne walked into the room where the angel was resting.

Father Richard was sleeping in the corner of the room. Megan had left for the night along with Father Carl. Anne got comfortable as she started writing the documentation for the Council. It was quiet with the occasional sound of what seemed like weeping from Devine. It was so hard to see someone so powerful be in so much pain. If only she knew what had happened to her.

275

Anne didn't know how long she was writing before she herself was getting a bit tired. She got to the window to gaze up at the sky. There was a moment when it felt as if she were looking at the same star in the sky. She got that feeling again. There was no way for her to hold back the smile. It was Kale.

"Are you okay?" Father Richard's voice was raspy from being tired. "Man, I hope I'm not coming down with something."

"You're probably just tired. It's been a long day." Anne did one more glance at the sky before turning to Father Richard.

"How's she doing?" Father Richard compassionately stared at the angel.

"I don't know." Anne grabbed a wet washcloth and wiped her forehead. "She's suffering, that's all I know. There are small teeth marks down by her feet."

The priest saw the marks when Anne lifted the blanket. "I bet my favorite RC that has something to do with what is going on."

Anne was confused. "RC?"

Father Richard laughed. "I race remote control cars as a hobby."

"I didn't know that." Anne covered Devine back up.

"Why don't you go home? I'll take the night shift until Alex gets home. Where is she anyways?" Father Richard saw what time it was.

"She is having a much-needed relaxing evening," Anne informed him.

"Good, she needs that." Father Richard smiled at the thought. "Go on home. I'll watch over her."

***

Alex was laughing with Kameron and his friends. Kameron continued his story. "And then Alex is holding onto me so tight that I could hardly breathe. Here we are, on the snowmobile, only going thirty-five, and I have her arms wrapped around my waist, praying to God she makes it through the ride."

Alex returned the laugh. "Man was not supposed to go that fast on snow!" Alex got up from the table. "I need to use the bathroom."

"I'll come with you." Midnight got up.

Komptin lifted his head as Alex motioned for him to stay. Kameron watched Alex leave with Midnight to the bathroom. Scotty stretched a bit. "She's a character."

"Yes, she is," Kameron told him.

"You guys are good together," Scotty told Kameron something he already knew.

Kameron immediately averted that conversation. "Have you ever had anybody in your life?"

"Not like that. Not all lovey-dovey." Scotty turned to see a group of guys congregating in the corner with United Won patches on their arms.

"Never a special connection with a girl?" Kameron asked him. "And not like that."

Scotty laughed as Kameron knew exactly what he was thinking. "Nope."

The girls returned from the bathroom laughing. Midnight scanned the crowd. "I want to dance." She stared right at Scotty.

"No, no way, not happening, I do not dance, unless it's horizontally." Scotty turned his head away from Midnight.

"Okay, there's an image I can't get out of my head. If you don't get out and dance with me, I will tell everyone about..."

Scotty immediately got up. "Okay, okay." He playfully covered her mouth. "But you can only use that so many times."

"But it's a lot of times." She dragged him out to the dance floor.

Alex sat back down in her seat next to Kameron. "You choose good people to be around."

"Only the best for me." Kameron gave her a shy smile. He couldn't help but think Alex was feeling a bit anxious. It was as if she had something on her mind but was afraid to ask. He touched her hand, and she took a deep breath. "Do you want to dance?"

Alex nodded as she fought back tears. "I do, Kameron." He gently escorted her onto the dance floor as they started to dance. It didn't last long until some yelling started to rise from the corner.

"You piece of shit. That costume is disrespectful." A guy pushed the man dressed as Darius King zombie into the crowd of United Won.

"This is not good," Scotty said as Midnight joined him next to Kameron and Alex. "Look, it's Qwai."

278

"I don't think he's Qwai anymore." Kameron motioned his head for Alex to look.

Alex turned to Komptin who was in the overwatch position. There was definitely a Dark present here. "Oh, damn it, really, now?"

The United Won leader came up to the group. "It's Halloween; we're all dressing up as monsters; Darius King was a monster."

"He was killed by a blacks hating cop!" a kid yelled from the back with a young girl at his side.

"Is that Moses?" Kameron tried to peek over.

Alex confirmed it. "I saw him earlier. He said his dad knew he was here."

"Doubtful." Kameron got his phone to message Grossman that his son was here in Copper Top.

"Who's Moses?" Midnight asked Kameron.

"My old supervisor's son. They had some issues with him." Kameron was trying to get a hold of him but he wasn't answering.

"You really think that one is a Demon?" Alex stared down at him. "You sure?"

The United Won group was growing equally in size as the supporters for Darius King. They were taunting each other as vulgarity and insults were being thrown at each other. The tension was increasing and one bad move from either side would result in a violent demonstration of strength. The four of them gave each other the necessary fighting room as this situation had no other direction to go but from bad to worse.

Qwai strutted up to the United Won group. "I, like my fellow brothers and sisters, are not afraid of you. You can't stop black people. Your fear of our superiority will not keep us down!" The crowd started to cheer him on behind him.

Mack Righteous stepped up to Qwai. "Here's your superiority." He punched Qwai in the face sending him into the group.

"No Demon would drop like that," Alex said as she got into a ready position.

The crowds attacked each other as the street turned into one massive fight. The four of them started to defend themselves. Alex turned to Komptin, who was on edge, motioning him to stand down. She thought she heard her name when she turned around. Then she was met with a hit by the leader of the United Won as she fell into the table where Komptin was. "Ow, that was a Demon punch."

***

Merik sat in the back behind some bushes. The fight between the primates was escalating quickly. Salamor hovered above him, being careful not to be seen by the Sentry who had her hands full herself. "Which one is she?"

"That one; next to the angry one." Salamor pointed to the young girl who was getting concerned over the riot.

Prontor, the Demon who just punched Alex, was disguised as the leader of the United Won. He and the Demon-infested Qwai started this fight to escalate racial tensions in the town. The girl with the pure heart backed up from the fighting near the bushes. Merik was like a cat ready to pounce. All she had to do was come a little closer. "If this doesn't work, we'll grab Alex's boyfriend," he whispered to Salamor.

Salamor turned to Merik as his body got sick. He flashed his red, glowing eyes as he floated next to the girl's ear. "Step back." The pure of heart moved closer to Merik. He adjusted his body just before wrapping his arm around the girl's body and covering her mouth. They disappeared into the Dark without anybody knowing.

***

Komptin barked to gain Alex's attention. "I know, I know!" Alex went after the United Won leader but was battling other normal humans to get to him. She checked on Kameron and the others. They seemed to be holding their own.

The Demon turned to Qwai. "You're a dead man!"

"Bring it!" Qwai yelled back. The Darius King supporters pulled back on Qwai as anger filled his body.

The cops came in with riot gear. They announced they were coming in before attacking the crowd to try to calm it down. "We'll gas you if you don't halt your actions," the cop announced over the microphone. The crowd continued to fight, prompting the police to force it to stop.

Kameron yelled out. "I don't feel like getting shot today. Drop to your knees and put your hands behind your head." Alex and the others dropped to their knees as the cops put them in zip ties. The rest of the cops were battling both the United Won and Darius King supporters. Kameron checked on where Moses was. He saw him getting arrested by a white cop. From his viewpoint, the cop was rough with him, but within the rules of engagement.

Komptin was muzzled and did not put up a fight as they were all separated from each other. Kameron, Scotty, and Midnight were the first of them to let loose after they were verified as federal agents. The three of them walked up to Alex who was still tied with her hands behind her back.

"Do you know this one?" the cop asked Kameron.

"Well…" He started to play off.

Alex gave him a playful snarky face. "Kameron."

"Yeah, she was with us." Midnight was touching a bruise on her face.

"She really is," Kameron smirked.

The cop wasn't impressed since he had too much to do. "Fine, she's clear to go."

Alex stood up by herself and pulled apart the zip ties that bound her hands. The cop stood there flabbergasted. "How did you…?"

"Oh, they were faulty." Alex winked at him. "Can I have my dog?"

"Of course." The cop ordered the release of Komptin.

Midnight yawned. "Guys, I'm tired, really tired."

"Ditto." Scotty saw what time it was.

"I should get some sleep as well." Kameron was thinking about getting into the hotel bed.

"Well, I guess my night is going to be trying to go find my friend who punched me across the face." Alex felt her jaw. "It really hurt." Alex made eye contact with Kameron when she turned to him. Her heart skipped a beat as he smiled at her, but it was a shy smile as if he was wanting something more.

"Be careful." He put his hands into his coat pocket. Scotty and Midnight both at the same time turned around to leave after watching the two of them.

"I always am." She stood there for a second before turning back around to head out to find the Demons that were out tonight. Alex took a couple of steps before turning around. "Don't you leave town without saying goodbye."

"You have my word," Kameron promised as he crossed his heart with his finger.

"Because…if you leave, and don't say goodbye. I'll kick your ass." Alex smiled at him. She took a couple more steps before turning back around. "I mean it."

Kameron resisted the urge to run after her when she turned back around. "Hey, Alex."

She quickly turned back to him. "Yeah?" Excitement arose from her voice. This was a first for Alex; she saw Kameron try to think of something but couldn't. Normally, as stoic as he was, he was actually frustrated with himself.

Finally, something came out of his mouth. "See you tomorrow." Then he turned around to join Midnight and Scotty who were leaning on the car.

Scotty watched the Lite Sentry go off to her hunt. "How'd it go?"

The only thing that Kameron could say was, "Stupid, stupid… just stupid."

***

Gron came back from scouring his office for more Lite Sentry blood. They seemed to run out faster than expected. "Kids eat too much," he quietly said under his breath. A pure of heart is what they needed; obviously, there wasn't one in the F.O.R. complex. Even if there was, there was no way for him to know without Salamor, and where he was, who knew? Unfortunately, again, he had to rely on Merik to find someone, which was a gamble by itself. Although, he did know where the twins would be. Maybe there was more to him than Gron initially thought.

"They will need to feed soon." Misluna gazed down at the shackles in the middle of the floor. "Then their growing will begin."

"How long before they can open the conduit?" A tranquil excitement came from his voice.

Misluna grazed her fingers on the children's forehead. "It's hard to say, but when they look like they are about ten to twelve years old, they'll be ready."

"Really, nothing more detailed than that?" Gron was getting irritated.

"Now, now, honey. We can't fight in front of the kids," Misluna snickered. "Opening a Dark Conduit without Vandor has only been done twice before."

"When did that happen?" Gron watched as Merik's car pulled into the compound, and passed the guards.

"Once in the 1800s, and another in the 1980s." Misluna saw there was hope in Gron's eyes. "Don't get excited. The early one was opened by the killing of a Lite Angel by the betrayal of another."

"And all fallen angels were banished inside of the Dark or killed." Gron rubbed his head with disgust. "Any chance of that happening again?"

"Zero, unless the Conduit of Lite is killed."

Gron got annoyed. "And if we could do that, then we wouldn't need to open the conduit." "What about the one in the 80s?"

"It was a tiny fissure that some kids unlocked with a role-playing game. They found Dark Texts that opened a tiny fissure. It was enough for an Infiltrator to get through.

"Where are those texts?" Gron didn't understand why they just didn't use those.

"Somehow, the texts were burned. Whoever got the Dark Texts in their body like me, didn't make it through the night, along with the Infiltrator that came out of the tiny conduit," Misluna explained.

Gron got worried. "You're telling me that if you die, everything dies with you."

"I'm translating them to paper, but it takes time." Misluna heard Merik coming up the stairs with a girl.

Gron was in a jam. Misluna should be here translating them all to paper, but she was the closest one to get involved in the Council. He needed to come up with a plan to get her out of there while getting someone else in her spot.

"Well, there is another way for the Conduit to open from the other side, but it's impossible. Even if it worked, finding the location would be like finding a needle in a haystack," Misluna told him. "It would be easier to open it this way."

"The Dark was overpowering the Lite in the area," Misluna stated. "The problem is, with one side of hate there usually is a victim, so there isn't enough Dark to produce it. It would help the twins open a bigger portal if we had that much hate from two large groups."

Gron smiled. "I love it when I kill two people with one stone."

Merik came into the room holding a small, teenage black girl by the waist and mouth to prevent her from screaming. He shut the door behind him while he threw the girl on the ground. "There you go."

Gron studied the girl. "You're sure she is pure of heart?"

"Bet my life on it." Merik confidently stood his ground.

Gron approached the girl to stare into her eyes. "You are." He rubbed the cheek of the young girl. "You may be right. She reminds me of Anne."

The girl trembled in fear as she couldn't keep her eyes off of the shackles on the floor. "Please don't rape me."

Gron was taken aback. "Rape? Please, I wouldn't do that to you, dear." The leader of the

F.O.R. rubbed her cheek before putting his arm around her.

Misluna came to the other side of Gron. "You're far too important to us."

The girl had a sense of relief to her. "Then why did you bring me here?" Out of fear, she looked around the room. "There's a better way to get a nanny than kidnapping."

Gron laughed. "Nanny. No." He pushed her to the ground and removed his tie to use it as a gag. The girl was put in the shackles as she screamed to get away. "This may hurt." Misluna took the baby girl from the crib as Gron took the boy. They placed them on the floor as both babies had glowing red eyes. They showed their sharpened teeth as they crawled to the feet of the girl. "I was wrong. This is going to hurt a lot." Gron put his arm around Misluna as they watched a baby bite into the leg of the girl.

***

It was late when Anne finally left the church to head back home. All she wanted to do was jump into bed to get some much-needed sleep. The feeling in the town seemed dark, but it was probably Anne's imagination. The only thing she could account for that feeling was the fact she saw Devine so beat up. The poor angel was defeated emotionally as well. Anne truly felt sorry for her.

Anne was bit hungry, so she decided to stop for a snack. She pulled into the gas station, where there seemed to be only one other customer. The food wasn't the healthiest, but she managed to find a banana and a snack pack of peanut butter to spread on it. The plastic knife was a bit flimsy. Hopefully, it would do its job. Anne smiled at the attendant. "How are you?"

"Got stuck working. I wanted to go to that street dance downtown." The young kid was ringing up her food.

Anne could tell he was disappointed that he didn't get to go. "Well, things happen for a reason." She was waiting for the total when she caught someone coming out of the bathroom in the corner of her eye. She turned to see Shawn staring at her. Anne's heart stopped as she had trouble breathing.

"Why do you keep stalking me, Anne?" Shawn pleaded. "Can't you leave me at peace? I don't understand why you keep doing this to me."

Anne couldn't answer as she was looking for her inhaler that was in the car. The counter was the only source of balance. Once she regained her balance, she grabbed the bag and rushed to her car.

"Hey!" the clerk yelled at Anne. "That girl didn't pay for her stuff."

Merik walked up to the clerk. "I'll cover it." He paid the clerk as he watched Anne fumble around for something in the car. He waved to her and blew her a kiss before she left in her car.

***

Alex was with Komptin as they strolled through town, but this was a dead end. The streets were pretty much empty since the cops raided that fight.

It irritated Alex that she couldn't sense the Dark like she could before. She would have been better prepared to fight the Demon. They continued to walk to the edge of Copper Top to see the woods.

She nudged Komptin with her leg; the massive dog gazed up at her. "Anything out there?" He flashed his eyes to confirm there was Dark about. "Good." Alex and her hunting companion began the hunt. She decided to head toward the F.O.R. Compound. The woods were quiet, not an animal made a sound. That meant something Dark was nearby. There was some noise up ahead. Alex ducked down low in the thicket of the forest as Komptin joined the crawl as well. "Well, this is a first," Alex told Komptin. There were two Infiltrators stalking through the woods for their next victims. The hunters of the Dark were going to be able to get the drop on them for once. Alex motioned for Komptin to stay as she circled around them. "Let's have some fun."

She moved through the woods as if she was a part of the forest. The quickness and stealth reminded her of how Osiah used to run while she was in training. Alex made it to her position. At just the right moment, the attack would happen. The two Infiltrators were heading into the kill zone. The moment was coming for the attack.

The first one passed Alex without any knowledge of her presence, but the second one was the one she was going after. It came into range, and Alex signaled Komptin to attack. He came running out and morphed into his hunting state. He gave a massive roar as the Infiltrator turned to face the gargoyle in a fighting stance as it returned a growl. The two charged each other. Alex came out of the bushes shooting a Lite Beam at the Infiltrator charging Komptin. The combination of the force of it running towards Komptin with Alex's Lite Beam caused it to fly through the air. Komptin jumped to grab it by the head in mid-air. They crashed to the ground as Komptin flipped his head, tossing the Infiltrator to the forest floor. He followed up for the easy kill.

The first Infiltrator attacked Alex but was met with a perfectly timed uppercut to its chin. It crashed to the ground. Alex quickly followed up by grabbing its leg. Her kick to the kneecap broke the leg. "You're not getting away there, boy." The Infiltrator howled in pain as it knocked Alex over with its claw. The two of them got up to stare each other down. "You got a hurt leg there, buddy," she sarcastically pointed to it. The Infiltrator looked down at his limp leg and bit it off. "Okay, that's gross."

The Infiltrator got down on three legs and charged Alex. The Lite Sentry didn't move as her eyes and fists glowed. When it came close enough, she landed a punch on top of its head, driving it into the ground. She instantly dropped her knee on top of its head, driving it deeper into the dirt. There was a big rock next to her that she picked up with two hands. The force of her throwing it on top of the Infiltrator's head cracked bones. Alex made a face of revulsion. "Ewww."

Alex stood over the Infiltrator as it couldn't move with its head stuck underneath the rock.

Komptin joined Alex with a little blood dripping from his leg. "You okay?" she asked him. He happily gave a gargoyle bark as they both turned their attention to the Infiltrator flapping his body about with its head still stuck under the rock. "What do you say? Should we put him out of his misery?"

The two of them headed back to the church after disposing of the stuck Infiltrator. The way back after a successful hunt was always mind clearing. Entering the church, the two of them went straight into Alex's office to check on Devine. She was lying down and she seemed to be sleeping. Father Richard was reading the Bible next to her. "Hey, how's she doing?"

"No change. The only sound she is making is as if she is crying," Father Richard told her. "Are you home now?"

Alex shook her head. "No, there's something I need to do. But Komptin will stay behind and watch her." Komptin flashed his eyes up at Alex.

"I was going to stay anyways. I'm too tired to go home. I'm just going to go and crash in my office." Father Richard stretched. "You seem happy."

"Had a good night, considering." Alex kissed Komptin on the forehead before leaving the church. Her heart was racing more than any hunt she was on. There was actually sweat starting to form from nerves. This was going to be it; it was do or die. One way or another, this night was going to change everything.

Alex knocked three times on Kameron's hotel room door. Kameron took a minute to come to the door. When he opened it, both of them said nothing as they embraced each other. He brought her into his room– as together they shut the door behind them.

CHAPTER ELEVEN

Alex lay in bed with Kameron's arms around her from the back. She felt so secure and happy. The squeeze from his arms meant he was starting to wake up. Alex shifted her body to get closer to him. "You up?" Alex finished a text message reply to Anne telling her about last night. Anne had mentioned that she needed to talk to Alex.

"Yah," he muffled. "What time is it?"

"Six." She put her hands on top of his.

Kameron sighed.

Alex's eyes got wide. "What is it?"

"Ugh, I don't know how to tell you this?"

Alex's heart stopped as her nerves went skyrocketing. "What?"

"I have to go to the bathroom." Kameron dug his face into Alex's hair.

"So do I," she laughed.

"Well, how about we do that separately, okay?"

"Sounds good. Me first." She moved with supernatural speed to the bathroom while laughing.

After they both got up and got ready for the day, with a minor detour, of course, they both went down to the lobby to grab some breakfast. They were eating when Midnight joined them for breakfast. "Morning."

"Morning, join us." Alex pushed the chair with her feet.

"Didn't want to interrupt anything." Midnight smiled at Kameron.

Kameron tried to play it cool but failed miserably. "How was your night?"

"Went straight to bed." Midnight put a small amount of syrup on her egg. "I checked in at work. Apparently, we're still on special assignment. Weston is trying to get us transferred under the CIA so we can report directly under him."

"That will make things easier." Kameron studied his eggs. "These taste fake."

"Probably powder," Alex said as she grabbed the syrup. A mound of a mixture of biscuits, waffles, pancakes, sausage, and bacon sat in front of her. Some of the ham and eggs were barely hanging on the plate.

"Where's Scotty?" Kameron asked her.

Midnight shrugged her shoulders. "Getting crabs, probably." Midnight looked ahead. "And the dead rises."

Alex immediately looked up but then was a bit relieved to see Scotty coming to join them for breakfast. He had bags underneath his eyes. "You look horrible."

"I'm tired. Apparently, the occupants of the room next to me were watching adult movies most of the night." He stared at Kameron.

Kameron embarrassingly gazed over at Alex. "It was a good movie."

"I bet." Scotty sat down, grabbing a part of the waffle from Midnight's plate.

She slapped his hand with a sticky fork. "Hey, it's a free buffet."

Alex saw Anne pull up in the parking lot. "Looks like we're going to have one more."

The other three saw who was coming. Scotty was watching her come in. "What is she doing here?"

"She said there was something to tell me." Alex was already about a quarter of the way done with her breakfast. She grabbed one more bite before grabbing another chair for her to sit down in.

With a tad bit of earnestness, Anne sat down. "Good morning, everyone."

"Hey." Alex hugged Anne. "What's going on?"

"Such a rough night. I ran into Shawn last night." Anne took a sip of her coffee.

"Are you okay?" Alex checked her over for any bruises.

"I'm fine." Anne smiled at Alex for her concern.

"Who's Shawn?" Midnight asked.

Anne turned to the group in a very low tone. "A very, very evil man."

Kameron read the reaction on Anne's face. He could tell who Shawn was. If he was able to do anything about it, he would. The only person at the table to do something about this man was Alex. "I understand."

Anne told the table about her interaction with him. "I just don't know what to do."

Alex continued to eat her breakfast. "Oh, I'll take care of it. Trust me."

Alex's confidence made Anne feel a little bit better. "Thank you, sweetie." Anne continued to drink her coffee. "So, how was your guys' night?"

"Well, funny you should ask," Scotty started to say when he stopped. "Uh oh, someone is in trouble."

The table turned to see two cops holding a legal-sized envelope. Anne got a sickening feeling in her stomach. "I forgot to pay for that food. I can't believe I did that."

Midnight turned to Anne. "Don't say a word. Let us see if we can run interference."

The cops approached the table. "Anne McClure."

"Yes." Anne politely stood up.

"I'm Federal Agent Midnight Solis," she pulled out her credentials. "Ms. McClure is actively involved with an investigation we are currently running. She informed us of the mistake she made last night after a long shift at work. She was going to go and apologize to the manager today and also pay for the goods taken."

The cop studied the credentials. "That's nice. But the food taken was covered last night."

"Really, by whom?" Anne was confused.

The cop handed Anne the yellow envelope. "By the man who filed the restraining order against you."

"What?!" Anne opened the envelope. "Shawn filed a restraining order against me! This is bullshit!"

Alex smiled at hearing Anne swear. "Anne." She put her hand on her friend to try to calm her down. Anne took the cue and sat down while taking a puff from her inhaler.

"Have a nice day, ma'am." The cop smiled as he left.

His partner stayed behind. "Little piece of advice. He's a good man, stop playing with his emotions. I don't know what I would do if someone did that to me."

"You did what you had to do, you can leave." Scotty stood up. The two of them eyed each other as the cop left. "Stupid local cops act like they have something to prove."

"Scotty," Kameron restrained him. "They are just doing their jobs. Granted, that last comment was unnecessary. The last thing we need is to lose the cooperation of the local sheriff."

Anne read over the restraining order in complete shock. "I can't believe he did this."

Alex appeared to be in disbelief. "Really?" Then a text message came in from Father Richard that they needed to get back to the church as soon as possible.

**

All of them arrived at the church to see Father Carl greet them at the door. "What up, padre?" Alex went to high-five him on the way in.

He didn't accept. "You just can't act respectful in any way," he just shook his head at Alex.

Alex turned back to him. "Not worth it."

Father Richard met them downstairs as they came into the church. "Good morning, Alex. Did you get done what you wanted to do?"

Alex nodded. "Several times."

Kameron just closed his eyes as he knew everyone was staring at him.

"I have some news for you," Father Richard told Alex.

"Is Devine okay?" Alex looked up the stairs towards her office.

"No change, but I'm glad there are a lot of people here." Father Richard put his hand on Alex. "Carl, do you have a second?"

"No, No." Alex's eyes got big. "Please, no."

Father Richard nodded. "Yep. You knew this day was coming."

"Ugh, are we going to tell him everything?" Alex pointed to herself.

"No, slowly, you'll probably be the last of it," Father Richard told her.

Father Carl came in from outside. "I was just talking to Megan."

"Please have her watch the phones. Can you join me just outside Alex's office?" Father Richard asked him. "You all might as well come to, you all are part of the Council now."

Scotty laughed, "Me?"

Midnight joined in. "Him?" She pointed to Scotty, laughing.

They all met in the tiny hallway outside Alex's office. Father Carl and Father Richard were up front. "Cardinal Joe wanted to be here for this, but he had an emergency over at the Vatican he had to attend." Father Richard slowly opened the door.

Father Carl walked into the room to see the angel asleep on the floor in Alex's office. "Who is she?"

"She used to be the Guardian of the Conduit of Lite." Father Richard wiped the sweat off his head. "Only the best guard the Conduit."

Alex moved to Devine to wipe her forehead. "She still is the best."

298

Father Carl didn't understand. "You're telling me she is an actual angel." He looked all around the room. "And you all know this?"

"All but Megan; she isn't cleared by the Council." Father Richard told him.

"Thank God for small favors." Alex moved some of the bright neon purple hair away from Devine's eyes.

"Is she going to be okay?" Scotty studied the being of Lite, lying beaten on the floor.

"Unknown," Father Richard told them. "The Conduit of Lite hasn't been seen since the night of the festival."

Scotty got a phone call. "Excuse me, but I have to take this." He left in haste. "Talk to me, goose."

Midnight watched him leave when she turned back to the angel. "How do we save an angel?" She took a gander around the room for answers that no one could give.

Father Richard moved over to Father Carl. "I know you have questions. I will answer what I can as we drive to DC to meet up with Cardinal Joe upon his return."

"When do we leave?" Father Carl asked as he stared down at Devine.

"Today; sorry for the short notice." Father Richard dropped the news.

"No big deal, I'm always packed for just an occasion." Father Carl had a bit of excitement in his voice. "Just need to swing by my apartment for my bug out bag."

Scotty came back into the room. Midnight and Kameron both looked at him with concern. All he did was lift his phone, saying he had the information. Kameron leaned over to whisper in Alex's ear. "I'll be back in a minute." With a quick kiss, he left with his friends.

Alex turned to Kameron with a smile. Kameron's touch was so caring. It felt good to be back where they belonged. She saw that Anne was smiling at the two of them. "I know."

"I need to call Council Legal regarding this." Anne lifted her envelope.

"Good luck." Alex smiled at Anne before she left.

Alex turned back to Devine. "Hey, how you doing? I don't know if you can hear me, but I'm right here. Can you tell me what happened?"

For a slight moment, Devine seemed to answer her. She just cried for a bit before mouthing, "No." Then she seemed to fall back into her sleep.

***

Kameron met Scotty and Midnight outside the church. Scotty didn't seem like he was particularly comfortable. "What did you find out?"

Scotty peeked over Kameron's shoulder. "We should talk in the car." He got into the backseat of the car so Midnight and Kameron could take the front. They both turned to look at Scotty who was obviously upset.

"What's going on?" Midnight asked.

"No good deed goes unpunished, that's what." Scotty leaned forward a bit.

"What are you talking about?" Kameron asked.

300

Scotty just shook his head. "I just got my stupid ass fired, that's what happened."

"What?" Midnight was in complete shock. "Why?"

"For helping out a church, that's why." Scotty leaned back in the seat as he tilted his head back. "What the hell am I going to do now?"

"Why did they fire you?" Kameron had a feeling he already knew the answer.

"Well, apparently, I had an unauthorized filing of a citizen's travel within the continental United States that violated the Conus Travel Security Act. I'm so screwed." Scotty put his hand over his head.

Kameron turned to Midnight. "Do you think the F.O.R. had it cut off?"

"No shit." Scotty raised his voice. He lifted his head up at Kameron. "Sorry."

"It's okay," Kameron assured his friend. "I'd be upset in your shoes as well."

"I think this confirms it," Midnight told the group. "They are protecting her."

"It's weak," Kameron pointed out.

"I need to report to HQ to turn in my creds and service weapon." Scotty was still in complete shock. "This just sucks."

Midnight put her hand on his leg. "Maybe you could work for this Council?"

"They're the reason I got my ass canned. The minute I start helping a religion, ugh." He just continued to shake his head. "I have to leave today."

"Are you going to return?" Midnight's voice trembled a bit.

"I don't know. I just don't know what I'm going to do."

Kameron had a sense of guilt for getting his friend fired from fighting this war. "I'll come with you to the airport. I just need to see Alex before I go."

"Please don't say anything," Scotty begged.

"I won't." Kameron got out of the car to head back into the church. He opened the door to see Megan staring outside the office window at the car. She turned to him and gave a smile as if she knew what they were talking about before sitting down at her desk. Kameron took a step into the entryway before stopping himself. Then, he did something completely ill advised. He opened the door to the lobby office where Megan sat.

"Can I help you, Kameron?" She sat back in her chair drinking her coffee.

"Ever find the rosary that you lost?" Kameron studied her reaction.

Megan's face had a cocky confidence to it. "Must have dropped it." She leaned forward. "Father Carl, is there something I can help you with?"

Kameron turned to see Father Carl come into the room. "Yes, I'm going to go home to grab my bug-out bag. There is a package coming for me, should arrive tomorrow."

"I got you," Megan told him.

"Thanks, don't know what I'd do without you." Father Carl left to get ready for his trip.

She turned back to Kameron who was now dead faced as he stared at her. "Is there something you want to ask me?"

"Not right now." Kameron started to leave the lobby.

"Hey, Kameron," Megan yelled out to him.

"What?"

Megan yelled out from behind her desk. "Be careful with the door, there's more than one way to close it."

***

Gron watched the twins feed on the young lady on the floor. They had doubled in size since switching their diet to a pure of heart. Gron nudged her with his foot to see if she was still alive. There was a little life left to her, but not much. There wasn't much of a mess from the twins' feeding. They were pretty clean. Gron couldn't help but think about how people complained about kids being messy; he didn't think they were that bad.

Someone knocked on the door to the baby's room. "Come on in."

The Demon known as Tressex came in. The group he led knew him as Qwai. "My leader, you summoned me?" Behind him was the leader of the United Won, formally Mack Righteous.

"Prontor, Tressex." Gron picked up the kids and put them in their cribs. They fell instantly asleep. Gron put a blanket on them and motioned for the two Demons to be quiet. "How are things going?" he whispered.

"Better than expected," Tressex informed him softly. "The primates are eager to hate."

Prontor took a peek at the kids while in his United Won jacket. "We are ready whenever you give us your command."

"Do you have someone in mind?" Gron adjusted the blanket on the male child.

"I got mine all picked out, easy choice." Tressex shivered at the sight of the children.

"And I have the target." Prontor watched as Gron dipped his finger in the wound of the young lady on the floor. She winced from the pain as he did it.

Gron gently put the blood inside both babies' mouths. "Helps them sleep."

***

Anne was extremely annoyed with herself. She hated it when she got cravings like this. All morning long, she wanted a House Caesar Salad from Kate's. She tried to fight it, but it wasn't working. She was debating on having it delivered but she was out running errands. Her conversation with the Council lawyer didn't go well. There was nothing that they could do.

All the evidence Shawn put on her was already documented. Anne had a hard time describing the night she laid with Shawn. Had she known he was a Demon, she wouldn't have done it; she shouldn't have done it regardless. Goosebumps covered her body, remembering all the details about that night.

After she talked to the lawyer, Father Partinello called her. He was supportive and insisted the

Catholic Council was informed. He didn't say that they understood, all he said was that we are all human. Anne hated that answer.

Anne pulled into the parking lot of the club. She debated whether she should even go in. There was still no apology given to Kate for leaving her crying at the park. Maybe her craving was God telling Anne it was time to make amends. She sat there in the parking lot for a while debating if she should go in or not. Then her stomach growled; she was hungry. She wasn't going to stay and eat; she was going to get it to go. Inside, the restaurant was busy. Anne waved to Dan when she walked in. "Hi, Dan. How's the baby and Jessica?"

"They're great, thanks. How are you doing?" Dan grabbed the menu for Anne. "Just you, or will Alex be joining you?"

"Just getting a House Caesar to go." Anne smiled. "Thanks."

"Okay." He turned to the hostess. "I've got this covered."

"Okay, Dan." She marked the receipt. "You need to get home, remember?"

"I know, I know." Dan checked for his car keys. "I have to go get my parents at the airport. As if Jessica doesn't have enough stress."

Anne gave a small laugh. "I'll keep her in my prayers."

"She'll need it. I'll give you a call to come see Little D." Dan took off out the door.

Two older ladies were behind Anne whispering to each other about Anne. "Isn't that the girl from the church who used that poor boy?"

Anne could feel herself get frustrated.

"Typical religious woman, speaks one way, does another."

The women continued talking to each other. "Between hypocrites and race riots…"

Anne could barely hear it, but she heard it. It seemed this whole town was talking behind Anne's back, which really hurt. There was nothing more important to her than being a good person. Her reputation was being tarnished.

Anne's heart stopped as she saw Shawn come out from behind a booth. He approached the office, acting as if he was nervous. Anne was the one who used her inhaler. Shawn spoke loud enough for everyone in the lobby to hear. "Miss, I called the police. I have a restraining order against her, and she's violating it."

The hostess saw as the police walked in behind the gossiping women. They parted the way for the police to approach Anne. "Anne McClure?"

All Anne could do was acknowledge without speaking.

Shawn stepped back as if he was intimidated by Anne. "She was in the parking lot sitting there for twenty minutes before coming in. I'm pretty sure she was stalking me and then came in to see where I was."

"It's true," the older lady confirmed the story. "I was waiting in the parking lot for my friend to join me and everything he said happened."

"I was debating on what I wanted to eat," Anne defended herself.

"Anne McClure, place your hands behind your back. You are under arrest for violation of an established restraining order." The cop grabbed Anne's arm and twisted it around. "Don't resist. I'm already having a bad day."

Anne was so embarrassed as Shawn watched her get arrested. "I'll cooperate."

"I wish there was another way for you to learn, Anne." Shawn acted like he was starting to cry.

"He truly loved her. Such a sweet boy," the lady behind her said.

Anne's mouth dropped open with shock.

Then to make matters worse, Kate came out from the kitchen to see what was going on. "I'm the owner. What happened?"

"This is none of your concern." The other officer stepped in and put his hand on Kate.

With a stern voice, Kate came out saying, "Bullshit, it's not my concern. That's my daughter-in-law you have handcuffed."

Anne was shocked at the intensity in Kate's voice. It was as if a mother bear was protecting her cub. "It's okay."

"Anne, anything you want me to do?"

"Call Alex," Anne said as she was getting escorted out the door.

Kate nodded. She turned immediately around to Shawn. She took a poster off the wall to give to Shawn. The paper stated they have the right to refuse service to anyone. "Well, you are no longer allowed in my restaurant."

***

Alex sat in the waiting area with Kameron and Kate. She was sitting next to Komptin stroking his head. Kameron was being quiet. Alex was in fear that he was regretting getting back together. Were they back together?

Kameron leaned in. "Sorry, I'm not talking much, work stuff." His hand interlocked hers.

Alex had a sense of relief, but then confusion. Did she say that stuff out loud and not know? Is Kameron psychic? Then reality hit when Anne got buzzed out from behind the glass door. All of them stood up to greet her. "How are you doing?" Alex hugged Anne.

"It was the longest five hours of my life." Anne was still in shock. "I have never been so embarrassed. Thanks for bailing me out."

"That was Kate." Alex pointed to Kale's mom. "My dad is seeing what he can do on his end."

"Thanks." Anne wiped a tear from her eyes. "Do you have a second?" Anne gently grabbed Kate's hand as they both walked out of the police station.

Both Alex and Kameron decided to give them breathing room. "He's really got her wound up." Kameron checked his phone to see that Scotty had reported to his job for the last time.

"What's going on at work?" Alex let go of Kameron's hand to get some money for an Apollo from the vending machine.

"Manpower issues." Kameron put his phone in his pocket.

Alex opened the can and turned to lean on the machine. The two of them stared at each other. "Are we back together?" Alex flat out asked.

Kameron didn't know how to answer. "I thought so. I hope so. The time we spent apart was absolutely horrible for me."

"Me too," Alex admitted. "Kameron, I should tell you something though. Some stuff that happened while we were separated."

Kameron put his hand up. "Alex, really, what's in the past, should stay there. You were in a bad situation; I wasn't free from error. The only thing that matters is the second after this, and all the others that follow."

Alex smiled at her boyfriend standing before her. "I still love you."

"I never stopped." Kameron shyly smiled.

Komptin barked, wagging his tail. Alex laughed. "Of course, we love you too." The two of them knelt to give Komptin some much-needed love as Alex and Kameron embraced each other with their dog in the middle.

The couple came down the stairs to the police station to see Anne and Kate crying as they held each other. "Now, there is something I am glad to see." Alex watched them hug. They came down to Anne and Kate, who were wiping their tears. "See, all it took was Anne to get arrested."

"Funny, Alex." Anne blew her nose.

"I have to get back to the diner." Kate rubbed Anne's arm. "Are you going to be okay?"

Anne smiled at Kate before hugging her again. "I'm so sorry again. I love you."

"Love you, too, Anne." Kate tried not to cry again. "Dinner tomorrow."

"Yes," Anne eagerly agreed.

Kate checked her watch. "I have to get back to work. Take care. And this…." Kate points to Alex and Kameron. "Good."

"I could go for some coffee," Anne suggested. "Plus, I have to go get my car."

"We'll get it after some coffee." Alex went to get her car. "Wait here, I'll be back."

Kameron watched Alex walk away with Komptin. They both seemed to have a little spring in their step. "You okay, Anne?"

"Really, I'm fine. Just this whole Shawn thing." Anne turned her attention to Kameron. "What about you?"

"I'm happy," Kameron let her know.

"So is she," Anne pointed. "First time in quite a while."

The group found an outside table in the park to have coffee. The fall air was giving them notice that winter was coming. Even though it was cold, it was nice to sit outside while the group of friends talked while Komptin slept underneath the picnic table.

"How was the big house?" Alex started to tease Anne. "Let's see your prison tats."

"I wasn't the first of us to get arrested," Anne pointed out.

"Prison changed you, Anne," Alex teased her.

She took a sip of her coffee. "Who is watching over Devine?"

"Malkaroy came to check up on her when I got the call from Kate. He told me Celestial is still recovering from whatever drained her. The Lite has no idea what it was, but it was full of pure Dark to take that much from her." Alex looked over at a white cop in uniform playing with his family. The cop's partner, who was black, was talking to his partner's wife while her husband was playing with the kids. Alex recognized them from her walk. They were the ones who were fixing up Sarah's old house.

"She was beaten really bad." Anne turned to the sound of laughing kids. "It's nice to hear that with all that is going on."

"She started acting weird back when I found her in DC," Alex started to tell the story. "She was so distant from everyone."

"I saw her a couple of times. The only time she said more than a sentence or two is when I told her what Shawn did to me," Anne added to the story.

Alex thought about it for a while. "I actually caught her having sex." The two of them looked at Alex with shock. "Well, not the actual physical act but evidence pointing."

"Poor girl is probably so confused." Anne finished her coffee.

"Sounds like she was raped." Kameron just stared straight ahead at the cops.

"What?" Alex turned to him, in almost anger. "No. How could you say that?"

"Think about it, Alex. Take out the fact that it's Devine or an angel." Kameron's attention was focused on something.

311

Alex and Anne both locked eyes. They both had the realization that Kameron may be right.

"Is that Moses?" Kameron saw him marching towards the cop with determination. "What's he…"

Before Kameron could draw his pistol, Moses put a gun to the back of the head of the white cop and pulled the trigger. The crowd screamed as the body of the cop fell into his wife's arms. The cop's partner pulled out his gun at Moses, screaming commands.

Moses confidently and calmly dropped his weapon down in front of the black cop. "I did our people a favor. Wake up, brother." Moses dropped to his knees and gently laid on the ground. The cop got that cold look in his eyes as he was about to become judge, jury, and executioner.

"Stop, Federal Agent Dutcher, holster your weapon, officer." Kameron showed his credentials. "I saw it, I saw the whole thing. Don't. Don't do this."

"He killed my partner." The cop was fighting back his tears. "What kind of monster would do that in front of his family?" The cop's finger went into the trigger guard.

Alex and Anne were standing up. Her nerves shot up as Kameron approached the officer. "I can't tell what he's saying to him. I swear if he gets hurt." Alex's eyes flashed. She watched as Kameron calmed the officer down. He gently took control of the officer's weapon before having to handcuff his good friend's son for murder.

***

Salamor hid in the shadows of the forest. He remained hidden until the twins were able to open the portal. A feeling of gloom entered the air. The precursor to overpower the Balance with Dark has begun. Soon, he would be home.

CHAPTER TWELVE

"What the hell did you think you were doing?!" Alex kept on hitting Kameron over and over again. He tried to cover himself, but she kept on hitting him. For a second there, her body burst blue. "Ugh!" The hitting stopped, but she continued pacing back and forth.

"I'm sorry." Kameron was half laughing at Alex beating him.

"I was never so scared." Alex hit him one more time. After one more deep breath, Alex calmed her nerves. "Did you tell Grossman yet?"

"He's on his way down now with his wife, but the kid's life is over." Kameron rubbed his shoulder where he was shot.

Alex had a sense of guilt running through her. "I thought I got through to that kid."

"Not your fault." Kameron saw Midnight pulling into the parking lot of the church. "Can we go back on church property? I'd feel a lot safer."

Alex shot him a reading look. "Yes. Just don't do anything that stupid again."

"I promise." Kameron grabbed her hand. The two of them met with Midnight inside the church. "Hey, how are you doing?"

"I've been better." Midnight grabbed a candy bar from her pocket. "I don't know how Scotty is doing, though."

"What happened?" Alex turned around to Komptin who was starting to pace a bit.

Midnight turned to Kameron, where he gave a subtle shake of his head to prevent her from saying anything. This was not the time to announce that they checked on Megan to see if she was in San Diego when the arsonist was murdered. "He was relieved of his duties and no longer employed by the federal government."

Alex was shocked. "What? Why?"

"Long story, but it wasn't his fault," Midnight defended her good friend. That was the first time she'd actually acknowledged to herself that he was her best friend.

"Maybe I can talk to Father Richard about getting him a job on the Council," Alex genuinely offered. For some reason, she thought maybe she was responsible for Scotty losing his job. Alex saw that Komptin was still pacing back and forth. "You okay, boy?"

Malkaroy came from down the stairs. "She is awake."

Alex turned her attention to the top of the stairs. "If you will excuse me." Alex left to go check on her friend. "How is she?"

"I need to go." Malkaroy started to rub his chin. "Apparently, sanctuary in the church is not for everyone."

"She hit you?" Alex smirked a little. "Well, I'm glad she's got her strength back. What happened?"

"I told her I needed to check her wounds." A ringing started to come from Malkaroy's clothes. He started to search for it but could not find where it was coming from. Inside his pocket, he picked up his phone, confused about what to do next.

315

"May I?" Alex gently grabbed it from his hands as she gently opened the old flip phone.

Malkaroy cautiously put it to his ear after Alex motioned for him to put it to his ear. "Speak." Malkaroy listened for a bit before answering. "Bring Tristan. He needs to get a little training."

Alex watched as Malkaroy fumbled around with his phone. "Problems?"

"Opportunity." The big angel was like a kid trying to figure out what to do with his phone. "Scarlett is safe inside the church. The pastor is watching over her, helping her through some stuff. I need to get Tristan introduced to Infiltrators. Where better than here?"

Malkaroy's training method reminded Alex of Osiah. The former Dark Sentry trained Alex by injuring a couple of Infiltrators so she could learn their style of attacks. There were a couple of times she had some pretty painful lessons. It prepared her for her virgin hunt the night that Joseph died. She came out victorious, but at times, it felt like a night of failure.

The big angel was just about to walk straight into the room where Devine was staying. Alex grabbed his hand before he opened the door. "What are you doing?"

"Going in."

"Malkaroy, we should knock first. I don't think startling her is a good idea right now." Alex guided his hand back to his side. She gently knocked on the door. "Devine, it's Alex and Malkaroy."

"So what?" she sharply said on the other end of the door.

"Can we come in?" Alex waited a bit before Devine finally answered.

"If you must," she coldly snapped back.

The two of them cautiously entered the room after Alex slowly opened the door. Devine was up and staring out the window. Her wings seemed to have a droop to them instead of up with pride as usual. The misty halo was faint, but present. Her clothes were still torn with stained neon blue blood on them. The bruises on her body were evident. It was truly a heart-wrenching sight to see her in such a state.

Malkaroy started to approach her, but Alex stopped him. He got agitated but complied. "Devine, now that you are up, you need to come home."

Devine continued to stare out the window. "I do not have to do anything that you tell me."

"It would be wise; the Golden Pond would heal your wounds. We can ensure you are back to your old self; it would be like nothing happened," Malkaroy offered.

"It would be like nothing happened." She just kept looking outside.

Alex wasn't sure, but she thought a tear dropped from Devine. "Devine, we are trying to help you through this, no matter what happened." Alex turned to Malkaroy. "I think it would be best if you go," Alex stated. "I got this." Alex knew if she was raped, then having a male in the room might not be the best thing for Devine. Malkaroy was about to object, but Alex sternly eyed him and pointed to the door. Defeated, he started to leave even though he wanted to comfort his sister. "It's okay. I'll take care of her." He thanked Alex before leaving. Alex took a moment before slowly walking over to her desk to sit down.

Devine just watched her by moving her eyes before staring back out the window.

"We can open that up to get some fresh air in here," Alex offered. The angel didn't say anything; she just continued to have the thousand-yard stare. "Do you want to talk about it?"

"There is nothing to talk about. Apparently, all I need to do is go home like nothing happened." Devine clenched her fist but then let it go.

Alex was almost one hundred percent sure now that what Kameron said was true. She pulled out her phone to message Kameron that she wasn't able to leave the room. Kameron informed her that he would be going back to his hotel room. As Alex knew him, he was going to go for a run to relax and probably get some much-needed sleep. The Lite Sentry put her phone in her desk as she grabbed some candy from the drawer. "Want a chocolate?"

"No, what I want is to be left alone," Devine nipped back at her.

Alex was not in her comfort zone. If she was raped, Alex couldn't imagine what she was feeling. How could she be empathetic to her? Was she to do tough love? Tell her it will be okay? So much was going through her mind about what to do. It wasn't as if she could call a counselor in this particular situation.

It was half an hour before Devine made a move. She closed her eyes and shivered before morphing her battle armor into a pair of jogging pants and a sweatshirt with a jacket on. The angel seemed to pull the jacket tighter around her. She moved back to the bed to grab the blanket. Devine wrapped it around her before going into the corner of the room, where she sat on the floor.

Alex didn't say a word. She didn't want to push Devine to a point where she would run off. She was going to do what it took to get her surrogate sister through this. She messaged Father Richard asking if she could close the church to everyone, including Anne, Megan, and Father Carl. That she would explain everything but right now, he needed to trust her. With a bit of hesitation, he complied.

"I'm here for you, if you need me. It's just us. Komptin is downstairs to make sure we are not disturbed. I'm not going to leave you, Devine," Alex reassured. The shivering angel just sat in the corner of the room into the night.

***

The twins were walking about. The boy had flat, jet-black hair, while the girl had long black hair that went down to her back. Gron watched as they finished off what was left of the pure of heart. Misluna sat in the rocking chair watching them as if she was their nanny. Their hands started to produce a black mist.

"What are they doing?" Gron asked.

"Just honing their skills," Misluna told him. "By tomorrow night, they should be ready."

Gron got excited. "This is good. Should we name them?"

"It wouldn't hurt," Misluna told him.

Gron watched them practice with each other as they sat on the floor. "What will happen to them when they open the portal?"

"If all goes to plan, they will use all their Dark power to open the portal. Basically, then they are normal kids." Misluna checked the message on her phone. "I was just told the church is closed until further notice, but it won't be long."

"I wonder what is going on." Gron was studying the kids, trying to think of some names.

"Who knows? I think the Sentry's boyfriend is on to me about that little San Diego thing." Misluna watched the boy with no emotion take a stuffed animal and twist the head off. "How about Darcel for the boy?"

Gron watched him throw the parts of the bear away. "I like it."

"Can I kill Kameron?" Misluna had a low-level excitement in her voice.

"Not until after our Master returns; can't have the Sentry going on a revenge rampage." The little girl also had no emotion on her face. She was still just sitting there as she practiced her portal skills.

Both the twins had pale skin, not Alex pale, but pale as if there was no blood running through their bodies. They both turned to the window as if someone was watching them but then turned back to what they were doing. Gron got up to check out the window to see if there was anything out there. There was nothing that he could see.

Gron turned back to Misluna. "But we'll have to kill the other two as well."

"Shouldn't be that hard, although, the male that is with him, you know, the one who looks like James Franco, he hates religion with a passion." Misluna continued to rock in her chair in the corner of the room.

"He would make an easy Demon once we get more Infiltrators." Gron made sure the door was shut. "We are running dangerously low. I had to pull them all back here for the portal opening."

"It will be worth it," Misluna assured him he had made the right decision.

Gron smiled as the twins went back to practice opening the portal. "Ciera is the name of the other." The girl just moved her head to Gron slowly, with deadness in her eyes, before turning back to her training.

***

Salamor made sure Gron didn't see him from the shadows. The twins were progressing on schedule. The portal would be open to the Dark Conduit, where his master would come to the world to offset the Balance. The Dark Myst wouldn't have much time to sneak back into the Dark. There he would be home, inside the Dark. Hopefully, his Master will be here and not care about his whereabouts.

This world would soon see the power of the Dark. The primates who infested this planet would feed the Dark to open the conduit. The Lite will try to protect it, for they still have hopes for saving His vision. Many humans will suffer as the angels die to protect them. They will put up a valiant fight. They won't survive. Salamor could feel his body start to hurt again. There was something he needed to check on.

***

The night was calm, quiet. It was something Anne was enjoying. She was on the deck at an outside table sipping on a glass of red wine, writing her report for the Council. Anne understood the reasoning why the Council didn't want electronic records, but writing her reports on a computer would be much easier on a keyboard.

Out in the field was a doe licking on a salt block that her dad leaves out. She seemed too peaceful as her tongue was grazing against the graining texture. The stars were bright in the night. The weather was starting to let everyone know winter was on the horizon. Her hands were starting to get a bit cold, so it was time to go in.

As Anne gathered her belongings, she noticed the deer had taken off back into the field. Anne thought she saw a pair of glowing eyes for a moment, but it was just some brake lights off in the distance. She needed to get into the house because her imagination was starting to play with her. The fear of having a Demon come after her didn't really bother her. She knew her faith would be able to protect her one way or another.

Anne locked her report in the safe that was in her room. It was time that she took a shower to get a good night's sleep. Devine was on Anne's mind, that poor girl. If she was assaulted like Kameron had thought, then she had a long road of recovery ahead, if she even could. Anne was in the middle of washing when the power went out in the house. Luckily, the nightlight in the bathroom kicked on so she could finish rinsing off before getting out.

The towel was nearby as she grabbed it to dry off. Outside the bathroom, Anne heard a noise hitting glass. She peeked her head out of the bathroom into her room. The sound was like small pebbles hitting the window from the outside. Anne went to find her phone to call Alex, but it went straight to voicemail.

Anne calmed herself down. "It was probably nothing," she thought to herself. Anne walked down the black hallway. None of the lights were working. The vibration from her phone scared her as she gave a small scream. The number was unknown. She answered it anyways. "Hello."

"How's our kitten?" Shawn's voice said from the other end.

"Shawn. I swear, when Alex finds you," Anne started to scream.

Shawn laughed on the other end. "You should really dry off better before getting out of the shower." There were two sets of tapping on the windows. One from her bedroom, the other from what sounded like the kitchen table. Anne was frozen in fear. She hung up the phone. She didn't know what to do. The door to the garage was near, but she was only in a towel. The door to the basement was nearby. She made it down the stairs in total fear. There were some jogging pants and a sweatshirt she put on from out of the dryer.

She had to get to her car and get to the church to find Alex. The sound of the door to the basement shutting stopped Anne's heart. She closed her eyes and prayed, for she knew she would be with Kale soon. She felt sorry for not being able to say goodbye to Alex. More tapping on the basement windows pursued as her name was being called by Shawn and another Demon.

The door started to shake as someone tried to break into the room. Anne started to breathe heavily. She needed to get her inhaler, but it was in her room. Between the banging of the windows and the calling of her name, Anne was near cracking from the pressure. Then it all stopped. It was quiet.

Anne waited for what seemed like an eternity before she decided to slowly go upstairs. The basement door creaked as she peeked through the crack of the door. Anne crawled on her hands and knees to her bedroom to grab her inhaler and keys. She took a puff of her medicine before rushing to the garage door. She fumbled with the car door before getting into it. The car started as she opened the garage overhead door.

As the door was opening, she noticed two sets of feet appear. "Oh God, no." Anne had given up hope of escaping. The door opened all the way to see Arome and Omeila standing in their battle gear. Their weapons were in hand as they both stared at Anne. They dissipated their weapons as they kindly motioned for Anne to join them. Anne got out of the car and slowly approached them.

Arome was the first to speak. "You are safe, Pure of Heart."

"One is vanquished, the other ran like the coward he is." Omeila surveyed the land to make sure there was no other danger.

Anne could do nothing but hug Arome. The angel was confused as he looked down at the primate, squeezing him tightly. Omeila shrugged his shoulders as he didn't know what to tell his brother. He just motioned for his brother to return the hug. Arome returned the hug, giving Anne a much-needed sense of security.

"What are you doing here? Is Celestial safe?" Anne didn't want to let go of the angel.

Anne felt a female's hand on her head. "I am fine, my child." Celestial appeared behind her.

"Not that I don't appreciate it, but what are you doing here?" Anne asked the Conduit of Lite.

Celestial escorted Anne back into the house. "I have something I must do. Arome and Omeila will ensure your safety tonight."

"But what about…" Anne started to argue.

"Shhh…" Celestial put her finger to her mouth before putting her hand on top of Anne's head. "You need some sleep."

Anne instantly started to close her eyes. "Maybe just a couple of…" Anne drifted off to sleep. Arome and Omeila caught her and carefully carried a sleeping Anne to her bed. They gently pulled the covers up to her head. Anne adjusted her body in a comfortable position with a smile on her face as she went into her slumber.

"Protect her, nothing is to happen to her." Celestial smiled at the young girl.

"She will be safe, my lady," Arome assured her.

"We will convert to stars before she is put to any harm." Omeila stood firm in front of Anne.

Celestial smiled. "Thank you both." Her smile turned to one of worry. "There is somewhere I must be that you cannot follow."

***

Alex stepped out of the bathroom. She came into her office where Devine wasn't to be found. Her heart stopped. "Devine?" Alex ran downstairs and passed the congregation to see Devine staring at the cross in front of her. The feeling in the room felt as if Devine was at a pivotal junction. "Are you okay?"

"What do you know, primate?" Devine continued to stare ahead of her.

"I'm Primate now?" Alex stood in the hallway. "Devine, I can't imagine what you're feeling…"

Devine morphed into her battle gear to face Alex. "NO! You are incapable. How would you know?" Devine started shouting judgment towards her. "You willingly give yourself to any male you come across. At least prostitutes make silver for their actions."

Alex started to get upset and fight back tears. "Really? That's what you think of me?"

Devine approached Alex with hate and contempt. "How could you allow that to be done to you? How could you look at your reflection without repugnance, such a filthy and disgusting creature?"

Alex stood her ground, combating the hurt. "I have made my mistakes, but they are my mistakes." Alex tried to be sympathetic. "Devine, I willingly did that. I may have been going through hard times, but I still made those decisions. They weren't forced on me."

Devine formed her bo staff and smashed it against the floor. "Nothing gets forced on me. I am Devine, former Guardian to the Conduit of Lite." Her bo staff disappeared. She softly spoke, "I should have done something. I am Devine." The angel stopped for a second as she didn't know what to do. "This house is no longer for me."

"You're not leaving." Alex stood her ground.

"Get out of my way, Sentry," Devine warned her.

"Powers or not, you're not getting through me." Alex gritted her teeth. Devine punched Alex across the face, knocking her down on the ground. Blood dripped from Alex's face as she pulled out a tooth. She could barely stand from that hit. "You're going to have to kill me, Devine. But I'm not willingly going to let you go."

"You cannot stop me." Devine stood eye to eye with Alex.

Alex wiped her mouth of the blood. "No, though she may have something to say about it."

Devine turned around to see Celestial in front of the altar with Komptin in his Gargoyle state. The purple-haired angel moved inside the row of pews. "No, no. Please."

"Devine." Celestial slowly started down the aisle. "I am here."

Komptin moved to the other side of the pews to prevent her from leaving. Devine returned back to the center of the congregation room where Celestial stood. "No, He hates me. That is why that happened. I am a filthy and vile creature."

"No. He still loves you. If He could, He would take back what happened." Celestial had tears running down her face. "I wish I could have been there for you. I failed you."

Devine fell to the ground crying. Celestial ran to her angel who wrapped her arms around the Conduit of Lite. Alex slowly approached the two of them but stopped as Komptin joined Alex. Devine broke down, crying uncontrollably in Celestial's embrace. Celestial guided her onto the floor. Devine lay on the ground as Celestial held her in her arms. "They tied me down, there was nothing I could do. I fought, I resisted, I called out to my Father, but He could not help me." Devine held onto Celestial's arm, almost afraid to let it go as the Conduit of Lite comforted her.

Alex, herself, started to cry as Devine was telling what happened to her. She couldn't help but put her hand over her mouth to prevent herself from crying out loud.

Devine continued to tell the story in Celestial's arms in a deep cry. "They tore my clothing, laughing. Then, he laid on top of me and he...he—" Devine was trying to say something but was having difficulty saying it. "He told me to try to enjoy it."

Celestial pulled Devine closer to her as she continued to cry. Celestial was wiping the tears from herself when she peered over to the Lite Sentry. Alex was bleeding but had a mixture of sadness and anger to her as she watched such a pillar of strength break down. Celestial stroked her hair. "We will work this out together."

"I am afraid to go home," Devine pleaded to Celestial. "I do not want to be judged."

"We are going to go home." Celestial kissed the top of Devine's head. "No one will judge you. You have an entire family of angels who support you."

"And a Lite Sentry," Alex added. "No matter what."

Devine started to shiver as she was trying to get warm by Celestial. She faced Celestial with tears still streaming as she barely got out, "There is more."

**

Salamor was in the room watching the Devine cry in the arms of the Conduit of Lite. The Sentry's hunting partner turned his head in his direction as Salamor laid in the shadows. The pain throughout his body increased as he saw how much distress the purple-haired angel had gone through. He found himself sick as she described what was done to her just so the arrival of the twins would come to be. He had the compulsion to leave as if he shouldn't be there. All he needed to do was keep his distance

329

until the portal opened. Then he could escape this Hell.

CHAPTER THIRTEEN

Alex went for a walk to clear her mind. There was a lot that got dumped on her last night. The only thing she could think about was how bad she felt for Devine. That, and if she ever ran into either Merik or Salamor again, she would kill them on the spot. She thought Salamor had actually converted to the Lite. Apparently, she has a track of thinking one way, but in reality, it's the total opposite when dealing with people.

Komptin seemed tired; she guessed that last night took a toll on him as well. Devine was now in Heaven with Celestial, trying to heal. If Alex was honest, Devine will never completely heal from that experience. Poor Devine, she basically went through all that alone. The fear of what was going to come out of her on top of dealing with the rape.

Her walk took her to Kameron's hotel where she thought she would look to see if he was in the lobby area for breakfast. No shock, he was. The thing that caught her by surprise was that Grossman and his wife were there with him. This was a good thing, because that gave Alex a good opportunity.

"Alex." Kameron got up and gave her a kiss. He pulled up a chair for her to sit down.

"Nice to see you again." Alex felt uncomfortable with apologies. She saw Grossman and his wife look at each other, speaking the way married couples do without saying a word. "Look, I need to apologize to both of you. I was a bitch the last time I saw you."

"It's okay." Michal gave Alex some relief. "You were going through a lot."

His wife, Talia, smiled. "Of course, actually we should be thanking you."

"Oh." Alex grabbed some food off Kameron's plate, but it was nothing but fruit as he was eating oatmeal.

Talia continued as she started to eat breakfast. "I understand that you were instrumental in getting Michal his new job at the Synagogue. I've never seen him so happy."

"I'm glad it is working out. I'm sorry about your son." It just clicked why they were in Copper Top.

"I can't believe he did that." Michal fought back tears. "I should have been a better father or something."

"We," Talia emphasized, "did our best. In the end, it was his own decision to pull that trigger."

"Was it?" Michal turned to Alex for an answer to a question she had to answer once before.

Alex had Komptin see if he was a Demon or not. Unfortunately, Moses performed that action all on his own. "It was."

"He is being arraigned tomorrow afternoon before a judge. Rumor has it, that the prosecuting attorney is a real hard ass." Michal hadn't put the two together yet since Johnson was such a common name.

Alex winced from hearing that news. She didn't even think about who would be prosecuting the case. "Yeah, rumor has it he even sent his own son to juvey."

Kameron nearly choked on his oatmeal when he put the two together. "Sorry. Wrong hole." He pounded his chest to get it down.

One of the customers turned on the news to a conservative news station. They were talking about how Moses was a Darius King supporter. The influence over him was the fault of that organization.

"Turn that crap off," another customer yelled from the other side of the room. "The Darius King Supporters are a legitimate group for ensuring proper rights are given to the black minorities."

"Right," another person yelled. "Forget the fact that Darius King what a thug, dealing with drugs, illegal firearm possessions, assault, and didn't listen to the cops' commands. I would have shot his ass too."

The manager came into the lobby. "Hey, can we tone it down? I'm going to have to ask you to leave."

The tension in the room was filled as customers were talking to each other about everything that was going on. Alex couldn't help but feel like this was all the fault of the Dark. "It feels like a volcano that's ready to blow."

***

Gron was preparing to meet with Prontor and Tressex. Everything was falling into place. The scheduled events should promote enough fear and hatred to give the twins enough Dark to rip open the portal. Gron opened up a map of the city to find a location close enough to the protest but not too close to expose the portal. The problem with exposing themselves to the public was that it would drive humanity to the Lite. The Dark needed to influence humanity slowly, underneath the radar.

Misluna walked into the room with the twins. Darcel was in black pants with a dark maroon shirt with a black suit coat. Ciera was in a black dress with black tights. In her long, straight black hair was a dark maroon headband holding her hair back. The kids had no expression on their pale faces. "What do you think of the children's clothes for their big event?"

"Great," Gron said as he went back to his map.

"What are you doing?" Misluna gazed down at the desk.

"Debating something in my mind." Gron took a sip of his drink. Then as he was studying the map, two little fingers pointed to the Purch-Mart building. The old Purch-Mart building would be a good fit. The inside was big and mostly empty. The room had a back way out for the Infiltrators and Vandor to escape to the F.O.R. Compound. "And answered."

"I can't wait to see when our Master crosses over." Misluna got excited.

"You can't go." Gron kept his head down at the map but moved his cold eyes towards his mistress.

Misluna was disappointed. "Why not?"

"You need to keep your cover. Also, too dangerous. I can't afford to put you in danger." Gron folded up the map.

"Oh, you care about me?" Misluna got all embarrassed.

"Once you translate the texts, then I don't care what happens to you." Gron put the map in the desk.

Misluna quietly agreed. "I see. Okay." Misluna grabbed the children's hands. "Come on. Let's ensure you are ready for tomorrow." The three of them walked by Prontor and Tressex as they came into the room.

The twins stared down at the two Demons with no expression. Prontor shivered as the kids left. "I don't get how I'm a Demon, but those kids scare the shit out of me."

Gron sat down in his chair. "I have the location of the protest. Tressex will start the protest at the far end of the Purch-Mart parking lot just before dark. Get that crowd going."

"Done. It won't be hard." The Demon flashed his eyes.

Gron just went on with the plan. "Fine. Prontor, you know what you have to do. After you get shot, I'll have Provisionaries remove your body. You cannot be seen in this town again. So, you'll be on a mission to kill Kaylee and Scarlett. You don't stop until both of them are dead."

Prontor turned to Tressex. "Just don't shoot me in the head."

Tressex smiled. "We'll see."

"It's unknown how long we'll have the conduit open, so keep the riot going as long as possible." Gron, for the first time in quite a while, was going to be able to relax, for everything was in motion. There was no one who could stop him.

***

Alex wanted to switch off the radio on the way back to the church. All the news could talk about was the influence of the Darius King shooting. It was causing so much havoc. The local stores were putting up their support flags for either Darius King or the United Won. She was about to shut the radio off when something else caught her attention.

The radio announcer came on. "Hello, this is a special announcement from Copper Top news." Alex's gut turned as this could only be bad news. The announcer continued. "We are here with Deputy Mayor John Gresin regarding an established curfew." There was a moment of silence when the Deputy Mayor got online. "Hello, citizens of Copper Top. During this time of high tension, I just need to recognize that there are feelings on both sides of this subject matter. I am asking you to use your best judgment in the upcoming days."

The radio announcer didn't say a word, it was as if he was stunned. "That's it. No curfew in affect?"

"I'm not going to infringe martial law on the good citizens of Copper Top," the Deputy Gresin resumed. "In fact, I want to take this opportunity to call for a special out-of-cycle election for a permanent mayor. In this time, we need stability. Let people speak for leadership."

"Is this your candidacy announcement?" the radio announcer asked him.

"No, I will not be running because I need to focus on my family. I am openly supporting Roger Somberson. His leadership and policies will no doubt put Copper Top back into the great city I know it is."

The radio announcer again seemed shocked. "Ah, okay. So let me get this straight. No curfew, you're asking for a special out-of-cycle election, and you're actively supporting Roger Somberson for mayor?"

The Deputy Mayor concluded, "Yes, and so should all of you."

Alex shut the radio off. "What the hell? What is going on in this town?" Her car pulled into the church where Midnight and Kameron were in the parking lot. They both immediately stopped what they were talking about when Alex pulled up. "You're lucky I'm a trusting girl. Otherwise, I might get suspicious of you two."

"That and you could kill us both in five seconds flat," Midnight joked.

"Three seconds." Alex winked at her. "What's going on?"

Kameron put his hands in his pockets. "We haven't heard from Scotty."

"Maybe Father Richard could check on him. They are in DC for the Council Priest indoctrination."

"That might not be a bad idea," Midnight agreed. "But I don't know how accepting he would be to them."

Anne joined them after pulling into the parking lot. "Good morning." For the first time in quite a while, she seemed as if she was rested.

"Hey, how was your night?" Alex asked her.

"It was really stressful at first, but then I slept great." Anne grabbed the keys to the church from her purse. "Did you hear about the Deputy Mayor?"

"It's just ridiculous; like that doesn't have the Dark written all over it." Alex was looking around for Komptin who was sleeping in the morning sunshine.

"How is Devine?" Anne gazed up at the office window.

"It was an emotional night. We should talk before Megan gets here." Alex went to go into the church, but she stopped to pet Komptin before going in.

Midnight and Kameron gave each other a concerned look before they both started into the church. Anne gently grabbed Midnight by the arm. "I was wondering if you could do me a favor?"

***

Alex sat at her desk with her feet on top as she leaned back in the chair. Midnight was leaning in the doorway watching for Megan as Kameron was keeping an eye out from the window. Anne sat in a leather chair in complete shock. Alex didn't even drop the big news yet.

Anne didn't know what to say. "That poor girl."

"Oh, there's something else," Alex confirmed with Midnight and Kameron that the coast was clear. "She gave birth to twins. They are now in possession of the Dark."

All three of them turned to Alex with fear in their eyes. Kameron asked what everyone else was thinking. "What do you know about the twins?"

"All I know is they are evil. Salamor was very interested in ensuring they were born and safe." Alex still couldn't believe he was involved in this matter.

"Salamor." Anne didn't expect that. "Have you seen him lately?"

Alex nodded. "Last I saw him is when he told me where your friend's body was. He's a sneaky little devil. Finding him will be difficult." The Lite Sentry turned herself to Anne. "I suppose there is nothing in the history of the twins?"

"Nothing I was able to translate, but I didn't get to read them all before they were stolen. I can reach out to the historian in the other sanctions, but something like that would be known to the Council," Anne explained.

"Whatever the twins are for, it's not good." Kameron stared out the window.

"What's on your mind, Kameron? I know that look." Alex was halfway to her boyfriend. It felt good to her to use that title.

"Just trying to put it all together." Kameron turned around as he heard Komptin come into the room. The German shepherd came to his side to lie by the window's sun. Kameron bent over to scratch his ears.

Alex couldn't help but be happy that her two favorite guys were back in her life. "I guess Komptin and I could go out and try to find Salamor. That won't be easy. He'll talk to me one way or the other."

Kameron turned around. "There's some stuff from San Diego that I need to tie up."

Anne got up from the chair. "I have an appointment I need to get to. I'll probably be out until late this afternoon."

Midnight watched as Anne left the room. "I'm going to try to see if I can get a hold of Scotty."

Alex and Komptin were all that was left. There was some time before she and Komptin needed to go out and find Salamor. Since she didn't have her senses, she had to rely on Komptin to find him. The Dark Myst wasn't a fan of the morning sun so he would be hiding in the shadows somewhere. That meant he could be anywhere.

In the meantime, she thought she would see if there was something constructive, she could do around the church. Alex made sure all the doors were secure before going into the congregation to take a moment to relax. It was just quiet... peaceful, almost like it was the calm before the storm.

"Alexandria," Devine's voice came from behind.

Alex turned around. "Devine." The angel was cleaned up as if she had a complete reset to her former self. Alex got up to greet her but kept her distance. "How ya doing?"

"My body is healed. I, myself, am working on it." The angel turned away in shame but regained her composure.

"It'll come in time." Alex smiled at her.

"I have the support of my family," Devine informed her. "All my family." She looked at Alex with a shy smile. "I do not know what I would do without them."

Alex caught the message. "It's what family does. We're there for each other, no matter what."

"There is something I must do; it is a first for me." Devine adjusted her stance.

"What's that?"

Devine summoned the courage. "I must apologize to you. I should not have hit you. The things I said..."

"Devine, it's okay, really." Alex tried to ease the burden off her.

"No. It is not. I played back what I said to you and cannot get that image of the hurt in your face from my mind." Devine was humble in her words.

Alex knew that lying wouldn't help the situation. "It stung what you said, I'm not going to lie."

"It is not what I think of you," Devine promised her.

"There was some truth to what you said." Alex got up to join her. "You just said it a little bluntly."

Devine put her head down. "May I still call you my sister?"

Alex put her hand on her shoulder. "This is what it means to be sisters." The two hugged each other tightly.

***

Midnight came up behind Anne. "Now, adjust your stance, putting your right behind your left for stability. There isn't much of a kick, but it will help keep it steady."

Anne moved her leg behind her. "Like this?"

"Are you comfortable?"

"It feels right."

"Good. Now put your left hand under your right. Only put your finger on the trigger when you're ready to shoot. Otherwise, just keep it on the side of the weapon." Midnight watched as she helped Anne.

Anne took a deep breath. "Okay, now what?"

"There's your target." Midnight put one of Alex's empty Apollo cans from the garbage on the way out onto a stump. "A common habit is to close one eye, but it is better to keep them both open."

"Okay." Anne was concentrating hard.

"Take a breath and squeeze the trigger on the exhale." Midnight stepped back from Anne.

Anne squeezed the trigger and hit the can on the first bullet. "I did it." Her excited voice made Midnight laugh.

"Good." Midnight got a message from Kameron to have her meet him at the hotel. "I have to go. I left extra ammo. Have fun."

"Thanks again." Anne watched as she left in her car. Anne stayed behind to practice. The shooting felt good for Anne, almost as if she had some control in her life. She knew that bullets couldn't kill any Demon, but perhaps slow them down a bit. Anne continued to shoot when Devine dropped out of the sky. Anne turned around. "You scared me."

"Not my intention. I was out looking for Salamor with the Sentry when I heard the noises." Devine turned to see the can with a bunch of holes in it. "What are you doing?"

***

Kameron sat in the hotel room debating if he should or shouldn't go through with his plan. He needed proof that Megan was part of F.O.R., not only that, but that she had something to do with the murder in San Diego of the arsonist that killed Lana. He was studying his notes, but there were no hard facts to put it all together.

Midnight knocked on the door to Kameron's hotel room. "Hey."

"Where were you?" Kameron went back to his notes that he had scattered over the small hotel desk.

"I had to help Anne with something. What are you doing?" Midnight picked up some of the notes Kameron was making.

"It was just announced on the Darius King website that they are going to hold a rally tonight to show support for Moses. In turn, United Won is going to hold a rally as well." Kameron pointed out.

343

"I talked to Alex's dad, the prosecuting attorney. He said that the cops are on standby, but no police presence will be authorized by the Deputy Mayor."

"This is just wrong." Midnight sat on the desk chair, dumbfounded. "What do you want to do?"

"I think we should scout the F.O.R. Compound. Just keep that between us." Kameron kept quiet. "If they are involved with this, this is the night they will be active."

"Shouldn't this be Alex's move?"

Kameron had this all plotted out. "No, she will be needed at the rally. She can handle what the F.O.R. will be doing."

"You want to break into the compound. We don't have a warrant; if we get caught, we're going to jail." Midnight knew that look on Kameron. He has already made up his mind.

"Midnight, if we get caught, we're going to get killed," Kameron corrected her.

She banged her head against the wall. "Okay, what do we need to get?"

***

Finding Salamor was a dead end. Not even Komptin could pick up the trail. Devine had searched north and east of Copper Top; Alex took south and west. There was no sign of him. Actually, there was no sign of anything Dark related. The sun was announcing to Copper Top that it was about to set. Alex had some time to continue the hunt when Komptin alerted to something. Alex flashed her eyes as she heard the cracking of the trees in the woods. It was too quiet to be anything but supernatural. Alex motioned for Komptin to go around while she came from behind. The target made itself known.

The Sentry got into a position of attack. Komptin growled enough for the target to break his concentration. Alex took advantage of this and ignited her fist, forming a knife. She wrapped him in a headlock and put her hand on the small of his back. "And like that, you're dead."

Tristan put up his hands in defeat. "I'm never going to get this."

Malkaroy came out of the woods, joined by Komptin. "Where did you go wrong?"

"I got distracted by the low growl. If I hear that, that means they see me…and there are probably more." Tristan was getting hard on himself.

"Hey, don't be hard on yourself. All my lessons were painful ones; some of them I shouldn't have lived through." Alex turned to Malkaroy. "When did you get in?"

"Last night." The big angel lifted his Sentry off the ground. "Weston is trying to find out all he can on the Darius King rally. He thinks it is being influenced by the Dark. Just looking for proof."

"Well, the United Won leader is definitely a Demon." She rubbed her jaw. "If Qwai is a Demon, then we have an issue on our hands. Why would Roger be playing both sides?"

"That's a lot of hate," Tristan came out of nowhere as he picked the leaves off his gray sweater.

"What did you say?" Alex and Malkaroy both turned to him.

"That's a lot of hate," he repeated. Tristan realized that everyone was staring at him. "What?"

Alex was about to talk, but she was stopped by Malkaroy. "Alexandria, we are being watched."

The Lite Sentry just moved her eyes around to see where it may be coming from. Alex called for Komptin. "I'm going to dinner with Kameron. Then going to hunt, maybe; we'll meet up later."

"Sounds good." Tristan waved. "Why did she leave?"

"She has something to do." Malkaroy turned to his Sentry. "Tell me what you sense."

Tristan closed his eyes. "It's Dark, whatever it is. Nothing like I've felt before." He opened his eyes again. "Are we under attack?"

"Not by anything that can physically hurt us, but just as dangerous," Malkaroy told him. "Do not listen to its lies. If you hear thoughts that seem like they are not your own, push them away." Malkaroy moved next to his Sentry as if protecting him. "Show yourself, Salamor."

Salamor floated from the shadows of the forest. "You will find nothing in these woods." The Dark Myst approached the new Sentry. "This one has much doubt. You will disappoint him. He knows you think he's not the hunter the female is."

The angel turned to Tristan, who seemed to be listening to Salamor. "Tristan."

"I'm not weak. I can be a strong hunter. Why do you look at me like a failure?"

346

Malkaroy turned to Tristan. "I do not think you are a failure. Resist his thoughts." Malkaroy grabbed his Sentry by the arms. "Those thoughts are not yours."

"Oh, they're his. You just choose to ignore the signs. He just wants your approval." Salamor got close to the Sentry.

Tristan looked to Malkaroy. "I'm sorry I'm not the hunter she is."

Alex's voice came from behind Salamor. "Not yet, but it'll come." Alex shot a Lite Beam at Salamor, pushing him against a tree. He screamed in pain from being pressed. Alex stopped and grabbed him by the throat with her glowing hands. She twisted around, slamming him into the ground. Then, she picked him up, just to throw him into the ground again. "That was for Devine, you piece of shit." Salamor tried to break free of the Sentry's grip but failed to do so. "Now, I'm going to kill you."

"I will tell you about the twins," Salamor hissed.

Alex squeezed harder. "What are they for?"

"The Dark Conduit," Salamor barely hissed out.

Malkaroy and Alex had fear in their eyes. Alex turned back to Salamor. "You told me Vandor couldn't come back for seventeen years, if only the proper ceremony took place."

Salamor still tried to get her glowing hand away from his throat. "You let me live, and I will tell you."

Alex was ready to kill him right there until Malkaroy stopped her. "Alexandria, we need to know."

347

Alex growled at the Dark Myst. "Just this once. You are going to die the next time I see you. Now speak!"

Salamor moved himself from the earth floor. "The Dark Texts contained a way that had never been done to open the Dark Conduit. It was said to be impossible to achieve, so it was never attempted."

"How?" Malkaroy asked.

"The Dark needed an angel of the Lite," Salamor whispered as if someone could hear.

"Devine," both Malkaroy and Alex said together.

Alex thought about it. "The twins must be needed to open the conduit. Oh, this is bad. Really bad."

Malkaroy turned to the sky. "I must tell Celestial. She will be needed when they try to open it. She can counteract the Dark."

"The Conduit will require a massive amount of Dark energy for the twins to open it," Salamor hissed. "Once open, I will be going home."

"That's your involvement, so you could go home!" Alex ignited her fists and flashed her eyes.

"Sentry, I did not put this plan into motion. I'm just taking advantage of it." Salamor growled back with glowing red eyes.

"Alex," Tristan said, holding her arm. "You promised. You would be no better than him if you went back on your word."

Alex screamed as she turned around in anger. Then she faced Salamor again. "You are truly a piece of work, you know that." She was able to calm down a bit. "Can we close it?"

348

Salamor started to sink into the ground. "That was not part of the deal."

***

Kameron and Midnight checked over each other's gear. They both were wearing black tactical gear. They inventoried the gear. They were wearing tight vests with a few necessary items that wouldn't make any noise. They weren't going for battle; they were going to recon. Midnight put her blonde hair into a tight bun. The only weapons they were taking were a small 9mm with extra clips.

"I really should call Alex." Then Kameron's phone rang. "Hey, I was just thinking about…yeah, come on up."

The door knocked, and Midnight answered it. "Hey, Alex. Kam, I'll be in my room."

Alex looked over at his get-up. "What are you doing?"

"Just a little recon." Kameron noticed Alex seemed a little distracted. "You okay?"

"I need to get to the rally. I don't have much time. If the F.O.R. is influencing both sides, we may have a serious issue on our hands."

"You do what you gotta do. I'm hoping to get answers for you as well," Kameron told her. The two of them couldn't keep their eyes off each other. "Come back to me."

"You as well." The two kissed each other before she left for the rallies.

Kameron met up with Midnight in her room as she was writing on a piece of paper. "What are you doing?"

"Last goodbyes and wishes. I have that funny feeling again." Midnight put it on the table for whoever was to find it. "I guess we should..." Then there was a knock on the door. "Maybe it's Alex." Midnight opened the door to Scotty dressed in all-black tactical gear.

"HQ took my phone, the number, and all my contacts. I couldn't call anyone because I didn't have your numbers." Scotty walked into Midnight's room. "I'm going to take those F.O.R. bastards down. They took my job." It finally clicked that Midnight and Kameron were in the same gear. "Why are you guys in tac gear?" The only answer he needed was Midnight giving him a hug.

***

Gron was debating on what to wear tonight. It did not seem like a night that he should be wearing a suit. He got a message from Prontor and Tressex that everything was falling into place. The sun was setting, and that meant that the time was coming to head out to the portal opening. There was a knock on the door. "Come," Gron commanded.

Merik walked into the room. "You wanted to see me."

"Yes, I don't know how you did it, but tonight wasn't going to happen without your help. I have another job for you. I need the Sentry distracted."

Gron put on a pair of pants with hiking boots. He put on a sweater that had a mixture of black and maroon on it.

"What do you want me to do?" Merik grabbed a drink from Gron's bar.

Gron decided it was time to send Merik to his death. He was done with his arrogant attitude. This way, he could kill two birds with one stone. "Go harass, Anne. She'll call Alex to save her. Then you can kill them both." Merik smiled as he didn't even finish his drink. He put it on the bar without a coaster before he left with a smile on his face. Gron rolled his eyes as he threw the whole glass away and cleaned up the water ring on his bar.

Misluna came in with the twins. "The kids are ready." They were in their garments and had expressionless faces. Their eyes had a slight red glow on their pale faces. "I wish I could be able to see you, but mommy has work to do." She knelt to fix their clothes. "You be good for daddy."

Gron finished his drink. "Get them into the car. It's time to get our master back."

CHAPTER FOURTEEN

Alex made it to the rally, where Qwai was soon to take the stage. There were a lot of people in the old parking lot of Purch-Mart. The supporters of Darius King were talking amongst each other. A couple of times, as Alex walked through the crowd, she was getting called racial slurs. She got pushed once; luckily, she had a good hold on Komptin before he tore them to pieces.

Poor Komptin. He was not enjoying this. The air was tense with hostility. What shocked Alex the most was that there were no cops around. Alex was getting nervous as one guy seemed to beeline right for her. She didn't know if he was a Demon or not, but she wasn't going down without a fight.

"Komptin," the man said as he knelt to pet him.

"You look familiar." Alex was relieved that Komptin knew him.

The man looked around the crowd. "I'm Weston. I saw your battle at the F.O.R. Headquarters in DC."

"Oh, that's right." Alex had to talk loudly from the music being played during the rally. "No offense, but aren't you an F.O.R. member?" Alex boldly asked him.

Weston laughed. "No, CIA. You actually work with my father."

Alex thought about it. "I do? Who?"

"Malkaroy," Weston told her as he got bumped by another member of the crowd.

"You're Malkaroy's son?" Alex somewhat laughed. "I wasn't expecting that. Does he know you're here?"

"Yah, I'm secretly working for the Council. I'm helping to watch over Scarlett while Dad trains his Sentry." Weston was eyeing the area with worry. "I'm just here to see how much of the Dark is influencing this mess."

The crowd started screaming as Qwai took the stage. "My guess is… a lot." Alex looked down at Komptin, who flashed his eyes when the activists took the stage. It was just confirmed to Alex that Qwai was in fact a Demon.

"A few hours ago, your fellow black brother, a brother who was just defending himself from a tool of white supremacy, was arraigned for murder." The crowd started to chant "Free Moses." Qawi was leading them on some more. "This racist judicial system failed to take account of the years of oppression this young man suffered." The crowd started to get rowdy.

Alex leaned into Weston. "There's something I need to look for."

"Be careful." Weston was watching the crowd become more belligerent.

***

Kameron, Midnight, and Scotty were outside the F.O.R. Compound, sitting in their blacked-out car. "Look, there's a bunch of movement going on inside the compound." They were watching a bunch of people get into cars.

353

"They must be heading off to that rally you told me about." Scotty was double-checking his equipment.

"The gates are opening." Kameron watched as the first car started to leave.

"It's a damn caravan." Midnight couldn't believe all the cars that were leaving.

Kameron was watching car after car leave. "That's a lot. That might be a benefit for us. I don't think there are many left in there."

"Hey, look," Scotty came in between them. "There's two cars breaking off going separate directions."

Midnight saw the cars veer off in the opposite direction. "Where does that lead?"

"Follow them, I'm staying here." Kameron got out of the car.

"What are you nuts?" Scotty tried to tell him.

"I need to find out what she knows." Kameron shut the door.

Midnight got mad. "She might be in there."

"But there might be a clue. I have to find something that links Megan to the F.O.R." Kameron started to head towards the compound.

The two of them watched as Kameron headed toward the compound. Scotty jumped in the driver's seat of the car. "I'm starting to get that feeling again."

Midnight turned to him. "You got crabs."

Scotty turned to smirk at her. "Cute." He started the car to catch up to the other two that ventured off.

Kameron was hiding in the woods in front of the main gate. There were two guards standing outside the gate shack talking. This was going to be a lot harder than Kameron thought. The only choice was to sneak around the perimeter to find a way in. In the far corner, he found a spot where the ground had eroded from the rain. This was going to be the only way in. The only way for him to squeeze through would be to cut some of the fence. The wire cutters in his pocket were able to cut enough for him to get through.

Part of the fence caught his pocket dropping his phone just perfectly on the rock to crack the screen. "Damn it." The phone was damaged to the point it was now a paperweight. Kameron tried to call Midnight and Scotty on his radio, but they were out of range. "I'm starting to get a bad feeling." He stared at the sky while on his back.

***

Alex stared at the Purch-Mart building. If the portal was going to open, it would have to be close to hate for the twins to open it. That building would hide all that was going on behind the scenes. The crowd started to get more restless as Alex was getting pushed about. Out of the corner of her eye, she saw a group of cars come in and park. In the third car, Roger came out with what Alex would assume were the twins. He held their hands as he escorted them into the building.

"What do you think you're doing here, white trash?" A woman grabbed Alex. It took everything not to throw her to the ground. There was no need to start a full-out riot. She managed to get away without initiating a bigger scene. Alex saw Roger deploy people around the building to protect them while they performed the ceremony.

She made it to the outskirts of the crowd. To her surprise, there was a familiar face. "Celestial." Alex bowed. "What are you doing here?"

"There is an overabundance of Dark present. I am trying to maintain the Balance the best I can." Celestial closed her eyes to have a slight glow underneath. "I will try to provide enough but if they open the Dark Conduit, there is no stopping Vandor from coming."

Arome and Omeila weren't in their battle gear but in clothes to blend in with the crowd. They seemed to be on edge. "This situation will turn at any moment," Arome said, on edge along with his brother.

Omeila surveyed the crowd. "These people are going to be their own demise."

Arome watched another crowd wearing United Won gear start to walk down the street. "That did not take long."

Alex changed direction to see what they were talking about. This crowd was being led by the Demon that punched her in the jaw earlier. "I suppose they aren't here to exchange cookie recipes."

* * *

"Ever wonder how we got involved in all this?" Scotty asked Midnight as they were driving with no lights. They were just far enough behind to make sure they weren't seen by the cars they were following.

Midnight saw a sign for a local power transfer station. "Why would they be going here?"

Scotty took a peek at the sign as they drove by. "They're a power-hungry organization."

Midnight turned to Scotty. "That was really, really bad." Midnight pointed to a spot to hide the car. "We better walk from here." The car was hidden from the road and couldn't be seen. Scotty and Midnight checked over each other's gear. "Ready?"

"I think we got the better end of the deal. All we have is two cars to worry about." They snuck by some other little buildings to come to the power station. "There's a guard, but he's not moving," Scotty pointed out.

Midnight and Scotty split up so they could approach the guard shack from both ends. They signaled each other for Midnight to open the door to the shack while Scotty covered. The guard's body dropped with two bullet holes in his chest. "Shit." Midnight pulled her weapon out. "This is bad."

Scotty also had his pistol out. "Do we go in?"

Midnight led the way to enter the power station through the guard shack. This particular station wasn't the main building that supplied the power; that was located in another town. This was just a junction for the power to be distributed so it wouldn't need to be manned all that much. They saw that the door was broken to get into the building. Midnight covered Scotty as he entered the building.

They walked down the hall, checking the doors to make sure there was no one in there. There was a set of maintenance doors at the end of the hallway that must have held the power junction equipment. Scotty and Midnight both entered the room to see a girl over-watching some people set what it looked like a bomb.

Scotty motioned to shoot them, but Midnight said no. The group set the bomb and passed the two agents hiding behind some equipment. They waited to ensure they left before approaching the bomb. "I suppose you don't know how to disarm this?"

Midnight was looking over the device. "Not a clue, but there isn't much time."

Scotty was covering Midnight as she studied the bomb. "We need to get out of here. This is way above what we're trained for."

"There's not that much wiring. We should be able to disarm it quite…" Then the doors slammed open, and shots were fired. A bullet grazed Midnight's arm as she ducked behind a piece of machinery.

Scotty returned fire but found himself hiding behind the bomb. "This is a stupid place for cover." He kept on dodging bullets. He returned fire but had to conserve them because he only had one extra clip. "Can you get a clear shot to get me out of here?"

"No, I was going to ask you the same thing?" Midnight picked hot shrapnel out from the back of her neck. "Hey Scotty, I'm starting to think that bad feeling is going to come true."

"Oh, no. We're good. What could possibly go wrong?" he sarcastically stated. "On three, go for that exit."

"What?" Midnight yelled at him.

"Just do it. Three!" Scotty got as much cover as he could to provide Midnight a way out. A bullet entered his arm, then immediately into his side. He dropped to the ground. He made sure Midnight made it to the door, but she got hit in the leg; it caused her to crash into the wall.

Scotty hugged the floor while shooting to prevent the others from following. They made it to the exit. The people shooting must have been looking over the bomb to make sure there was no damage. This gave them much-needed time to come up with a plan of escape.

Scotty tried to lift Midnight up as she limped down the hallway. "I don't think I'm going to be able to finish my needlepoint." They saw some shadows on the door glass. Scotty shot at them to hold them back. His gun was empty as he reloaded his last clip.

"How many you got left?" Midnight checked her weapon.

"Eight." Scotty shot and hit one of the guys as they opened the door. "Six."

"Leave me. I can cover you while you go tell Kameron what's going on." Midnight was now starting to lose a little color in her skin. "I'm bleeding bad."

"Yah, well, I think I'm a couple of quarts low myself." Scotty shot a couple more times down the hall. "I'm out." They made it into an office door that was left open.

Midnight peeked out the window. "There's a company van out there." They looked around the office. "Thank God," they said as they both saw a key box on the wall marked "Vehicles." They both laughed at their fortune. Midnight picked up a chair and busted the window to climb out. She gave Scotty her weapon. "Hold them off. I'll start the van."

Scotty agreed as he helped Midnight get over the window. He immediately turned around, and he shoved her out the window as he got shot again in the upper shoulder when the F.O.R. came into the room. His body dropped below the window as the group approached him. He went to shoot himself in the head, but the gun clicked. "Of course," he said in between breaths.

A girl came up to Scotty. "You killed two of my people." She stuck her finger in Scotty's wounds. Her glowing red eyes told Scotty she was a Demon. "Where's your partner?"

Scotty was huffing and puffing. "Dead."

"Nice try. No body." The Demon stood, staring down at him. "Bring him."

Midnight fell into an emergency egress window from a basement room. The window was open, as she managed to get into it. She heard Scotty get hit with something before he went silent. She managed to limp out of the basement room and back upstairs. It was quiet, there was no sign of life, just bodies lying on the ground. Midnight made it out the side door just as she saw Scotty get thrown into the trunk of a car. The cars sped off in a hurry as Midnight cried as she was limping to get away. The power plant blew up, causing a force of air to throw Midnight onto the ground. Pieces of metal and wood engulfed her body as she laid down face first on the ground with the burning building behind her.

***

"Darius King isn't a role model!" Mack Righteous started to scream. "He was nothing but a thug, like all you people!"

"What do you mean, 'you people'?" Qwai yelled back through the microphone. "You fear us because we are superior, we are chosen, we excel at everything better than you." The crowd started to cheer for Qawi.

"The only thing you are better at is becoming cheap real estate!" The United Won leader screamed. "And defending a criminal who shot a cop right in front of his family."

"He is a victim. Oppression was his only crime– for being black in a white man's world." The crowd started to chant louder for Qwai.

Alex turned to the Conduit of Lite, who was trembling. "Celestial, what's wrong?"

Her nose started leaking golden blood. "I cannot do it. There is too much hate; the Dark is feeding it. The Balance is altering."

The Darius King crowd parted like the Red Sea for the United Won leader to get a clear view of

Qawi. "We are the only ones who are protecting a peaceful way of life. You want the destruction of our culture."

"You have no culture!" Qwai yelled. "You are a soulless shell of God's creature." The crowd started to chant, "Won is Done."

The United Won crowd started to retaliate with screaming of their own. The two leaders both looked at each other and gave each other a nod. Alex's nerves shot up. The crowds screamed at each other with nothing holding them back.

Celestial opened her eyes. "I have failed."

The United Won leader got onto his microphone. "We will do what we must to protect our land."

Qwai fed the fear, "Are you threatening us? You will not like the result!"

The United Won leader yelled back with support from his crowd. "Let's see the best you got." Then the power suddenly went out, sending the crowd into a panic, and Qawi pulled out a gun. He shot the United Won leader twice in the chest. A couple of people screamed while the crowds charged each other.

Alex was fending off whoever was attacking. They were purely in a defensive posture. Celestial dropped to the ground as Omeila and Arome protected her the best they could. "Do not kill any of them," Celestial pleaded.

"Easier said than done." Alex blocked a punch from one of them. She grabbed the arm, twisting, and tossed him into others. The others started to beat the man she threw. Alex went to stop them, but Celestial stopped Alex.

"You must stop the Conduit from being opened." Celestial had worry written on her face. "Arome and Omeila will protect me."

Alex debated if she should leave her or not, but then realized she was right. She started off to get inside the building. As she fought through the crowd, she ran into Weston, who was trying to get away from some attackers.

Malkaroy made it to him to get the attackers off his son. "There you go."

Weston stood up and wiped the blood off his lip. "Thanks, Dad. Where's Tristan?"

"He is holding his own." Malkaroy pointed like a proud parent.

Alex approached the two of them. "We need to get into that building." She pointed to the Purch-Mart. "I'm pretty sure those are Demons protecting the perimeter."

"We will distract them so you can get in. Tristan!" Malkaroy yelled. "Time to go to work." He motioned to him the plan. Tristan punched someone who was attacking before heading to the building.

***

Anne was sitting in the living room reading when the power went out. She calmly put her bookmark into the book before closing it. The house was dark, with only the night sky to light inside it. Her phone was on the kitchen table. This was her only source of artificial light. The house was quiet as some scratching on the windows caught Anne's attention.

"Anne," Shawn's voice whispered from the house.

Anne stopped as she started to shake when she put herself next to the wall. There was a small knock on the window, but when Anne looked, there was nothing there. She slowly walked backward but knocked over the lamp. She jumped when the glass from the bulb broke. Another knock on a different window startled Anne. "Anne, I see you."

"Shawn!" Anne cried out in fear. "Leave me alone!"

Anne grabbed her keys from the key rack to get to the garage. Her hands were shaking so badly that she kept locking and unlocking the door. The door in the back of the garage door broke open. Anne turned around to see Shawn with glowing red eyes. "How can I leave you alone when we are meant to be together?"

"Shawn, please, stop!" Anne got into her car. She pushed the garage door opener and took off, scraping the roof of her car on the garage door. Anne was driving as she tried to catch her breath. A sudden hit from behind with a car with no headlights jolted the car. Anne turned to see a pair of glowing eyes in the driver's seat. It could only be Shawn chasing her. Anne sped up the car, leaving Shawn a bit behind. A moment of relief was welcome but didn't last long when Anne's tire blew. The car veered over to the side of the road. Anne fumbled about to get out of the car when a pair of headlights pulled over behind Anne.

A man came out of his pickup truck. "You okay, young lady?"

"Yes, I just got a flat and…" Anne screamed when Shawn came behind the man and snapped his neck. Anne took off running through the woods, stumbling about. The only direction she knew where she was, was the park. Shawn was in the woods calling out her name as she ran. She tripped over a log; she crashed to the ground, scraping the top of her head.

Shawn confidently strutted up to her with his eyes glowing. "Anne."

"Why are you doing this?" Anne pleaded.

"Because I love you, Anne," Shawn snickered. He flashed his eyes as his mouth grinned with his sharpened teeth.

Anne screamed. She got up and started running towards the park. She was crying and running out of energy when she approached the clearing from the woods. Shawn was behind her. He called to Anne in a calm, eerie tone. Anne went back to running but she had no energy left. This was it. Ironically, she ended up by the cliff overlooking the lake.

"Oh, Anne. You picked our spot," Shawn said as he approached her. Anne turned around to look down at the cliff. "Don't jump, Anne. I just don't know what I would do without you," Shawn sarcastically told her.

Anne turned around as she started to hyperventilate. She tried to grab her inhaler, but she was so nervous it dropped out of her hand. She dropped on her hands and knees as she tried to catch her breath.

Shawn slowly walked up to her and grabbed the inhaler. "You won't need this much longer." He crushed it with his hands.

Anne's gasping for air was getting worse. The pathetic attempt of Anne crawling to get away caused the Demon to laugh. Shawn turned around to watch her head slowly towards the parking lot. "Pathetic Anne, do you really think you can get away?"

Anne's heavy breathing stopped as she stood up. "No. I just needed to be over here." Anne pulled out a gun from a concealed holster.

"A gun, really?" Shawn approached. Anne shot at him, hitting him in the shoulder. "You shot me!" Shawn's eyes were a steady red glow. "I was going kill you quick, but now, I think I'm going to savor every last minute of this." Anne shot again and then several times. "Stop doing that, that hurts!" Shawn screamed.

Anne took a deep breath. "I only have one bullet left."

Shawn stopped as the bullet holes leaked black blood. "I'll give you a choice, use it on yourself or suffer for a very, very long time."

Anne stared at the gun. She started to raise it towards her head but turned it towards Shawn. With a single pull of the trigger, she shot Shawn in between the legs. Shawn grabbed his crotch and screamed in pain. "Oh, you bitch!" Shawn stumbled to get up. "You are going to pay for that."

Anne put the gun back in her holster. She stared at Shawn, ready for whatever he was going to do. "I'm ready, Shawn, are you?"

"Stop calling me Shawn. I am Merik! And there is no way you can kill me!" He flashed his eyes.

"No, there isn't, but she can." Anne pointed behind Shawn.

Shawn turned around to see Devine fly up from the cliff. She stabbed him with her Lite Bo before decapitating him with the sharpened end. The body dropped to melt into the ground. Devine landed next to the spot where Shawn's head rolled. She spit on it with loathing before it liquefied into the ground. She stared for a second before turning to the Pure of Heart. "Are you hurt?"

"I'm fine, how are you doing?" Anne took in a deep breath.

Devine turned to the spot where the demon melted. "He took something from us, something we will never forget."

"Yes, he did." Anne took a deep breath. "But it's how we live on, that is what matters."

"I will be fine, so will you, but if there is ever a time we may need to talk about it," Devine put her hand on Anne's shoulder, "we have each other."

***

Kameron hid behind a small workshed. He was trying to find a way to get into the main building. There was no doubt cameras were everywhere. It wasn't if he was going to get caught, it was a matter of when. He just hoped he could find something in the main office that connected Megan to the F.O.R. and possibly that murder. There were lights illuminating the main building area. He was going to get caught if he rushed over. Then, it must have been an act of God, the power went out.

There was a garbage can near the building that he could jump onto. From there, it looked like access to a room. The window was open, so that could be his way in. He circled around the building to come to the dumpster from the side. He quietly closed the lid. It made more noise than he wanted. He hid in the shadows when a guard turned around the opposite way, starting a conversation on the phone. This was the opportunity he needed to take advantage of.

Kameron hopped on top of the dumpster and pulled himself up onto the roof. He slowly snuck up to the window. It was big enough for him to get through. He stubbed his toe on something metal on the floor. "Son of a…" he tried to keep quiet as he hopped to the other side of the room. "What was that?" He took out his flashlight and saw a set of iron shackles on the floor in between two cribs. A sudden chill rushed down his spine. "How did I get myself involved in this?" he questioned himself as he opened the door just enough to peek down the hallway.

The passage had battery-powered lights giving little illumination. They seemed to be shining on the paintings in the hallway. Kameron saw the first painting of the man who had Alex by the throat while inside that church. That was Vandor; hopefully, they could stop him from returning. The other painting was a picture of a handsome man. The man had blackened eyes while sitting proud.

The next picture was that of Roger Somberson in his signature black suit and red shirt.

Kameron got to the top of the stairs when he saw a young man approaching in a F.O.R. uniform. There was no way Kameron wasn't going to get caught. When the kid saw him, he went to scream, but Kameron covered his mouth. He wrapped his arm around the kid's neck. "Stop fighting it, kid," he whispered to him. The kid fought for a bit but then lost the battle. Kameron dragged the kid to the middle of the hallway, near the wall to get him out of sight. The kid would wake up with a massive headache, but at least he would wake up.

He cautiously treaded down the stairs, where he found Roger's office. There were others coming so he rushed to get in there. He silently closed the door to the office before making it over to the desk. The desk had nothing to pinpoint Megan as F.O.R. Things were not going to plan, as he was waiting for the computer to boot up. A map of the town, then a circle around the old Purch-Mart building was marking the portal location.

He tried to log onto the computer, but it was password protected. He took out a USB from his pocket able to try to bypass the security. He rebooted the machine so the USB would initiate its decryption program. He saw an empty shelf that seemed to once hold empty orbs. He couldn't help but think this was the location of the orb Alex had told him about. The one that Gron had taken while in Brazil.

The computer was broken into, and Kameron was searching for anything that could connect

Megan to the F.O.R. "Come on, come on." He was eagerly reading anything he could find. "I need something to show you are connected to the F.O.R."

"How about just asking?" Megan was in the doorway with multiple guards pointing guns at him.

Kameron instinctively went for his gun, but he knew for a fact that he wouldn't make it alive. "Would you have told me the truth?"

"Oh, hell no, but it would have been fun watching you squirm as you asked." Megan had blood all over her hands and clothes. "You would not believe the kind of night I was having." Megan dug her hand into her pockets and pulled out a bloody tactical hat.

Kameron couldn't see if it was Scotty's or Midnight's. Very slowly, he got up from behind the desk. He looked out the window at the fire in the direction of where his friends went. "What now?"

"I let you go." Megan threw him her keys to a car. "Here you go. It's parked out front, facing the main gate. It's the dark maroon one."

Kameron was confused. "What?"

"Kameron, you're in a no-win situation here. No matter what, we will win." Megan fixed herself a drink. "I either get my master back or you lose Alex. Win, win." Megan took a sip of her drink. "What are you going to do?"

"Why would I lose Alex?" Kameron asked her as he showed her one of the keys.

"The other one." She pointed it out to him. "The only way to close the portal is to close it from the other side with the blood of a living Sentry. So, either Vandor comes through and closes it from this side, or Alex takes a little trip." Megan walked by him to gently pat him on his butt. "You better get moving there, sport." Kameron ran out of the room.

"You let him go?" The guard was confused by Megan's actions.

Megan sat down on the couch. "The portal is already opening, there's no way he'll make it on time."

Kameron was driving down the road as fast as possible when he saw Devine and Anne walking down the road. He slammed on the brakes and opened the door. "Do you have your phone on you?"

Anne shook her head. "No, why?"

"I need to get to Alex, ASAP!"

Devine looked confused as she turned to Anne.

"As soon as possible," Anne answered the question.

Devine turned to Anne. "Head to the church, you will be safe there."

Anne went to the car, but before Kameron let her in, he hugged her. "Don't ever change who you are."

Anne returned the hug. "Kameron, what…"

But before he could answer, he went to Devine. "Let's go." She grabbed him and took to the sky.

***

Alex was fighting a Demon alongside Malkaroy. They couldn't use their Lite in public, so they were letting most of the Demons live. Komptin was at Celestial's side, helping Omeila and Arome keep her safe. People tend to stay away from police dogs, in fear of getting bit.

Tristan was doing pretty well, considering… though Alex and Malkaroy were keeping most the Demons on them. Alex grabbed one of the Demons from behind and bent him backward. She jerked her body, breaking his neck. All the humans were distracted, so Malkaroy concealed Alex as she stabbed the Demon with her Lite. "We need to get inside."

"I got you covered," Tristan said with blood dripping from his mouth. Malkaroy turned to his Sentry with worry. "Seriously, it's okay." He elbowed a guy in the face who was charging him.

Alex and Malkaroy went into the empty building only to see the portal opening. The twins had black mist coming from their hands. The fissure in the corner was growing. Roger turned to see Alex. He sighed before stepping in between her and the twins. He started to walk toward her with his glowing red fists and eyes. He was joined by four other Demons and three Infiltrators.

Malkaroy ignited his whip and sword while Alex ignited her fists. "Who do you want?" he asked the Lite Sentry.

"Roger. It's time that he and I have a little talk." Alex matched the direction of the Dark Sentry.

Roger pointed to the Demons and Infiltrators to attack Malkaroy. Roger moved away from the battle so Alex and him could be alone. Alex attempted to shoot the twins with her Lite Beam, but Roger shot one of his at Alex sliding her across the floor. Alex slowly got up to see Roger studying the fissure.

"I thought you would have more Infiltrators here than three." Alex brushed off her clothes. "You must be running low."

"That will change in a bit." Roger wasn't attacking Alex. He was just ensuring the twins weren't interrupted. "Shall we?" He motioned for her to come to him.

"We shall." Alex swung at Roger, but he blocked it and punched Alex in the face. It didn't knock her out, so she countered with a kick. He blocked it with his leg. Alex punched him in the nose and then took his arm and flipped him over her body. She tried to punch his face while on the ground, but he moved out of the way.

She generated another Lite Beam to shoot at the twins, but Roger tackled her to prevent her from hitting them. Alex flipped him off of her but then was tackled by an Infiltrator. Alex ripped the creature's jaw apart and jabbed a Lite Spear into the black beast's chest. As it disappeared, Gron punched Alex in the face. He picked her up and threw her across the floor. She dug the knife into the floor to prevent her from moving any farther.

Roger attacked Alex, but she blocked the punch and countered with an uppercut that sent Roger flying backward. He crashed onto the floor, then shook off the cobwebs. All that mattered was the portal, so he got back up for an attack. Alex punched him back down on the ground. Alex picked him up and then slammed him on the ground again. "Oh, this feels good."

Roger started laughing. "Do you feel that? Oh, wait, I'm sorry. I forgot– you can't." Roger checked his bloodied mouth.

"Funny." Alex got her stance ready for the next attack. "What am I supposed to feel?"

"It's too late!" Roger started laughing as he was coughing on his blood.

Alex looked up to see the twins put their dark hands on both sides of the fissure. They pulled it apart to see the conduit open. Black fog spots started to come out of the Dark Conduit. Alex stood there in shock. "Oh shit." One of the black spots seemed to have an outline red around it.

Roger got up from the ground. "Those are all Infiltrators. And that is just the beginning." Roger ran over to the Conduit, awaiting his master's return.

Malkaroy finished killing the last of the Demons when he joined Alex by her side. Tristan was beaten up badly but was able to join Weston from outside. "The whole town is on fire. It's just one big riot out there!" Weston told her.

"Arome and Omeila took the Conduit of Lite home. It was too much for her," Tristan told Malkaroy. Komptin came into the building in his gargoyle state with a massive roar.

"How do we close it?" Alex was in shock as all those black clumps of mist poured into the room. Most of them didn't stick around; they left the building. Alex just saw her hunts become more violent with each one coming out of the portal.

Malkaroy shrugged his shoulders. "I bet he knows." He pointed to Salamor, who was hiding in the far corner. Out of the Dark Conduit came an angel. His eyes were completely black with black fog as wings. Instead of a halo, it looked as if he had black mist in the shape of horns. Malkaroy could not believe his eyes. "Azrael."

"Who?" Alex watched as Malkaroy started to approach him. She couldn't help but notice the look of concern on his face.

The Dark Angel surveyed the area. "Send the Caliginous to secure the area for Vandor," he yelled into the Conduit. The man in dark angelic armor was studying the surroundings when he saw Malkaroy appear. "Long time."

"Yes." Malkaroy approached Azrael. "It is nice to see you again."

"Is it?" Azrael formed an axe in one hand and a sword in the other.

"You can still make this right." Malkaroy adjusted his stance.

Azrael took a moment. "The primates need to be ruled over. They are far from equals to us." The Dark Angel noticed the two Sentries in the room. "I will kill all of them."

The massive Lite Angel saw the determination in his former brother's eyes. "I know of one that you will find difficult."

"Do not speak of her name. She is no threat!" Azrael got into a battle stance.

"I was not talking about her." Malkaroy flared his sword and whip. "Shall we?"

Azrael nodded.

Malkaroy flung his whip, catching the hand of Azrael with the axe on it. The Lite Angel went to swing with his sword, but Azrael pushed it out of the way and blocked it with his. He was able to push the angel off balance with the sword. He took that moment to cut off the arm holding the whip. Malkaroy screamed as the Lite Whip disappeared, and his arm fell to the floor. The Dark Angel took his axe and decapitated Malkaroy. His head rolled before disappearing with the rest of his body.

Tristan and Weston screamed at the sight of Malkaroy's body dropping. Tristan ran towards the Dark Conduit to attack the angel. Azrael actually had a look of concern in his eyes as he pointed to the Lite Sentry. "Stop him!"

A group of Demons attacked the Lite Sentry. Alex and Komptin tried to stop his suicide vengeance. Then out from the Conduit, a Caliginous appeared to secure the room. The twins were still holding onto the fissure with difficulty. Alex and Komptin both stopped in their tracks. Komptin jumped at the Caliginous as he easily threw the gargoyle dog across the building. While that was happening, Alex shot a Lite Beam at the Demons, who were about to kill Tristan. She was able to pull him out of the way before it was too late.

Weston helped grab him. "He's barely alive." He started to pull him out of the building. "Are you coming? We need to retreat!"

"We need to close this portal!" Alex saw Salamor reaching the portal. "Salamor!"

Gron turned to the Dark Myst. "You're alive!"

Azrael gazed up at Salamor. "Our Master will deal with you when he comes."

Alex didn't know what to do. She noticed the twins were having a hard time holding the Conduit open. Alex turned around to see Celestial with Arome and Omeila in full battle gear. Her eyes were glowing gold, along with her hands. "I cannot prevent this much longer."

Arome and Omeila went after Azrael. He met them in front of the Conduit in full battle.

The Caliginous saw that Celestial was unguarded. He started to charge towards the Conduit of Lite. Komptin started to limp towards the battle but was attacked by Demons that came into the building. Alex stood in front of the Caliginous. "This is going to hurt." The Caliginous went to strike Alex but was stopped by Devine holding her Lite Bo. Alex immediately backpedaled to Celestial to guard her. Alex was the only form of defense for her.

Salamor stopped as he was going to enter the Conduit but then shouted out, "Sentry." She looked up as he pointed to the other Sentry being dragged out of the building. He then pointed to the Conduit.

Alex understood what he meant. She turned to the nearest Demon to her. "Hey, you piece of shit. You hit like a little…" She was smacked across the face onto the ground. Alex got back up. "You call that a hit. That was like…" She got hit again on the ground. "Ow." Alex was annoyed. "Will you just hit me in the nose?" The Demon complied as it hit her in the nose to start bleeding. "Thank you." Now Alex went on the offensive to destroy the Demon.

Devine was battling the Caliginous. She couldn't help but think of Ariel. Soon she will be joining her sister. This Caliginous was powerful as he continued to battle the angel. She got punched on the ground, and blood dripped from her body. The Caliginous grabbed the angel's body and threw it against the concrete wall. Her body left a small indentation before she fell to the cement ground. Komptin was battling against the Demons on the other side of the building so there was no way for him to rip open the chest to expose its heart.

Salamor was just about to enter the Conduit when he saw Devine get thrown against the wall. A sickening feeling came over his body again as he watched her crash onto the floor. He moved towards the Conduit again but stopped. He watched her get punched while on the ground by the Caliginous. Alexandria shot a Lite Beam at the Caliginous to distract it enough for Devine to roll out of the way. He hesitated before skipping over the Conduit and rushed over to the angel. "Devine."

"Are you not going home? Do you come to watch me join my sister?" Devine barely stood. She made eye contact with the purple eyes of the Myst. He spoke to her inside of her mind. "You will die."

"Perhaps someday, you will forgive me for what I did to you." Salamor turned to the Caliginous. He rushed to the monster and entered the monster's body. The Caliginous used its own monstrous hands to rip open its own chest to expose its heart. "Now, I cannot hold this."

Devine stood up and threw her Lite Bo into the heart of the Caliginous. The mixture of the

Caliginous and Salamor's voices melded as they screamed as it disappeared into the ground. There was a faint purple glitter that floated in front of Devine.

Celestial couldn't hold it any longer as she dropped to the ground. Alex turned to Celestial and gave her a hug. "I appreciate everything you did for me."

"Alexandria." Celestial could barely talk. "What are you going to do?"

Alex let go of her as she wanted to say goodbye to Komptin, but he was clear across the building fighting Demons. She shed a tear as there was no way for her to say goodbye to him. Alex turned to the Dark Conduit and cracked her neck. She was about to run until she heard, "ALEX!" Kameron came running into the building.

"Kameron." Alex hugged him. "There's something I have to do."

Kameron gently grabbed her face. "I know. I just wanted to tell you that I love you."

"I love you, too." Alex started to cry.

Kameron pointed to her chest. "You hold me in here. You got it. You'll get through this." Kameron kissed her.

Alex turned when Celestial yelled for her, "Alexandria." She pointed to the Conduit.

Roger yelled out with victory in his voice, "He's coming!"

Alex locked eyes with Kameron. "I have to go." Alex turned around and started to run to the Conduit.

"Will you marry me?" Kameron yelled out.

Alex stopped and turned around. "Yes, now you hold onto that," she said with tears running down her face. With a final big breath, she started to run towards the Conduit.

"I will." Kameron pulled out his gun and shot Alex in the leg. She crashed to the ground holding her leg in pain.

Vandor fully appeared from the Dark Conduit. "If you think you are worried about me, you have no idea what is coming." That was directly for Alex and Celestial as they stared at Vandor.

Kameron ran toward Alex; he knelt to her. "You just made me the happiest man. I love you!" He kissed her again before rubbing her blood over his face and hands. He ran towards the Dark Conduit. Before anyone could stop him, he tackled Vandor back into the Conduit. They both disappeared.

Alex screamed as her body was engulfed with a fiery blue flame as she reached out for Kameron. The twins screamed as they lost control of the Conduit, and it slammed shut. Alex continued to yell for Kameron as Azrael screamed along with Gron. The Guardians of the Conduit realized Celestial was not guarded, so they fell back to protect her. Azrael took a moment to see the Lite Sentry on the ground, screaming for her love. He then retreated from the Guardians of the Conduit with the help of Gron with the remaining Dark to head back to the F.O.R. Compound.

Komptin limped over to comfort Alex, who was crying and screaming uncontrollably. Devine approached Alex to help her up, but the Lite Sentry's body was limp; she couldn't help but shout in pain. Arome and Omeila helped the Conduit of Lite to her feet. Celestial motioned she had to go to Alex. No one knew what to say as they watched Alex cry on the ground as she pounded the floor in a glowing body of blue. Sirens from outside were in the distance as the flickering lights of the burning town were in the background. Alex remained on the floor, crying out loud for the man she loved.

CHAPTER FIFTEEN

Alex sat at her desk, sipping on a glass of Apollo and ice. Her throbbing leg was resting on a cold metal folding chair on the side of her desk. Dr. Smithon had to rush down to perform first aid on her and Tristan. Tristan was resting somewhere on the grounds. The boarded-up church had no power and there was an eerie coldness to the air. It was just cold enough for Alex to put on Kameron's old Secret Service sweatshirt. The bullet that Kameron shot her with was sitting in a medical jar in the middle of her desk. She just stared at it while she brought her drink to her mouth. In the background the flames from the riot were in the distance. A mixture of sirens from multiple response agencies seemed to be a common sound this night. Unfortunately, gunshots could also be heard. Luckily, they seemed to be far from the church. Komptin had his massive gargoyle head resting in the bed the Kameron made him. The battle wounds he endured covered his body. The only sign of hope Alex could see through the smoke was a glimmer of a purple star.

She could hear the stairs creaking before a knock on the door. Alex just continued to stare at the bullet laying in the jar. "Come on in, Anne."

"Hey, sweetie." Anne barely peeked in the room, half not knowing what to expect.

"You can come in." Alex turned her attention to the sound of a gunshot that was a little too close for comfort. She remained stoic but Anne jumped at the sound. Anne had her arms folded around her, trying to warm herself as she was in the sweatshirt Kale had given her.

Anne sat down on the chair next to Alex's desk. "I just got a call from Weston; he said the police found a severely wounded woman at the power plant. They are taking her to the hospital. Dr. Smithon is heading there now."

Alex just moved her eyes over to Anne. "Midnight?"

"Hoping so." Anne gazed at the bullet on her desk, almost afraid of touching it. She just left it alone. "Any word from Celestial or anybody?"

"She just left. He's not in Heaven. She looked pretty drained." Alex continued to stare at the bullet. The sounds of sirens were still heard in the distance. Alex finally moved to pick up the jar holding the bullet closer to study. "It was a long shot."

"Alex, I wish I could have been there." Anne tried to give some sympathy.

"No, you don't. It was bad, really bad." Alex put the jar down. "Malkaroy is a star now. Devine barely survived, Tristan was severely beaten, who knows what happened to Midnight, and Kameron…" Alex stopped herself from thinking about that. "There was so much hate out there." Alex wiped a tear from her face. "Celestial was legitimately scared and defeated. Like all hope was lost."

"What do you want to do now?" Anne softly asked her best friend.

383

"Well, first, I'm going to finish my drink, heal my leg. Then, I think I'm going to find Roger, beat him to the point of death, stop, let him heal, and then beat him again, repeat, and repeat until the pain goes away, then, when I feel like it, beat him again." Alex stared at the window to the purple star that was being blocked by the black smoke. "Who's Azrael?"

Anne was taken aback a bit at that question. "Former Guardian of the Conduit. He was the one who opened the gate for the Dark to confront the Lite on Earth. That led to the battle where Celestial was almost killed by Vandor and Osiah. He was one of the original Guardians to the Conduit of Lite, until he was banished."

Alex just stared out the window. "I thought the Guardians came in pairs."

"He killed his brother, Javan, in the 1800s." Anne put her knowledge of Council history to work. "Why do you ask?"

"He came through the portal and killed Malkaroy. He was battling Arome and Omeila but escaped with Roger." Alex took another sip of her drink as she stared out the window. There was a bit of a pause. "Do you think He hates me?"

"Roger? Without a doubt." Anne kind of chuckled until another gunshot came from outside followed by sirens.

"No... God." Alex stared at the window as the sun was starting to tease its arrival.

Anne got serious. "He's incapable of hate."

"I feel like I'm failing as a Sentry. Constantly cold, no connection to the Lite. Failure, after failure. I'm surprised he hasn't sent someone to relieve me of duty." Alex took another sip of her drink. "What does He see in me? When He was able to see me."

Anne put her elbows on the knees as she leaned forward. "He sees what we all see; a kind, passionate, caring woman who sacrifices herself through pain and suffering for the people she loves and those she doesn't even know."

Alex wiped the snot coming down as she was crying. "Just feels like I'm constantly failing."

Anne closed the door to the office after making sure no one was coming. "I'm going to tell you something that I'm not really supposed to indulge."

Alex wiped her eyes and nose. "What's that?"

"You have gone through more than any other Sentry at your age. There were Sentries out there that had never even seen a Demon, let alone fought one." Anne shared with her.

"I've had Komptin's help with many of those. I'm the only Sentry who has him." Alex took her leg off the chair to limp over to her hunting partner. She gave him a loving pat on his sleeping body. He rolled over on his side so she could lean on him comfortably. Alex sat on the floor to sit up against her massive friend.

Anne got up to join her on the floor. "He draws his strength from you." They both leaned on Komptin as Alex put her head on Anne's shoulder.

Alex was taking refuge in Anne's comfort. "How are you holding up with the whole Shawn thing?" Alex closed her eyes as Anne was holding her.

Anne smiled. "Fine. I shot him in the nuts. Then Devine sliced his head off."

Alex snorted through her nose with small laughter in between her tears. "I wish I could have seen that." Komptin lifted his head to see the two girls lying on him. He flashed his eyes and rested his head back on the bed Kameron made his as a pillow. "I don't know how I'm going to get him back."

Anne couldn't help but think there might not be a way to get him back. That was something Alex didn't need to hear right now. What she needed was her best friend. "I'm sure if there was a way, both of you will find a way to get back to each other." Anne now stared at the jar on top of Alex's desk from across the room.

"He asked me to marry him." Alex put it out there.

"Wait, what?" Anne sat up a little bit to look at Alex who continued to stare at the jar across to the room. "Are you serious? When? What did you say?"

"I said 'Yes,'" Alex was playing back that moment. "Then he shot me."

Anne returned to her normal position leaning on Komptin as she resumed being a pillar for her friend. The faint sound of Anne's phone vibrating could be heard. "It's Father Richard." Alex adjusted herself so Anne could answer the phone while still leaning on Komptin. "Yes, Father." Anne listened for a bit. "It's bad, the main road into town is closed. You'll have to come in from the east." Anne continued to listen to Father Richard.

386

"Alex, Father Richard wants to know how you're feeling." Anne handed the phone over to Alex.

"How am I feeling?" Alex answered with a determined voice. "I'm pissed off." Alex handed the phone back to Anne.

She listened for a bit before saying goodbye. "They'll be here in an hour." Anne put her arm back around Alex to hold her.

More faint sounds of sirens and gunshots could be heard in the far distance. The smell of the town burning filled the room. They sat for a bit before Alex finally spoke. "I really hope he's not suffering."

POST END

Kameron screamed in pain. The ropes around his wrists felt slimy and tight. There was no time. It seemed as if he had just gotten here but been here forever. The black torn suit he was wearing felt dirty. Deep inside the black that surrounded him there were people screaming nearby. They offered no help or comfort. The air burnt like tiny paper cuts of sulfur down his throat. The only light was a dull red; it was shining on top him so he could barely see the worms come out the wall to enter his skin. There was a coldness to him, but he couldn't stop from sweating tiny moments of heat covering his body.

The small man in front of him was in a monk's outfit that was all black. His eyes were black against his pure white face. The sound he was making was nothing like Kameron had heard before. The creature came up to Kameron, studying him. The cold hands were forceful as he moved Kameron's face from side to side. The black monk picked up a rod with a glowing red end.

Something covered Kameron's mouth, he couldn't tell what it was. If felt flat but could stretch, the taste of it was salty. The thought of trying to think what it was got interrupted by the burning piercing of the rod iron entering Kameron's body. He wanted to scream into the flap over his mouth, but it muffled the cry for help. More of the slimy rope substances moved across his chest to make sure it pinned him against the wall that appeared to move. The creature pulled out the rod and then studied Kameron's reaction. The creature made a sound and then pointed to the left of Kameron. A light shined on a girl in the military jacket with an F.O.R. patch. She had two bullet holes in her chest and one in her head. They were forced to look at each other. "Why did you do this to me?"

Kameron tried to look away as the young lady had some of the worms from the wall enter her body. Kameron's face turned towards the creature. It's face got closer to his, speaking in a language he couldn't understand. Then the creature's eyes got big as a blue light came from behind through his chest. The only emotion the monk had shown was shock before falling to the ground. Kameron couldn't see where he had fallen. The silhouette of a woman approached with her fists lit in a neon blue glow. "Alex." Kameron managed to speak out.

"No," the lady came into the light. She had light brown hair and dressed in renaissance Viking clothing. She untied Kameron from the binders. "My name is Cara."

www.ingramcontent.com/pod-product-compliance
Lightning Source LLC
Chambersburg PA
CBHW050025030726
47506CB00001B/123